KISS TOMORROW
GOODBYE

KISS TOMORROW GOODBYE

E.C. SHEEDY

KENSINGTON PUBLISHING CORP.
http://www.kensingtonbooks.com

BRAVA BOOKS are published by

Kensington Publishing Corp.
850 Third Avenue
New York, NY 10022

All Kensington titles, imprints and distributed lines are available at special quantity discounts for bulk purchases for sales promotion, premiums, fund-raising, educational or institutional use.

Special book excerpts or customized printings can also be created to fit specific needs. For details, write or phone the office of the Kensington Special Sales Manager: Kensington Publishing Corp., 850 Third Avenue, New York, NY 10022. Attn. Special Sales Department. Phone: 1-800-221-2647.

ISBN-13: 978-0-7582-1563-5
ISBN-10: 0-7582-1563-0

First Kensington Trade Paperback Printing: October 2007
10 9 8 7 6 5 4 3 2 1

Printed in the United States of America

For Tim, as usual—and for always

Chapter 1

Joe Worth appreciated seriously fine woman flesh when he saw it—and what walked a few steps ahead of him was up there with the best of it. Made him wish he could strap on a tool belt and whistle. The high heels and skirt—short enough to be interesting without shouting about it—were an added bonus. As was the hair. Damn near to the middle of her back. And that darkish blond color that looked real instead of salon metallic. Then there were the legs . . . showgirl quality, endless and shapely.

A devout leg man, Joe experienced something close to awe.

Hell of a way to start a morning.

"Coffee, tea, me—or her," a booming voice said from his right.

"Definitely her." Joe jutted his chin in the direction of legs unlimited, then looked down at Riggs. "But I'll settle for the coffee—preferably with less sludge than yesterday."

"Picky. Picky."

Donny Riggs, a small guy to start with, who barely managed to clear the kiosk countertop from his wheelchair, ran the coffee shack a block from Joe's office. On a good day his coffee hit the psyche with the silk and heat of good-morning sex; on bad days, a mug of crude oil with curdled cream would be an improvement.

Joe took the coffee Riggs handed him and studied the donuts. "Today's? Or last year's?"

"Suddenly you're a gour*met?*" He accented the final T and shoved a donut into a paper sleeve. That was the thing with Donny Riggs, you ask about the food, you've bought the food. "Here." He handed Joe the donut. "You don't like it. Bring it back. Comes with a one month guarantee."

Joe took the donut, capped his coffee cup, and handed him the usual fiver. "Tell me again why I buy this crap from you."

"One of two reasons. My scintillatin' personality or my wheelchair gig."

"The chair's too obvious. It's the scintillating thing. Definitely." He headed down the street, taking the same hallowed path as the long legs that had enamored him seconds before.

"Hey, Joe."

Restraining a sigh, he turned back. He knew what was coming; Riggs hadn't missed a morning yet. "Yeah?"

"Your horoscope says you're in for trouble today. Says something left behind is coming back in your life that will seriously affect your future and ya can't avoid it."

"Good to know." He made to turn.

"It also says something that looks like a simple puzzle on the surface is nothin' but a nest of snakes. You better be careful, it says"—Riggs jabbed the morning paper he had spread out on the counter—"or you'll be—and I quote—ensnarled."

"Great. Thanks." He lifted his coffee cup in salute and turned the corner. Joe wasn't worried about snakes, and the only thing coming back into his life was last month's bills. Which, thanks to the check he received yesterday, he was able to pay and then some. Temporarily at least, he was ankle deep in clover.

Snakes and ensnarling aside, he was planning a damn fine day; the morning setting up next week's job, which would start with his joining Zern, his partner, on a yacht in

Spain—*not hard to take*—and the afternoon at the gym. Okay, so he wasn't so keen on the gym thing but keeping in shape was part of the job. No one hired bodyguards from the before pictures.

Joe rounded the corner and walked the half block to his office. The building was ten floors, and he was on the fourth; he took the stairs.

The door to his floor opened on the end of the hall farthest from his office, and he'd cracked it barely an inch or two before he spotted Legs—standing outside his office door.

The day was getting better and better. He stopped to admire the view.

Legs reached for the knob on his door then, as if she'd touched a hot element, abruptly stepped back and ran a hand through her long hair, brushing one side of it behind her ear. She looked nervous. No. Beyond nervous. Scared.

And the face that went with that Grade-A body didn't disappoint. The woman was eye-blasting beautiful.

Beautiful + scared = client.

Interesting . . . Joe watched her make another attempt at the door, back away again, then finally—and he could damn near hear her inhale half of Seattle's supply of air—she opened the door and walked in.

Joe stepped into the hall, uncapped his coffee, and did a taste test as he ambled toward his office.

If Legs was the trouble Riggs predicted—bring it on.

April closed the door behind her and looked around Joe Worth's reception area.

It was a long, windowless room painted a pale institutional green. Amid the green, there was a reception desk with no one behind it, some battered filing cabinets, bench seating along one wall, and a coffee table piled high with magazines. A blood-red movie poster touting *Kiss Tomorrow Goodbye*, featuring a mean-mouthed James Cagney in lurid, fist-raised detail, hung crookedly behind the bench. The place looked like something from a thirties crime novel—not a computer in sight. She wondered if it was intentional—and if she'd made the right decision coming here.

But Cornie said their mother, Phylly, was in trouble. Big trouble. Enough trouble that Cornie bussed in from Vegas on her own and landed on April's Portland, Oregon, doorstep. Enough that she convinced April they needed to go to Seattle ASAP—a city April never expected, or wanted, to see again. And, damn it, it looked as though the girl was right. So, even knowing Phylly would freak at her being here—here she was. About to talk to Joe Worth.

Rumor had it, when the going got tough, family came through. She wouldn't know about that, but she was anxious enough to give it a try, because Joe Worth was definitely family.

Lifting her eyes to the old ceiling, where a fan spun without enthusiasm in the warm August afternoon, she prayed silently: Forgive me, Phylly . . .

"Can I help you?"

April nearly fell out of her stilettos. She was so busy second-guessing herself, she was still gripping the doorknob and hadn't noticed a young man enter from a side door.

She settled herself and stepped into the room. She might not want to be here, but she wasn't about to advertise the fact. "I'm here to see Joseph Worth."

The young man—he wasn't much more than twenty—settled his fashionable metal-rimmed glasses on his nose, smiled at her, and glanced at an open scheduler on the desk. "Sorry, but I don't see an appointment here."

"I don't have one."

"And she doesn't need one."

The voice came from behind her, and she turned to see a big man enter the room—fill it—and approach the desk in long easy strides. When he stepped a little too close to her, she moved back, and looked up into his sharply assessing, very curious eyes and a gaze that settled on her like cool water.

There was no doubt this was Joseph Worth. Those eyes— a pale silver blue—were instantly recognizable. Set in the family genes, Phylly said. As was the height. The man was at least six feet three. Even with her wearing high heels, he was taller than she was. No mean feat when, barefoot, she stood five-ten.

"You're Joseph Worth."

She put out her hand and he took it, held it, and nodded, his gaze unwaveringly direct. She had the brief thought they were playing some kind of macho who'll-blink-first game. If so, Silver Eyes would lose. When it came to men, April stopped *blinking* years ago.

"I'm April Worth," she said. Ignoring how small her hand was in his, she tightened her grip, and shook firmly. "In a roundabout way, we're related."

One eyebrow arched and he frowned. "A kissing cousin, I hope."

"Afraid not." *Not even close.*

"Damn!" He withdrew his hand, eyed her closely. "You don't by any chance have anything to do with snakes, do you?"

She couldn't tell if he was serious or not. "Worked with a few in my time," she said, "but only the human variety."

"Lots of those around." He half-smiled and added, "You want a coffee?"

She nodded.

He looked at the young man. "Meet Kit, the purveyor of all caffeine-related products and resident genius." He gestured to a door. "He holes up in there with his stuff." The door said *Genius.*

Kit grinned at her. "That 'stuff' being computer muscle—his being of the more mundane variety."

April smiled. "Nice to meet you, Kit. And it doesn't look

like you're doing too bad in the 'mundane' department yourself." Where Joe Worth had height and breadth, Kit was closer to five-ten, compact and wiry. His arms were lean, tan, and looked stronger than they needed to be to punch computer keys.

"All Joe's fault." He grimaced in Joe's general direction. "He keeps dragging me to the gym. He calls it a job perk."

"What do you call it?" she asked.

"Death by dumbbells."

"And he loves every rep," Joe said, not a trace of sympathy in his tone. He set the plastic cup he was holding on Kit's desk. "Riggs hit an all-time low this morning. Any chance you've got backup?"

"Just dripped its last drip."

"Good. Use those new delts of yours and bring some in, will you?" He gave April another curious look, and smiled, one of those fake-friendly salesmanlike smiles of a man hoping to do business. But it was enough of a smile to light his eyes and indicate good humor, which pumped up her hope quotient. Maybe he would help. Although in what capacity, she couldn't be sure, but at the very least a man in his job—a bodyguard—surely had some connections he could call on, or advice he could give.

She trailed him toward a door, the top half of which was opaque glass with the word *Guardian A* printed across it in the same script used on Kit's. Next to his office was another door; it read *Guardian B*.

He saw her glancing between them. "My partner, Julius Zern. He's on a job." He opened the A door and stood aside for her to enter.

"And the letters?" she asked. "Do they mean anything?"

"Nope. A is whoever's in the office. We figured we needed a pecking order a client would relate to."

"Ah . . ." Hell, what else was there to say? "So you're both . . . guardians." Which she took to be a fancy name for bodyguard.

"Uh-huh."

She had the sense Joe Worth was much more than that, and it occurred to her that, in a bizarre kind of way, he and Phyllis were in the same business.

Inside his office, outfitted in the same bland yellow oak décor as the reception area, he took off his suit jacket and—surprise—put it on a hanger before hooking it on an ancient coat tree. His waist was narrow; his shirt was pale blue—the color of his eyes—and his shoulders, now shifting under soft cotton, were immense. *Guardian, indeed.*

He stood behind his desk, nodded at one of the two wooden chairs in front of it and said, "Sit."

She sat.

Sitting himself, he leaned back in the chair far enough that she envisioned an undignified tumble, but he obviously knew the chair's limits and remained upright. Morning sunlight slanted through the one window in the room and illuminated his desk surface. A surface that made the expression "neat as a pin" inadequate. Definitely *not* like Phylly. "You don't spend much time here, do you?" she asked.

"Mornings when I'm around. Otherwise this place is Kit's home away from home." He didn't add more on the subject, instead saying, "You want me to ask questions," he said, "or do you just want to get to it?"

April set her tote bag beside her chair, crossed her legs, and met Joe Worth's gaze with one she hoped was equally as calm. Again, her stomach did a pitch and roll. God, if Phylly knew she was here, she'd—

April had no idea what she'd do, but it would involve copious bloodletting.

No going back now. Forgive me, Phylly.

She cleared her throat. "I'm here about—"

Kit interrupted, walking into the room with a couple of mugs on a black plastic tray. Another surprise. The mugs matched.

As Kit handed them coffee, Joe Worth's eyes never left

hers. *Quiet eyes*, she thought. Intelligent and . . . patient. The eyes of an unhurried man, or a man who'd learned the payoff that came from shutting his mouth and opening his ears.

When Kit was gone, she started again. "I'm here about your mother. Phyllis Worth?" She didn't know why she phrased Phylly's name as a question—as if she were talking about a stranger. Which she was—at least to Joe. Still, it was stupid and made her sound tentative and insecure. *Which I am.*

Phylly's name hit the room like an arctic wind, chilling the room palpably, and Joe Worth's interested gaze iced up along with it. "I know who Phyllis Worth is," he said. "And I know *what* she is. What I don't know is who you are— what your connection is?"

April couldn't sit still any longer, so she got up and took her coffee mug with her to the window. His question was valid, but she wasn't sure how he'd take her answer, or even if it was the right one. "You could say, I'm your . . . sister."

He stared at her as if she'd handed him a live virus. "I might have a sister, but what I don't have is a mother." His face set to mean, like the poster in his outer office, he got up, came around to the front of his desk, and headed for the door.

He was going to throw her out—without hearing what she had to say. She didn't intend to let that happen. She'd promised Cornie; she wouldn't let her down.

She caught him by the arm and got in his face. "Yes, you do, *Joseph Jonathan Worth*. You have the same mother I do, and she needs your help. She's in trouble. *Serious trouble.*" April played her ace. "Life and death kind of trouble."

He stopped, looked at her long and hard, before dropping his gaze to where her hand still gripped his bicep. His very hard bicep.

She let go, and he strode to the door and opened it wide. "Get out of here, Legs—go tell someone who gives a damn."

Chapter 2

Henry Castor was enthusiastic—about his new Seattle penthouse, his new Mercedes, his new everything, including the excellent scotch he was trying hard not to swallow in one boorish gulp. After tonight, he'd have the money to be a classy guy. He might as well start acting like one.

He made a silent toast to Victor Allan. After all, everything good that was about to happen to him he owed to anal old Victor. He'd even given Henry options, two surefire routes to megacash, but no contest really. The man in front of him—fancy on the outside, shit on the inside—was his kind of guy. A guy with a lot to protect and a lot to lose. Which made him plan A. Yeah.

But Jesus! Who'd have thought Henry Castor, the backroom guy, would be sitting in the library—*a goddamn library, for Christ sake!*—being offered booze in a crystal glass by none other than Quinlan Braid. One of the richest men in Los Angeles. Hell, all of California! A man the newspapers referred to simply as Q, and the man who was about to give Henry his heart's desire. A brand new life.

No more strong-arm stuff.

No more bloodied knuckles.

No more Victor telling him what to do.

Henry downed the last of his scotch, noticed the pulled threads on his suit cuff, and tucked his arm inside the chair.

"Are you comfortable, Henry?" Q said.

"Yes, sir, Mister Braid." Might as well be respectful. Not that it mattered, because when this meet was over, it would be Braid calling him sir. Yeah.

"Good, then we can proceed." The tall, imposing man smiled down at him. At least Henry thought it was a smile. Odd how the rest of Quinlan's face didn't join in with it, though. Like it wouldn't dare a wrinkle on his smooth California tanned skin.

The man with eyes so dark they looked black had to be over fifty, but looked ten years younger. *Money did that*, Henry thought sourly: Fancy spas, lots of good sex, the best food, the best of everything. Not for Q, the sweaty back-alley gym, wilted salads in the local diner, and a case of cheap beer on the weekends. Or worse yet, one of those celebratory bottles of crap wine Victor handed over when a job went to his liking. Wine that had gotten even worse since old Victor's business started going downhill, while Quinlan here lived larger than large and looked like a god-damn movie star while he did it.

Henry couldn't wait to do the same. Although given his five-feet-eight inches of height and super-sized muscle mass, he'd have his challenges.

Deciding it was time to get things rolling, he held out his glass. "Any chance of getting this topped?" He liked the idea of Quinlan pouring for him.

"Certainly." Q poured the amber liquid—to the halfway point—and smiled again. Funny that smile. Looked like it was cut into his face with dull scissors.

Q sat opposite Henry on a fancy leather sofa, about a thousand feet long, and sipped from his glass. His black eyes studied Henry over its rim—as if he had pus on his face or something. "You mentioned Victor Allan's name," he said. "Or perhaps it's more accurate to say you used the name as a ticket to my study."

"That I did. Yeah." Henry took a swig of scotch, and ignoring the coaster on the fine cherrywood side table, set down his glass—ready to talk business. "Always good to have a mutual pal, huh?"

"May I ask the nature of your relationship to Victor?"

"Business partner." He pressed two fingers tight together, held them up. "Like this. Yeah."

"Really?" Q sipped from his glass. "Odd Victor never mentioned you." Q eyed him as if he was a crumb on his shirt front. Like Victor always did.

Because Victor didn't think I was good enough for the front office as he called it. Always telling me my blood ran too high, that I had "anger-management issues" or some shit. Like that didn't work for him. Yeah. I was the hired help, the backroom hammer, the guy who kneecapped the seriously overdue and pulled out fingernails when a monthly installment was missed. "You're my enforcer, Henry. My back-alley guy. No point in you mixing with people not of your ilk. Plus, you look like shit in a tuxedo." Henry never did get that "ilk" thing.

Remembering Victor's words, all the crap he'd taken, Henry's mood darkened. *All those fuckin' years . . .* and the bastard turned on him, tried to phase him out. *"Times have changed,"* he'd said. *"New blood, Henry, that's what I've got now. Fresh, young talent, who can set things up, make things happen."*

Years of resentment lodged in Henry's chest like a heap of coal. "Not surprised he didn't mention me. No." He jumped back into the conversation game. "I more or less worked in the field, you know. Wasn't around much. Yeah." He smiled, even though he didn't like either the guy's tone or his pointy eyebrow. Made the back of his neck heat. This asshole was Victor all over again, looking down his skinny nose at him, thinking because he had muscle he had no brain. Well, he'd showed Victor and he'd show him.

"And now Victor is gone," Q said, not looking as if he gave a shit.

"Six weeks now. Yeah." Henry said, as happy at the thought today as he had been sitting in the dumbass's study watching him bleed out. "That's why I'm here."

Quinlan cocked his head. "I see."

"Here's the thing. I'm not sure you do *see*. But I'm going to set that to rights."

"And how will you do that?"

"Like I said, Victor and I were partners. Shared everything, you know. Like those two musketeers—"

"Three. There were three musketeers. You'll have to excuse me, I like exactitude."

Henry didn't get it but neither did he care. "Whatever. The thing is we were 'all for one and one for all,' or however that goes. If you get my meaning." Henry met Quinlan's eyes. He expected a trace of alarm, instead he saw amusement. *Cold cocky bastard.* He added the clincher, something sure to get his attention, "You remember that big safe of his? Behind the sliding wall in his office? Damn door in that baby was thick enough to take mortar fire." He shook his head in real appreciation. "And now—since Victor's sad passing what was in that safe is all mine. Yeah." Henry's heart thumped a couple of times before it settled. He held the fancy scotch in one hand and gripped the chair arm tight with the other. *Here we go . . .* "Including some stuff about a young Quinlan Braid. Interesting—*illegal* stuff."

After a few seconds of silence ticked by, Q smiled again. This time the smile actually warmed his tan, tight-skinned face. "You killed him," he said, his voice soft as cotton.

"I didn't say that."

"You didn't have to." Q got up from his chair and walked the few steps to the fireplace. He set his drink on the mantel, and looked down on Henry. "Sooner or later someone was going to do it." He nodded approvingly. "And, yes, as the chosen one, you'd do nicely. Exactly who Victor deserved." He rested his eyes on Henry, looked him over good. Henry couldn't be sure, but he thought he saw a trace of respect. "What do you want?" Q asked.

"Two million."

The rich asshole didn't even blanch. Didn't answer either.

"A one-time payout, and I'm on a sunny island a million miles from here," Henry said, waving his hand around Q's fancy digs. "Out of your face. *Forever.* You go along with things, don't make trouble, and you'll never see this mug of mine again. Yeah."

"Do I look like I was born yesterday, Henry?"

"I mean it. Two mil and I'm gone. Chump change for the big Q. A new life for me."

"Beside the fact that two million dollars is never 'chump change,' I see no cause to concern myself with providing you a new life." He looked at his watch, like he had an appointment or something, like Henry was keeping him.

Rage balled in Henry's chest. He rolled his head; even Henry Castor knew it wasn't the time to let his temper get the best of him. "Look, I know an ace when I got one, and I know enough not to waste it. So let's not bullshit each other. I saw your file in Victor's safe, and I checked you out. You're a busy man—a big man, with big-time friends. You got what they call a public profile. Hell, you're developing half of California. Everything legit as hell. The way I figure it, you livin' here in the Hills"—he again waved a hand around the fancy study—"you won't want the likes of me showing up, splintering kneecaps . . . bothering your rich buddies, interfering in your day-to-day business. So I thought, Henry, the smart thing here is to lay down the ace. Do a one-shot deal. Let Q get on with his business."

Nothing in Q's expression changed. If anything he looked like he was going to laugh. "And why," he asked, "if

Victor had such an 'ace,' do you think he never played it, Henry?"

Victor was a spineless asshole, that's why—and you scared the shit out of him. You and your millions. But not Henry Castor. "Saving it for a rainy day maybe. Yeah."

"No. He didn't play the ace for two very good reasons, first because he didn't have one"—he leveled a clear-eyed gaze on him—"and second, he understood considerable harm would come to him should he try." Quinlan stepped away from the fireplace. "Now if you'll finish your drink, I'll show you out."

"Not 'til I get what I came for."

"You'll leave with what you came *with*, Henry, a potentially fatal case of greed."

It was Henry's turn to smile, and if it was smug, who the hell cared. He was about to rattle this frigid asshole's chain. "I got a lot more than that. I've got schedules of payment—times, dates, places—from you to Victor mostly. Big payments for bad stuff. Coke. Crack. The big H. Yeah. He sourced it. You moved it—a lot of it. And you know, Victor liked that *'exactitude'* idea as much as you do, 'cause he kept records of everything, always writing in those journal things of his. Insurance he called it. But—"he shrugged—"your business being mostly drug deals, you're right, not much proof other than old and, very dead, Victor's scribbles."

Henry had wasted weeks going through those fuckin' journals. He'd been looking for a pot of gold in what Victor called B & E Inc. The initials stood for blackmail and extortion. If Henry hadn't been involved in one way or another with all of Victor's clientele—until the new help had arrived—he wouldn't have made sense of any of it. But he did, and what he found was that most of what was in the journals was useless crap. Outdated. Yesterday's news. Half the clients were dead, for God's sake. Victor didn't need new *staff*, as he liked to call his new hires, he needed fresh meat, new victims. There was only one real payday in the whole mess, and Henry was looking at him. "And it's not like you and Victor did the UPS thing and signed on a dotted line or anything," he said, getting back to business. "One of your high-priced legal types would make the drug crap disappear like that." He snapped his fingers.

"Your point—if you have one?"

"My point is I'm not talking about drugs, low-level shit. I'm talking about a bit of stink that *nobody* can make go away . . . except yours truly here." He took an easy breath, starting to enjoy himself. "You remember that shipment you and Victor planned to send offshore?" He watched Q's face closely. No expression. "Turns out that shipment never left the great US of A. Seems Victor fucked-up big time, but didn't tell you. Figured what *you* didn't know wouldn't come round and bite him in the ass. Said best to let dangerous dogs sleep or somethin' like that." *Pure yellow-belly, old Victor.*

Henry let his words sink in, saw the first crack in Q's plastic face, a tiny tic in that steely jaw of his. He savored it a moment, before going on, "That shipment? She's what? Maybe thirty something now. Probably seriously pissed about what happened back then, her taken from her mommy and all. And now, being all growed up, she's likely ready for a little revenge." He shook his head. "For a man like you, all legit and all, that's big-time trouble." He nodded his head, rubbed at his jaw. "Get that kind of pissed-off female talking to the press—about that career you and Victor set up for her . . . Yeah, trouble." He left the rest to Quinlan's imagination.

Henry gave him credit; he didn't waste time on denials. "And you know where the *shipment* is, I take it." His eyes didn't narrow, they pierced. Sharp black lights, with an even blacker center.

Henry considered whether to flat-out lie and say yes or

tell the truth. He looked into Q's hard face and stone cold eyes, and opted for truth. "Let's just say I'll know if I need to know. Won't take more than a couple of days at most." *And I'll have her singing like a canary an hour after that— if you don't cough up the two mil.*

"If I understand you correctly, you want money *not* to locate her."

Henry made a shooting gesture with his index finger. "Got it in one. You put the money in my bank account, I leave her be, and she leaves you be."

"What makes you so sure you can find her?"

"It's what I do." *And goddamn well, too.* "Plus, I have a source—a pipeline, you could say, that'll take me right to her. More of a chute . . . yeah." He slid one hand off the other in swift gliding motion and grinned. "Like I said, two days tops."

"And this 'pipeline' of yours, where is it?"

Henry gave him a vacant stare. "I wasn't born yesterday either." He stood on his too-short legs and squared his thick shoulders. Christ, why was he always looking up at these bastards? He hated that, hated how it poked at the gut-ball of anger rooted low in his stomach.

The confidence in Henry's voice came easily, and it looked as if Quinlan picked up on it. He took a few paces away, stopped, and left his back to Henry. Henry damn near heard the whir of cogs and wheels in his brain. He had him. Henry Castor was about to become a rich man! Yeah.

Without another word, Q went to his desk and pushed a button near its base; a drawer opened where Henry hadn't seen a drawer.

He took out a whack of cash and a cell phone. He handed both to Henry. "Expenses. And an untraceable cell. Keep me informed as to your progress, and call me immediately when you find the girl."

"You want me to find her?" *What the hell . . .*

"I want you to find her and bring her to me."

Henry snorted, laughed. "Like I'm working for you?"

"You are now."

"Not exactly what I had in mind." He might be holding a nice wad of cash in his hand, but he didn't have to count it to know it was nowhere near Bingo!

"Nor I, but unfortunately your avarice and my natural tendency for self-preservation necessitate our unholy alliance." He stood over Henry, as tall and rangy as Henry was short and thick. He didn't blink. "I repeat, find the girl, Henry, bring her to me—and you get a four million dollar payday." He looked at the money Henry held in his hand, probably a few grand. "Consider that a signing bonus."

"Four mill—" Henry didn't know whether he was pissed at himself for underestimating the value of his information or so fuckin' excited his tongue had tangled. He slipped the cell phone into his pocket and slapped the cash he was holding against his thigh. "You want I should finish her?"

"By that I take it to mean, would I like you to kill her?"

Henry winked. "Hell, when I find her . . . I'm there, she's there—makes sense, Q."

"Do not call me Q." Quinlan's black eyes got blacker. "And, no, I do not want you to kill her. What I want you to do is restrain your dumb-animal instincts and do your work quietly and methodically. When you find her, bring her to me. In the course of your investigation under no circumstance will you attract attention to yourself *or me*. Do we understand one another?"

Henry eyed him, simmering about that dumb-animal remark. "I get it. You want to do the job yourself, make sure there's no loose ends—that exactitude thing."

"What I do and why I do it is of no concern of yours." He paused. "Do we have an agreement?"

Henry shrugged. Hell, Q could fuck her to death, use her for target practice, or slice and dice her for a goddamn salad, Henry didn't give a shit. It was only a woman. And with four mil in his jeans, he'd be far enough away, her screaming wouldn't keep him awake nights. "You just cut yourself a deal." He held out a hand. "I like you, Quinlan, I like the way you think. Yeah."

"Unfortunately for you, Henry, I can't say the same." Ignoring Henry's outstretched hand, he gestured toward the door. "Get out of my house."

Henry's rented Navigator sat waiting for him at the bottom of the five broad steps leading to the doors of Q's house—goddamn castle more like it. He got in the SUV, lit a cigarette, and leaned his head against the headrest, too pumped to drive. Four million bucks for finding one dumb bitch. Damned if his heart wasn't near to beating itself right out of his chest thinking about it.

He put the key in the ignition and started the car. Three minutes later he'd cleared Quinlan Braid's gates and they'd closed behind him.

Henry's thoughts went immediately to the job at hand. *Piece of cake.*

A few days ago, him wanting to be on firm ground before meeting Q, he'd made a couple of calls, confirmed his pipeline was still living in Las Vegas with her kid, so he knew exactly where to start. All he needed was her address, then it was one, two, three. Go to the pipeline, squeeze out the information on the misplaced shipment, and . . .

Shut down the pipeline—permanently.

He nodded to himself. Yeah. It wasn't often good business and getting even made such a perfect couple. Henry was proud of himself. He'd spent weeks going over the old crap in Victor's safe—all that damn reading and figuring had damn near killed him. For a while there, he thought maybe he'd wasted his bullets on Victor, that his getting back at him for being pushed aside wasn't going to be as sweet as he'd hoped. Then he'd found Quinlan Braid's name and a piece of information as good today as it was twenty-odd years ago. And he was the only one who had it.

He frowned suddenly, and his throat tightened.

From here on in, Braid would probably have him followed—or try to. While Henry figured he'd have no trouble making, or shaking, a tail, he didn't want some asshole hired by that freeze-dried prick Q finding out a Vegas bitch was his connection. That happened—and they found the shipment—Henry'd be dead two seconds later. Not going to happen. He'd cover his butt and he'd cover it good. Nobody was taking advantage of Henry Castor—ever again. Yeah.

In the end Q would pay or Q would die. Henry chuckled to himself. Hell, there was always plan B. Q didn't know why that girl-shipment never went out on time, that Victor dithered like an old woman when he found out exactly what he had locked in his basement. Victor built his life on secrets and lies, his and other people's. His stock in trade, he called it. The sharp-brained bastard never shared the goods unless there was something in it for him—and he was fuckin' ruthless in procuring it.

None of which mattered now. First things had to be first and first was Henry nailing down his pipeline—and that girl.

He drove along the lush, tree-lined street, careful to drive slow to not attract attention. But his mind was racing.

What was that ad line again? *What happens in Vegas, stays in Vegas.* Lucky for Henry, that when their sequin-and-feather days were over, so did old-time showgirls like Phyllis Worth—his direct connection to four million dollars.

And an added bonus—getting the chance for payback against that Vegas bitch. Yeah.

Chapter 3

This was her third hotel room in less than a week. She was running out of favors, and she was no closer to figuring out what to do than she was when she flew out of her apartment.

God, it was hot out there! August in Las Vegas, the closest the sinless would ever get to hell's fire.

Phyllis Worth's heart thumped in her chest like a rabbit on crack—had since she'd crossed The Strip ten minutes before. Being out in the open made her feel like target practice, had every nerve in her body quivering like a crazed thing. She had to settle down, get a damn plan.

She tossed her suitcase and makeup bag on the hotel bed and walked to the window. Outside, the man-made cities of planet Vegas bustled and glowed; some sprawling, others thrusting upward toward the sun they attempted to rival: Wynn—fifty stories high, all of it gleaming bronze, thumping its massive chest and saying to the sun, "Right back atcha!" Then New York, New York, Paris, and the shadowed canals of Venice. Phylly loved them all. Las Vegas was her kind of town. Her home.

A home she might have to leave because of one teeny-tiny mistake she'd made when she was a dumb kid.

Okay, flat-out stupid kid, and in her twenties at the time, not much of a kid either. If you added scared out of her mind and greedy, maybe the words *teeny-tiny* didn't exactly fit the event that was about to change her life. Impulsive, ignorant, and vain more like it. And if that weren't enough, she'd gone on to compound it.

She went to the minibar and got herself a cold can of Coke, rubbed it over her forehead.

"Think, Phyllis, think!"

Yeah, right . . .

Damn it, she hadn't been able to think with any kind of logic—never her strong point at the best of times—since she'd heard from Elena, Victor Allan's housekeeper, telling her that Victor was dead. That vile Victor was maggot meat, didn't bother her in the least. He might have lived high, had all the money in the world—at least back then—but he was still the worst of low-life scum, one of the many of his type that passed in and out of her life from the time she spotted her first erect penis; a flag she'd too often mistaken for love, with the usual miserable results. No, she hadn't cared about Victor dying for a second. Hell, it had been years since she'd laid eyes on either him or Henry Castor, that sicko-thug partner of his—but when Elena told her Henry had emptied Victor's safe, it could mean only one thing; he'd taken over Victor's business.

That got her attention.

That and a strange phone call to her boss, Rusty Black, a few days ago—a bogus credit check—had set her packing. Henry would want the journal.

Damn Victor anyway, and that obsessive-compulsive urge of his to keep records—of every friggin' thing in his life! But then what the hell would you expect of a blackmailer and extortionist? Information was the blood he lived on.

She should know; she was one.

Okay, maybe she hadn't used the information in the journal—and she certainly hadn't made a career of bilking people, but when things were tough, she'd used the journal itself against Victor. Of course, he'd paid. It was her having that journal that kept Victor off her and April's case. Without it . . .

But all that was years ago. Her heart lurched in her chest. While Victor was okay about paying her for her silence, even occasionally begging her to come back to him, Henry's approach would be more lethal. That asshole hated her, pure and simple.

Henry Castor was mean as dirt. Vicious and incredibly stupid—a bone-deep nasty, who was unpredictable, vengeful, and violent. She'd considered handing the journal over, but it was too risky. He'd think if she knew what was in it, she'd be dangerous—or a competitor, which was even worse. Besides, Henry had wanted her dead years ago, ever since the April thing—Victor told her that—and she didn't figure his intentions had changed. He'd had it in for her since she'd kneed him in the groin, hard enough to shove his balls up and under his eyelids, when he'd come after her during one of her money pickups at Victor's. It had been her third visit and her last. Eight grand in total from her life of crime and not a penny of it was worth it. Funny how it was all tied up with the only good thing she'd ever done. The April thing . . .

When her thoughts stalled on that memory, she shook her head, shut her eyes tight, and forced it back.

Henry wouldn't care about that, not after all this time. No way. After the first year, Victor hadn't even cared. At first he'd been crazy mad, but after a year or so, it was like he'd forgotten the whole damn thing. One time he'd even said she'd probably saved his ass. No, Henry was after the journal; she was sure of it. With revenge as an appetizer.

The phone rang and—thank God—ended her irrational attempt at being rational.

She picked up the phone and set the unopened pop can on the bedside table. "Hello?"

"Phylly? You okay?"

"I'm good. Thanks to you." She sat on the edge of the bed, rifled her bag for her cigarettes. "I really appreciate the comp, Marcie. I know the town's busy."

"The town's always busy, and I'm glad to help. You'll be okay in that suite for two days, then you'll have to move to the Mirage. Annie says she can take you for another two."

God, she hoped to hell she'd figure something out before it came to that, but it sure was good to have friends in front-desk places. She lit the cigarette. "Hey, as a lifestyle, this isn't bad, you know. A great hotel, room service—a minibar. And all for free. I know people who'd kill for this." She tried to smile, tried to believe her own words, drew in some nicotine instead. Actually, she hated being holed up like this; she liked people, bright lights, action. But given her current situation, she couldn't risk being seen until she figured a few things out. And a disguise was useless; at six feet tall, she stood out like an oak in the Sahara. She took another drag.

"I hate to rain on your parade, girl, but you're in a nonsmoker."

"Shit. Sorry."

"Hold on a sec." Muffled, unintelligible sounds came down the line, and when Marcie came back she sounded rushed. "Don't forget, while you're here, you're Mrs. Rhonda Lott. She's the comp who canceled. Got that?"

"Got it." Easy, she'd known a Rhonda once, smart, kind, and superorganized. Everything she wasn't.

"And don't overdo the smoking thing, okay?"

Overdo? She'd been smoking like a hell-fiend for days. "I won't." She inhaled deep. Marcie, who'd conveniently not recorded Rhonda's canceled reservation, had ensconced Phylly in one of the best suites in Caesars. Her years in Vegas had given her some good friends—friends she didn't want to leave. "And thanks again. I owe you."

"And I'll collect. But I gotta go. There's about a million Japanese tourists about to assault the reception desk. Call if you need anything." She paused. "Or if you need to talk, Phylly. I'm here."

Phylly knew she was fishing, and that she was doing it with the best of intentions, but talking about Henry Castor would be like sharing a toxic needle. And no way did she want anyone else in his sights. "Thanks, I'll remember that." Phyllis hung up the phone, and stripping off and dropping her clothes as she went, headed for the shower. She tossed her cigarette in the toilet bowl, flushed it, and watched her Lucky Strike swirl into oblivion.

She wasn't much of a believer in omens, but that cigarette eddying its way down watery depths until it disappeared hit her damn close to her miserable heart.

She closed the toilet seat, sat on it, let her nerves off-leash—and cried like an abandoned baby.

When that got old, she showered, and put on the plush hotel robe. Hugging herself in its soft warmth, she murmured, "At least I'm going out in style."

The phone rang again, and she picked up, listened.

"Phylly?"

"Hey, Rusty." It was her boss at Hot and High, the costume design and repair shop she worked for. Rusty, moving from showgirl to entrepreneur without a blink, had started the business over fifteen years ago. In the beginning it was mostly alterations and repairs, but now—with the addition of April's talent—Rusty had moved like a caffeine-charged cheetah into design. She was a take-no-shit, leather-tough, ferociously loyal friend—the best friend an ex-showgirl like herself could have. It was Rusty who taught her to sew—a talent she never knew she had—and Rusty who'd given her a full-time job when she'd finally hung up her feathers and glitter ten years ago.

She got right to it. "A guy called for you. Said he was an old friend of yours."

"Did he leave a name?"

"Nope. Said he wanted to surprise you. He left a number though and said to tell you all he wanted to do was talk. You want the number?"

Phyllis sucked in some air, put her hand over her thumping heart. "No."

Silence.

"I kind of figured you wouldn't. Besides, he sounded a little too much like that guy making that bogus credit check. Real pushy type. And you know how I like those." She paused, and Phylly envied her the long pull on the cigarette she heard coming down the line. "Anyway, I told him you were away on vacation—like you wanted me to—but I don't think he bought it. He kept asking when you were coming back, and when I said I didn't know, he wouldn't let it go, asking for numbers, addresses, where you were, the whole bit. That's when he gave me the number. The jerk wouldn't get off the phone."

"What did you do?" Phyllis fisted her hand in the lapels of the robe, drawing it tight to her throat.

"I told him to fuck off and quit wasting my valuable time."

Trust Rusty not to waste words. "Thanks."

"You going to tell me what this is all about?"

"I can't . . . not until it's over." The less Rusty knew the better—and the safer—she'd be.

"Fair enough. God knows we've all got secrets. But maybe you should think about calling the cops." She huffed a heavy exhale down the line. "I can't believe I just said that."

Before Rusty went on to the showgirl circuit, she was a working girl, and she had no love for the men in blue. Nor did Phyllis, knowing full well her story of theft and blackmail wouldn't serve to inspire them to work on her behalf. "That's a nonstarter anyway."

"Then get the hell out of town, Phylly, and *stay* out of town until we can figure things out. Tommy will be back tomorrow, I'll talk to him. He'll know what to do."

"I don't want to bother Tommy with this, Rusty." Tommy was Rusty's brother, a pit boss at the Sandstone, a small casino downtown; he was all slick and slide. Phyllis had no doubt he "knew people" as he constantly claimed he did, and more than once he'd saved her showgirl ass from some stage-door creep. But this situation was beyond Tommy. And his "people."

"He won't mind." A pause. "He can at least get you out of Vegas for a few days. You know he's got a thing for you."

Exactly. "I can't leave Cornie." The minute she said it, she knew she was wrong—and she knew what was really driving her nuts about this whole rotten situation. *She'd have to leave Cornelia*—and not for just a few days hiding out on The Strip. Christ, what was wrong with her brain? Staying in Vegas, she was putting her daughter at risk! She had to leave, she had no choice. *Why in hell had she taken that damn journal? God, she was as bad as Victor.*

"You can't *not* leave Cornelia. What if this idiot decides to use her to get to you? Have you thought of that?"

She just had, and the thought congealed the blood in her veins.

When she didn't answer, Rusty went on. "Look, here's what you do. Call Cornie and tell her to stay a few days longer with April—"

"What do you mean April? She's supposed to be with you." She felt her eyes widen, heard her voice rise.

"She hopped not long after you took off, called me from Portland. Said if you called 'not to worry—that she was with April. I think she's picked up on the fact you're in trouble."

Phyllis's heart plunged to her stomach. "You should have told me, Rusty . . . Jesus, she's only fifteen. I'm going to skin her."

"Fifteen going on a hundred. And I didn't tell you because I couldn't find you myself for a couple of days—how many damn hotels have you been in?" She sounded pissed, and Phylly didn't blame her. "Besides," Rusty went on, "what did you expect her to do? You disappearing like you did, leaving that dumb note about you being away for some . . . business reason. You seriously underestimate that kid, Phylly. You should have talked to her—at the very least called her sometime in the last few days." She paused. "You thought she'd think you'd taken off with some guy, right?"

Rusty was right, and scared as she was, Phylly didn't want her daughter to think a man was involved in her leaving—again. Cornie had seen enough of her mother's "stupid-man-stuff," as she called it, to last her lifetime. "I had to take off, and I just thought the less said, the better." Phylly went on, "You know how Cornie is. A whiff of trouble, and she'd have stuck to me like glue." She twirled a piece of her long pale blond hair. "I thought she'd be okay, that she'd stay with you until I got back. Like we planned." She hadn't called her because she didn't know what to say, and she sure as hell hadn't called April. She was too damned . . . embarrassed. Phylly figured what she had to do, she had to do alone.

"Teenagers don't do plans, you know that. Plus she's scared. Hell, I'm scared. And damn it, you should quit playing Joan of Arc and call her."

"But she's okay? You said she called from April's." At least Cornie had gone to the right place—and the right person.

Portland, Oregon, was a weird place for April to have gone to study theater and costume design, but she said she'd follow Blanche Reevis—with her string of costume design awards—anywhere to study under her, and Portland, Oregon, of all the damn places in the world, was that anywhere, for the next few months. April was so damn smart, a cool plan-ahead type—exactly the qualities Phylly needed right now. She wished she could run to her like Cornie had. Would have, if it weren't for her tangle of lies, lies April would despise her for. As far as April knew, Phylly's relationship with Victor had ended that awful night. *If she knew what I did . . .*

"Yes, she called. She's fine. As it turns out, she did the right thing going to April's. Like the right thing for you is to find a safe place as far away from Vegas as you can get—and stay there until this guy, whoever the hell he is, gives up."

He won't give up. He'll never give up. But, damn it, Rusty was right about Cornelia. It was best she stay with April. There was only one teeny-tiny problem. "I don't have anywhere to go, Rusty." Christ, she sounded like a kicked puppy. *Get a grip, Phylly!*

"Then find a place! And find it fast. Somewhere you can figure your way out of whatever mess you're in." She stopped, spoke to someone in the office, then, "And when you do, call me, April, and Cornie. You got that?"

"I got it." Phyllis hung up the phone, closed her eyes, but no matter how hard she thought about it, she didn't know a single soul outside of Las Vegas.

She was almost forty-eight years old and she had nowhere to go and no one to go to—

Except . . .

No, she couldn't. Jesus, she'd broken his heart—or so he'd said.

She walked to the window, pulled back the heavy drapes and again stared down at the glitter and crowds. What had he said, fifteen years ago, when she'd refused to leave Vegas with him?—"When you're in trouble, don't take it to the ones you love, baby, take it to the one who loves you—and that will always be me. I won't come to you, but I'll be there if you need me."

The *there* he'd referred to was a house on the west coast of Vancouver Island in Canada. Nothing between his house on the beach and the shores of Asia except a few thousand miles of the northern Pacific Ocean—or so he said. She'd never seen it.

Noah Bristol had only been in Vegas a couple of months, doing some special speeches or seminars at the university—and when he wasn't doing that they'd been in bed.

God, it was a sexual firestorm.

She'd never forgotten him; her most unlikely lover, a botanist with a hundred initials behind his name, who'd just sold a successful business, bought himself fifty acres in the middle of nowhere, and was about to turn himself into what he called a wilderness gardener.

She had no idea how any of his life or his plans turned out. All she remembered was the choice she'd had at the end of their too-short time together: Life with him in the cool green of a remote rain forest or a life without him wearing feathers and tights under the hot gold lights of Las Vegas. He was ten times smarter, two inches shorter, and the most magnetic man she'd ever met.

And a spectacular lover . . .

She'd been thirty-three, still in good shape—dancing and strutting-wise—and unwilling to give up what she still thought was an exciting and glamorous life, so she'd turned him down. Phyllis never regretted her decision, but in the thrall of a sleepless night, she'd often revisited it. In the end, she'd done the right thing, she was sure of it. A showgirl and a wilderness gardener? Glitter and dirt. It would never have worked.

Fifteen very long years. Jesus! He was probably married with ten kids. What if he wasn't? What if what he'd said to her was true: *I love you, Phyllis Worth. I'll never love anyone as much—or in quite the same way again.*

He'd written her a couple of times, but she hadn't read or answered his letters. Too confusing, too much to say, too many weird secrets she didn't want to share. And, God knew, words weren't exactly her thing. He'd stopped writing—which was understandable, and just as well.

But there'd been that postcard he'd sent her—just a couple of years ago: *Still here. Still remembering. Love to see you again.* And signed *Always, Noah.* She'd shown it to Rusty.

The window in front of her became a screen, playing a bad movie: She saw her ignorant, uneducated self walking into his arms. A lost gypsy, asking to stay, even as she tried to decide what to say to him, what to tell him, about all those pesky teeny-tiny secrets of hers. Like how she was a thief, kidnapper, and blackmailer—and how she'd had his daughter nine months after he'd left and never bothered to tell him—because she'd thought it would complicate her life. *Her stupid life!*

She sighed to release the building tension in her chest and leaned her forehead against the window.

What the hell . . . she might as well stay true to herself, be the selfish bitch she always was. It wouldn't be hard to find out if he was married. After the postcard, she'd checked on where he lived. Tofino was a micro-town. A village on the shores of the end of the earth.

The perfect place to hide.

All she had to do was keep her big mouth shut. And that she knew how to do.

She went to the desk, made an airline reservation—and arranged a car rental. All they'd need was a signature when she got there. No problem.

And she'd keep her promise to Rusty; she'd call April and Cornie when she got . . . wherever the hell she was going.

Chapter 4

"What the hell's the matter with him? Doesn't he get it?"

"Watch your language, Cornie," April said, "or I'll get out the soap." April looked around the clean but ugly motel room. "And chances are good the soap in that bathroom"—she gestured with her fork to a closed door—"will peel the skin from your tongue."

"Promises, promises." Cornie bit into her hamburger, chowing down as if she were a logger after a third foodless shift.

"And stop with the smart-mouth. I'm tired and cranky, which means I'm likely to do you physical harm, if only to lower my stress level." Stress caused by being back in the city of her earliest memories—none of them good. A city she never expected to see again. Didn't want to see again. Three days here—in this miserable motel—first trying to find Joseph Worth, then waiting, after he'd ushered her out of his office, for him to return her calls. It was too long, both time-wise and emotion-wise.

She and Cornie sat opposite each other at the Formica-topped table under the motel room window of their second floor room. As a fifties retro piece the damn table was worth more than the room. The view from the window showed a setting sun and a half-empty parking lot, its concrete rid-

dled with oil stains and fissures. Not the most scenic view
Seattle had to offer.

At least it wasn't raining.

April remembered the Seattle rain, remembered watching it pound and bounce on the torn pavement in the alley
below the ratty apartment she'd lived in with her mother
after her grandmother died—a grandmother she barely remembered. Her mother she remembered too well. And Gus,
her brother. She'd never forget Gus. For a long time, she'd
blamed him for what happened, until she was old enough
to understand how young he was, how powerless he'd have
been to stop them from taking her away.

She stared out the window, touched her hand to the knot
in her chest.

History. Ancient, nonrevisable history.

April had learned some things living with Phyllis Worth:
Life was about forward movement and there was no going
back, not to men, not to family, not to a place. You learned
to forget and you learned to look out for yourself, because
no one else would—or could.

Not even Gus . . .

But April intended to look out for Cornie, until Phylly
showed up—and she'd do it without any help from big
brother, Joe Worth.

Cornie had smiled at her idle threat about the motel
soap, but the smile didn't stick. "I don't get it," she said.
"That guy's her son. He's my freakin' brother. Which I find
extremely weird, by the way." She took another bite of her
burger, chewed, then reached for the carton of milk she'd
brought into the motel room along with her hamburger and
April's sorry excuse for a salad. "And you know, April, you
should have told me I had a brother. I shouldn't have had to
find out by going through Mom's things."

"Which you shouldn't have done in the first place, and
something your mother is going to be seriously pi—ticked
off about."

"I had to do something! Her disappearing like she did? Not saying when she'd be back, that she had '*business to take care of*.'" Cornie pulled a disbelieving face. "Mom never has 'business' I don't know about. Work or otherwise. She's a production supervisor for Rusty—nine to five. Not exactly a traveling salesman type. And hell—heck, I've been paying our bills and running the house stuff since I was ten, ever since she figured out I could count better than she could."

"Still, you should have left her stuff alone. Everybody has things in their lives they want kept private, Cornie. Even your mother." *Especially your mother.* And my mother, too, she added to herself, the hole of worry in her stomach deepening. Because if being a mother meant giving you life, caring, and protecting you, Phyllis Worth more than qualified. Hard as the early years had been, Phylly never let April go. She'd held her, loved her, bandaged her scrapes, and healed her damaged heart. She'd raised April, haphazardly maybe, but as best she could, keeping her close through the good times and bad. "Tears and laughter," Phylly had said to her once. "That's what life is all about and knowing one is coming on the heels of the other is what keeps a woman sane—more or less."

What April felt for Phylly was about gratitude, yes, but so much more. It was about loyalty—and love. Love given as a child to her very own guardian angel. And a bond that had grown stronger with every year they were together. If Phylly was in trouble, April would get her out of it—any way she could.

"Yeah, Mom has secrets all right, like a brother I never knew I had. She should have told me."

"Maybe she should have, but now that you know, what's the good of it? He's not going to help us find your mom, and finding her is what we have to focus on." April's heart fluttered, and her thoughts went back to her growing concern, grown deeper since she'd talked to Rusty. After that conversation the faint hope that Cornie was overreacting—dramatizing—her mother's disappearance had died.

Oh, God, Phylly, where are you?

"Yeah . . ." Cornie sipped more milk then she sighed. A thoughtful look replacing the defensiveness of a few moments ago. "I know Mom can be a certified flake sometimes, and at first I thought"—she shrugged—"it was just some guy she'd met. But, now I don't think so. I don't know what to think. She's been gone almost a week, April." Her gaze was wide when it met April's.

"You're just scared—"

"I'm not scared. I'm just, like . . . mad, I guess."

"So because you're mad—which I don't believe for a second—you rifle through your mom's things and hop a bus to Portland so you can make me 'mad,' too." She tried to smile, lighten things up a bit.

"I didn't know where else to go." She attacked her burger again. How Cornie could eat like a ravenous wrestler and stay so thin bordered on the incredible. Lucky for her she was going to have the Worth height. "No one in Vegas would tell me anything," she went on. "I didn't plan on discovering some big family secret. But if Mom didn't want me to find out, she shouldn't have kept his birth certificate—or his business card." She stopped eating. "Where do you suppose she got that anyway?"

"Can't imagine." But April knew Phylly kept track of her son. Always had. She'd had more than one friend check on him over the years, but even when she knew where he was, she never attempted to contact him. She'd been frantic when he'd left the army because for a couple of years she'd lost track of him. When a friend found him again settled in Seattle and brought back his card, Phylly had looked at it, held it to her breast, and cried for an hour.

Cornie tilted her head, eyed April, looking peeved. "I thought he might help, and I figured you'd know about him. That with a bit of pressure from a difficult teen—that being me—you'd cave and tell me stuff." She finished her burger and wiped her mouth with the paper napkin. "So?"

"So, what?"

"Spill. Tell me the whole sad story of Mom's teen pregnancy. Did her parents kick her out? What?" Her words sounded tough, uncaring, but her eyes were alive with curiosity and hurt.

April couldn't help her. She knew about Joe, had since she was in her teens, but she didn't know very much. Phylly might be a major motormouth about everything else in her life, but never about her son. Or why she'd given him up. "I don't know the 'whole sad story,' as you call it, and even if I did, Cornie, I'd tell you what your mother would want me to tell you." April made a zero with her thumb and index finger. "Besides, I've done enough already, I went to see your long-lost brother, didn't I?" She pushed her unfinished, thoroughly unpalatable salad away from her. "And that was an all-time bust."

"It's not your fault he's an ass—"

"Cornie!"

She rolled her eyes. "Let me rephrase. It's not your fault he's a horse's rounded rear end." She frowned then and added, "You shouldn't have told him you were his sister."

"Not exactly a lie, Cornie." April had thought Joe thinking of her as a sister of sorts would be a good way of getting him on board. Major miscalculation. He wasn't interested in her as a sister, and he sure as hell wasn't interested in his birth mother. April didn't want to admit to Cornie that she understood his bitter feelings, his bone-deep reluctance to dig into a part of the past long buried. You can't heal the past, after all, so why try to resuscitate it. In that, she and Joseph Worth were on the same page.

"God . . . *dess*, April. Don't you get it? You wasted all that"—she made a sweeping gesture that took in April from her head to her toes—"by letting him think you were related." She abandoned her food and got up. "You should have—"

April held up a hand. "I really don't want you to finish that sentence. There's way too much Vegas in you, sweetheart."

Cornie widened her eyes theatrically, shook her head. "And I always thought *you* were the smart one. Guess there's only one thing to do." She went to her unmade bed and sat on the edge of it. "I'll go see him myself." She looked directly at April. "Did you tell him about me—his real-life sister?" The last sounded plaintive—a bit wistful.

"He was too busy showing me out of his office to give me the chance." April pushed away from the table, rose, and walked to the bed. April knew—although Cornie would never admit it—that even in the confusion of her mother's disappearance, she'd been excited about finding a brother. For a girl who'd never known her father—and had a series of uncles—it was natural. Cornie wouldn't admit it, but she'd expected more from Joe Worth and she'd been disappointed.

Damned expectations! They let you down every time. April touched Cornie's silky hair, which was nearly as long as her own, but Cornie's was raven dark and ruler straight; her own had a tendency to curl. "His loss, Cornelia Vanessa Worth. Definitely his loss."

Cornie shrugged, shifted from under her hand. "It doesn't matter. I don't care about that. What matters is Mom, and finding out what's going on. He should help us."

"He's not a private investigator. He's some kind of bodyguard. Calls himself a guardian. I honestly don't know how much help he'd be anyway."

"Maybe none, but he should try. He's . . . *family.*"

There was that mysterious word again. "He's *blood*, Cornie. That doesn't make him family. We build those ourselves. Like your mom says, families are made, not born." She paused. "I didn't tell you, but when I spoke to Rusty, she said—" She hesitated, wondering how far she should go, how honest to be, or whether a well-intentioned lie would serve better than the truth.

Cornie donned her mulish look. "Don't even think of not telling me everything—or repeating Rusty's line about how I shouldn't worry, everything will be fine—with no friggin' explanation at all. I'm not a kid, so don't treat me like one."

April sighed. "No, you're definitely not a kid." Anyone as steeped in the inner world of the Las Vegas showgirl— which thanks to Phylly and her coterie of dancer friends, Cornie surely was—left kid status behind somewhere in the third grade. As April had, virtually growing up backstage, she'd had an up close and personal look at the good, the bad, and the ugly from the age of ten. April remembered it well. Backstage: Awash in bottles, jars, and atomizers; spangles and mile-high plumage; flesh-colored spandex, barely there thongs, and inch-long eyelashes. Not to mention PMS, cat-mean jealousy, angst, and naked ambition. Backstage was masquerade on overdrive, and it came with a full cast of witches, bitches, and angels. Phylly fell into the angel category, some shadows on her wings, but an angel nevertheless.

"Tell me what Rusty said, April. Everything."

"She said she thinks your mother is being stalked. And that's why she's in hiding." April thought this was as likely a scenario as any other, but what bothered her was that Phylly was no shrinking violet. It would take a very *special* stalker to make her cut and run. There'd been a lot of men in her life; Phylly would be the first to say "too damn many," but she'd practically been living a nun's life for the past few years, so whoever this guy was, the relationship had to be old. That left a lot of suspects. "A stalker's a possibility," she added, not wanting to add her own worried thoughts to Cornie's.

"No way! Come on, April, Mom's a drama queen. We'd be the first to know if she was being bugged by some guy. She's had her share of 'stalkers' over the years, and she wasn't scared of any of them. She either took care of them herself or she called in her personal militia. Tommy. It would take Freddy Krueger—or worse—on her case, before she'd go underground like she has."

Cornie was on the mark, as usual. The girl had no stars in her eyes when it came to her mother, but it didn't diminish her love for her—or her fierce protectiveness. There were times April wondered which of them was the mother. "More like above ground," April said. "She was being comped at Caesars when Rusty talked to her."

Cornie's face brightened then shadowed. "Was?"

"She left last night."

"For where? No, don't tell me. If she left Caesars—that's Marcie's place—she'd have gone to—"

"She went north. She went to Canada."

Cornie blinked and her head jerked straight. "Canada," she repeated as if she were struggling with a geography exam. "Why would she go there?"

April hid her own concern with a shrug. If she'd had any doubt Phylly was in trouble, her going to Canada laid them to rest. Phylly was Vegas through and through, so whatever—or whoever—made her leave had to be damned bad. "I don't know. She didn't say."

"Then how did Rusty know?"

"She used the company credit card, bought a ticket to Vancouver."

"Vancouver . . . that's in British Columbia. Just across the border." Her eyes widened, something suspiciously like moisture coating their surface. Cornie, strong, stubborn, and super-smart, never cried. She quickly brushed away the tears. "Then we're going there. It's a three-hour drive tops."

"And do what? Just because she flew to Vancouver doesn't mean she's staying—not that we'd find her among the two million or so other people who live there, I might add. All it means is she's most likely on the west coast—somewhere."

April ran a hand through her hair, shoved it roughly behind her tri-studded ear. "Without a plan of some kind, it would be a complete waste of time running up there."

"We have to do *something*!"

"I know." *But Canada's west coast?* She thought she knew everything there was to know about Phyllis Worth—the men, her time on the showgirl circuit, going from job to worse, and back again. But never once had she talked about anyone or anything in Canada. "Rusty made her promise to call us when she got . . . wherever it is she's going."

Cornie shook her head and didn't spare the vehemence. "Not good enough. In the note she left me, she said she'd call. That was days ago. No call. If we can't go to Canada, we have to go back to Vegas," she said. "We have to talk to every single person who knows Mom. Go through her stuff again. If there's a link to someone there, we'll find it."

"I'll go to Vegas," April said. "And I'll take care of it." She didn't add that Rusty said Phylly didn't want Cornie in Vegas because she was concerned as much for her safety as she was her own. But it was past time for both of them to get out of Seattle, and this rotten motel room, which she'd only stayed in this long so she could humor Cornie—by making useless calls to Joe Worth—and figure out what to do. And the more she thought about it, the more obvious it was; it was important to find Phylly, but it was even more important to find out what the hell was going on. Put some kind of face on whatever trouble she was in. "I've got a friend in Portland, you can stay—"

Cornie shot to her feet. "No way. I'm going with—"

A loud knock interrupted. Probably the room cleaners. She headed for the door, already lost in thoughts of where she'd start back in Vegas—and how to make sure Cornie was safe while she was there.

She opened the door on the last person she expected to see. *Joseph Worth.*

Chapter 5

Joe strode into the motel room without an invitation, put his hands on his jeans-clad hips, and eyed the two shocked women. Well, one woman and one kid. He shot a glance at Legs, and didn't bother hiding his irritation. The woman had lied to him. "You're *not* my sister," he said. He looked at the girl, who'd shot up from where she was sitting on the bed to stand beside Legs. "You are."

Both of them stared at him as if he'd fallen on their picnic table from a high branch. Both of them opened their mouths and closed them again.

Good. Joe liked the element of surprise, almost as much as he liked to satisfy his curiosity. And why Legs hadn't told him the truth definitely had him curious.

"So . . ." he said, deciding to get right to it. "Why the big lie?"

"It wasn't exactly a lie. It just wasn't exactly the—"

"Truth? Yeah, I got that." He nodded. "And all because your adopted mommy dearest and her real one"—he nodded at the kid—"ran off with her latest?"

"Hey!" the girl said. "You don't know anything about anything—so shut up, okay?" She copied him, slamming both hands on her hips, and shooting him a death glare.

"True enough, which is why I'm here. To find out." He looked at the kid, considered her carefully. Pretty little thing.

But not so little. Already maybe five-seven or eight. Light blue eyes—like his—but not his hair. Hers was black. Jet black. He wondered who her father was? Wondered if she knew. With a mother like hers—a showgirl at best, with the worst unthinkable—probably not. "You're Cornelia, right? Age fifteen. A decent student. Semi-serious basketball player. Likes horses better. Born and raised in Vegas. Have I got it right?"

She looked as if she'd rather chew wet leather than answer. "And you're Joseph—"

"Joe. Joseph was some kind of saint. I'm not."

She ignored him, repeated, "Joseph, age thirty-one, born in Seattle, April fifteenth. Pawned off sometime later to the open arms of Washington State."

Three years later to be exact. Phyllis took her time dumping him. He lifted a brow. "A kid who does her homework. I'm impressed."

"What are you doing here?" Legs asked, stepping in his and the girl's sightline.

"Other than being pissed off at being suckered, I'm not sure yet. Filial loyalty, maybe?" *In a pig's eye. What he owed Phyllis Worth was womb rent plus a buck for the ice cream sandwich she'd left him holding when she'd dropped him off at a convenient ER and walked out on him.*

"I doubt that," April said, her tone dry.

"He's here because of me," the girl said, stepping out from behind Legs. "He's curious. After he checked you out, found out you weren't his sister"—she eyed him smugly—"which made him a happy man, he found out about me and decided he'd pretend he wanted to meet his little sister, so he could see the sexy blonde again without all that icky family stuff getting in the way."

It was Joe's turn to blink. "Jesus!"

"Don't swear." She gestured with her head in Legs's direction. "She doesn't like it." She flopped back down on the bed and put her hands behind her as a brace. From there she gave him a crocodile smile—all teeth, no heart.

Joe looked at Legs. "She always like this or is it something in my winning personality?"

Cornie answered. "You don't have a winning personality. You're a jerk. I've got a missing mother, and a jerk for a brother. Great!" She let the brace of her arms collapse and fell back on the bed.

April, who'd been watching their exchange with an expression that bounced between shock and amusement, said, "While you're stretched out there, Cornie, stuff that pillow in your mouth, would you?" She turned to Joe, and her face got all tight and suspicious. "You checked us out. Why?"

"I check everybody out, Legs. Especially women who claim to be sisters while sobbing about how the mother who dumped me—pretty much like the kid there said—suddenly needs me to keep her sorry butt alive."

"You're the one with the sorry butt." Cornie's voice from the bed.

"Cornie, for God's sake!" April's face flushed when she glanced up at him, and her eyes snapped with irritation.

Green eyes. Yes. Definitely green, not the dark hazel he remembered from yesterday. It didn't get much better than a green-eyed blonde, and dressed in jeans and a Tee—not one that showed her midriff sadly—she was hotter and more beautiful than he remembered.

"You need help strangling her?" he said, tipping his head toward the bed the kid was lying on.

"No, I can manage fine. Thanks." She shot a holding glance toward the girl before turning back to him. "What you can do is tell us why you've changed your mind and are willing to help."

"Who said I was?" Just because she was right was no reason not to make her sweat a little. And maybe the kid had him pegged. Maybe Legs was why he was here. Wouldn't be the first time his cock went on autopilot—but it had been a long time. Hell, he wished it were that simple. It wasn't.

He was here because, after he'd bounced April out of his office, he'd thought things through and decided it'd be damned interesting to clap eyes on his mother, after all—and get a couple of questions answered. From what little he knew about her, she'd be easy enough to find. A quick run through her little black book shouldn't take more than twenty-four hours. He didn't buy for a moment this was the life-and-death situation Legs made it out to be.

"You're here, aren't you?" She shot him a sharp look. *Smart eyes*, he thought, *and direct. Don't-mess-with-me eyes.* "And you know, Joe, one *kid* is all I can handle right now, so I'd appreciate an answer mano a mano. What are you doing here?"

Man to man? Not exactly what he had in mind. "I've decided it's time to meet Worth, get a few things off my chest." Hell, he was between jobs, semi-flush with cash. Why the hell not?

She eyed him, all wary eyes and distrust. "That's it?"

"That's it." He slid his gaze over her. "Although the kid's right. You not being a sister is definitely an added incentive."

"Told ya," Cornie said, giving him the evil eye. "He's a jerk. And you're the carrot on the stick."

April either shook her head at him or the kid's tangled metaphor. He didn't know. Then she closed her eyes and drew in a long deep breath. As a woman praying for patience, she was picture perfect. "I do like carrots," he said. He managed not to smile, when she opened her eyes and tried to kill him with them.

"That said, I think we understand one another. Always a good place to start." With that she went to the phone, put her hand out, and said, "Your credit card please."

"Excuse me?"

"I need to book three tickets to Las Vegas." She made a gimme gesture with her fingers.

The kid shot to her feet. "I'm coming? And I don't have to stowaway?"

April Worth shifted her attention from the telephone pad and gave Joe the once over, from toes to head and back again. "You can definitely come, Cornie. We've got ourselves a supersized bodyguard. The way I see it, it'll take a small, well-armed army to hold off big boy here." She met his gaze, her own cool and defiant. "All the carrot has to do is stay one step ahead."

He handed her his Amex. Smiled. "I've got a long stride, Legs." He winked his best wolfish wink. "A very long stride."

He heard the word "jerk" mumbled again; it seemed his sister had a severely limited vocabulary. Legs shot him a narrow-eyed glance.

"What you've got, *Joseph*, is a bloated ego and a small brain"—she looked pointedly at his crotch—"most likely in your pants." She met his gaze, her green eyes jewel-hard. "And if you call me Legs again, you'll lose even that."

Cornie giggled. "You better listen up. Better men than you have tried and failed." She shook her head, smiling so hard it looked to break her face. "You don't know what you're in for, big bro."

Bro . . .

Joe's mind locked on the word and his stomach got queasy. He looked down at . . . his sister. She might as well have been a multilimbed alien for all he knew about her. Then it hit him—smart-mouth was a living, breathing, honest-to-God relative. Legs might not scare him, but this teenage girl who shared a DNA strand with him made his nape prickle and his stomach sink. He felt like a kid who'd found a monster in the closet and didn't know whether to beat it with his bat or give it a cookie.

"We leave tomorrow," April said, handing him back his card. "Pick us up at noon, please. We'll be ready."

He pulled his eyes from the girl and looked at the woman. She stood watching him, her arms crossed, her expression speculative and laced with amusement. "You can go now, Joe."

Obviously April Worth wasn't averse to giving orders, and any other time he might have called her on it, but not today. Not now. All he wanted to do was get his ass out of here. Now—before this follow-that-cab scenario he signed on for started to play out. He had some thinking to do—about just what he was getting himself into. He'd gone along this far without that mysterious construct called family. Maybe he should leave it at that, because he didn't like the effect this sass-mouthed teen nightmare had on him. "Happy to," he said. He slipped the card back in his wallet. "I've got a date with someone who appreciates small brains."

Her lips twitched. "I'll bet."

Heading for the door, and with nothing to do but continue the charade, he gave a few orders of his own. "Tonight, you and . . . Cornball here, make a list of everything you know, think, feel about where dear mommy might have gone. And people. Who she knows—men and women—and how long she's known them. You got that?"

And while you mess with that, I'll decide whether or not to show up tomorrow.

Legs said nothing. The girl got up and walked to stand in front of him. "I have a name, you know. It's not 'kid' and it's not Cornball. It's Cornelia. My friends call me Cornie." She eyed him with no mercy. "So far you don't fall into that esteemed group."

Henry Castor sat in his rented Taurus, smoking and dreaming about the new Mercedes set for delivery next week in Seattle. He'd even kicked around the idea of renting one when he got to Vegas, but he figured this job didn't warrant such a quality vehicle and might attract attention. His plan was to get the job done and be out of this town two seconds later. *You're mine, Phylly baby, just as soon as I talk to your boss. Yeah.*

And, thank Jesus, it'd started to cool down. Whole damn day over a hundred. Shit! He couldn't wait to get back to Seattle where you could breathe the air without scorching your lungs. He lowered the air-conditioning, and watched the parking lot slowly empty out. He figured by eight, eight-thirty at the latest, she'd be alone up there, and judging from how fast the staff was hightailing it out of the building, he looked to be right.

Hot and High took up the second floor of a two-story building in a kind of a light industrial district, not far from McCarran Airport. The area already looked mostly deserted, but they worked late at the redhead's place.

Henry knew this was the design studio of Rusty Black's business, because the building where all the sewing stuff happened—and where Phyllis Worth had worked before she up and disappeared on him—was farther out. He'd done a good look-see before setting up this unscheduled *appointment* with the redhead. If she wouldn't talk, her payroll records would talk for her. He huffed out an irritated breath. Chances were the damn records were on a damned computer. He hated those things. Didn't understand them, didn't want to.

He got out of the car and headed for the building.

He already didn't like Rusty Black, didn't like any woman who told him to fuck off—to his face, on the phone, or any other way. Probably one of them lib-type ballbusters. He hated those bitches. His blood boiled around his neck even thinking about them.

He took the stairs slowly, listening hard to hear if anyone else was hanging around. Nothing.

He passed through a tiny reception area and crossed a carpeted work area filled with drafting tables at odd angles, filing cabinets, and a scattering of computers. The lights weren't out, but they were dimmed. There was a giant movie screen-type thing on one end of the place, and her office at the other. It was glass with slatted blinds. One of the slatted sections was open, and he saw her plain enough, sitting at her desk, working in the pooled glow from a high gooseneck lamp; her red hair, copper bright under its light, swung loose over the papers on her desk.

He didn't bother to knock, just walked right on in.

She had a pencil in her hand and was drawing something; took her a second to register him when she looked up.

"Who the hell are you?" she said.

He closed the door, locked it, and gave her his best bullshit smile. "I'm the guy you told to fuck himself." He figured she'd get scared at that, maybe take a step back. Didn't happen.

"I tell lots of guys to do that. Which one are you?" She looked at him as if he were shoe shit.

"The one that doesn't like it." He walked to the window and closed the one blind that was open.

She watched him, real calmlike. Too calm. The blood was boiling in his neck again. "Ah," she said. "You're the asshole who's looking for Phylly."

"The very one."

"And you're doing the little office lockdown thing, because you're planning to beat the crap out of me if I don't tell you where she is." She put her pencil down and stood. Loomed. "Well, you better think again, mini-dick, because I don't plan on making that easy for you."

Jesus, the woman was a giant, a fuckin' Amazon. She had at least seven inches on him. Damned if his blood didn't jelly some. He took in air, spread his legs, and cupped his crotch. "No need to go and insult a man's equipment, Red. And for your information, there's nothing mini about it. Yeah."

She rolled her eyes.

Putting one hand in his pocket, he lifted the other and waved it, damn near cheerily. "How about you just tell me where Phyllis Worth is, and you and I go our separate ways"— he nodded at the papers on her desk—"you to your little pictures there and me to find Worth. Just want to talk to her is all. Nothing to worry about on that score."

She snorted, like a goddamn mare, put her hands flat on the desk, and lowered her head enough so she could look him square in the eye. "*How about you* getting the hell out of my office, before *I*"—big accent on the I—"beat the crap out of you?"

Henry pulled out his shiny new Glock. "I don't think so."

"You son of a bitch!"

He had her attention, or at least what he had in his hand did. "Where's Phyllis Worth?"

"As far away from you as she can get—which is a long, *long* way from Vegas."

"Something a little more specific would be good."

She shook her head, eyed the gun in his hand. "I hate to repeat myself, but . . . Go fuck yourself!"

He fired. He didn't mean to exactly, but damned if his finger didn't convulse on that trigger. Yeah.

She stared at him, her face white with shock, then she lifted a hand to her shot-up shoulder, now pulsing blood down the front of her white blouse. "You son of a bitch!" She slumped back into her chair, blood slipping and sliding through the fingers of the hand pressed to the wound.

Henry wanted to kick his own ass, knew damn well his putting a bullet in her was a bad idea, bound to attract the boys in blue. Q wouldn't like that, but there was no going back now. "There's more where that came from." He put both hands on the gun, steadied it. He always shook a bit after he fired. Never told anybody that though. Always figured it wasn't how you felt about things that mattered, it was how you performed. Henry Castor always performed. "So, how stupid are you, bitch? Here's your second chance. Where's Worth?"

Her face, white before, was chalky now. It looked as if the damn bullet had aged her twenty years. Not a killing shot though. Not yet. He took aim at her chest, and for the first time she blinked.

"Worth," he repeated. "Where is she?" Jesus, she was going to pass out on him. *No fuckin' way!*

Instead, she struggled to her feet, put her face inches from his. "Where you'll never find her." She gave him a dragon's smile. "Now get your sorry ass out of my office, before I—"

He fired again.

Chapter 6

Quinlan Braid placed his hands on his patio balustrade and looked down; already the egos and their satellites were gathered in their selected herds on his lawn and patio. It was the Los Angeles A-list—an awkward, unwieldy mix of politicians, moneymen, and movie people who pretended to admire one another while each sat on his own smug perch, convinced it was the highest of them all.

Catching sight of Giselle, his groin tightened, and his gaze followed her lush form as she wove her way through the crowd to the patio below, where she joined two of his guests. She wore white as he'd instructed her to, and she looked like an angel—which, of course, she wasn't—at least not in his bed. Giselle Morrisey was the best he'd ever had.

She looked up, saw him, and waved, the gesture bordering on childlike. "Hurry up," she mouthed.

He nodded. Giselle would enjoy the formal evening—another reason he'd proceeded with it. Keeping her amused served to stave off his own boredom.

Back in his bedroom, he lifted his chin and straightened his black tie. With so much on his mind, he'd considered canceling the event—spending the evening in bed with Giselle. It wasn't as if he needed these people anymore. He already had their money. But he'd planned this party months ago as a way of showing the expected gratitude for his guests' investment in his last financial offering. A deal that had gone very well. Fifty million dollars domiciled in an offshore, zero-tax regime. Tax relief for them. Immense profits for Braid Enterprises.

He studied his tie in the mirror. Perfect. As was the catered food, the music, and the lights and candles artfully illuminating the grounds of his lavish estate.

Yet, he hesitated, loath to join his guests and curry favor no longer necessary to him, when the matter currently of most importance in his life was his own past—brought back to him in living color by Henry Castor.

He had to deal with the man, of course, but the prospect was not without its concerns. The measures required might well be severe, and Q was disquieted by the thought that he might have grown soft over the years, his instincts dulled by the security that gates and money provided.

Opening a narrow drawer in a tall marble-topped bureau, he surveyed the symmetric row of folded, monogrammed Irish linen hankies. He selected one with double-seamed edging and placed it in the inside pocket of his jacket.

He was ready—prepared, physically and mentally, for the evening ahead.

All he needed was his shoes, given to Jerald to shine exactly twenty-one minutes ago.

Where was the man?

He reached out a hand toward the keypad on his dresser, was about to touch Jerald's call number, but again hesitated. So unlike him, these delaying actions, but he couldn't settle himself.

Perhaps an added moment of reflection . . .

He walked to the French doors leading to his private patio. Not the patio looking down over the pool area where close to a hundred and fifty people waited for his arrival, but the secluded balcony he used for drinking his snifter of cognac and smoking the one cigarette, a Nat Sherman classic he allowed himself each night before retiring. A thoughtful, analytical time, it appealed to his sense of order.

Henry Castor, on the other hand, was chaos—a yawning sucking chasm pulling Quinlan into a past he'd left far behind. He'd brought back to Q the one transgression—in years of many—he'd never forget. It was his basest moment; the moment when greed erased his soul—and it bore no statute of limitations.

He remembered Victor twisting Robert Browning's famous words, poking at Q's initial reluctance to become involved—in one more job. "'Ah, but a man's reach should exceed his grasp,' Quinlan, my man," Victor had quoted. "Or what's a hell for?"

That final reach had given Q the last of the funds he'd needed to start the legitimate life he'd planned—as far from Victor and the streets of Seattle as he could get. Except for a minor matter or two, Q hadn't had serious dealings with Victor Allan since.

Yet that last reach had brought him Henry Castor.

In Q's first life, Castor would have been dead within five minutes of their meeting—perhaps during it. Things were so much simpler then, kill or be killed. Take or be taken from. Now there were complications.

Castor was a thug, a man driven by violence and avarice, and Q had played into both with the offer of a four million dollar payday. Right now the rabid beast was in Las Vegas. According to Quinlan's source—ironically a connection he'd made through Victor—Castor had gone there directly from their meeting. The town—loud, crass, and gaudy—did not run to Q's taste, nor as far as he knew, did Victor have any business there.

All of it together made him uneasy.

There was far too much of the *street* in Henry Castor: The poor diction, the drugstore cologne, the furtive eyes— windows to an even more furtive spirit. The man appeared to lack basic intelligence. Worse yet, he was unpredictable—as was the teeming, tourist-infested town he'd gone to.

That such a man was in a position of power—albeit temporary—over Quinlan enraged him, a rage he stifled, considering unbridled anger a weakness as dangerous as Castor himself.

He'd known his share of Castors and their type. As a young man, during his years in Seattle, he'd been one of them—but shrewder, more ambitious—until he'd risen above them all, and got what he wanted—enough cash to begin a life within the law. Almost.

What he and Victor had done in those heady, dangerous days, they'd done together. Drugs mainly, some smuggling, contract killings—whatever was necessary. All of it lucrative and planned to the last detail.

Q's finale was to be the girl. The little girl in the torn jeans and too-big green shirt.

Now Castor—and that girl—threatened everything: The Braid name, its hard-won legitimacy, and its moneyed connections.

A possible prison sentence.

Idly, he rubbed the teardrop shaped birthmark under his chin. A conviction would, of course, prove difficult, given the elapsed time, a child's memory as testimony—his money. But he would not risk the possibility nor the notoriety that would inevitably follow such an accusation.

Of course, Quinlan Braid could disappear. Some cash transfers, a flight plan, a new identity. . . . Although complicated it could be arranged, but it would mean leaving Giselle. He was reluctant to do that.

Nor, given the nature of Henry Castor, would his leaving be a guarantee of safety. The man was a mongrel, a back-alley cross between a bloodhound and a bulldog—as his investigation of him had confirmed. There was only one way to deal with the cur—put him down, and Q had the right people in place to do exactly that. How ironic that it was Victor who'd supplied them.

Yes . . . when Q had what he wanted—the name of Castor's pipeline, Castor was a dead man. As was the girl.

Murder wasn't new to Quinlan. His personal tally was eight in all: Six men and two women. He remembered the godlike challenge of it: The intense planning, the anticipation, the flawless execution, the feel of hard cash slapped in his hands, the extreme level of excitement. . . . The blood.

Even now his heart beat stronger at the thought.

The nostalgia for those long-ago days surprised him. *Perhaps because I excelled at it—or because I felt more alive on the streets than I ever have in a boardroom.*

Unsettled, he terminated his odd thoughts and reminded himself that murder was messy business, and the risks were high. Risks he could no longer afford. No, this time he'd be the one paying the killer while his own hands remained clean. He would witness the girl's death, ensure there were no loose ends, but that would be the extent of his personal involvement.

He heard laughter and brighter, louder music coming from the pool area. He could delay no longer, and there was no need to; his decision was made.

As Q reentered his bedroom, there was a double rap on the door.

"Come in, Jerald."

Jerald entered the room soundlessly on the soft-soled shoes Q required all his household staff to wear. "Your shoes, sir."

"Thank you." Q took the shoes, new John Lobbs purchased on a recent trip to London, and turned them in his hand, admiring the gleam of fine leather before sitting on the bench at the foot of his bed and slipping them on. "Has everyone arrived?"

"Yes, sir. All one hundred and fifty-six." He paused. "Is there anything else I can do for you?"

"Yes. Tell the orchestra to finish forty minutes earlier. I've decided on an earlier end to the evening." If he couldn't eliminate his boredom, he could at least lessen it.

Q noticed a trace of surprise cross Jerald's face, and he understood it. Jerald, through their long association, was aware of Q's assiduous adherence to schedule. How rare it was for him to initiate a last-minute change. To his credit, Jerald adjusted quickly. "I'll see to it."

Q watched him go, briefly grateful for Jerald's unshakable loyalty. So much better than a dog. So much more advantageous. And all because one of the women on Q's kill list was of Jerald's choosing—the mother who'd abused him from birth. Jerald had been thirteen when he'd arrived on Q's doorstep. He'd offered eighty-six dollars and a lifetime of servitude in exchange for a simple garroting. It was one of the best deals Quinlan ever made.

On the way to his party, at the top of the stairs, he paused, took note; his heart beat steadily in his chest and his mind was clear. His decision had calmed him, given him a sense of purpose. He again considered the numbers.

Three people were to die: Henry Castor, his mysterious pipeline, and most important, the girl—that dangerous misplaced shipment from his first life.

The girl whose name he couldn't remember.

He ignored the tremor in his chest when he thought of her—of her beautiful, terrified green eyes.

Pity? Remorse?

Impossible. He'd taken her life over twenty years ago; what he was doing now was merely putting a signature on the death certificate.

Chapter 7

"Jesus, this place is a mess. And I *am not* sleeping on that." Joe glared at the sofa—short with high arms, its cushions askew, magazines dripping from it to the floor—as if the thing had jaws and a double row of teeth, then he looked at April. "I'd be crippled for a week."

April barely glanced at Joe. She hadn't been in the apartment for two or three months—and she hadn't missed Phylly's casual approach to housekeeping. To neat-freak Joe, no doubt the mess was doubly unappealing, adding to his already low opinion of his birth mother.

Although, when she looked at Joe's large frame and the sofa's small one, she had a twinge of empathy. "Take the bed, then. I'll take the couch."

What she got in response was a grimace.

Well, too damn bad for him! She didn't care where he slept. They had no choice but to make the best of things, and it made sense, if they were going to go through Phylly's things, to stay at her and Cornie's place, a modest—very messy—two bedroom apartment about a half hour southeast of The Strip. Although she had to admit the place was worst than usual. Even Phylly generally closed drawers when she opened them. God, she really had left in a hurry.

Cornie, who'd been listening and watching from the kitchen doorway, said, "For what it's worth, little bear is sleeping in her bed, so have at it, guys." With that she disappeared into the kitchen.

"Not exactly Martha Stewart, is she?" Joe said, the second Cornie was out of earshot.

"You're determined not to like her, aren't you?"

The gaze he slanted her way was not attached to a smile. "I'm determined to get a good night's sleep," was all he said. "So how about we take a room at the Mirage? That way we can both have decent beds." He paused, set his cold-hot blue eyes on her and grinned like a wolverine. "If we shared one of them, we'd be happier still."

April resisted rolling her eyes, instead choosing a sweet tone. "Do you work at being obnoxious, *Joseph*, or were you born with the talent?"

"You know the family lineage better than I do. You tell me."

She let that go. They had to talk about Phylly sometime, but now wasn't the time. April had barely slept since Cornie arrived on her Portland doorstep with the news of Phylly's disappearance, and right now, she was too tired to scale the wall of resentment Joe had built around his mother. All she wanted was for him to lay off the tease and innuendo. Not only could she do without it, it had a false ring to it, as though he were playing the part of the idiot wolfman purely to irritate her. No man who was serious about seduction would be so blatantly obvious—or stupid.

She was absolutely sure Joe Worth was not stupid.

And I'm mad as hell at myself for finding the idiot attractive and amusing in spite of my better judgment.

Not that it mattered what she felt. Joe was wasting what little charm he had, because other than finding Phylly—priority one!—all April wanted to do was get back to Portland and start her theater internship. She'd waited over a year for Blanche Reevis to accept her, and Rusty had given her six months of leave to study under her. April had a lot of hard work ahead of her, exciting work, and she had no room in her plans for a fast-talking, silver-eyed body-guard—who hated his mother. Her mother.

"I think you should give serious consideration to my Mirage idea," Joe said, sitting on the sofa and spreading his arms along its back. "I'd be a lot more comfortable than this." He patted a sofa cushion.

She tilted her head then shook it. "You don't even like me and you want to take me to bed. Why is that?" It wasn't the first time since leaving Seattle that she wondered if she'd made a mistake, having him come along. Cornie wanted it, yes, but it wasn't as though they'd bonded as siblings. They were like a pair of alley cats fighting over the last sardine. "Well, are you going to answer me?"

"I was thinking?"

"Hard for you, is it?"

He grinned. She hated to admit it, but she enjoyed the humor in his eyes. She liked men who didn't take themselves too . . . seriously. Then again there were those who used humor and a quick wit as a shield to keep you out. Another time—or more of it—and she might've made the attempt to learn which kind of man he was. Or at least figure out how he managed to irritate and attract her at the same time.

"You weren't thinking," she said, giving him a straight look. "You were studying my ass."

"Guilty. And those legs of yours go right up to it. Amazing, how that works."

With no answer to that, she shook her head.

Hell, it would take a semi load of super glue to bond anything to this man. That made her feel bad—for Cornie's sake.

"And who said I didn't like you. I don't even know you"—he got up from the despised sofa—"except that you don't like peanuts, white bread, or mushy tomatoes."

"I thought you were asleep." What he'd described was the excuse for lunch they'd bought on the plane earlier today—five dollars' worth of awful. "But you're right, you don't know me. Not enough to either like or dislike me." She crossed her arms. "Which means you have . . . issues. About me"—she jerked her head to where Cornie had left them for the kitchen—"and maybe about her."

Joe had taken to wandering the room, touching, lifting, turning, and studying the knickknacks and cheap prints on the walls. God knows he had lots to look at; Phylly's place was basically secondhand, junk-sale chic. The woman loved stuff. His back was to her when he said, "Real men don't have issues."

"No, but boys do. Boys who wonder why a mother takes in a stray—like me—and keeps her, but lets her own son . . . go."

When he turned to look at her, there was nothing of the boy about him. He was all towering, glowering male, with an expression so hard and uncompromising, she almost took a step back. Almost. He closed the short distance that separated them and stopped directly in front of her. "You know what I think?" His low voice was soft, at odds with the darkness in his eyes.

"Not a clue, but by the look on your face, I'm guessing you're about to tell me." *He was too close . . .* April forked her fingers in her hair, shoved it behind her ear.

"That I am." He reached out his hand, touched her hair, and brought back the strands she'd put behind her ear. Smoothing them down over the swell of her breast, he leaned forward. "I think you should mind your damn business and leave those issues you're so concerned about to Phyllis and me." He picked up a few strands of hair, twirled them between his thumb and forefinger and watched his own play as though fascinated. "Until now, I'd have said, your legs were your best feature. Now"—he took in a heavy breath—"I'm not so sure. You have great hair. Long. Heavy. The kind that sweeps across a man's chest during sex. Or lower if he's really lucky." He lifted some strands to his nose, breathed her in. "Smells like honey and roses." He put his face to her ear, his breath a warm storm across her cheek, her neck. "And you smell like . . . Paris."

She pulled back, her stomach fluttery and untrustworthy. He was still holding her hair when their eyes met. "You're trying to change the subject," she said.

"Actually, I'm making a pass. I must be slipping if you didn't pick up on that." He let go of her hair and smiled, all trace of his earlier irritation gone. The man was definitely in charge of his emotions.

And too damn sure of himself. "Save your clumsy passes for someone who's interested, because I'm not."

"I think you are." He bent his head, lifted her chin and—

He would have kissed her if she hadn't jumped back like a frightened hare, while he grinned like a painted mask. *Damn it!* He was playing with her, deliberately trying to antagonize her. "Has it occurred to you, we don't have time for—"

"Sex? There's always time for sex."

She shook her head. "You're crazy."

"But in a good way, don't you think?"

She opened her mouth, but her jumbled thoughts wouldn't let her form words. "I think . . ."

The phone rang, or rather the "Happy Birthday" song played; Phylly's idea of fun.

Thank God!

She took a step back, shot him what she hoped was a sobering gaze. She'd had guys coming on to her for as long as it was legal—and before, but she'd generally felt as though there was something honest behind it, however misplaced. They either wanted sex or some kind of connection. But Joe Worth struck her as the kind of man who didn't want anything except one-upmanship. She didn't like it—freaking butterflies in the stomach aside.

"You going to answer that or do you have to wait until the candles are lit."

"This conversation isn't over." A lame attempt at the last word and she knew it. He arched a brow and went back to his in-depth study of Phylly and Cornie's acquired artifacts. She found the phone under a scarf and last month's copy of O, the Oprah magazine. She picked up the phone. It was Leanne, Rusty's cousin and her assistant at Hot and High, returning the call April placed when they'd arrived at Phylly's apartment.

"Leanne, hi, I—" She'd didn't get to finish . . .

And she couldn't grasp what she was hearing.

April again thrust her hair behind her ear, and holding it back, she sat heavily on the unlovely sofa. "My God! When?" She listened hard, nodding, tears filling her eyes when she lifted them to Joe. She raised her hand against his questioning gaze, shook her head.

He watched her silently, hands on hips.

April closed her eyes, listened intently, not wanting to miss a word, while her heart sank in her chest. "When will we know? . . . How is she now? . . . Good. Yes, I know she's tough, but—tell me everything." Finally, she nodded. "Good idea. I'll call the hospital. Thanks, Leanne, and God, I'm so sorry."

April clicked off the phone and sat like carved marble on the sofa. She couldn't think, couldn't process . . .

Joe took the phone from her hand, set it on the side table. "What's going on?"

"That was Leanne from Hot and High, where Phylly and I work. She says—" She swallowed so hard it hurt her throat.

Cornie came into the room carrying two bottles of water. She stopped abruptly when her gaze met April's. "What? You look like a zombie."

"It's about Rusty."

"Who's Rusty?" Joe asked.

"She's my mom's boss," Cornie said.

"And mine," April added. "And our best friend."

"Geez, April, what happened?" Cornie asked.

April's eyes started to water, and she took a second or two to settle herself down. "Rusty's in the hospital, Cornie."

"Oh, my God! Was she in a car accident. What?"

Taking a breath, April said, "She was shot. Last night at work."

"Shot! Like with a gun?"

April could only nod. "The cleaning people found her. Shortly after ten last night." She stood, started to pace.

"Jeez . . ." Cornie sat on the other end of the sofa, clutching the bottles of water to her chest as if they were pillows. The condensation dampened her Tee. "But she'll be okay, right?"

"Leanne said she was shot twice, that she lost a lot of blood," April said. "She had two surgeries during the night. They're hopeful, but . . . don't really know, yet. She hasn't regained consciousness."

Cornie's eyes were wide. "Does this have anything to do with Mom? Do you think?"

"I'm not sure what to think, except—" Joe was going to get his wish for a better bed, because no way was she having Cornie stay here. She looked at Joe. "Book us those rooms, would you? But not at the Mirage. We'll go downtown, the Sandstone."

If Joe had any questions, he let them lie. "Done." He took his cell out.

Looking at Cornie, April said, "Pack your stuff, kiddo."

Cornie frowned. "We just got here."

"And now we're leaving. We're going to see Tommy. He'll know more about what happened." And April was suddenly very sure they'd be safer away from this place.

"You *do* think what happened is about Mom." Cornie's face went stubborn—and pale. "It could have been just . . . like vandals or something?"

Joe, who was on the phone, raised a brow, waited for her answer with as much interest as Cornie.

April had opted for the "something" or more specifically the *someone* who was looking for Phylly, and after what happened to Rusty, she saw no point in keeping Cornie in the dark. If information was power, Cornie needed the protection. "If it was vandals or a random robbery, the police don't think so. They said whoever was in Rusty's office was looking for something specific, that nothing was wrecked or broken—except her computer. They said it looked as though it had been kicked in. Other than that nothing is missing, and the search 'appeared methodical and professional.' Their words."

Cornie went paler.

"I don't know if any of this has anything to do with Phylly—not for sure anyway." She paced a few steps, her knees feeling like warm toffee. "But I think it's smart to *act* as though it does until we know different." *And even smarter not to be sitting ducks in Phylly's apartment if whoever shot Rusty decides to show up.*

"She's right." Joe shoved his phone in his pocket. "We're set. I've got a suite at the Sandstone."

"Why?" Cornie asked. "Why can't we stay here?"

"We will"—Joe's tone was brusque—"for the next hour. We're going through everything in this place, then we're out of here." He looked at Cornie. "You check your mother's room again, see if anything's missing—" When it looked like she was going to backtalk him, he held up his hand. "Later for the teen crap, okay?" He shifted his gaze to April. "You check the closets, any storage areas—and wherever the hell else the woman might keep stuff."

"When did God put you in charge?" Cornie blurted.

April would have asked the same question—if they had more time. But his instructions made sense, so she decided to let his machismo tactics pass. *For the moment.*

He ignored Cornie and walked back to where he'd been nosing around the room earlier. "But before you get started, do either one of you know anything about this?" He took a picture, maybe eight by ten, off the wall, held it out for them to see.

"That's been there forever," Cornie said. "I think some guy gave it to Mom. She likes it, says it's peaceful."

April took the picture from Joe's hand. Although it had hung on Phylly's wall for longer than she could remember, she'd never paid much attention to it. Now, she studied it closely. It was a watercolor of a beach. Not a sunny California beach, but a gray misty one that seemed to go on forever; the beach was bordered by tall trees—maybe fir or cedar—but the scene was anything but peaceful. The trees were bent back from a fierce wind, and waves the height of houses were rolling in from the ocean. It was titled, appropriately enough, *Storm Watch.* "Doesn't mean anything to me," she said. "And I don't remember Phylly ever saying anything about it."

She handed the picture back to Joe, who was all business now, as if the last ten minutes, and his earlier quasi effort at seduction, had never happened. "You're sure?"

She nodded. "But Cornie's right," she added. "Phylly's had the picture for years. What about it?" She was puzzled.

Staring at it, he said, "Maybe nothing . . . but you said Phyllis went to Canada, right?" He studied the picture again. "This looks a lot like a place my partner and I went fishing a few years back. I could be wrong, but I'm betting this is a picture of somewhere along the British Columbia coast. Its extreme west coast."

Chapter 8

Giselle was in the shower when Q found her. Behind the clear glass panels, water sluiced over her nakedness, a warm river of water that pinked her pale skin and blurred her curves. She had her face turned up to the water's rushing source, eyes closed, like a child facing the sun. She ran her hands through her long dark hair and held it behind her head, her arms wings above her shoulders.

Q let his eyes roam over her slowly, knowing her body, lush and toned, was his for the taking. Any time. Any way.

His body, already hard and aching with need, was demanding that taking now. He ignored its clamor, setting his primal urges aside, he chose instead the trial of waiting, to savor his latest possession.

Giselle's breasts—large, as he preferred his breasts—were accented by a twenty-two inch waist, her buttocks were firm, smooth from oiled massage, and her legs were slender with ankles in perfect proportion to the curve of her calves.

Giselle was the best thing to come into his life in too many years to count. A sad commentary, given his hard work and incredible success, yet it was true. She was his most valued possession—absolutely flawless.

Beyond the public ideal lay private perfection, again all his: Her soft mons pubis—which he insisted she have waxed—full labial lips, the moist warm depths of her vaginal orifice, enclosed by pulsing walls of tender flesh and sinew. All of it set to simmer or boil by a single perfect switch—her delicate but fiercely sensitive clitoris. That was his, too, this paradoxical sexual center of woman, both mechanical and magical, or as close to magic as Q allowed himself. He wasn't a man for magic.

When they'd met, Giselle had much darker skin, overly tanned from her time under the California sun. In the month she'd been with him, it had faded somewhat. Q had insisted she stay out of the sun and have regular whole body treatments at St. Maline in Beverly Hills. Pale skin was more to his liking.

Giselle loved the spa, especially the famous people she saw there, and Q was alternately amused by her enthusiasm and aghast at her commonness. That she was still here, that he'd let her stay, almost a month now, occasionally astonished him. If he'd had a heart, he might have said she warmed it, but dead things repelled heat. So he'd come to believe it was more a matter of convenience and his own maturity; he'd become too jaded, too weary for the constant search for new diversions, female or otherwise.

Giselle was simply easy, that was all. A young woman who'd entered his life at the right moment in time. That she'd brought with her an edge of uncertainty further intrigued him. For all her obvious enjoyment of a lavish lifestyle, she had something of the butterfly about her, causing him to be somewhat concerned she might exit his life as easily as she had entered. He wouldn't let that happen.

Her streak of commonness concerned him, of course, as he had no liking for the crass and ordinary, but she was an apt student—most of the time—and willing to oblige him. With time, and his continuing efforts, her rough edges would be as smooth as her spa-pampered skin. As denuded as her pubis. Giselle had balked when he'd made her first appointment for a Brazilian body wax, but Q was immensely satisfied by the results, the shimmer of her pale creamy skin. Certainly worth any discomfort she'd endured.

She turned the water off, again slicked back her hair, and stepped out of the shower. She smiled immediately when she saw him. "Hey, I thought you were busy shuffling papers."

"I was." *Shuffling papers worth ten million dollars*, he thought, but knew she wouldn't be interested. While Q was avid in his efforts to amass money, Giselle only cared about spending it—and in the past few days, she'd been doing even less of that. "I'm done." He wrapped her in a large towel, kissed her wet hair. "Feel good?" he said, squeezing the soft warm terry around her shoulders and rubbing her back.

She turned in his arms, locked her hands behind his neck, and went on tiptoe to kiss him. "Feels wonderful. You feel wonderful." Grinning at him, she said, "Wanna fuck?"

He spun her around, smacked her towel-draped bottom. "You know I don't like your using that street language." And he hated that it aroused him, that she aroused him more than any woman had in years. He was fifty-five years old, past the time merely looking at woman made his testicles ache. But then everything was different with Giselle.

She laughed. "You might not like me to say it, Mister Quinlan-Q-Braid, but you sure like to do *it*." She kissed his cheek—as if he were an old uncle—and gave him a seductive, teasing smile. "And you sure know *how* to do it." She finished toweling off and let the terry drop to the floor.

"Thank you," he said. "It's heartening to know I satisfy you."

She laughed, turned to the mirror, and ran a comb through her dark hair. "It's not heartening that you've been so busy lately." She again pulled the comb though her hair. "Who was the ugly guy I saw leaving here the other night? You were huddled in the library forever."

"No one you need to know about."

She faced him in the mirror. "He sure didn't look like your usual pack of friends—all tricked up in their fancy suits and shiny shoes. I thought he was rather interesting."

"Then I'll bring him back for a ménage à trois. Would you like that?"

She grimaced, gave her hair another stroke, and reached for a jar of lotion. "He's not *that* kind of interesting."

"Then what kind of *interesting* is he?" Quinlan watched her closely. It wasn't like Giselle to ask questions about his business, his friends.

"Hit man-interesting or thug-interesting. Weird-interesting. I don't know. And I don't care." She turned, propped her buttocks on the counter. The position put the best of her on show, again highlighting her recently waxed genital area. "I care about what you're going to do about this." She stroked herself boldly, lifted her breasts.

"What would you like me to do?" Quinlan refused to show his excitement, refused to gratify her in that way. That he felt like tossing her to the floor and ramming himself to her core, he would keep to himself. That he wanted to make her happy, he also ignored. Such feelings were dangerous.

She played with her nipples. "Whatever you'd like to do. What's behind that zipper of yours has probably got some good ideas."

"Too many to pick just one."

He was filthy hard. Loved it. Hated it. To ease himself back, he picked up the towel she'd dropped on the floor, put it in the hamper, not taking his eyes off her naked body. She knew he enjoyed looking at her, and she rewarded him with a full frontal stretch before spreading her legs slightly and running a teasing finger through her exposed crease. "How about starting right about here"—she flicked her clitoris and her eyes closed. When she started panting, she looked at him from under heavy lids. "You sure you don't want to . . . copulate?"

His breath hitched. "Even I have to admit that particular

word lacks cachet." He walked to where she stood in front of his vanity, replaced her finger with his, stroked until she sighed and closed her eyes again. Then he lifted her, set her bottom on the cold granite top and spread her legs. "Wider, Giselle, and hold them there."

"Oh, yes . . . Not a problem, baby." She leaned back, braced herself on her elbows.

He separated her labial lips, played with her until her juices were hot and heavy, then bent his head to kiss her hardened nub. With what touching she'd done to entice him, and if she'd been playing with herself in the shower, as she often did, she was already well primed.

He gave her one deep stroke with his tongue. Took her firm, distended clitoris between his lips and sucked. Hard.

It was enough. Her body convulsed, and she came on a wild shriek.

Giselle wouldn't do well in a motel room.

Q had come to know it made for better sex for him if he brought her to an early release. After his shower, they would go to his bed, where he'd build her tension again, sustain it—and his—until that one blinding moment when for a few seconds, longer if he did things right, his world and its ugly creation left his consciousness.

He stepped back, his penis an iron rod behind the zipper of his slacks.

When Giselle opened her eyes, they appeared unfocused. Her legs were still open, and he could see the moisture glistening on her hairless mons, the shine of it on her inner thighs. She smiled at him, then let her head fall back. "You are so-o-o good at that."

He got a facecloth, dampened it, and started to clean her up. "I'm good at everything. I thought you knew that by now."

She let him wipe her, but when she looked at him, the sexual mist was replaced by curiosity. "I never know if you're being funny or not."

"I'm never funny."

She took the cloth from him, tossed it in the sink, and closed her legs. "Well, that was funny, because you're not good at everything." She looked serious, when she added, "You're perfect, except . . ."

He waited.

"You're so . . . unreachable."

He helped her down from the counter, got her a robe, and helped her into it. "I'm right here. An arm's-length away from you. I'd say I'm very reachable."

"That's not what I mean and you know it."

He tied the belt on her robe and started to take off his clothes. "What do you mean?" Of course, he knew. It wasn't the first time he'd heard the accusation, but women liked to talk after sex, so he'd allow it. It cost him nothing to oblige. He took off his slacks, folded them, and hung them over the brass valet.

She looked at his erection and frowned. "That"—she pointed at his engorged penis—"is what I mean. Like, how can you do what you just did to me, and just, I don't know"—her frown deepened— "just act all normal while your cock's the size of a, uh . . . a Yule log."

The image sat between them as hard as the reality between his legs. He looked down at his heavy jutting appendage. His Yule log . . .

His lips curled and he clenched his jaw tight, but then his chest hurt. He looked up from his erection, into her wide blue eyes, and he . . . laughed. And laughed. The sound of it bouncing off the tile and marble in his bathroom. The sound of it like rap at a funeral. The sound of it painful to his heart.

Q swallowed some air and held his breath, worked to save himself from the hurricane in his lungs.

He had to stop his eyes from watering, regain his decorum, but it hurt. The effort to stop laughing made his throat burn and his stomach ache.

Jesus!

When he managed to draw a proper breath, he looked at Giselle. She eyed him warily. "You're not having a heart attack or something, are you?"

He shook his head—his oddly light head. Laughter . . . he shouldn't be laughing. Quinlan Braid didn't deserve to laugh.

"I'm fine." He turned his back on her and headed to the shower. "And I don't like the word cock, Giselle. It's crass."

Before he could turn the water on, the phone rang.

"I'll get it," Giselle went into his bedroom and got the phone. Holding the phone to her breast, she said, "It's a woman. Should I be worried?"

That she didn't look the least worried, Q found faintly annoying. "Give me the phone, Giselle—and some privacy, please."

"Whatever." She handed him the phone. "I'll be on the bed. Naked. You can tell that to whoever's on the other end of that line."

He didn't have to, because she'd spoken loud enough to be heard on the first floor. "Go."

She went, laughing, and Q put the phone to his ear, his gaze following her, watching as she dropped the robe and climbed onto his bed.

"Yes?" With difficulty he brought his attention back to the telephone—the woman speaking from the other end.

"You asked me to report any, uh, problematic behaviors, Mister Braid."

"Go on."

"Then I think this qualifies: Henry Castor attempted to kill a woman last night and I think the chances are good, he'll try again."

Chapter 9

Henry Castor swigged down the last of his coffee and eyed the buffet; he liked those eggs Benedict things, but his gut couldn't handle a fourth. Plus, they were probably getting all hard, lying there in their steel bed.

For about the fortieth time, he thumbed through the address book he'd set in front of him. Nothing. What kind of friend didn't have another friend's name and address in her goddamn book?

One who didn't need to because she knew it by heart, dumbo.

His bile rose, and his anger, only a sliver under his skin at the best of times, was directed at himself. He thought about checking through the rest of the names in the book, maybe calling on a couple of them, but figured it was a waste of time. And dangerous, because after last night with the redhead, the fewer people who knew he was looking for Worth, the better. Yeah.

He'd fucked up with Rusty Black!

Why the hell didn't he give her his fist instead of a bullet? Why the hell did he let her get to him like that?

A fuckin' woman!

A woman with a piehole she wouldn't goddamn shut. Not that it was his fault he took her down. No way. Between that mouth of hers and the powder he'd put up his nose before going in there, he'd been off his stride. No more of that shit until this job was over. When he had his four mil, he'd swim in the damn stuff.

He'd thought about going back to Worth's old job, the chorus line at Bally's, see if there was something there to give him a lead, but decided it was a waste of his time. Worth hadn't worn a headdress and feathers for years, and if anyone was around who remembered her, they weren't about to tell some guy who wandered in the stage door and started asking questions. In Vegas no one answered questions, unless you were a cop or connected—and neither of those was a guarantee.

Nope, Rusty Black was his only connection—and he'd fuckin' shot her because she'd got in his face. Now he had a bigger problem. The useless piece of ass wasn't even dead—and if she did make it, she could ID him. Jesus!

If that bitch doesn't die, I'll kill her.

He'd already called the hospital from the payphone in the men's washroom. They wouldn't tell him anything, of course, but he'd learned two things: she was hanging on and she had a brother. Tommy Black. *A damn brother . . .*

The penny dropped, and he quickly waved over a waitress. "Sweetheart, do me a favor, will you?" He smoothed a twenty on the table. "Get me a phone book." He smiled as if he meant it, tapped the bill. "I'd appreciate it."

She smiled back. "You got it."

Took her a few minutes. "There you go." She plunked it on the table. "Anything else?"

"Just coffee, sweetheart, and keep it coming. And a couple of those Danish."

When she left, he opened the book to the B listings. Shit! There had to be twenty, thirty Blacks with the initial T. There was always the chance the guy's phone number was unlisted, but considering his sister's wasn't, he might be in luck.

He was on the fifth Black when the cell phone Braid had given him rang in his pocket. Like he needed *him* right now. He pulled out the cell and connected. "Yeah."

"I haven't heard from you."

"'Cause I've got nothing to say, that's why." He stuffed the last of the Danish in and washed it back with some coffee.

"My orders were that you work quietly, under the radar so to speak. You think your attempt to kill Miss Black complies with those instructions, Henry?" A pause. "I think not."

"How the hell did you know about that? Who the fuck are you talking to?" Henry darted his eyes around the busy restaurant.

"Spare me the foul language. I don't like it."

Henry was about to say he didn't give a rat's ass what he liked, but didn't—maybe because this damn call out of the blue had him spooked. This guy was a freak. "What do you want?"

"I want to know if Miss Black is your pipeline."

"No. A bit player, a piece of the puzzle. Nothing to worry about." He was talking too fast. Not good.

"And did she tell you what you needed to know?"

Henry wasn't going there. "Everything's under control, Quinlan. Quit worrying."

"Until this relationship of ours bears fruit, I will worry, and I will watch. Get used to it, Henry. Perhaps if you keep your payday in mind, my presence in your life will be more palatable." He paused. "Answer my question. Did you get the information we need?"

"Yes," he lied.

"There, that was easy, wasn't it?"

"Easy! That bitch made me, and her waking up, blabbing to the nearest blue suit puts me smack on their APB list."

"Irrelevant. She remains of importance to me—as a piece

of that puzzle. And her untimely death would attract attention. And should it come down to your personal safety—may I remind you, you'll have ample funds to leave the country."

"I don't like it."

"You don't have to like it. You just have to do as I say. Stay away from Miss Black. Is that understood?"

"Sure, if that's what you want."

"And from here on I'd prefer to hear from you with more regularity. Twice a day is a minimum—late morning and early evening. I like to hear about the day's events, particularly as they affect our partnership." He clicked off.

Henry muttered the word "shit" under his breath and slipped the phone back in his pocket as casually as possible. Again he scanned the restaurant, trying to spot his tail. No way.

Whoever was on his ass blended in with the hodgepodge of tourists and garish yellow and green wallpaper in the restaurant like they were glued there—as elusive as that twenty million promised by the Big Mama slot machine at the casino entrance.

He told himself to calm down, reminded himself he was safe enough as long as Q didn't get Worth's name. Q got that? Henry was roadkill.

Which is why the prick wanted him to stay away from the redhead. Q wanted her to wake up—and talk. Henry's every survival instinct quivered to life, and a brutal, self-protective rage boiled in his chest. Rusty Black might know where Phyllis Worth was—but she also knew his face. She could nail him for attempted murder.

Which meant she wasn't going to wake up. Ever.

Which meant he had to find her brother.

He went back to the phone book, started dialing.

The third call in: "This is the University Medical Center, can I speak to Thomas Black, please?"

"He's not here right now. Is this about his sister?" a panicky female voice asked. "Can I take a message?"

Bingo!

By the time Henry got off the phone, he had a direct route to Tommy Black, at the Sandstone casino, downtown Vegas.

Henry was back on track.

On his way out of the restaurant, he dropped the Quinlan phone in a trash can. He had a brand new plan: Find Phyllis Worth, get her to tell him where the girl was, then kill the bitch. The girl he'd keep alive for a time—as far away from Q as the planet allowed. Yeah.

He smiled, feeling on top of things for the first time since he'd shot the redhead. Had to love it when a plan came together. And he had a hell of a plan.

He would find a hole somewhere, stash the girl, prep her to chat with Q—and then it really got good. Goodbye four mil. Henry was going to bleed that ice-faced fatcat Quinlan Braid until his last red drop.

Then he'd bleed him again.

Chapter 10

"You come into an inheritance during the cab ride?"
April was speaking to Joe's back, because the second he'd tipped the bellboy, he'd started prowling the spacious suite. He looked out the windows, checked the bar and compact kitchen, then headed for the main bedroom. If he'd heard her he was too engrossed in room reconnaissance to answer.

Cornie said, "If he did, there's no complaints here." Then she dipped her shoulder and let her backpack slide to the floor, while managing to hold on to the battered box she'd brought from home; the one she hadn't finished going through before they'd left the apartment.

April watched her disappear into the second bedroom, carrying the box.

Okay . . . Unless she wanted to share a bed with Cornie, which from past experience was like sleeping with an octopus wearing hunting boots, it looked like the sofa for her. At least it was a step up from the one at Phylly's.

She dropped her bag on the long soft sofa, and followed it with her butt and a sigh. Through the open bedroom door, she saw Joe checking out the mattress with the thoroughness of an engineer checking a launchpad for a space shot. Although she had no idea what made Joe Worth tick—obviously a comfortable bed was high on the list.

What wasn't on the tick-list was the reason for his sticking with her and Cornie on their search for Phylly. He didn't give a damn about his mother, that much he'd made plain. Maybe it was all about his facing her down and having his say, his shot at revenge for Phylly abandoning him. But, frustratingly, whatever his goal was, he didn't seem to be in any hurry to reach it. He was there, with them, but he really didn't seem to care very much. Damned confusing.

Even so, her heart lurched at the thought of what Phylly had done to Joe, the pain it must have caused—perhaps was still causing. She never did get the full story on what had happened. Why Phylly let him go like she had. She'd only heard bits and pieces, snippets Phylly doled out when she had a maudlin moment or one glass of wine too many. Neither situation came along very often, particularly in the past few years when, as Phylly said, she'd finally grown a brain that matched her boob size.

Oh, Phylly, where are you?

April leaned her head on the sofa back and took some deep breaths. She knew mentally chewing on Phylly's bizarre vanishing act was fruitless. Two hours of searching the apartment had netted a big zero. There wasn't a note, a letter, or any other scrap of paper relating to Canada anywhere to be found, other than the picture Joe had taken from the wall. When she'd asked him what he was doing with it, he'd said he was "checking it out." How he was checking it out, she had no idea, other than it involved his resident genius, Kit, back in Seattle. Joe would have to talk for her to know the details, and Joe didn't do conversation. He did one-liners and innuendo.

She lifted her head to see him prowling the main bedroom, exploring it as if he suspected it was seeded with land mines.

Her heart tripped in her chest, and she rubbed at it, shifted her gaze to the clear bright sky outside the window. A white hot day with no relief in sight.

She really hadn't expected an answer to her joking question about his having an inheritance—other than an evasive one. Joe, despite his macho flirting and come-ons, wasn't one for letting anyone get personal. Maybe he was just another "bed-'em-and-beat-it" kind of man. Having married one—her biggest life mistake so far—she sure as hell wasn't looking for another.

After that misguided matrimonial adventure at age twenty-two—paid for with two years of hellish regret—she'd graduated from Love Knocks College with a PhD. Since then she'd taken it re-al slow when it came to men, a species she had an abiding fondness for but didn't quite trust.

Points for Joe included his not wasting that sexy mouth of his prating on about himself, but it would be nice if he'd answer a question or two, maybe drop the big-tough-guy façade—and even nicer if she didn't find herself so . . . amused by him. She wasn't kidding herself, she knew damn well what it meant when a woman had trouble keeping her eyes off a man and got that jumpy feeling in the stomach when he looked at her. It meant caution, dangerous curves ahead. It meant get a damn grip.

Cornie came back into the room after her quick tour of the second bedroom. "Nice place. But that inheritance question of yours, April? I don't think so. I think Joe here is doing the credit card mambo."

"Know the steps well," Joe said, ambling back into the living room and shrugging off his leather jacket. April marveled again at his shoulders, broad and military straight. And there she was again—looking at him, admiring him—she looked away . . . *Damn it!*

And she hadn't had sex in—

God, where had that come from?

She worked to shove what she recognized as a shot of pure, unadulterated lust back into the brain mist it came from. Talk about bad timing!

"Or maybe there's more money in muscle than we figured?" Cornie wasn't going to give up.

Joe arched a brow, then tossed his jacket over the bag April had put on the sofa earlier. "You don't like it, there's always a Bugs-R-Us motel behind The Strip."

"It's fine," April interjected, trying to shut Cornie up with a firm stare. "Just fine." It went way beyond fine, actually. Joe had booked them into one of the luxury suites at the Sandstone: Two private bedrooms, a den with a giant-size TV with a bar big enough, and well stocked enough, to annihilate alcoholically whatever team might be playing on its big screen. The suite had a sitting area larger than the apartment she'd abandoned in Portland.

Portland! She leaped to her feet.

"God, I totally forgot." April put a hand to her head. "I didn't pay my rent on my apartment! And I didn't tell my landlady I was leaving. When Cornie came, told me about Phylly, I just . . . God, she'll think I've skipped." She headed for the phone on the bar. Her landlady, not one to waste time when it came to collecting money, was probably already showing the place to potential tenants. Damn! April needed that apartment until she finished her theater internship. It was cheap, tacky as hell, not in the best part of town, but it was all she could afford.

"Will you call about Rusty, too?" Cornie said. "See how she is."

"I will." April knew Cornie was concerned for Rusty—and anxious to see if she had any word on Phylly. She walked back to where the girl stood and gave her a hug. "Quit worrying, Cornie. Rusty will be all right. Everything's going to be okay. And we *will* find Phylly."

"I know." She took in a big breath. "Make your call, Sis—"Cornie eyed Joe, her expression shifting to mock evil—"and while you're doing that, Joe and I will bond over *Killer Blood Bats*." She waved a CD in front of them. "I brought it from home."

Joe frowned. "What the hell's that?"

"Ah, a greenling. They're the best kind," Cornie said.

While April dialed and smiled, Cornie walked over to Joe and took his hand. "This way, macho man." She led him past April to the den, waving the disk again before plugging it into the video game console. "I'm going to beat your as—butt."

April wasn't sure, but when she saw Joe look down at their joined hands, she was sure she saw the blood drain from his face.

"I learn fast," he said.

"That's what they all say." Cornie gave him a wicked grin.

Joe gave her an assessing look, then glanced at April. She nodded, hoping he would see that Cornie needed the diversion.

"Chicken?" Cornie goaded. "Afraid to die in a pool of bat blood?"

"Those are fightin' words, Cornball." Joe looked at April, and said, "You owe me." How he figured that, she didn't know.

Cornie gave Joe a few terse instructions, and in seconds the bodyguard and the "kid" were hip deep in red-fanged bats.

When Ellie Mack, her landlady answered, April turned her attention away from the dueling duo. She made her apologies and promised a check would be in the mail immediately. Ellie wasn't happy, but she grumped that she "guessed that would be okay—this time."

She was about to hang up, when Ellie added, "By the way, there was some guy here looking for you."

April's heart sputtered for a beat or two. She didn't know a soul in Portland, had arrived barely a month before she'd left again with Cornie for Seattle. "Did he leave his name?"

"Yeah, but I don't remember. Should've wrote it down, I suppose."

Yes, that would have been good. "What did he look like?"

"Tall. Dark hair. Good-looking on one side, bad scar on the other. Kind of along his jaw like."

"When? When was he there, Mrs. Mack?" She kept her voice calm, ignored the chill that danced at the back of her neck. Could it be someone was trying to get to Phylly through her?

"Maybe a couple of days after you left with that girl."

"Okay, thanks." She turned the information over in her mind, didn't like how it finished up.

"If he comes back, you want I should tell him where you are? I've got caller ID, you know. It says you're in Las Vegas." She sounded proud of herself, as if she'd mastered the technical universe.

"No," April said, too quickly. "Don't tell anyone anything. I'll be, uh, leaving here tomorrow morning anyway."

"Right after you send me that check, right?"

"Right. Thank you, Mrs. Mack." She put the phone down.

Joe strolled into the room and headed for the bar; he took out two Cokes. Lifting them, he jerked his head toward Cornie, and said, "The bat demon thirsts. I guess it comes with racking up a high body count. That girl has the eye of a sniper and the tactics of a SWAT commander." Neither of which seemed to displease him.

When she didn't answer, he arched a brow. "Something I should know?"

"A man was at my place in Portland. A man with a scar."

"And?"

"I don't know anyone with a scar."

He set the two Cokes on the counter, studied her face, his own expression flat, unreadable. "You're sure?"

"I'm sure."

"They've connected the dots then—between you and Phyllis Worth."

"Maybe." She nodded toward where Cornie sat in the den, immersed in the game. "Or worse . . . they followed Cornie—and are *after* Cornie."

Joe's jaw set hard, and he followed her gaze to the teenage girl in the den. When his eyes again met hers, they were concerned, protective—and dark with purpose. The kind of eyes you didn't want to see in a shadowed alley. "Then they'll be making a big mistake."

For the first time since Cornie had insisted April find Joe—against what she thought was her better judgment—she was glad she had. If it was Bronze-age female thinking to appreciate having a big strong man in your corner, color her copper. Especially when you had the two people you loved most in the world in that corner with you. She thought of Rusty clinging to life in the trauma center at University Medical, and wrapped her arms around herself, again feeling cold—almost impossible to do in Las Vegas in August.

"I just don't get it." She met his gaze. "Who wants Phylly so much they're willing to kill to find her?"

He was silent for a long time. "I'm new to the family, remember. But the way I see it, there's only one person who can answer that question. And that's the lady herself." He rested his hip on the sofa back, crossed his arms. "And the person that might help us find that particular lady is—"

"Rusty." April let out a breath, irritated and impatient. "Who we can't see until tomorrow." *And maybe not then unless she improves during the night.*

"Yeah, so until then, I say we kick back, relax, and enjoy what the Sandstone has to offer."

Joe eyes were still, but she saw the tension in his body, and he was right—given they had no other choice. April took in another deep swallow of air and told herself to take his good advice. She nodded at him. "And for me," she said, "the first of those Sandstone offerings is a shower, immediately followed by food."

He gave her an unreadable look, then stood away from the sofa. "While you have that shower, I'm going for a run."

"A run? It's a furnace out there."

"One of the reasons the treadmill was invented—along

with air-conditioning and hotel training rooms." He headed for the door. Once there he stopped. "Put the security lock on, don't let anyone in, and don't order room service. I'll take care of that when I get back." His eyes skimmed over her, a sudden lick of flame. "Enjoy your shower." He was gone, stopping long enough to give Cornie, now soloing on the bat game, her Coke and the same instructions he'd given to April.

April had half-expected some double-edged comment from him, about saving water by showering together, but again Joe surprised her. He hadn't looked the least interested; he'd looked preoccupied. And, no, that was *not* disappointment stirring listlessly in her chest. It was . . . surprise he hadn't followed true to form, by being glib and suggestive.

She secured the door and headed for the shower.

Just as well, he'd taken that magnificent bod of his off to the gym, because she'd didn't at all like how her mind—and other parts of her body—responded when she looked at it, or into those silver eyes of his. Joe Worth was a definite babe-magnet, knew it, and relished it. April guessed demagnetizing him wasn't in the cards. He was the kind of guy a woman played with—at her own risk. Not that she was averse to risk—if she knew the odds.

A few minutes later, stripping off her clothes and covetously eying the triple-shower heads in the gymnasium-sized stall, she was more determined than ever to learn about the real Joe Worth. For Phylly, for Cornie . . . and for herself—she wanted to know those odds.

She stepped into the shower, and in moments water was cascading over her naked body. She closed her eyes, enjoyed, and refused to dwell on the fact that, in true Las Vegas style, the marble shower was opulent, out-sized, and definitely built for two.

Henry checked into the Sandstone Hotel and Casino and got the last crap room they had, eighth floor, and a fuckin' mile from the elevator.

He wasn't in the room ten minutes before he was pulling gym shorts from his bag. He needed a workout, something to peel away a couple of layers of frustration and maybe wash away the bitter taste in his mouth. He hated having to work in a strange town—even if it was Vegas. He hated that he had to wait, kill time instead of people, when what he wanted was to get the job done and get the hell out of here.

Not going to happen.

He couldn't pick up Tommy Black until tomorrow, and his planned hospital visit to the sister had to wait until much later tonight. He couldn't risk gambling, because he knew himself well enough to know he'd get carried away, maybe attract attention. All he had left to pass the time was a workout, maybe a massage . . .

Maybe a hooker later.

The idea of that lifted his spirits.

But right now, he was going to the gym, burn off his shit—pretend he was a regular guy on a holiday in *Lost Wages*. Yeah, that was him, all right. Mister Everyman. He snorted.

He stepped into the hall, looked both ways.

One thing about going to the gym, he'd spot anyone trying to follow him. He smiled inside. *Whoever the hell Q had on him, he better be prepared for a good sweat.*

At the thought of Quinlan Braid, his black mood returned.

If that bastard thought he was going to get the better of Henry Castor, he'd been spending too many years in that mansion of his snorting money dust.

In the elevator, he slammed the palm of his hand on the button marked spa, and in a thoroughly pissed-off state watched the numbers drop along with his mood.

One thing was for sure, if he didn't work out, he'd end up punching out the goddamn wall.

Chapter 11

Coming out of the shower just off the exercise room, Joe damn near walked over the guy. Although how he didn't see him was a mystery, the man was damn near as wide as he was high, and he had muscle mass that would be the envy of every gym rat from here to the east coast. "Sorry. I didn't see you," he said.

The man stepped back, and a flash of irritation lit up the hard-ass gaze he leveled on Joe. Just as quickly the anger seemed to disappear, as if the guy was pushing at it. "No problem," he said. "I should have looked where I was going." He scanned Joe's naked body. Nothing sexual in his eyes, more like envy laced with admiration. "Shit, you're in good shape. How much do you bench?"

"Not as much as you, obviously," Joe said and wrapped a towel around his waist.

"One rep max five hundred." He flexed his arms and a bicep popped that rivaled a hot air balloon. "Losing it now, though. The age thing sucks." His expression soured.

The guy was in his forties somewhere, Joe guessed, reaching for his clothes; he had a mean look about him that probably had been etched at birth. A nasty ass, for sure. "Yeah."

The little guy eyed him. "Not that you'd know about that." Again that spark of irritation as if he'd been short-changed in some way—and Joe was to blame.

With no answer to that, even if he wanted one, Joe shrugged and finished dressing. He didn't like the guy, and unless he had it wrong, the jerk had serious anger-management issues—and a mile-wide competitive streak. The kind of guy who always picked a fight with the biggest guy in the bar—which, unfortunately for Joe, was usually him.

"Not much of a talker, are ya?" he said.

"Got people waiting." Joe headed for the door. "Enjoy your workout." He headed for the door.

"Asshole," the guy muttered from somewhere behind him.

Joe smiled and kept on going. His thoughts quickly leaving the muscle freak and fast-forwarding to getting upstairs.

He wanted to be in the suite. He wanted to be with April—be there in time to see her skin all soft and pink from her shower. See her long hair, damp and clinging to her neck . . . just plain see her.

He'd kept his workout short, but he was edgy, still felt as though he'd been gone too long. Not that security was an issue. He hadn't told April, but he'd arranged for a guard on their floor while he was in the gym. He wasn't about to take any chances with either the Cornball or April. A woman who was getting seriously under his skin—so seriously he was running out of the usual gags and one-liners he used to keep his distance and keep it light. Somehow the flirting was flatter than—as Belle Bliss, the wickedest witch among his foster mothers always said—piss on a plate.

The elevator doors yawned wide, and he stepped into the glass and gilt enclosure, immediately shooting an arm out to hold the doors open for three women who'd hailed him down. They clattered into the elevator with him, clutching drinks and slot tickets, and wearing enough perfume to set off a smoke alarm.

They'd all had too much free booze and kept shooting glances his way.

Finally the blonde said, "Are you, like . . . somebody?"

Inwardly he grimaced; outwardly he smiled and looked longingly at the numbers panel on the elevator. *Three.* "Nope."

"You sure do look like somebody. Like maybe a movie actor or something."

Four. "Nope," he said again.

"Maybe not, but I'll bet you know how to party." She ran a red painted fingernail down his arm. "We're on nine."

Five. "My tough luck, because I've got a wife and five kids on the next floor."

"Liar," she said, without a trace of rancor and smiling when she added, "But you can't blame a girl for trying."

Six. Joe stepped out of the elevator, looked back at the three women. "And I hate to think what I'm missing. Thanks for the offer."

"Anytime, big boy, and . . . if you change your mind just you come on by: Nine. Four. One. Five. Otherwise known as Parties-R-Us." They all laughed, the door closed, and Joe let out a breath. It wasn't the first time women had come on to him, and while it was great for the ego, it always made him vaguely uncomfortable.

"If you're done with your pickup routine, you might be interested to know that Cornie's gone."

He turned to see April glaring at him. He didn't bother responding to her sarcasm. "Damn it, I told her to stay put."

"Then you might as well have put the spurs to her mulish teenage butt."

While April appeared calm, Joe's heart beat like a damn jungle drum. "Where is she?"

"She went to a friend's place. Raina Danson, a girl whose parents run a trail riding stable this side of the Red Rock Canyon. Raina's dad picked her up. The minx arranged it before we left Phylly's apartment. Then slipped out when I was in the shower. She's staying the night."

Joe hit the elevator button. "We'll go get her."

April shook her head. "No, I think we should leave her there. I spoke to the family—which boasts three grown sons by the way—and told them enough that they'll be sure to look out for her. Plus it's a long dusty road that leads to their place, so they'll see anyone coming from a mile off." She nodded her head. "She'll be safe there. Raina's dad will bring her back tomorrow morning—after we see Rusty." She shoved her hands in her jeans' pockets. "And I think she needs the horses—the distraction."

The elevator door opened and closed, and two people dressed for the evening gave them an annoyed look when neither of them got in. Joe didn't care. "I don't like it."

"It's not for you to like or dislike." She lifted her chin. "She'll be fine."

"You're sure?"

"Absolutely."

It struck Joe then, what strong women he'd hooked up with. He hadn't yet seen April flinch, although he knew she was frantic about Phyllis, and the same with Cornie. She was the most independent—obstinate—young girl he'd ever come across—not that he knew many young girls. But it wasn't raw stubbornness, with the Cornball, it was savvy and a keen intelligence. The Worth woman had done one thing right at least. She'd raised a hell of a daughter. He looked at April . . . two daughters. He wondered again what had brought the women together, what had made Phyllis choose April . . . over him. *Shit!* Even thinking those kind of thoughts made him feel like his hair was sticking up and he was wearing overalls. Cursing himself, he got back to the subject at hand. "I still don't know how she got past—"

"Him?" April gestured with her head to the security guard standing a few doors down from their suite reading a newspaper. "Piece of cake."

"Great. Las Vegas security at its best."

She gave him a funny half smile, as though she were enjoying herself at his expense. "You didn't tell him to stop anyone from going out—just coming in."

"Maybe because most of my clients are smart enough to stay put when I tell them to stay put."

"Then they're not Cornie."

"No, they're not Cornie," he agreed. Cornie was one of a kind, and a hell of a bat killer.

She raised her eyebrows. "Now, that's progress, Joe."

"What?"

"You said her name."

He looked down at her, easy because she was barefoot. Toes pink as roses. "And you said mine—without that snarly little twist you usually tack on."

"I do not snarl or twist."

He touched her still damp hair, smoothed some strands behind her ear. "I'll bet you do. And I'd bet you growl, too—and moan. I'll bet you're wild as hell—given the right incentive."

She went still as morning.

They were standing outside the door to their suite, face-to-face, the air between them suddenly sharp and weighted, and despite the power of air-conditioning, heating to flash point. He touched her ear, ringed the delicate shell of it with his forefinger. When her breath hitched, he knew it wasn't just him feeling the undertow. The pull. The reckless wanting, coming from nowhere and heading . . . God only knew where. And it wasn't all about his cock, predictably rising to the moment. And it wasn't about getting a quick fuck, more of what he'd had too many times to count.

This pull, this thing, with this woman, seemed askew, like a sloping unmarked path. Different. Unknowable. Hell, he didn't know what it was about or where it came from; all he knew was he liked the feeling as much as he liked the pulsing in his groin . . . the warmth in his chest, and the intrigue in his head.

With April, all systems were go.

"You know," he said, his voice sounding low to his own ears, "what's on my mind, don't you?"

That little lip twist again, an irritating, beguiling half smile. "No. I don't have a clue."

He grinned. "Then maybe I should show you."

"Try words first. They're such a challenge for you."

She was playing him. He liked playing—especially when he had an edge. He slipped his other hand to her shoulder and with her delicate neck between both hands, he stroked her jaw with his thumbs. Her skin was soft and silky from the warmth of the shower. "I, Joseph Jonathan Worth, would very much like to kiss you." *Then I want to do a hell of a lot more. I want you naked, and doing some of that twisting and snarling you say you don't do, where we can make the most of it. Because I think you're a match for me, April Worth. I think you'll give me as good as you'll get. Which I'll make sure is so good you'll never forget it.*

She met his gaze, her own curiously thoughtful. "Not that I have anything against kissing," she said, her tone as low as his. "And I think you and I could be . . . interesting." She touched his mouth, smoothing three fingers over it with a touch so soft he wondered if he imagined it. "But I'm not going there with you until we talk . . . straighten a few things out."

He tilted his head, slid one hand across her straight shoulder, which luckily for him was bared by one of those skinny strapped things that made a man want to lift that quarter inch of fabric with his little finger and slip it down and over the arm—which he did.

Get it off. Get everything off.

His blood was running too high. And those words she wanted? Not a problem. Small hurdles on a track where the race belonged to the sprinter who jumped the highest. "Okay." He took a step forward, backed her against the door, and leaned close enough to see her irises darken, smell the woman mystery under the flowery scent of soap, and hear her sharp intake of breath. "Exactly what kind of *things* would you like straightened?"

"Joe, this is not talking." She narrowed her gaze but didn't look the least intimidated by having six-feet-three-inches and two-hundred pounds of man in her face. She looked determined—and she was breathing heavy. Which he took for a good sign. A very good sign. He ran a finger along the edge of her top, over the swell of her breasts, one still covered by cotton, the other partially exposed by the dropped strap. Breasts he couldn't wait to get his hands on—his mouth on.

"You were saying?" His eyes followed his finger, trailing the top of her semi-bared breast, and his ears deadened to anything except the blood pounding in his ears. For a second or two—he was losing it fast now—he watched the rise and fall of her breathing, his erection seeming to pulse and grow in an identical rhythm.

Oh, Jesus . . .

"For one thing—"

He took her face in his hands and kissed her silent, a first taste, then another, until their mouths knew each other. Until he felt the blood beat in her throat, his own heart slam against his ribs, and the weight and length of him behind his zipper set up clamor enough to draw a goddamn crowd. He groaned against her lips, slid his fingers into her hair, held her mouth to his.

Oh yeah . . .

He kissed her again, deeper, then deeper still. Sliding his hands across her shoulders, down her arms, he clasped her narrow waist, then cupped the roundness of her ass. Pulling her rough and flush to the desperate demand between his legs, appeasing it with body against body.

Too many clothes . . .

She gave him her tongue and he took it, sucked, and gave back. No angel kisses now. Just the devil's own hard need.

She put her arms around his neck, lifted herself on her toes, crushed her breasts against his chest and gave into the kiss fully.

Her mouth was hot heaven and he wanted more.

More. He swept her mouth, her lower lip with his tongue. Tasted the peppermint flavor of her toothpaste.

More.

He lifted his head, looked into her eyes—as blindly glazed as he was sure his own were—and whispered close to her mouth what his body dictated, "I want you, April. I need you."

He heard her drag in a rocky breath. "We're in the hall," she said and blinked. "We're still in the damned hallway."

Laughter came from somewhere behind them. A couple stood at the elevator, the woman had a hand over her mouth. The elevator doors opened and they got in. The guy held the door open long enough to stick his head out, smirk, and say, "Y'all have a nice evening. Hear?" There was more laughter as the doors closed.

"Oh, my God," April said, her tone a mixture of shock and confusion. "I can't believe we did that." She put her hand in her pocket and pulled out the room's keycard, but her hand was shaking so bad they'd be out here a week before she got them inside. She glanced at the guard down the hall; he snapped the newspaper up to cover his grin.

Joe took the card from her, slid it in and out of the slot, and opened the door. "And I sincerely hope we do it again—real soon." He closed the door and reached for her.

She evaded him with catlike ease, and held up a hand, palm out. "Down boy! We need to talk."

Her eyes were wide and kind of gauzy and the flush on

her face was hot pink. He liked it, liked what it meant. "We just did that."

"You call that talk?" She touched her still moist lips.

"Works for me." He reached for her again.

She eluded him, again, her wide eyes narrowing dangerously.

Shit! He put his hands in his pockets, and with every nerve, muscle, and sinew in his body readied for sex, he figured it was best to keep them there.

April stood back from him, not breathing too steadily herself, and dropped her eyes to his crotch—his goddamn bulging crotch. Her looking at him had him stifle a moan and the big boy in his jeans consider another hurdle jump.

Her eyes met his then, and she said, "I knew this would happen."

"Happen? Did something happen?" he looked at his staggering erection. "Maybe somebody should tell Bigfoot down there."

She smiled, and he could see she was trying not to laugh. "You're not mad."

He thought about that. "I would be if I thought what we did back there"—he gestured with his head toward the hall—"failed to qualify as foreplay." He watched her face. "Did it?"

She thought a moment, moistened her lips with her tongue, and shook her head. "No."

He nodded. "Round one, then. Do you want a drink?"

"Just some water—and that talk you promised."

The woman was a pit bull.

Joe headed for the bar, working to cool down as he walked. He wanted to bed this woman so bad his damn teeth hurt, along with a million other parts of his anatomy, but he knew when to push, and he knew when not to. Although he didn't much like the idea of that talk she was so keen on. Talk, to a woman, generally meant digging in old hard ground, a lot of work for no return.

On the other hand, if he went along with her, maybe he'd learn a few things. Ever since she'd mentioned the scarred man who'd come by her apartment, he'd wondered if her connection to his mother had played a part in Phyllis's disappearance. Now was as good a time as any to find out—nothing else currently being on his damned agenda.

He put his hands palm flat on the granite surface of the bar counter and set about turning the tables. "Fair enough. We'll talk. But you first."

She frowned. "Me?"

"You." He reached for a couple of glasses. "You can start by telling me how you came to be Phyllis Worth's daughter."

Chapter 12

April, still trying to rein in her hormones and get back to a semblance of sanity, stared at Joe, who, after laying down the question she hated above all others, had set about clinking ice into tall glasses and pouring water from the large bottle of Evian he'd pulled from the fridge. He was as unhurried and casual as if what had happened between them in the hall took place last week instead of mere moments ago.

She turned her back on him, walked to the window, and stared out at the lights of Fremont Street, her thoughts jumpy and haphazard, like pebbles scattering over glass.

Obviously, Joe Worth rallied fast.

Too bad she couldn't do the same. She stood like a statue at the window, wanting—the dew between her legs telling her exactly *what* she was wanting—and wondered how things had got so out of hand so damn fast. She was no shy virgin, but she'd never been sucker punched by a kiss before. Never.

She hugged herself tight. *April, you'd be the biggest fool in the universe if you give more meaning to that kiss than it deserved. Until you know more about Joe.*

She took some quiet but very deep breaths, got herself—somewhat—under control, somewhat rational, and reactivated her caution light.

Men liked sex. No secret there. Every woman in every chorus line in Vegas knew that. If April's three years on the line had taught her anything, it was to not get light-headed because a man wanted you. Like Phylly once said, it didn't mean you'd won the damn lottery. From the time she'd come to live with Phylly, she wanted to be like her—she just couldn't figure out exactly what Phylly was. An angel yes, but crazy weak-headed when it came to the male half of the population.

By the time April was sixteen, she was spooked by Phylly's parade of men, her on-again-off-again romances, her romantic highs, lows, and broken dreams. Spooked, too, by Phylly's constant admonitions to "not do as I do—but do as I say." Be smart, she'd say and find yourself a nice guy and settle down. Which appeared to be the last thing in the world she herself wanted. But watching Phylly play with men, with sex, looked so emotionally dangerous, she'd taken her advice—and married the first man who'd asked her. She'd pegged Royce as strong, decisive, and ambitious, and she'd been wrong on all counts; he was cold, mean-spirited, and selfish. When she'd finally realized that the last man on earth she wanted to father her children was her husband, she'd left—both him and the showgirl life—and went to work for Rusty at Hot and High.

Now, given that her man-for-a-lifetime idea hadn't worked any better than Phylly's man-of-the-week system, all she had left was wariness and confusion. Not good launching pads for a successful male/female relationship.

"Here." Joe came up beside her and handed her a glass of water.

"Thanks." She took a deep drink.

"Shoot," he said, taking a drink himself, and like her, looking down at the lights in the street below, glittering to life as the sun reluctantly gave up center stage.

April turned to face him, studied the determined line of

his jaw, the intensity in his gaze, and decided to do something she hadn't done in a very, very long time—take a leap of faith. She would trust Joe Worth—at least partly. Maybe because he was his mother's son, or maybe because she needed to trust someone, and he was handy. Or maybe because he was simply Joe, a man she'd come to like, more than she'd planned to. Still, she didn't meet his eyes when she started her sordid little story. What she did was take a deep breath. "Your mother rescued me from a pedophile when I was nine years old."

His gaze filled with sick shock then questions. After a short silence taken, she expected, while he attempted to digest the indigestible, he said, "Other than telling you the idea of you . . . of *that* makes my stomach turn, I don't know what to say."

"I wouldn't expect you to." She kept her gaze on the glittering, pulsing lights outside, the effect pleasingly hypnotic. "And if it's all the same to you, I'll stick with the abridged version." She glanced at him. "The only reason I'm telling you this is because I want you to see another side of your mother."

He studied her a moment, then nodded.

She went on, "I was being . . . held in a house in Seattle. When Phylly figured out what was going on—"

"What was she doing there?"

His question caught her off guard. "I don't know," she lied—or edited. She wasn't sure which. What she was sure of was that Joe didn't need to know everything, that parts of her story—and Phylly's—were best left in the past where they belonged.

Don't say his name. Ever. Phylly's rule.

She realized she'd stopped talking, that Joe was waiting, still as marble, for her to go on.

"Some people came to the house one night—and Phylly was with them. I heard music. I suppose, like a lot of . . .

those people, he led a second life, something close to normal—at least on the surface of things." She shot him a glance. "All I know is your mother got me out of there, and I'll never forget it." *Middle of the night. Out the basement window. Running wildly down the street. Winter. Dogs barking. No socks. Scared . . . Cold. So cold. The red light of a taxi. Finally a taxi.* "We just ran. She didn't look back and neither did I."

The way he was looking at her, she thought maybe he hadn't bought into her claim of not knowing why Phyllis was in the house that night, that he was going to ask for a better explanation; he didn't. "What you told me, sounds like the abridged beginning of Part Two—the you and Phyllis part. How about Part One? How did you come to be in that house in the first place?"

"It's ugly, Joe." Everything inside her tightened, twisted.

"It doesn't get much uglier than what you just told me." His silver eyes were quiet and watchful, telling her she couldn't stop now.

Oh, yes it does. She swallowed, searched her mind for a starting point. "For a few years my brother and I—"

"You have a brother?"

"*Had* a brother." His interruption rattled her, set her off course. She loved/hated thinking about Gus, but talking about him, about what happened, was new to her. Scary. She'd left it all behind for so many years.

"No other family?"

She shook her head. "A grandmother—we called her granna—who died when I was eight or so." *Just Gus . . .* And on that long-ago night, she'd lost him. "At least no one I know of."

He lowered his head, lifted her chin so their eyes could meet. "You should know I'm having a hell of time resisting the urge to put my arms around you."

She wanted those arms. *Oh, how she wanted them.*

"Keep resisting," she said, "or that 'Part One' you're so interested in will never get told."

"You sure about that?"

She straightened her shoulders. "I'm sure."

"Go on, then." He cupped her shoulder briefly, let his hand slide off her. "I'll save my questions—and keep my arms to myself—until you're done."

"Thanks." She got her direction again, held it, determined to keep her voice firm, her emotions trimmed. "Both my mother and father were addicts, so for most of our early years Gus and I lived with our grandmother, a custody thing probably. And that was okay. Better than okay, really. I loved her. So did Gus." She stopped. "But when she died . . ." *Everything changed.* April rubbed her forehead when the old images came: Granna, being carried out of their snug apartment, an old man at one end of the stretcher, a young man at the other, complaining because the ancient elevator wasn't big enough. Granna sleeping under the white sheet, Gus beside her, his silent tears making rivers on his handsome face, his hand holding hers so tight it hurt. She let the memories drift back to where they'd come from, deep in her heart, where she guarded them jealously, and where she so often replayed Gus's words: *It'll be okay, April, I promise. I'll look after you no matter what.* It was a promise he couldn't keep.

One look in Joe's eyes reminded her she'd stopped talking again, but true to his word, he hadn't prodded, hadn't interrupted her thoughts. She went on, "When Granna died, our mother came for us. I remember wondering who the strange lady was. If I had seen her before it had to have been when I was very young, because I don't remember recognizing her. And for a while, I was excited about the idea of having a real mommy and daddy."

Now that memory brought only pain.

"About six months later, my father died"—April met Joe's gaze briefly—"from an overdose. After that my mother went a little crazy, I guess. She owed money or needed drugs, I don't know which." Her mouth was dry, her lips, even though equally as dry, fused together. She tried to dampen them. "She was down to her last . . . saleable asset."

"Which was?"

"Me."

"Jesus!" The word came out of his mouth on a low growl.

April paused again. "I remember a tall dark man coming to get me . . . he wore a red wool cap." She stalled on the nonessential memory. But, in the grayness of a dirty kitchen oddly bleached and shadowed by the light from the bare bulb over the kitchen table, the cap was so bright, so vivid. She'd never forgotten it. "I remember my mother standing in the corner watching. She had her arms wrapped around herself, and she was thumping the back of her head against the wall."

"And your brother?"

"He wasn't home. There was never much food in our, uh, house, so Gus used to go out sometimes to get us something to eat. Sometimes from the alleys behind the restaurants . . . wherever." She didn't want to think about that. "Anyway, even if he'd been there, there wouldn't have been much he could have done. He was barely twelve years old." *But he would have fought for me. I know he would have done that, at least. He would have tried. Not like the woman who was her mother who watched her go—lost in space and banging her head on the wall.* "After that night— after the man took me—I never saw him, my brother, or my mother again."

"Did you look?"

She nodded. "For Gus, yes. Phylly had someone do some checking about a year or so after I came to live with her." *When she thought it was safe.* "By that time, my mother was dead—same cause as my father—and Gus had disappeared."

"In the system?"

"No. There was nothing."

"And that was it? You let it go. Your brother and the piece of shit you were sold to."

There was nothing accusatory in his tone, more a level-headed grasp of an ungraspable situation, but the words were nettles in her brain.

"Yes." She gave him a level gaze. "We let it go, because there wasn't a choice. I didn't want to be taken away from Phylly, and there wasn't a chance in hell she'd have been given custody of me. She was straight with me about that from the beginning. That no one in authority, be it police, social workers, or judges would go for the idea of a young, out-of-work dancer taking a nine-year-old girl across state lines." *Plus there was the money she'd "borrowed" from the man who'd locked that nine-year-old in his basement— a man masquerading as an oh-so-proper citizen—but who had friends in all the down and dirty places.* April knew it was the illegal types rather than the legal ones who terrified Phylly the most.

The man Phylly had taken her from was seriously connected and cared even less than Phylly about crossing state lines. Then there were the outstanding charges against Phylly, like the boss from the club she'd been working in wrongly accusing her of stealing the bar cash. Joe didn't need to hear that. It was ancient history now, but back then, as Phylly said later, her life was such a mess. There were a hundred reasons for her and April to fly under the radar.

"Why do I have the feeling you've left out as much out as you put into that story," Joe said.

"My story. My way."

Silence.

"Fair enough," he finally said, but he didn't look pleased about it.

She went on. "I did look for Gus again, a couple of years ago, but"—she lifted a shoulder, tried to look as though the disappointment of not finding him wasn't a shadow on her soul—"nothing. It was as if he'd vaporized."

"What was his name—obviously it wasn't Worth?"

"Hanlon. August Hanlon. Both of us were named for our birth months."

"Hm, clever," he said, but for a moment he looked distracted.

April shook away the sadness that came with thinking about Gus, and determined not to speculate on her brother's fate, she went on. "Anyway, from the time Phylly took me out of the house that night and brought me here"—she gestured to Planet Vegas outside the window—"it was just the two of us—until Cornie came along." An addition they'd both been crazy happy about and still were. April was seventeen, Phylly thirty-three, when Cornie made three, and April had been a hybrid mother/sister to her ever since. With Phylly still working chorus and the crazy hours that came with it—and still a bit crazy herself—when Cornie entered their lives, most of the household jobs and child rearing was left to April. And she'd loved it. They'd made a family. The first she'd ever had. She looked at Joe, about to tell him that, but stopped herself. Afraid talking about how good things were between her, Phylly, and Cornie would be rubbing salt in his own childhood wounds.

If Joe wanted to ask anything about their family connection, he didn't. He ran a hand over his jaw, looked away, then set his half-full water glass on the table under the window. Pacing a few steps away, his expression deadly serious, he turned back to ask, "Who took you that night? Do you remember?"

Her heart stone hard in her chest, she answered, "Oh, I remember him all right, every hard line in his face. I remember he had creases in each earlobe, like seams, and a dark spot, right here"—she touched directly under her chin—"a birthmark shaped like a big teardrop—or to be more specific like those drawings of sperm. And I remember he had the coldest, blackest eyes I'd ever seen."

"A name? Did you hear his name?"

"I never heard it." She left the window and walked toward the center of the room. She was done talking, and done answering questions. "All of that was a long time ago, and to be honest, I've tried to forget it ever happened. Thanks to your mother, I almost succeeded." Maybe she and Phylly had raised denial to an art form, but it had worked so far, and there was no point in messing with success. Or disturbing deep-freeze memories.

"Not good enough."

"I'm hungry. Shall we have room service?"

He stood in front of her. "That's it? We leave it there?"

"We leave it there."

When he gripped her arms, she tried to pull away. He didn't let her. "Tell me one thing," he said. "Did the bastard who took you"—the muscles along his jaw went taut—"touch you?"

April couldn't stop the quivering, the return of icy fear, but she shook her head. "No. I wasn't meant for him."

Joe frowned, continued to hold her arms, his grip easing somewhat, but he didn't take his eyes off her. "I don't get it."

She again tried to pull away, and this time he let her go, but he remained standing over her, a wall of avenging masculinity. "I was a luxury item, a green-eyed blond child, without a soul in the world who'd come looking for me." She stopped. "The night Phylly took me was the night I was supposed to be put on a ship for southeast Asia—to my new owner."

Chapter 13

With every word April said, Joe's gut had tensed as if taking a blow, and he'd had a hard time keeping his mouth shut and his hands off her. He wondered if she knew how she looked telling her story; her wide eyes looking away from him—childlike, as was the constant swallowing and straightening of shoulders, as though what she was saying would get her in trouble somehow. Either that or she was terrified of losing control, determined to keep her more fragile self together—while keeping everyone else out. April Worth had taken the art of composure to a whole new level.

She turned away from him and headed to the bar area. Once there, cool as the granite countertop she stood beside, she said, "Shall I order dinner or would you prefer to go out?"

It was as if she'd put up a stop sign, closing off memory lane, a road she hadn't liked traveling in the first place. "I take it we're done talking," he said.

"I'm done. We haven't started on you yet," she said, adding, "Dinner. In or out."

"In."

She picked up the phone, raised a questioning brow.

"A steak. Medium. Some vegetables."

He watched her place their order and wondered how the hell he was going to eat. Christ, he'd thought his childhood was a butt-pain. Hers was a damn heart attack.

Joe knew what it was like to be an *unnatural*—meaning having an indecipherable childhood; only pieces and bits of anything remotely normal—but having to *be* normal in spite of it.

Her own mother had sold April for cold hard cash—and if Phyllis Worth hadn't come along and got her out of that house, she'd have been in a container heading to the far east. And one of the ugliest most abusive lives a young girl could know. He looked at April, tried to ignore the constriction in his lungs, the uneven beat of his heart, the damned irony of it all—for the first time in his life, he had something to thank his mother for. It might not be enough to obliterate that melting ice cream sandwich, but it sure as hell was something.

"I'm going to freshen up," she said. "Dinner will be thirty, forty minutes, that okay?"

Joe thought she was more than fine just the way she was, but he understood the drill. She needed space. "Fine." He walked toward her. "What you told me . . . Getting past that. It's a hell of a thing." He stroked her hair.

"It was a long time ago. And as to that 'getting past it'? Life doesn't really give you a choice."

"Maybe you're right, but it's not fun dragging it up again."

"True." She paused and a slight frown creased her forehead. "Made me feel like that nine-year-old girl again." Then touching his face, she added, "Now, I'm going to get my act together for dinner, and come back here all grown up."

He turned her hand, kissed her palm. "Good, because I'm a lot more comfortable around consenting adults."

She gave him a quick smile. "I'll bet you are."

He watched her disappear into the bedroom.

He didn't know a lot about kids—on a personal level— but the idea of someone hurting a child, *trafficking in them*, made him dangerously angry.

In the last two years, partnering with Julius Zern in Guardian, protecting families—particularly the kids—had become a large part of their business, and it took them all over the world. But generally the work was for wealthy, high profile parents who were afraid of kidnappers and ransom notes—not sickos with travel plans.

Joe's relationships with kids might have been all business—one game of video bat battle hardly counting—but he liked them and he respected their innocence. He'd even taken a bullet for one once. Because kids weren't meant to be hurt. By anyone. Anytime. Ever. Period.

But out of all of April's story, one thing stuck like a burr in his brain. He couldn't pinpoint why he was so sure, but he was; this trouble with Phyllis Worth meant trouble for April. It was connected. All he had to figure out was how.

Joe went to the phone, dialed Kit. Got Julius instead. "What are you doing there? I thought you were in Mexico City with the Milonos."

"Was. Nick Milono's meetings went better than expected so the family decided to come home early. Plus one of the kids wasn't doing so well with the air down there," Julius said, his unusual bass-toned voice more gravelly than usual.

"You sound like crap."

"Feel like it, too. Got a head cold. Where the hell are you?"

"Vegas." Joe tried to visualize his partner, six-foot-four and outweighing him by twenty pounds, being broadsided by a cold virus. Normally it would take the offensive line of the Oakland Raiders.

"Nice. Who's the client?"

"Not so nice—brutally hot. And there is no client." He rubbed his jaw. "And if it's all the same to you, I'll leave the complete story for a stool in a dark tavern and too many beers."

"Your call."

"Is Kit there?"

"No. He's going out with . . . what do you call those beautiful creatures with curves? Been so long, I forget."

"Kit's got a date?"

"Yeah. He's caught himself a live one."

"You feeling sorry for yourself?"

Julius laughed. "Hell of a thing, Kit getting all the babes."

Joe looked again at the door April had gone through. *Not all of them.* Not that Julius had trouble getting women— when he bothered. Which, from what Joe could see, wasn't very often. The occasional tall, leggy creature showed up in his life for a month or two, then she was gone, and Jules never seemed the worse—or better—for it. A story there, Joe figured, but he never pressed. Zern's business until he decided otherwise. Plus, the guy was a work freak and, like Joe, most of his life was lived coming and going.

Since the two ex-army buddies set up Guardian, their business had grown steadily. In the current climate, there was no shortage of demand for well-trained muscle, sharp eyes, and even sharper brains. They knew they'd made it when their phone started ringing with calls from families in places like Saudi Arabia, China, and, of all the damn places, Iceland. If the family was important, and they had a travel itinerary, they called Guardian.

"While you're sitting there feeling hard done by," Joe said, "could you do me a favor?"

"Name it."

"See what you can find out about the name Hanlon, Gus or August Hanlon. Out of Seattle originally, but could be anywhere."

"That's a pretty blind search."

"All I got." And if anybody could find out anything, it would be Jules. The man had friends in all the right places, high and low.

"I'll do what I can. And I'll get Kit on it when he gets down from his love cloud."

April walked back into the room—all grown up, just as she'd promised, and suddenly Joe had to concentrate on breathing.

"You still there?"

"Yeah, I'm here. Thanks, Jules." Joe lowered his voice. "I'll call you tomorrow."

"Is she pretty?" he asked.

Joe's mind blurred about the time he saw April stroll into the room wearing some strappy little black dress that showed enough leg to bring a man down from a hundred paces. He was having trouble un-blurring it. That dress would slip off like silk from warm marble. If he was real lucky, she'd be thinking exactly the same thing. Distracted, and without looking away from her, he said, "What was that?"

Julius laughed. "Forget it—and enjoy. But remember—be careful out there." He hung up.

Joe followed suit but left his hand on the phone, his eyes never leaving April. He had no intention of "being careful." Hell, his defenses were already breached, all that was left were a few crumbling walls.

And the black dress had pretty much finished those off.

Giselle caught Quinlan unaware. Coming up from behind him, she covered his eyes with her soft hands, and whispered in his ear, "Guess who?" She nipped his earlobe.

He covered her hands with his. "A beautiful young woman who—I thought—was doing what she calls her 'spa thing'."

"I love it when you're wrong." She took her hands from his eyes, kissed his head, and walked around to face him.

He was sitting in one of the double lounges beside the pool, his papers and files neatly stacked beside him on a round glass table. A plate of cheese and a large bowl of fruit sat in the middle of the table, along with a glass and a fine bottle of Burrowing Owl Merlot. A new wine he'd only recently discovered.

Earlier, Quinlan had taken his work—today mostly research reading—outside, intending to enjoy the soft breezes of early evening, the sunset and, finally, the cooling air.

He was also expecting a call from Las Vegas and preferred to take it privately on his cell. Since Henry had stopped calling, he was forced to rely on the reports of his hired hands. So far such reports had yielded little, other than the fact that Castor had worked out earlier in the Sandstone exercise room, then procured himself a prostitute. The lack of news had Q unsettled.

Giselle reclined on the lounge beside him, obviously intending to stay—with no apology about disrupting his work or his concentration. That he didn't mind alternately irritated and surprised him. In truth, he welcomed the diversion.

"I've come to talk to you," she said, closing her eyes. "Oh, but this is nice." She stretched, putting her hands above her head, and wiggling her toes in the last of the sunlight touching the base of the lounge. "You do know how to live, Q." She said the last with her eyes still closed, an impish grin on her face.

Quinlan frowned. Her toenails were painted black, making him think of street punk and rebellion. He'd need to speak to her about that. But not this moment. This moment he would enjoy the stirrings in his loins, the sight of her woman's mound, high and round, enfolded in fine white cotton.

He liked the way the waning light played on her hair and pale skin, making her look fragile and ethereal. He liked the bikini she wore, a thousand dollars worth of white fabric and lace that showed off every inch of her smooth skin, high on the thigh and skimming the rounds of her buttocks. But not a thong. Quinlan didn't like them and refused to buy them for her, considering them excessively immodest. He had no wish to see her parading around his friends at the pool in a state of near nakedness. She was for his eyes only.

He marveled, as he always did, at the paradox of her, her disingenuous playfulness and the intensity and wildness of her response to him in bed. She delighted him and troubled him. He was perilously close to a new and uncomfortable emotion—an emotion he'd always believed was the downfall of the stupid and careless.

"What is it you want to talk about?" he asked, knowing his own desires veered away from talk to another more interesting activity upon sight of her. Unfortunately, those thoughts were also inopportune, given the only privacy they had was the lounge canopy, not enough to conceal them from the second floor of the house. With a staff of four, there was bound to be someone looking on.

"I'm going home," she said. "Later tonight, I think."

The words hit him as if they were cold sharp stones, alphabet pieces he needed to assemble before he could understand their meaning. "Home?" he repeated, subduing his shock and an inexplicable surge of . . . disappointment. *No.*

Momentarily unable to add more to his inane echo, he finally said, "I don't understand."

She opened her eyes, turned her head to look at him. "Home—as in the place I grew up? Dad, brothers, a sister, all that stuff." She smiled at him, oblivious to his confused reaction. "Dad's fifty-sixth birthday is next week, and one of my brothers has arranged a party. It'll be wild. And a big surprise for Dad."

"I see." He swallowed, seeming to have trouble clearing his throat.

"It'll just be for a few days. It'll be fun. God knows there's never enough of that!" She reached across Q, picked up the half of a peach he'd left on his plate, and took a bite.

She knew he hated her eating from his plate, yet he let her transgression slide.

She was going away. While his brain processed her words, his stomach muscles clenched.

"Mmm, this is good," she murmured.

The peach juice made her lips shine, and she tongued it from the corners of her mouth, momentarily disturbing his concentration. "I didn't know you had . . . siblings," he said.

She took another bite of the peach, smiled before answering. "Siblings? Why does that word sound so right coming from you." She put the peach pit back on his plate. "Yes. I have siblings, Q. Two brothers and one sister."

"You never mentioned them."

"You never asked. Too busy fucking me, I guess."

"Giselle, I've told you I—"

"I know, I know, you don't like the word . . . just the act." She grinned briefly. "You know, for such a totally fuckable man, you're a real prude." She rolled over and swung one leg across his crotch, then she raised herself above him on her knees. "And, by the way, that was not a complaint." She undid his belt, unzipped him, and slid her hand inside his pants, stroking him over his silk boxers.

When she found him semi-erect, her grin widened. She yanked his boxers down, so quickly his breath caught. "Looks like I have some work to do," she said. Enfolding his penis in her hand, she pumped him, slowly tightening her grip.

His body bucked, and he briefly closed his eyes, before clasping her hand, stopping its work. "*No!* Not now, Giselle." He clenched his teeth, swallowed. Quinlan refused to let sex—his body's demand for it—cloud his thought process. And while it had been growing increasingly difficult with Giselle, he considered his self-imposed rule inviolable. "No," he said again for her benefit—and his.

She looked surprised, shrugged, and rolled off him.

Q did up his zipper and belt. "This idea of yours, about going home. I'm against it. I thought you understood. I don't like plans being dropped on me without proper consultation."

"What's to consult? I'm going home for my dad's birthday. What's the big deal?" She sat up, yoga-style, looked at him, her eyes questioning. Alert.

"The big deal, as you put it, is that I expect to be considered when you make decisions that affect me and my household."

She looked at him in what he could only call bafflement. "You're kidding, right?"

"You know I don't kid."

For a moment, silence took its place between them on the lounge. A silence of weight and sharp edges.

She got up, stood over him, and tilted her head. He stood to face her, the lounge solidly between them. "And I don't think I'm going any further with this conversation," she said. "Because if I do, there'll be a winner and loser. Not a good thing for a relationship of convenience like ours. So I'll just say again: I'm going home. I'll be back—when I get back. As long as you don't say another word about 'consultation' or how *my* decisions affect *your* freakin' household."

"You're being childish, Giselle. I don't like it."

"And you're being an asshole, Quinlan, and I don't like that." She stomped off with all the pageantry of a spoiled heiress.

He watched her go, then took the first step to follow her—to set her straight about his requirements. His phone rang.

He checked his call display: Las Vegas. He drew in an impatient breath and watched Giselle disappear into the house before he answered.

"Mister Braid? Mercy here."

"Yes?" Q had hired two people to tail Castor: Mercy was one of them, Charity was the other. It was Mercy who'd originally called him to tell him about Victor's death. She'd wanted him to know of her and her sister's availability for any work that he might have. It seemed Victor's death had seriously cut into their income. On Victor's recommendation he'd hired them once before to locate some particularly time-sensitive SEC filings that he'd needed before they were made public. He'd been impressed with their work—and he'd made a fortune. Their dealings, all arm's length, suited Quinlan. "Is there a problem?" Q pulled his gaze from the house where he could see Giselle pacing, see her pick up the phone.

"Henry Castor just got into a cab. I'm right behind him."

"Good."

"No. Not good at all. He's headed for the University Medical Center."

Quinlan closed his eyes—*the hospital where Rusty Black lay, barely alive.* Obviously the blundering oaf intended to correct his first botched effort and kill the woman—against Q's specific orders. *Or he'd lied. Perhaps Miss Black was more than the "bit player" Henry claimed she was. And perhaps he hadn't got the information he needed from her during their earlier encounter.*

He worked to make sense of it. But only one thing appeared certain: Henry Castor was an idiot; worse yet, he was a loose cannon. Tension hot and sharp clutched at his spine. He detested unpredictability.

"What do you want me to do?" Mercy asked.

"Give me a moment."

Quinlan walked toward the pool, stood gazing into its pristine water. All Henry had that Quinlan didn't at this point was the name of the mysterious pipeline—the person who would lead him to the girl. That name was all Q needed to remove Castor from the game. Therefore, his decision was either to protect Rusty Black from the murderous fool at all costs and elicit the information from her himself at a later date—both time-consuming and risky—or let Henry do whatever he planned to do—and see where the blood-soaked path led him.

"Mister Braid?"

"Do nothing," he ordered. "Let him proceed with whatever his plans are—but do *not* lose him." He hung up, thinking about Castor's bloodied path and whether or not the footprints he made on it would lead to himself.

If Castor made any more mistakes ...

Slowly massaging his nape, Quinlan considered a fallback plan, one requiring his personal involvement. Something he hadn't considered until this moment. The thought brought an unexpected surge of excitement.

Hands-on killing ... it had been a long time.

He'd been young then, hungry and ambitious. Today he was fifty-five years old, feeling the weight of his years and a growing boredom and complacency. His old appetites for sex, money—life itself—had waned.

Until Giselle ...

Giselle who'd ignored his demand that she stay. He felt a chill, a shortening of his breath. Perhaps Giselle sensed his graying spirit.

Perhaps revisiting those youthful times, involving himself directly in activities that had his blood pumping and his testosterone boiling would invigorate him.

Perhaps taking Castor's miserable life would renew his own. He rubbed his forehead. It was insane, worse, highly impractical, to consider murder as some form of cosmetic surgery for an aging spirit.

Dear God, the risk! It was unthinkable.

Again, he looked up, toward Giselle's window. It was dark. She was gone—and she hadn't said goodbye.

Chapter 14

April couldn't eat another bite; she'd barely managed half the chicken Caesar salad she'd ordered as it was. Damned hard to eat with Joe's blazing silver eyes fixed on her as if she were the main course and the steak in front of him—the size of a welcome mat—was an appetizer.

They sat across from each other at the table room service staff had set for them by the window. Outside, the lights of Las Vegas danced, rolled, flickered, and burst like eternal fireworks. Not content to rival the stars, they obliterated them. The night was glass clear, the sky a blue-black curtain, nothing more than an inky backdrop for the heat and bold radiance below it.

Like this dinner was a backdrop, a setting for seduction; normal on the surface, all shimmer and fire underneath.

April knew her town, her world within a world, knew that outside this room there were thousands of milling people, winning and losing, laughing and loving; inside was only a man and a woman, both edgy, expectant, and . . . hopeful.

Sex was in the air—the thrall, the flesh and heart need for that crazed physical union that could mean so much—or so little.

Joe Worth's intentions had been plain since he'd kissed her palm and looked into her eyes—and April sensed those intentions had magnified a hundredfold over dinner.

Earlier, when she'd left the table briefly to call the hospital—happily to discover Rusty's condition had improved—his eyes had never left her.

Sex was in his eyes, in his unwavering gaze, the ease of his waiting, while it sat in April's mind like a mauled daisy, should I, shouldn't I, should I, shouldn't . . .

Inside, April felt as flashing and glittery as the Sandstone's bulb-studded canopy a few floors below where they sat. *A woman thing*, she thought, *this dithery bit*, although new to her. As though what was stirring between her and Joe was . . . new. Different. Which made it the tiniest bit scary.

Joe showed no inclination to dither. Earlier, when she'd asked him if he wanted dessert, he'd met her eyes and answered for them both. "We won't need it."

She'd looked away from him and smiled at that. The man was awfully sure of himself.

She liked that about him, but then she liked most things about him—including his spectacular body. She'd heard somewhere that women weren't turned on visually as quickly as men, that their lust was born in their minds and vivid imaginations and that it took time. Whoever said that, obviously had never seen Joe. Tall, lean, and powerfully muscled, he was prime cover material for *Men's Health* magazine—or *Playgirl*. Among other things.

His smile, at once seductive and teasing.

The way he kept things light. His quick mind, and even quicker tongue. The way he listened, tilting his head, seeming to draw the spoken words deep, consider each of them pure gold.

The way he was starting to like Cornie . . .

What troubled her were his feelings toward Phylly. Thinking his animosity toward her might be too deeply ingrained in him for a reconciliation made her uneasy; it would be awkward at best—painful at its worst. She didn't want her loyalties tested, by her loving Phylly, owing her everything, and Joe not caring at all—or worse holding fast to his anger and resentment. A hard body was one thing; a hard mind and heart were something else entirely.

She gave herself a mental shake. *He'll come around.* She was sure of it. Once he met Phylly and settled a few things, he'd feel the same way about her as April did. It was the natural thing, for sons to love their mothers. Yes, everything would be fine.

And she *was* going to bed with him.

All they had to do was keep it simple. She wondered if simple sex was an oxymoron, while her tummy, full of thrashing butterfly wings, told her what was between her and this man passed the simple mark at hello.

Maybe she should stop thinking and start acting.

"You want a penny for what's behind that smile?" He leaned back in his chair and picked up his wine.

"A penny doesn't get you much in this town." She met his gaze. "I'm not sure I want to make you that happy . . . yet."

His lips turned up. "You think you know what will make me happy?"

"I like the odds that I do." She leaned forward and put herself in the game. To April, sex was a team sport. Besides, she hadn't put on this black dress for nothing. "Want to bet?"

He studied her a moment, his eyes full of humor and seduction. "No . . . I think the fix is in." He looked where she wanted him to look, the low neckline of her dress then back up to meet her gaze. He gave his wineglass a couple of turns. "And I'm okay with that."

"Just okay." She picked up her glass, sipped. Her mouth was as dry as the desert surrounding Vegas. "Does that mean you'd rather have a nice long talk—like you promised?"

"Oh, yeah," he drawled. "I'd much rather have a long,

meaningful conversation about now than hot sex with a beautiful woman."

She kept her face straight, barely.

He went on. "Just so we understand one another. That *Okay* means I've been hard since you walked back into this room in a dress not meant to be worn around any living man for more than ten minutes—and me only five."

She put down her wineglass. "You know you've been staring, don't you?" She noticed Joe hadn't done any better putting a dent in his dinner than she had. "All through dinner."

"You wanted me to stare," he said.

She laughed. "Got me there."

"Besides, I wasn't just staring, I was calculating."

She arched a brow.

"Estimating my best time to get you out of the damn dress, into that bedroom"—he jerked his head to indicate his room of choice—"and begging me for more of what I can't wait to give you." He leaned forward.

"Begging, huh?"

"Isn't that what you want, April?" His voice was low, his eyes glittering. "Sex so good, you can't get enough of it?"

His whispered question touched her like an early flame, licked at her waning reserve of cool.

Begging for more from Joe Worth? Oh, yes, she liked the idea of that. Sinking into sexual hunger; bone and muscle softening, turning to liquid . . . releasing, letting go—so wild with need she hurt from it. "Begging for it would be a new experience for me," she managed to say, "and a challenge for you." One she had every confidence he was up to.

He smiled. "You want to know what I want?"

"I'm not sure. Is it legal? Does it require ropes and chains? Duct tape . . . rubber duckies?"

He shook a slow negative. "None of the above. I'm a basic kind of guy. All I want is you. Naked. Then I want to make you wet—all slick and juiced. I want you moaning, and moaning and—"

"I get that." And if he didn't stop talking, she'd be panting like a puppy in the Sahara. He didn't stop.

"And I want you to come when I'm so deep inside you, I'll feel every quiver and spasm. Then I want to start all over again. Taste you. Tongue you. That's when the begging starts." His eyes shifted from silver to a dark moody gray. "Are you *okay* with that?"

April swallowed, shifted in her chair, and pressed her thighs tight against the pulse and moisture between them. She swallowed again before she spoke. "You're good, Joe Worth. You're very good. Ever consider phone sex as a second career?"

"I'm good when I want to be." He stood, offered her his hand, his eyes again glinting with humor. "But as someone somewhere once said, you ain't seen nothing yet."

When she took his hand, started to stand, he jerked her hard to his body, slid his hands to her buttocks and pulled her flush to the cradle of his hips—the steeled thickness behind his zipper. He kissed her hard, deep, and possessively. "Christ, I've been wanting you since the day you set foot in my office." He took a male-sized get-a-grip breath. "Couldn't stop looking at you then, can't stop now." He held her face between his hands. "But before we take this to the next level, do I need condoms?"

Through her own already labored breathing, she managed to say, "That depends on you. I'm on the pill, so I'm okay, if you're okay." She looked at him, waited. "You are okay, aren't you?"

"Clean, cautious, and checked." He lifted her chin. "Good to go?"

She nodded, brushed her mouth over his, and whispered against his lips, "Good to go," she repeated, adding, "I want you to make love to me, Joe." She kissed him lightly again, smiled against his lips, and started unbuttoning his shirt. "And I think I'll start the begging early, if that's okay?" She ground herself against his erection.

He swallowed hard, and she saw the tendons in his throat go taut. He gripped her by the upper arms, held her a few inches away from him. "Not going to make me work for that? The begging thing?"

She undid the last button, shoved his shirt aside, and flattened her hands against his broad smooth chest, licked each of his nipples. Her reward was his sharp intake of breath. "You have your agenda and I have mine," she murmured.

"Which is?" he pulled her close.

"Make you hot and make sure you never forget me."

His eyes turned serious. "Then your work is done." He took both her hands in his and tugged her toward the bedroom.

Once there, the only light was from the street below, a blending of night sky and neon that left the room a low-fire red with flashes of gold from the sign on the casino across the street.

Joe stripped off his undone shirt . . .

Dear God! She damn near salivated. He tossed the shirt and gripped her shoulders. "No zipper in that thing, right?" He nodded at her black dress.

When she shook her head, he started peeling it from her shoulders. In seconds it joined his white shirt on the floor.

He unhooked her bra, ran his hands up her back, caught her bra straps with his thumbs and let it drop. When his hands came back up he filled them with her breasts. "You're perfect." He bent his head kissed each breast in turn, his breath searing against her oversensitized skin. When he squeezed her breasts gently, the last iota of her cool evaporated. Already breathing hard, she feared she'd embarrass herself and climax before they even got to the good stuff.

Pulling back, she traced his one tattoo. Starting above his

elbow a multicolored serpent, perfectly rendered, curled around his bicep and ended at his shoulder. In its smiling mouth, a single red rose. "This?" She tapped the rose.

"Army," he said.

"And this?" She ran the palm of her hand over his erection.

His sharp intake of breath was all the answer she got. He stepped back from her and stripped off the rest of his clothes; shoes, socks, slacks, and briefs were a heap on the floor in record time. Obviously Joe's neat tendencies didn't extend to stripping for sex. His frank nakedness left her, wearing nothing but her black lace hip thong, the most overdressed one in the room.

She dropped her gaze to what stood tall between his muscular thighs, and tried to slow down her breathing.

He was . . . fabulous. Male beautiful. She moistened her lips and continued to stare, her slow breathing exercise abandoned, giving way to a soft panting.

The length and breadth of him, fully erect, was the tiniest bit daunting—for about a half second.

He didn't—couldn't—miss where her attention was focused.

"Okay?" he said, arching a brow, and looking as though he knew damn well everything about him was okay. A word he had a definite fondness for.

She reached out, caressed him from stem to tip with one lazy finger, savored another quiver of growth. "Grade A."

She started to peel off her thong—he stopped her. "Not yet. I like it on you. I like imagining you." He smiled. "For about the next two minutes." He backed her to the bed, took her face in his hands, and kissed her. With one hand flat against his heart, she closed her eyes, let his tongue have her, and savored the wild pounding rising from deep in his chest. The second after that she was on her back—flat to the bed with Joe's . . . fabulousness pressed hard against her pubis, his eyes, now a deep sex-drenched blue, boring into hers. "No more talk."

He took her mouth with his, shifted his weight, and ran his hand down and over her belly. Slipping it between her thighs, he pressed them open and stroked her over the silk of her panties. When he discovered she was wet, he groaned, and slid his hand under the silk to where she pulsed and lifted. Parting her crease, he played with her, using a slow back and forth motion that had her twisting, reaching for more in a physical demand he find her center, touch her there.

He didn't. He penetrated her with a finger, then two . . . teased her to a slick frenzy and held her down while he did it.

Sliding down her body, he kissed his way to where her body screamed for him to be, took off her panties, and raised her to his mouth. He took her burning, pulsing nub silkily, voraciously, unrelentingly.

Her body bucked, roared its need, and she pushed herself shamelessly against his marauding mouth and tongue. She couldn't breathe, didn't want to breathe. She dug her heels into the bed, gave herself over to him.

Changing his pace, he tongued her once, long, slow, and luxuriously then sucked her deep . . .

She clamped her hands over her mouth, screamed into her damp palms, and came in a blinding searing rush, her body imploding, pulling into itself as though to hold and extend the riotous pulsing . . . make it not stop . . . ever. She tried to close her legs, contain the after-tremors.

For a moment Joe let her, watching her face, with an intensity, a singular interest that made her close her eyes against the burn of it. His voice was husky when he said, "Open your legs, April. Open wide for me."

Oh, yes . . .

Joe entered her in a smooth easy plunge, held himself still and in deep. Then in three powerful thrusts, he came inside her with a rasping, uneven groan. His head buried in her shoulder, he cursed softly. "Jesus," he said, finally. "That was . . ."

The space between them filled with the sound of ragged breath, his and hers.

"Okay," she finished for him, running her fingers through his thick hair and managing a smile with what little strength she had left.

Her own heart and brain were numbed. She could hear; she could think; she could feel; what she couldn't do was make sense of what was going on inside her. The tumult of it. She closed her eyes against the awe and alien dreamlike wonder that pulled at her, and forced herself into the now. Good sex was good sex, she reminded herself—but it did blister the brain. And the condition was always temporary.

You sound smart, April, now act smart. Enjoy the moment and quit with the awe and wonder.

Joe's weight, leaden with completion, rested on her for only a moment before he rolled to her side and pulled her close to his big muscular body.

"That was so far past 'okay,' I left orbit." He closed his eyes, rested a forearm across his face.

She kissed his tattoo and ran her hand over his heaving chest then down, stopping above his depleted sex. "How long will it take you to reenter earth's atmosphere?" She ran her hand back up his chest then straddled him, settling between his thighs.

He gripped her shoulders. "Whoa, aren't you the impatient one?" When her hair brushed his shoulder, he added, "Not that I'm complaining." He played with her hair, letting long tendrils slip across his palm—catching them in his fist. He drew her face close to his. "And in answer to your question, I'm seeing the curvature of Mother Earth, as we speak."

"Good"—she kissed him lightly, a bare touch of her

mouth to his—"because not being sure how long this, whatever it is, between you and me will last, I plan on making the most of it."

Joe frowned. "What the hell does that mean?"

"That means, Joe, that this night of debauchery isn't going to alter my universe." She forced a smile and made herself sound stern and committed. Always the best way to tell a lie.

He rolled over her, pinned her beneath him. "Afraid I'm going to offer you a ring and picket fence just because we—"

"Fucked," she said, and hid the hard swallow she needed to get down the knot in her throat.

He stroked her hair back. "We did that all right." His eyes were an inky blue in the blinking red and gold reflections pouring into the room from the street below. "But if there's a chance there's more going on here than either of us expected, you should know I'm good with that."

"Don't, Joe," she said, feeling panicked. "Don't make something out of this. Just don't, okay?" *It's too soon, way, way too soon.*

"Okay." He smiled at her, his easy capitulation not matching the knowing, teasing glint in his eyes. "How about I do this instead?" He slid down, took a nipple in his mouth and suckled gently. April felt it to the soles of her feet.

"That's a very good beginning." She sighed and arched to his mouth.

"And this?" He slid a hand down between her legs, found her clitoris with the precision of a master.

She craned her neck, reached for a breath but couldn't find one. And when he stroked and rolled her hot clit between his fingers—nor could she find any words. She moaned.

Still playing her, he lifted his head. "No more talking?"

"Not a word," she gasped. "Not another word."

Chapter 15

Morning sun, blinding bright and screaming of the heatwave outside, poured into the bedroom.

Would've been smart to close the blinds.

Joe, facing the white brilliance, kept his eyes shut, concentrating instead on the warm body pressed against his back. The sun, the late morning hour, the need for coffee and food, not one of them was a rival to the hand sliding over his hip and between his thighs to check him out. A woman who liked morning sex—his kind of woman.

She closed her hand around his morning salute, stroked him slow and easy. "You awake?" she asked, kissing his shoulder.

"I sure as hell hope so." His body did what it had to do when it got primed, and pushed into her hand. She obliged with a not so gentle squeeze that sucked out a good share of his lung's oxygen. "Because if I'm not, and I wake up and find out what you're doing to me is a dream." He bucked into her hand, then rolled onto his back. "I'm fucked."

Her hair was a wild tangle, her eyes were gleaming green in the brightness of the room. She was smiling—and she took his damn breath away. *He was fucked all right . . .*

"And not in a good way." She pumped him gently.

He had about a nanosecond's worth of control left before his caveman came out. He held on to it. "You got it."

She squeezed and ran a finger over his tip. "Want to shower?"

He covered her hand—the one stroking his erection. "Can I take this with me?"

"That's the plan."

Hell of a plan . . .

The phone rang.

Joe closed his eyes and cursed. He didn't want to answer it, but one look at April's face told him that wasn't an option. He picked up.

"Is April there?" Cornie asked, her words rushed, a little shaky, as though she'd been crying. "I *need* to talk to April."

"For you. The Cornball," he said, bracing himself for what he knew was coming. He held the mouthpiece to his chest, added, "This is going to end badly, for Sparky down there. I know it."

April kissed him quickly, smiled, and muttered something about his being a "big boy now" and released his clamoring cock.

She took the phone from his hand, and sat on the edge of the bed. In seconds her face was tight with concern.

Joe and Sparky had dropped off the radar.

Joe figured if someone wrote a book titled *The Top Ten Ways to End Perfect Sex*, his sister's call would rank number one—ending as it did, what was about to be the hottest morning sex of his life with the abrupt and stunning force of an arctic tsunami.

The kid's timing was flat-out brutal.

April, rapt in whatever Cornie was saying, got up from the bed and walked to the window. Getting his breathing under control—along with the rest of his anatomy, he didn't move. Instead he took his own sweet time studying her. Naked. Gloriously naked, she stood looking out at her town through the filmy drapes. The perfection of her lit like a tray of diamonds in the morning light.

She looked back at him, with what he liked to think was regret at what she was missing.

"She okay?" he said, his voice sounding like a dump of gravel.

April both frowned and nodded. "It's about Phylly," she mouthed, then gave her full attention back to the phone.

When he finally got it—that she wasn't coming back to bed, that their day of wine and roses was over before it got started—he left her to Cornie and headed for the shower.

Five minutes later, he was back in the bedroom, with a towel around his goddamn determined erection, and a brain he'd managed to shift from piss-off number one, *coitus interruptus*, to piss-off number two, the search for Phyllis Worth. A woman, that despite her having done a good deed getting April out of a hellish situation, he felt nothing for, and wanted nothing from, other than an answer to the what and why surrounding his birth and her dumping of a three-year-old boy in an ER room and never looking back. He'd keep his word, help April and Cornie get her back, but that was it. Game over. Hell, if nothing else, the woman was worth saving for the satisfaction of walking out on her and never setting eyes on her again. But to do that, he needed to find her and keep her safe.

Why thinking about her made him feel as if he were picking at a crusty old scab, he didn't know. Maybe it was some damn inner-child shit. Not that it mattered. Because Phyllis Worth didn't matter. Not to him. But she mattered to April—and that carried major weight. Way too late for hearts and flowers about his mother. Milk and cookies she wasn't, and he'd learned to live with that. He'd let her go years ago—and he didn't want her back.

April though . . .

April was something else. Somehow, she'd settled into

him, and he liked it. Liked how it made him feel. He didn't exactly know what it meant yet—had no fucking idea what to do about it—but he intended to find out, which meant keeping her out of danger—Phyllis's danger.

April hung up the phone and stared at him, frowning and chewing on her lower lip. She walked the few steps to the bathroom, put on a robe, and came back into the room tying the terry belt. "Cornie thinks she knows where her mother is."

Joe, in a final admission of defeat, dropped the towel from around his hips, and pulled on briefs. "And?"

"With a man . . ."

Surprise, surprise. "Who?"

"Other than his name's Noah—which means nothing to me—she won't say any more until she gets back here. She's afraid if she does, you and I will take off after Phylly and leave her behind. Anyway, it's probably nothing." She shoved her long dark gold hair back—and when she did, Joe's thinking snagged on the moment it had first brushed his shoulder.

Like living silk . . .

"Apparently she found an old postcard in that box she carted out of the apartment—signed by someone named Noah. I think it's the name that has her so upset." She paused. "Cornie thinks she knows about every man Phylly ever dated. She's always been a little obsessed about them." April played with the tie on the robe, wrapping it like a bandage around her palm then releasing it. She was thinking hard, he guessed, but not about to share it.

"Does she?" he asked. "Know them all?"

April glanced at him, hesitated. "No. Phylly's smarter than that. She was also discreet—particularly after Cornie was born."

"Which leads to question number two: Who *is* the kid's dad? Does she even know?" His stomach felt as if it were full of glass. And he had a major jolt of empathy for the kid.

"No. And neither do I. Phylly never talked about him."

"Then the kid's looking for him." Looking for him in every face, in every corner, wanting to know the unknowable. "She's the right age for it. Maybe she thinks this Noah guy is him."

April didn't say anything, kept playing with her belt. "Anything's possible, but it's a stretch, even for Cornie—the date on the postcard is less than two years old." She stopped, looked at her watch. "She said she's arranged for a ride back to the hotel, that she'll show us the card when she gets here—if we promise to take her with us."

"You ready to make that promise?" He pulled on some jeans.

"Not without knowing what we're getting into."

Joe agreed. "If there was a guy named Noah in Phyllis's life, who's the most likely person to know about him?"

"Rusty. Definitely Rusty."

He dug out a Tee from his bag, trying not to think of how many men had traipsed through Phyllis's life. Even if he did plan to ask her who his father was, chances were she wouldn't know. His stomach did a roll and twist.

Joe was no monk and definitely not a stone-throwing kind of guy, but the thought of his mother's busy past made his bile rise. He supposed that made him some kind of sexist, but there it was.

"Something wrong?" April asked.

"Not a thing." He grabbed her by the back of the neck, kissed her hard and deep, and let her go. That last part wasn't easy. "Now let's go see your friend Rusty—before I get a better idea."

Chapter 16

Phyllis, who'd temporarily parked her rented Ford Focus in a no-parking zone, looked at the map for the hundredth time since her first bad motel coffee—at frickin' six-thirty in the morning! The last time she'd met up with that time of day it was coming-home time, not getting-up time. And the damn map, with its line and squiggles, was useless. She needed to ask for directions.

She pulled back into the smattering of early morning traffic and a drizzling rain. Rain. In August. Who knew? At least it made everything nice and green. She liked that—and the flowers everywhere—but not much else. What the hell people did here after the sun went down, she couldn't imagine. Took pills to ward off terminal boredom maybe. The trees, the water, the cloudy skies, reminded her of Seattle—where she'd spent just enough time to make the mistake that had her on the run now.

Victor Allan. What the hell had she been thinking? No answer to that one.

She glanced at the seat beside her, patted the rust-colored carpetbag, and took a breath. At least she still had the journal. Maybe, when she had time to think clearly, she'd figure out a way of using it to protect her—and Cornie. God, she couldn't stand it if anything happened to Cornie because of her past, her stupid, self-serving choices. Thinking about it made her crumble inside, so she shook the thought away. Cornie was with April. Cornie was safe—and somehow, Phylly Worth would get herself and everyone she loved out of this unholy mess.

Not for the first time she questioned her crazed decision to come here. Even if Noah was still single, there was no guarantee he'd be filled with delight seeing an aging show-girl on his doorstep. Calling would have been a good thing. *Calling would have given him a chance to say no.*

Uh-uh. Crazy or not, she'd committed herself to going to him, and that's what she was going to do. One thing she'd found out, the man lived miles past nowhere—exactly the kind of address she needed right now.

To get there, she was heading to a place called Horseshoe Bay to catch a ferry, instead of stepping up to the bar at the Horseshoe Club in Vegas, where she damn well belonged.

According to the kid at the last gas station, she had another fifteen to twenty minutes of driving, and she'd be at the ferry. When she got there, she was going to call April, tell her she was okay—and for Cornie not to worry. She really wanted to talk to Cornie, but knowing her kid, she'd just get mad—or worse, insist on coming along. That girl was a dog with a bone when she set her mind to something, and Phylly wasn't up for the fight. For now it was best any talking that needed to be done, be done through April. Besides, Cornie would ask nonstop questions; questions Phylly wasn't prepared to answer. Yes, her being here and Cornie being as far away from her as possible right now was the best thing.

Hell, all she needed was Cornie along when she knocked on Noah Bristol's door. Christ, wouldn't that be some big drama! The man would have a heart attack.

But before she called April she'd call Rusty, and—

God! There was a Starbucks! She glanced at her watch; she had time. She'd get a *real* coffee and call Rusty. Damned irritating using payphones because she'd been too rushed to remember to grab her cell charger. Probably just as well she didn't have it, because by now Cornie would be calling every fifteen minutes.

Five minutes later, luscious dark coffee in hand, she dialed Hot and High.

Ten minutes after that, her hand shaking, tears making black rivers of her mascara, she got it together enough to call Tommy.

Joe paid the cabby, joined April on the sidewalk, and looked up through the staggering August heat at the University Medical Center. Rusty Black was on the second floor, ICU.

Joe hoped to hell this visit was worth it, that they could get some kind of confirmation of what Cornie found in her mother's things, and that April was right about Rusty "knowing everything." He also wanted to hear back from Kit on the picture he'd taken from Worth's apartment. If it did tie in with the postcard the kid had found, they'd at least have a direction to go in.

If Rusty Black could fill them in on the details of Phyllis's love life—which he was beginning to think should be in the *Guinness Book of World Records*—and they could tie *that* into the card, things would be even better.

They were heading to the main entrance when April's cell phone rang. She answered it and stopped so abruptly, he was two steps ahead of her before he noticed.

"When?" she said, shoving her hair behind her ear the way she always did when she was tense. "She was getting better. She was going to be okay. What happened?"

Whatever she was hearing, it wasn't good. She looked like death. Joe waited, watched as she gave her full attention to the caller, her eyes widening before welling with tears. "Tommy, I'm so sorry."

Finally, she nodded, her expression vacant, and said,

"No. Leave that to me, I'll tell her." She clicked off the phone. When she lifted her gaze to his, her face was ashen. "Rusty's dead."

Joe put his hand on the back of his neck, shook his head. "Jesus," he said. When he looked at her again, saw how wobbly she was, he took her arm and led her to a bench near the hospital entrance. "Sit," he said—the single word a flashback to when she'd walked into his office just days ago. "Can I get you something. Water?"

"No. Thanks."

"You sure you're okay?"

She shook her head. "No. I'm not okay. Rusty was my friend. She was Phylly and Cornie's friend. She was tough, smart, fun, and"—she swallowed—"she had the biggest heart in Vegas. I owe her. We all owe her."

Still sitting on the bench, she looked around vacantly, a thousand expressions crossing her face at once, from confusion to sadness, grief to frustration—then tears. Tears that quickly gave way to anger. "But the last thing she'd want us to do is get weepy and useless." She took in a breath, got to her feet. "We have to get back to the Sandstone. Tommy wants to talk to us, says it's important, and I"—she took another, even deeper breath—"have to tell Cornie about Rusty." She looked at her watch, her expression distracted, unfocused. "Raina's dad will be dropping her off any time now and I want to be there." She paused. "What happened to Rusty—it's going to scare her."

"She's already scared. She's just too stubborn to show it." *Like you.*

"But this . . ." She looked up at the hospital where the woman they'd intended to see now lay covered by a white sheet. "I'm not sure she can cope. Her mother running off . . . Now Rusty dying. It's a lot for her to handle."

Joe was having a bit of *handling* problems himself. Truth was, he didn't give a damn about Phyllis Worth, and doubted he ever would. She had saved April, but all in all that seemed to be it in the righteous department. Nothing else so far had raised his opinion of her. He was having a hard time drumming up sympathy for a woman who left a friend to take the blows meant for her, a woman who'd run off to some guy rather than stay and face whatever music needed to be faced—and a mother who had no trouble leaving her young daughter alone and scared shitless.

Joe didn't like cowards—and Phyllis Worth had all the hallmarks of one, a selfish one at that. In the end it was all about what was easiest for her. The world according to Phyllis Worth. April said he had issues. Not a chance. He didn't know his father, and he didn't know his mother, but he'd discovered there was something a lot worse—like finding out one of those missing parental units made your stomach turn. "The kid will handle it, because she doesn't have a choice." The words came out harder than he intended.

"Like you did." Her look was blade sharp.

"Leave it alone, April."

She didn't. She went on. "I understand your feelings. At least I'm trying to, but you have to get it through that thick head of yours that Cornie and I love Phylly. She's not perfect—who the hell is—but she did right by me and right by Cornie."

Joe thought the last was debatable, but he wasn't in the mood for a verbal war. "Fair enough," he said. "Now let's go." And he'd let the subject of Phyllis Worth drop; it was the best he could do. "I'll get us a cab." When he started his turn, she grabbed his arm, just as she had that day in his office when he booted her out.

"We need to talk," she said.

"We talked last night."

"I talked, you listened. Then we slept together and the talking stopped."

"Yeah, I remember that part." He slanted her a gaze, and

she looked away briefly. For such a frank, strong, and sexually assertive woman—*Thank God!*—she did have her bashful moments.

He saw a cab heading their way and lifted his hand. She grabbed his arm, pulled it down, and gave him one of her mulish looks. She had degrees of them, he'd noticed. This one hit pretty high on the scale. "I thought you wanted to be there for the kid," he said.

"Damn it! Her name is Cornelia, *Joseph,*" she said. "Or better yet, Cornie. I thought you at least had that figured out. She's your sister, and no matter how many times you call her 'the kid' that isn't going to change." She still held his hand, but softened her voice to say, "She didn't have anything to do with what Phylly did to you. She wasn't there—in case you haven't registered that little fact." She met his eyes, her face stern, but her tone was still soft when she added, "Don't you think it's time you quit being such a horse's ass? About Cornie . . . about your mother?"

He liked her hand in his, but he didn't like what she said—too damn right and logical. At least about the kid.

She cocked her head, one side of her hair shimmering gold under the brilliant sun, and waited for him to answer. Something in her face said this was a pass or fail question.

What Joe wanted was to reset the clock to preshower time and pick up where he and April left off—which had nothing to do with anybody's mother. "Let's just find the damn woman," he said, "and worry about the horse's ass part later."

She looked at him a long time. "Don't think I won't hold you to that."

Her cell phone rang again. She covered one ear and turned away from the traffic—and him. Two seconds later, she snapped her phone closed, and grabbed his hand.

"Get the cab, Joe. Phylly just called Tommy."

Chapter 17

Tommy was waiting for April and Joe in the 24/7 Bar at the Sandstone. Despite the early hour, he was nursing a drink, and even in the perpetual dimness of the bar, he looked angry and pale. He stood when they reached the table, and April wrapped her arms around him. "I'm so sorry, Tommy. We all loved her so much."

He gave her a hard, brief hug but immediately straightened away from her. Like his sister, he wasn't much for sentimentality. "Yeah. Well, somebody sure as hell didn't."

"Do the police have anything . . . say anything?"

His sneer was slight, but his meaning was clear when he shook his head. "No. Just that it looks like whoever shot her went back last night to finish the job." He stopped, took a breath. "Used a fucking pillow."

April froze. "I didn't know. I just thought . . ."

"Don't know how the bastard got in. Fucking security. Damned joke." Tommy had a coffee in front of him. He lifted his cup and took a drink, the cup quaking in his grip.

April's heart iced in her chest. Cold-blooded murder. A pillow held to Rusty's beautiful face until her lungs screamed for air. Until she died. "Oh, my God." Her eyes flooded with tears. Joe picked up a cocktail napkin from the table and handed it to her.

"Seems like God was otherwise occupied last night,"

Tommy said, looking away for a moment and swallowing hard.

"Tommy, I—" She had no idea what she was going to say, and was glad when he cut her off with a shake of his head.

"It's okay." He coughed and rolled his head, an obvious effort to leave the emotional part of this meeting behind.

Tommy Black was in his early fifties, a slight man with a thin face and graying hair above his temples, good-looking in a slick Las Vegas way. His claim to fame was a computer for a brain, an invisible set of X-ray eyes that could spot a bad play at a table in the next town, and some supposed heavyweight connections here and in Los Angeles, that everyone who knew Tommy assumed were more boast than beef. Add to that he had a soft spot for Phylly that went way back and got softer with every "no" she said to him. April had asked Phylly once, why she didn't take Tommy up on his offer, and Phylly said, "I love the guy, all right, but the thing is he doesn't need it. He loves himself enough for both of us." But despite his amorous intentions and Phylly's lack of them, they were friends, Rusty their bond. Rusty . . . April took a deep breath and wiped away her tears with the napkin Joe had given her. He put his hand on her shoulder, squeezed.

"Like I said," Tommy went on. "I've got to go—meeting the cops at the hospital—so I don't have a lot of time." He looked at Joe, raised a "who's-he?" brow in April's direction.

"This is Joe . . . Worth," she said, hesitated, then added, "Phylly's son." God, she felt like she was outing a celebrity gay.

"Yeah?" he studied Joe, his eyebrows raised. "Didn't know she had a son."

"Not surprised," Joe said.

"You look like her some. Around the eyes."

Joe said nothing.

"You helping to look for her?" he asked.

"Yes," Joe said, adding as if to forestall further questioning, "I'm sorry about your sister. That's rough—and damned ugly."

Tommy nodded, his face grim. "It'll be someone else's *ugly*, real soon. I've already made the calls. Important people. Whoever killed my sister is going to pay. Big time." Even in grief, Tommy puffed up.

April knew he was referring to those mysterious sources he was always going on about. But as there was nothing to be said in reply to his threat, idle or otherwise, both she and Joe let it pass. "You said you heard from Phylly," she said, thinking it best for Tommy if she led the conversation away from Rusty.

He nodded. "Sit down." He gestured at the chairs around the table. They all sat, and he pulled one of his business cards from his pocket. "She must have had her radar on or something, because she called the business, looking for Rusty, less than five minutes after I'd told Leanne about Rusty's passing."

To April the word "passing" jarred, too serene to describe what happened to Rusty. The word made it sound as if she'd died quietly and at peace instead of screaming for a last breath while her murderer held a pillow to her face. April shuddered.

Tommy went on, "When Leanne filled her in, Phylly called me. Crying about being sorry, going on about how it was all her fault. No idea what she was talking about. But this is where she called from, said something about getting on a ferry." He passed the card across the table and flipped it over. There was a telephone number and an address on the back. "That was maybe an hour ago tops. I had one of the security guys run a check on the number. It's a payphone in a place called West Vancouver. In British Columbia. Very ritzy, he says." He looked at April. "The place mean anything to you?"

"No." She shook her head, studied the number as if it were a sonar blip. It remained meaningless.

Joe looked at the card and frowned, but said nothing.

"So," Tommy said, leaning back in his chair. He looked mean and angry. "My sister gets herself killed because some creep is after Phylly. That right?"

April didn't know what to say, wasn't sure of her truths. "It's a possibility, Tommy. We don't know for sure."

"I'm thinking we do know," he said. "According to Phylly, the creep's name is Henry Castor." He looked at her hard, searching for confirmation.

She shook her head. "I've never heard of him."

"What about Allan? Victor Allan?"

April's mind numbed, and the hair on her arms stood straight and icy, as if chilled by a sudden wind. She couldn't think, couldn't breathe.

Victor Allan . . .

She knew the name all right—he was the man who the black-eyed man had taken her to for shipment. She hadn't heard the name aloud for over twenty years. Back then, Phylly said it was a game and they both had to play. They'd pretend the bad man didn't exist, that he'd never been real—and the first one to ever speak his name again would lose the game. Phylly had given her a big hug, told her if she played the game good enough, she'd make "nasty, mean old Victor go so far away he'd never come back." Then, Phylly told her, she'd never have to be afraid again.

April had played the game with a vengeance since she was nine years old. And while she'd never forgotten the black-eyed man, she'd pushed Victor Allan—and his camera and ugly instructions—out of her universe.

Pretend he doesn't exist . . .

"You okay?" Joe whispered from beside her, his deep voice laced with curiosity and concern.

She blinked, swallowed, and looked at him. He was blurred around the edges. She blinked again. "Yes . . . yes, I'm fine." She shifted her hazy gaze to Tommy. "Where did you get that name?"

"Phylly said Castor worked for Allan," Tommy said eying her closely. "I take it you know this Victor guy. So who the hell is he?"

"Yes, I . . . know him. From a long time ago. He was a—" *What was he?* She couldn't think, her mind blocking the reloading of the nightmare, the blanks, surges, and confusion of it—the terror. A chill shimmied up her neck, and she barely suppressed a shudder. What was Victor Allan?

Victor was a fiend.

A stranger. Terrifying. Smiling. He'd given her cookies. A peanut butter sandwich. A big room. A giant bed . . .

He'd smiled at her, started taking pictures . . . asked her to take all her clothes off. When she'd said no, he'd reached for her, torn her shirt . . .

She'd bitten him. Hard as she could. There'd been blood. Then she'd kicked him where Gus told her it hurt the most.

He'd thrown her in a dark room filled with bottles. Left her forever. Hungry. She'd been so hungry. Then he'd come back for her.

She'd tried to kick him again. No use.

He'd beaten her, cut her lip, stripped off her clothes—and she'd cried, and cried, and—

April touched her mouth, felt the blood, the hot thickness of her lip today as if she were back in that room. As if Victor stood looking down at her . . . panting. Glaring. Pulling off her clothes. *The flash and click of the camera.* His sick and terrible pictures. Then he'd tossed her back in the basement—she'd skinned her knee, but could only feel it, not see it, because he'd unscrewed the lightbulb, so she'd be in the dark.

Two days later Phylly came and took her away. And the forgetting game began.

When she didn't answer, Tommy sounding impatient, said, "He was what? What were you going to say, April?"

She rubbed at her tight throat, all the words bunched up in there like living things in a sealed coffin. She coughed, brushed her hair back—got a grip. "Victor Allan was an old boyfriend of Phylly's. Phylly called him the Titanic of her mistakes. He was from Seattle."

Beside her Joe muttered a curse, shook his head.

She knew what she'd said sounded ugly, but it was the truth, and this wasn't the time for lies or pretending—no matter how well they'd worked in the past.

Pretend he doesn't exist . . .

"Yeah, well now he's a very dead old boyfriend," Tommy said.

"What?" She was still trying to put herself in conversation central, trying to connect fully. A glance at Joe's questioning eyes told her she wasn't doing so well, and the ache in her stomach confirmed it. She flattened a hand over its tension, the threat of nausea. Phylly was right, she should never have said his name. He was back. Victor Allan was back. She looked away from Joe, to Tommy. "What did you say?"

"I'm saying, somebody beat the crap out of him, then put a few bullets in him for good measure." Tommy picked up the coffee mug in front of him, downed it, and stood. "Phylly figures it was this Castor character, and that now he's after her."

"That doesn't make sense." April looked up at him, not trusting her legs enough to stand. Tommy couldn't know, but there was no reason for anyone associated with Victor to come after Phylly, not after all this time. If anything it was dangerous and would stir up things best left unstirred.

"Phylly ever make sense?"

April didn't reply. "Did she say where she was going, Tommy? Give you any names?"

"No. Just gave me some bull about how she was going where she couldn't be found for a while. That when she figured things out, she'd be back. Said it was safer if you didn't know." He nodded at the business card in April's hand. "If I were you, I'd start there. And while you look for Phylly, I'll be looking for Castor." He stopped again and sealed his lips into a straight seam. "But right now, I'm going to take care of my sister. Then it's back here to get someone to cover my tables for a few days." He turned away, took a few steps, and turned back. "You find out anything, I want to hear it. We straight on that?"

April nodded.

When he was gone, Joe sat down again in the seat opposite her. "Look at me," he said.

"What?" she said, deeply mired in the muddy thoughts of the past and trying to climb out. Weak and shaky, she met his speculative gaze, and took a couple of deep breaths.

"You don't just look like you've *seen* a ghost, you are one—ever since you heard the name Victor. And considering I'm on this roller-coaster ride with you, maybe I should hear about him."

The fear kicked in. She couldn't say his name. She wanted to go back to being nine years old, pretending Victor didn't exist—which, if Tommy was right, he didn't. Not anymore. Being dead made things final—and made the job of burying him even deeper a whole lot easier. *Deny, deny, deny . . .*

"April, talk to me."

"There's no connection—" *There can't be, not after all these years. Impossible.* "It's been too long."

"You're not making sense. What's too long?"

His blue eyes settled on her with laser intensity. *Deny, deny, deny.* Her chest knotted and she could barely breathe. "Victor Allan"—the name dried her lips as it passed over them—"was the man in the house Phylly took me from."

She swallowed, kept her eyes locked to Joe's. "But that was over twenty years ago. And with Victor Allan dead"—this time the name came easier—"it doesn't make sense that someone is looking for her now—about *that*."

Joe, now sitting across from her, went silent for a time, then said, "*'That'* was kidnapping a child with the intention of selling that child outside the country—and God knows what else. And given there's no statute of limitations on kidnapping, my guess is Allan's murder has made someone very, very nervous." Joe leaned forward. "You're sure you don't remember this Castor guy?"

She shook her head. "No."

"But you do remember the man who brought you to Allan's house, right?"

"Yes."

"Then Phyllis must remember him, too."

April saw where his thoughts were taking him. He was thinking she was a threat to someone, particularly the man who'd brought her to Victor. "No. She never saw him. Phylly came to the house over a week after he took me there."

"So that makes you the only one to have seen him." His jaw flexed and firmed. "Tell me everything you can remember."

She didn't want to, didn't want to remember. She forced herself. "When he took me to the house that night—I saw Victor give him a briefcase—money, I presume now, and the second he had it he headed for the door, and—"

"Go on."

I'd forgotten. How could I forget? "He looked back at me, I remember. He'd tied me to a chair . . . He said—"

"What?" he urged, when she didn't finish.

She couldn't finish because the memory was resurfacing from the deep place. Buried there along with Victor Allan's name and those ugly days in his basement. Phylly called it the dung heap of memories; to April it was more of a black hole. But she'd never forget the man's hard, tight face; it was burned into her. She'd know him instantly. His face was fixed, flat—like plastic—except for the one moment before he walked out the door, when he'd looked at her— "Sorry, April girl," she blurted, the words rushing out of her on a heavy breath. "Yes, that's what he said, '*Sorry, April girl.*' I remember being surprised he knew my name." *And the way his faced changed when he said it.* "Then he left. I never saw him again."

Joe let out a disgusted breath. "Sweet guy. A briefcase full of cash and five cents worth of conscience."

"Either way, Phylly never saw him. So she's no threat to him."

Joe went very still. "No, but you are. Which means whoever's after her is trying to find you."

April gaped at him. "You're crazy."

"Makes perfect sense to me."

It made a cockeyed kind of sense, but not enough for April to swallow his logic whole. "But why? Why after all this time would the guy be worrying about me? He doesn't know who I am, what I am, or where I am. Nor I him. Why would he take the risk of stirring things up?"

"Maybe somebody did the stirring for him."

Click. Her heart staggered in her chest. "Someone who knew about Phylly stealing me from Victor." She swallowed. "Henry Castor."

He nodded. "The guy was in business with Victor Allan, cut from the same cloth. Which means he's probably figured out a way to turn Victor's loss—you—into a profit for him. *If* he can find you."

"And he thinks the person most likely to help him do that is—"

"Phyllis Worth. She's a means to an end, April. Not the main target."

Like Rusty. Rusty was a means to an end, too. Oh, God!
When she thought of Phylly in danger—again—because
of her, panic kicked in. She jumped to her feet, almost
knocking the table over in her haste to . . . do something.
Anything.

Joe stood beside her. "Easy," he said.

She picked up the business card Tommy had given her,
clutching it as if it were a connecting cord between her and
Phylly. Then she waved it at Joe. "We're going to visit a
telephone booth."

Joe eyed the card then her. "That's brilliant—as long as
she etched the next clue in the glass."

"It's a start," she said.

"So's a laxative—and we all know how they finish up."

"This isn't funny, Joe."

"No, it's not, but be reasonable. That phone booth could
be in the middle of nowhere."

He was right. She was stubborn. "Phylly doesn't do
nowhere."

"And even if it isn't, who the hell is going to remember a
woman making a phone call?"

On that point he was wrong. "A six-foot tall, blond and
beautiful woman, with a fan tattooed on her ankle and five
diamonds studs in each ear? A woman who doesn't know
how to walk without her stilettos?"

Joe looked annoyed. "Okay, maybe it's a possibility, but
all she did was use the damn phone. It's not like she pitched
a tent in the parking lot. She'll be long gone."

"You don't know that."

He went quiet. "What I know is that Phyllis Worth isn't
the only one in danger here, and that Castor wouldn't waste
his time looking for her if he knew where he could find
you"—his eyes fixed on hers, held—"a fact that makes me
very unhappy with said Mister Castor or any other asshole
who has you in his sights. I won't have you hurt, April. You
got that?"

"Joe, you don't have to—" She wasn't sure what she was going to say, but she knew it had something to do with her taking care of herself, as she'd always done. But something in his face stopped her.

Ignoring her hesitation, he went on, "I also know Phyllis is self-protective enough to look out for herself—until she gets to wherever she's going—which I doubt is a phone booth in a place called West Vancouver. Tommy did say something about her getting on a ferry, remember?"

She eyed him, calmer now, but irrationally irritated by his cool common sense put in a place where hers should have been. She was also a bit flustered at her reaction to his stern gaze and concern for her. The thing was she wanted Joe to look out for her—and she wanted to look out for him. She had a dim idea what that meant, but now wasn't the time to figure it out. "You're right," she said, trying not to sound grudging. "We have to talk to Cornie—see that postcard."

Joe nodded toward the bar's entrance. "Speak of the devil."

Chapter 18

The entrance to the bar was nothing more than a yawning gap that led to the casino room floor. April followed
Joe's nod to see Cornie walking into the bar—as if it was
legal—at age fifteen!

April shot to her feet.

"Cornie, what are you doing here?" She took the girl's
arm, hustled her out of the bar, and towed her down an
aisle lined on both sides with slot machines. "You know
damn well you're underage!"

Joe followed a step or two behind, but was wise enough
to say nothing.

When they'd cleared the casino, and were standing off to
the side of the hotel reception area, April was still gripping
Cornie's arm; she shrugged her off.

Joe glanced at both them in turn, and said, "I've got
some calls to make, so I'm going upstairs." Another quick
glance at April, and he added. "You need a bodyguard, to
protect you from Miss Cornelia Worth"—he smiled briefly
at both of them—"you know where to find me." He headed
for the elevators.

Cornie crossed her arms, her eyes, red-rimmed and puffy,
stayed on him until he was out of sight.

"God," April said, "I can't believe you did that. Tommy'd have a fit."

Not the least chastened, Cornie said, "I got tired of waiting. I saw Tommy on the way out. He said you were in there."

"Maybe, but it didn't mean *go in there*."

"Rusty's dead—who cares about a stupid bar!" Her eyes brimmed with tears.

The teenage logic left April in silence, and her tears led to a hug. Taking Cornie in her arms, she held her fiercely. "I know." They clung to each other, ignored the curious looks of the gamblers and guests—the here-today-gone-tomorrow people that were the town's stock in trade. Neither of them cared.

As one they pulled apart, Cornie snuffling and swiping her cheeks with the backs of her hands; April doing the same with her fingers pressed to her cheeks.

Cornie took a breath and reached into the back pocket of her jeans. She handed April a postcard. "If this isn't where Mom's gone, I'll eat that." She dipped her chin toward the card.

April turned the postcard over and read: *Still here. Still remembering. Love to see you again. Always, Noah.* She turned it back to the picture side. A fierce ocean, a large wave, high and poised to pound the shore. Under it, the words *Tofino, BC*. It looked very much like the print Joe had taken from Phylly's wall. "Where did you get this?"

"When I went to Raina's place I took the box from home and went through it. The card was in a pink envelope—like it was special."

"It might not be anything, Cornie. You know what a pack rat Phylly is." What she said was true enough, and she didn't want to raise Cornie's expectations—but it fit. All of this fit. Except they needed a last name . . . *Bingo!*

April took out her cell, dialed.

"What are you doing?"

"Calling Tommy." Why hadn't she thought of this before? Rusty might know the deepest details of Phylly's love life, but Tommy probably kept a detailed dating log.

When Cornie started to speak, she shushed her with a raised hand. "Tommy, it's April. I hate to bother you, but could you answer one question for me? Does the name Noah mean anything to you? Cornie found it in Phylly's stuff, a postcard from a place called Tofino. . . . Really?" April glanced at Cornie then away. After what Tommy had said, she had a million questions for him, but not now—with Cornie's eyes glued to her. "No, this has nothing to do with Rusty. But it might be a clue as to where Phylly's gone. . . . If I find out anything, anything at all, Tommy, I promise I'll call." She clicked off and again looked at Cornie. "Your mother once dated a guy named Noah. Noah Bristol." That was all she needed to know right now; the rest was Tommy—talk and conjecture.

"When? How long ago? The date on the card is only two years ago. I don't remember a Noah. Do you?"

April shook her head, tried to look as if she were doing a memory search instead of figuring out how to avoid that how-long-ago question. No way she wanted to go there, open a path that neither of them had time to walk on. She decided, for now, to throw her off scent. "Was he the one from San Francisco, do you think? He was here with that dentist's convention . . . maybe three years ago."

"No, that was Nathan Pond." Cornie took back the card, studied it for what April was sure would be the millionth time.

"Right." April took her arm, relieved her diversion worked, and led her toward the elevator. "Doesn't matter anyway. We've got the name, we've got a starting point, and we've got Joe's help. We're going to find Phylly." She didn't bother to mention that the *we* she was referring to was her and Joe. If she'd learned one thing, it was never to start a war of wills with Cornie one second before you had to. If Cornie got so much as a whiff of Tommy's opinion—that Noah was her father, and opinion was all it was—there'd be no holding her back. The girl made *The Little Engine That Could* look like a used car with a cracked block.

Cornie tugged her arm free from April's grasp, stopped. "Joe doesn't care about Mom, you know. The only reason he came here was to get you in bed." Her statement was made without heat or accusation.

"That's not true." *I hope* . . .

"Have you? Slept with him yet?"

"That's not your business." The words shot out of her all starchy and prim. Unfortunately, they were accompanied with rapidly heating cheeks. "Damn it, Cornie, you really are . . . too much at times."

She shrugged. "I knew if I left you two alone it would happen," she said. "We should tell him to get lost." She lifted the postcard—and her chin. "Now that we have this, we don't need him."

April knew it was her disappointment talking. Tough as Cornie was, she'd expected more from Joe, at least a trace of brotherly concern. So far, all Joe had dished out was indifference. She was hurt, although a flock of crazed and hungry blood bats wouldn't get her to admit it.

April took her by the upper arms, met her willful gaze. "We might not need him, but Phylly might. Have you thought about that? It was your idea to find him, remember. Well, we found him. And he's here to help—whatever his reasons." She stopped, knowing the only thing that worked with Cornie was the truth. "But you're right, he doesn't care about Phylly the way we do—he has no reason to, and he doesn't know her like we do. When he does, when your mom and he get a chance to set things straight, that will change. He'll come to love her as much as we do."

"You believe that?"

"Yes, I do." *I have to*. She smoothed some strands of Cornie's dark hair off her face. "He already loves you—he just doesn't know it, yet."

Cornie tilted her head then shook it. "You know it's way too early for drinking, right?"

April smiled. "Come on, smart-mouth, let's go. I've got plane reservations to make."

And I've got to figure out how to keep you safe and as far away from Noah Bristol as possible. It was bad enough April had broken Phylly's trust when she'd found Joe. The can of worms—aka Noah Bristol—was all Phylly's.

Phylly just made the ferry, and after it left the dock, packed with holiday travelers and a zillion RVs, for the first time in days she felt safe—if only for the hour and a half it would take to cross whatever water she was crossing. After that, she had maybe a three-hour drive. If things went according to plan, she'd be in a place called Tofino—well beyond the edge of her known universe—by early evening. With even more luck, she'd have located Noah Bristol's house before the sun went down.

Her car was on the second deck at the front of the ship, and although the bridge allowing the cars to drive on was pulled up below, from there she looked out over a gate to a broad expanse of calm water. She wished some of its calm would settle into her. But more than that, she wished she could claw back the years that had brought her to this frightening place in her life, and erase the rash, selfish living now causing pain—*and death*—to those she loved. She closed her eyes against the tears and murmured, "Forgive me, Rusty. Dear God, forgive me. I didn't know. I didn't know."

She grasped the steering wheel, her knuckles bone-white from her grip and leaned her forehead against her knuckles and wept, and wept and . . .

* * *

Joe hung up the phone, picked up the notes he'd made while talking to Julius and Kit, paced for a few seconds, then strode to the window. The cheap watercolor from Worth's wall was exactly what he thought it was, a beach area on the west coast of Vancouver Island, somewhere along the twenty-five or thirty miles of its west coast accessible by land.

From here to there, with a stop in Seattle, the usual airport crap, and *if* he and April made good flight connections, he figured travel time to be a minimum of seven hours.

He shook his head. Trust his mother to head for one of the remotest parts of the largest North American island in the whole damned Pacific Ocean—and to have attracted the undivided attention of one mean motherfucker who had no trouble killing his way to get what he wanted.

It had taken Kit less than ten minutes to confirm that Henry Castor was as bad as they come with a sheet to match, a total of nine years supported by the state of Washington for armed robbery, extortion, aggravated battery, and assault. And the charges that didn't stick were worse: Assault with a deadly weapon and attempted murder. After the nine-year stint, he had hooked up with Victor Allan, described in the obit Kit ferreted out from *The Seattle Times* as a self-employed businessman. Some fuckin' business! Selling kids and God knew what else.

An old boyfriend of Phylly's. That's what April had called him. *Jesus.*

Joe pushed the light drapery aside, stared down into the busy street. He didn't like where this mother-quest was taking him—or the mixed emotions marching along with it.

The knot in his gut was baseball-size, and Phyllis Worth put it there. Thinking about what the hell she was doing with scum like Victor Allan in the first place only made the knot thicker.

Not going there—or to any other guy in Phyllis's past, present, or future. No point.

Plus he had other things to think about.

Like how this thing between April and him might just go the distance. And while it felt damn strange, it also felt right. Very right. And that going-the-distance thing? It was an untried road for a guy who'd gone it alone for as far back as he could remember. Something he'd never wanted— hell, never considered—before April walked into his life on those endless legs of hers. He wanted—needed—the time to see where it would take them.

What he didn't want was April at risk—or Cornie—or, goddamn it, Phyllis Worth. Because if the crazy woman mattered to April and his sister, she mattered to him.

He'd stood watch for cautious businessmen, celebrities and their families, politicians, but none of it was personal. He'd never felt the fear himself, the bone-deep worry at having someone you cared about hurt—or worse, taken from you—until now. Until April, Cornie, and his jelly- brained mother. Now he was watching out for his own, and it was so damn personal it made his brain ache. It changed everything.

When he heard voices coming down the hall, he checked his notes, committed the address Julius had given him to memory, and shredded the hotel stationery he'd written it on.

The Miami address, a long shot that might or might not be a lead to Gus Hanlon, April's long-lost brother, belonged to a woman called Dinah Marsden. But the woman was somewhere in Europe, and would be for at least a month, maybe more. Unable to confirm Julius's information, Joe would keep his mouth shut about it.

What April did *not* need right now was false hope.

The last bits of paper fluttered into the wastebasket as April and Cornie walked into the room.

April didn't waste any time. "Show him the card, Cornie." Before it was in his hands, she added, "His name's Noah Bristol and he lives on—"

"Vancouver Island."

Cornie gave him a dark look, through red-ringed eyes. The kid looked rough. "Trust Mister Know-it-all to . . . know it all," she blurted the last as if she were too tired to create her usual kick-ass sarcasm.

"Cornie—" April started.

Joe touched her shoulder. "It's okay. Besides she's wrong. I didn't know the name, and I was barely within twenty miles of the place. Having this"—he lifted the card—"will make all the difference." He coughed. "Thanks, Cornie."

Cornie's eyes narrowed, and April's eyebrows raised. Jesus, you'd think he'd dropped in a French curse rather than the kid's—Cornie's—name.

"Go pack, Cornie," April said. A small smile turned up her lips, and she did that gimme thing with her fingers in his direction. "It's airplane time," she said.

He dug out his card and handed it over. "One thing about you two, you're not cheap dates."

April took the card, glanced at Cornie. Her smile widened. "We're Vegas girls. We don't do cheap."

When Cornie went into the bedroom to pack her things, April drew Joe to the far end of the living room. "We can't take her with us to Tofino."

"Why not? She's safer with us than here alone." Doubly safe when he picked up what was waiting for him across the border. If there was a country on earth where Julius couldn't arrange the necessary *artillery*, Joe didn't know its name.

"It's complicated, but it would be better if she didn't come along. I'm going to call her friend at the ranch, see if she can stay there."

"I've got a better idea." He walked the two steps to the

phone, dialed. "Kit," he said into the phone, looking his fill at April for the first time in hours. Damned if his breathing didn't snag in his throat. "You've got your first real job. Maybe even get to use those new pecs of yours. . . . I'll drop the client off later today and fill you in then. And call Julius, tell him I want you and the client to stay at his place—Yeah, the Zern Bunker." He listened, glanced at April. "It's . . . my sister. She's fifteen—so don't go getting any eighteen-year-old ideas. Her name's Cornelia." He gave a few other instructions about time and place, then added. "And get that computer game, the one with the bats—that's the one. I should have known you'd have heard of it. . . . Uh-huh? You think? Well, I say prepare to get your ass whipped. . . . Yeah, see you." He hung up.

April smiled at him. "I think I love you," she said.

His damn heart stopped.

She went on, as if her breezy declaration was the equivalent of "Can I have mayo with that?" "You didn't have to do that, you know. Not that anything about staying behind is going to make Cornie happy, but the game thing . . . that was nice."

He didn't bother saying he'd happily kill a few dozen dragons for her, that a phone call was nothing. "The warning was 'nice.' The game thing was simply a sedative to get Kit through the next few days with Cornelia." He handed her the phone. "Better get started on those reservations, but just get us to Seattle, I'll have Kit take it from there."

She took a step closer, stood on tiptoe, took his face in her hands and brushed her mouth over his. "When I say you're nice, you're nice." She kissed him again, and this time he kissed her back, taking what time he could—which wasn't enough.

When he pulled back, he knew he'd better speak before his vocal cords seized up completely. "If being nice gets your mouth on mine, I'm not going to argue." He sucked in a lung-filling breath. "But considering we don't have the time to take this where I'd like it to go—and there's a minor in the next room—I'd say your timing is seriously off."

Her face turned sober. "You're right."

"Yeah, damn it. I'm right as hell."

April dialed the phone, glanced up at him. "Is Kit really only eighteen?"

He nodded. "Last birthday."

"Even so, you don't have to worry about Cornie—and those 'eighteen-year-old ideas' of his."

He tilted his head, waited.

"Cornie plans to stay a virgin until she gets married."

Joe lifted a brow. "I've heard that before."

"Not from Cornie." She turned to the phone and started to book their reservations.

A half hour later they were in a cab heading for McCarran.

Chapter 19

Henry made Tommy Black, with his pit boss slick and silk suit, within ten minutes of stepping into the Sandstone's casino area. Now all he had to do was wait for him to finish his business in the pit.

Sitting at a slot machine that had a good view of the tables, Henry slid in a hundred-dollar bill.

Fifteen minutes later, Black left the pit. About time, too. Henry was already down eighty bucks.

Black walked past him, stopped at a blackjack table a few feet away from Henry and his mermaid-themed slot, and spoke to one of the dealers, giving Henry time to give him a solid once over. The guy looked like a pushover, and it sure as hell looked like the sister got all the looks in the family—and the height. Black wasn't much taller than Henry and probably forty pounds lighter.

When Black left the table area, Henry cashed out on the slot and followed him out of the casino. A block down, he turned the corner onto a less busy street, stopped to take a short cell call, then picked up his pace. Henry knew exactly where he was going. The Sandstone was an old casino, refurbished in the last five years, but that didn't include employee parking. This ancient, three-story lot a couple of blocks off Fremont was as good as it got.

A half block before the lot, Henry made his move. Stepping up behind Black, he centered his Glock on a kidney.

"Keep moving," Henry said, leaning close enough to spit the words right into his ear.

"What the—" Black jerked, turned.

Henry stabbed him hard with the gun muzzle. "I *said* keep moving. Do what I say and you won't get hurt." Henry prodded him again, this time easing off. "Just go where you're going." When they'd made the turn, Henry hustled Black to his own rented Taurus, which he'd parked in the shadows along the back end of the lot. It was early enough that this part of the lot was empty, but knowing this town, it wouldn't be for long.

At the Taurus, Henry dug out his keys, opened the driver's side door with his left hand and said, "Get in."

Black didn't move. "If it's money you want," he said, his voice shaky, "I've got about four hundred on me." He made a move for his pocket.

Henry lifted the gun a fraction. "Keep your fuckin' hands where I can see them. I don't want your minus-piss money. Just get the hell in the car, and keep your mouth shut until I tell you to open it."

He didn't move but sweat clustered on Black's forehead. Even in the shade of the parking garage, the August heat made it hell-hot. When it looked like Black was going to open his yap again, Henry planted the gun barrel in his cheek and pushed hard enough to leave a tattoo. "Get the fuck in the car!"

He got in.

Circling the front of the car, his eyes and gun on Black, Henry made for the passenger seat. Settled there, he took a good look at Black's face. The guy oozed fear, looked about ready to shit in his pants. Obviously the sister got the guts, too. Again Henry scanned the lot. A woman entered from the other entrance, medium height, dark hair, sunglasses. She didn't seem to notice them, just got in her car, and drove out the entrance she'd walked in from.

Henry flipped Black the keys. "You drive."

Black's hand shook so bad he could barely get the key in the ignition. When he did, he looked at Henry, ran his tongue over his lips to dampen them, and said, "Where? Where do you want me to go?"

Henry smiled, lowered the gun, and rested it on his thigh. He settled his sunglasses more comfortably on his nose. From this angle, one shot would gut the bastard. Make a hell of a mess of his new suit though. "Out aways. Somewhere we can talk private."

"What do you—"

"Drive."

It wasn't long before Henry found what he needed, a patch of isolated desert: Sand, rock, scrub, and not a soul in sight. Nevada's geography didn't disappoint; north on old route 604 was enough emptiness for any man—or a convenient disposal. "Turn here."

Black turned.

Henry let Black drive the pitted road for maybe five minutes—until the dust got to him. Good enough. "Stop here, and get out of the car." An old falling-down shed, piles of rock, and debris from what looked to be an old excavation did the job of hiding them from the road.

Outside it was white-hot. Blinding. Had to be a hundred and twenty out here and not a cloud or shadow in sight.

He'd better get this job done fast or the sun would stew both their brains. The two men stood facing each other.

Not wanting to waste a second—in hell's own heat— Henry shot Black in the knee.

Black dropped like a stone, smashing into a jumble of sand-covered planks propped against the shed. Hell of a racket. Henry, thinking he heard another sound in the din, one that didn't belong, swung around and did a quick scan of the tan and gritted landscape.

Nothing but his own nerves and the Mojave.

Black cried out, "Jesus, who the hell are . . . you? What . . . do you want?"

"I want to know where Phyllis Worth is."

He opened his eyes, looked confused as hell, then he said, "Fuck you."

Henry was impressed at the late-breaking display of guts, but he was undeterred. Saying nothing, he looked down at him, watched him twist and moan, while the dust swirled and clung to his black suit, sticking in dark clumps to where the blood soaked his pant leg. Pain always heightened after the first shock, so Henry watched him a minute, giving the little shit time to see how serious his situation was, but when sweat beaded on his forehead and started dripping under his arms—staining his expensive silk shirt—his limited patience ran out.

Damn the bastard. He'd just bought the damn shirt.

"Tell me about Phyllis Worth," he said. "I want to know everything you know—and it's fuckin' hell-hot out here, so don't waste my goddamn time. If I'm in a generous mood, you'll walk out of this"—he gestured with the gun to Black's blood-gushing knee—"well, crawl maybe . . . with nothing worse than shit-stained underwear." Henry gave a little shove to his sunglasses. Sweat had them slipping down his nose. "Which, by the way, is a lot better deal than I gave your whore of a sister. Yeah."

Black's eyes, which he'd again closed against the pain, opened. "You sick bastard."

Henry pointed the gun at his other knee. "That I am—now talk."

Walking back to his car, Henry slipped the Glock into the inside pocket of his suit. Damn fine piece, he hated the idea of tossing it somewhere in this wasteland, but no way was it going on a plane. He'd pick something up on the other side of the border. Yeah.

Rounding the corner of the shed, his thoughts focused on a place called Tofino, airplanes, mega mils, and the sweat drilling itself out of every pore in his body, he again pushed his sunglasses up his sweat-slicked nose.

Then he blinked, blinked again; the glare, with the sun centered high in the sky, made the sand look wavy and unstable. But she was there. He wasn't imagining things.

What the fuck . . .

The dark-haired woman wearing sunglasses, a baseball cap, turned-up jeans, and sneakers—and built like a Hollywood couch slut with muscle—was leaning against the driver side door of his car. And she didn't look like she was going anywhere. They were maybe ten, twelve feet apart.

Quinlan's tail. Had to be.

Henry stopped, pulled some Mojave-fried air into his lungs, and slid his hand inside his suit jacket.

"Leave it be, fat boy." She raised a hand with a pistol in it and aimed it at his chest.

Fat boy. Henry's blood surged. He glanced at her gun hand. Steady. He pulled out his hand, empty, raised it and the other one. *Fat boy . . . What the fuck was it with bitches these days? Goddamn ball-breakers!*

"Do I know you?" Recognition sparked in the back of his overheated brain. There was something familiar about her.

She shook her head, snorted, as if she was pissed at him.

"Name's Mercy." She smiled at him. "A real misnomer, by the way."

The name meant nothing to him, and he had no idea what the hell a misnomer was. But he knew he was in deep shit. "You're Q's bitch." He stated the obvious, knowing if she'd heard Black spilling his guts seconds before, she knew everything she needed to know—and Henry was dead meat. Expendable.

"He thinks so." She pushed away from the car and

jerked her chin in the direction he'd just come from. "He dead?"

"Last I checked." He rolled his head, got psyched to rush her. If he was going to take a bullet, he'd try to take it where it did the least damage, so he could take her down. "What the hell do you want, bitch?"

She rolled her eyes. "A little on the slow side, aren't you? I want in, dick-brain . . . say seventy/thirty? I guess you know who gets what."

What the hell . . .

She took a step toward him, her face as grit hard as the sand they stood on. "Although thanks to your sophisticated interrogation techniques and your big mouth, I have pretty much everything I need to go for the gold on my own."

"You're the fuckin' hooker I had—"

"And you're the worst fucker I ever had the pleasure to know." She leveled the gun at his heart. "So? Are we partners, fat boy, or is it 'Bye-bye, Love'."

Nobody was touching Henry Castor's four mil. Nobody! Least of all a shit-mouthed skank named Mercy. His brainwaves blood-red, Henry put his head down for the tackle.

Mercy blew it half off. Half was enough.

Henry had a last disjointed thought: *A woman did me. A bitch . . . a goddamn hooker! . . .* before he ate the desert dust at his killer's feet. *Yeah . . .*

"You dumb asshole! You stupid freak!" Mercy cursed, grimaced, kicked Henry's shoulder, and stomped her booted foot. "Fuck!" She screamed.

Still cursing, she spun away from Henry's lifeless, crumpled body, then immediately back again. She stared at the body at her feet for a long time, her lips twitching and jerking as if they were on strings tied to a brain doing heavy calisthenics. Finally, she blew out a heavy breath, straightened, and firmed her mouth.

She pulled a wafer-thin cell phone from her tight jeans

and punched in a number while watching Castor's brain leak onto the sand.

"Charity? . . . We have the info we need—most of it anyway. And we're in for the full payday . . . Castor's out of the picture . . . Yes, as in dead. . . . Well, things happen." Her voice hardened. "It was him or me, Char. And we both know who I like better. . . . Quit worrying. Everything will be fine—better than fine. . . . A place called Tofino. In British Columbia somewhere." She shook her head. "We know enough, the rest we'll find out soon enough—which means bringing Q along."

The voice on the other end of the phone got so loud Mercy lifted the cell from her ear. "There's no damn risk! I'll take care of things. I always do, don't I? All you have to do is go on ahead. Find a guy named Noah Bristol. The woman's most likely there already." She frowned. "No! We do it my way . . . Fuck Q—which by the way sounds like both a plan and a hell of an idea considering the slime I've been messing with. And getting into a man's pants is a damn good way to get into his pockets."

She kicked some sand over the gore oozing from Castor's cratered skull, listened, and raised an eyebrow. "Yeah, yeah, I know he's a control freak. They're my faves." Her full lips curled, and she raised a brow. "Don't get jealous on me, babe. We've both got our parts to play. But like I said, I've got to go. Just get your hot little ass to Tofino. ASAP." She clicked off.

Before she left, Mercy walked around the shed and put two fingers on Black's neck where a pulse should have been—and still was.

She put a bullet in his head, making him and Henry a matched set, and muttered. "Dumbass didn't even get this right."

Two minutes later she went back to her car, parked just behind Henry's. She got in, flashed up the air-conditioning, and focused on her next move. It was important that she be word perfect.

Again she took out her cell phone and dialed.

"Mister Braid? Mercy here."

Q's phone was set to speaker, and because he was alone in his office, and confident enough in Mercy's discretion that she'd couch her words, he left it that way. "You're calling early."

"Yes. I thought it best."

Her usual businesslike voice came down the line, terse but deferential. Q was pleased with the woman's work. So far his relationship with Mercy and Charity—two exceedingly unimaginative pseudonyms in his opinion—had exceeded his expectations, and as always, those expectations were high. "Your report," he demanded. Leaning forward, he balanced his elbows on the desk, and interlaced his fingers.

"May I speak freely?" she asked.

He didn't like the question, but again checking his locked office door, he said. "Freely, but carefully. No embellishments, please."

Some silence came down the line, along with a rush of exhaled breath. "Mister C. disposed of the Black subject, but unfortunately he spotted me." A pause. "I apologize for overstepping my mandate, but when he came at me, it was him or me." Another pause. "It was him."

Q put his head in his hands, briefly feeling overwhelmed. He wasn't mourning the loss of Henry Castor; he was concerned about his next more. "I didn't employ you for that purpose."

"No, and I hope what's transpired here hasn't inconvenienced you."

"Inconvenience is an understatement." *I need that woman's name.* Without it his life, everything he'd built remained at risk. He wanted to pound his desk, throw the telephone against the far wall. He did neither.

"However, as they say, all is not lost," she went on as though he hadn't expressed his disapproval. "I witnessed his interrogation of the subject—and I have a name. Perhaps a destination. And from your instructions, I believe this information was your primary goal."

Q quickly picked up the phone, pressed the receiver to his ear. "The name," he demanded.

"Phyllis Worth."

He wrote it down, and even though it meant nothing to him, he was calmed by the act of writing it. Knowing his cause was not lost with the death of Castor, his heart again found its rhythm. "Go on."

"According to the man Black, the Worth woman, a former showgirl and employee of his sister, Rusty, disappeared over a week ago. He said she knew Henry Castor was after her and that he wanted something she'd taken from Victor's house. When Black spoke with her—just this morning apparently—she was already in Canada, on the west coast. He believes she was going to an island, a place called Tofino."

When she paused, Q, busy processing this new information—so much more than he'd hoped for—waited for her to go on. He appreciated that she took the time to get her thoughts in order. He found her style of speech, clear and confident, reassuring. Faintly arousing. It was, in fact, a style much like his own.

After a moment, she continued, "I hesitate to make suggestions, Mister Braid, but—"

"Yes."

"The situation has grown more complicated. There are other people looking for the Worth woman—her daughter and her son." She stopped. "While I'm happy to continue my surveillance work and assist you in any way you wish—

for the appropriate payment, of course—I thought you should know about their, uh, entry into the situation, as it might require you to take a more direct involvement from this point on."

"Will you hold for me, please?"

"Certainly."

Q hit the hold button on his phone, set the receiver down, and stood. He went to the window and looked out over his perfectly manicured lawn, his sun-drenched gardens. He considered the added number of people now in the equation. Every one of them upping the stakes, increasing the risk. Now, even Mercy knew more than was appropriate. So many loose ends.

His direct involvement?

That's what she was suggesting—and exactly what he'd been contemplating since Giselle had walked out on him.

He rubbed at his throat, again turned the idea over in his mind, too aware of the adrenaline now releasing into his bloodstream and the danger it posed to logical thinking.

Yes. It was necessary.

And why risk hiring an outsider, perhaps another henchman the likes of Castor, whose swath of carnage had done nothing but make a serious situation dire, when he himself was expert in such matters.

With Giselle away for the next few days and only one pressing business matter he could easily deal with tonight, there was no reason for him not to take matters into his own hands—and many reasons why he should.

He'd known it would come to this, the need for him to act on his own behalf—as he had so many years ago. Back then he'd needed a stake, seed money on which to build his fortune. He'd found that stake in drugs and murder, and he'd taken himself from destitute to well beyond solvent in less than five years.

Q closed his syes, filled his lungs.

He'd lived by his brains, brawn, and gritty perserverance—and he'd never been more alive. Felt more vital. Finding the child Victor wanted and delivering her to him was to be his final piece of business. Two days after its completion, believing the operation successful, he'd left the Seattle streets, laundered his money, and become fully legitimate. Almost.

He'd had nothing. Now he had everything.

Again he looked out over his serene gardens, his ideal life—the absolute quietude.

I want more. I want to feel again.

And while he might be in the clutches of misplaced nostalgia, he was sure of one thing: There was no one better able to look after his interests than himself. He could do it. And he would do it. Mercilessly and ruthlessly. That he would enjoy it was an added bonus.

He went back to his desk, picked up the phone. "I'll be in Las Vegas tonight. We'll talk more then."

"Good. But you should know, Mister Braid, that Charity and I *are* experienced in termination work."

She was smart, this Mercy woman. Considering he hadn't said a word about "terminations." "I know."

"From Victor?"

"Yes." Something inside him settled. If the mysterious Mercy, a woman that like her sister Charity he knew only by reputation and a numbered account into which he'd deposited some very sizable amounts, proved to be as interesting as she sounded, he would include her—and perhaps bed her. It would take his mind off Giselle. "As I said, I'll be in Las Vegas tonight. I'll call you with the time of my arrival after I've talked to my pilot."

"I'll be waiting, Mister Braid. I'm looking forward to our meeting." Her voice, unless he'd imagined it, had deepened, turned intimate. Intriguing—and vaguely familiar.

"While you're waiting," he said, "make yourself useful, Mercy, and find out everything you can about the Worth woman and that town you mentioned, Tofino. If she has a connection to it, I'll want to know who or what it is."

"Of course. Anything you want, Mister Braid." Again the voice was smoky, vaguely sexual.

"One more thing." He put the brief sexual tug aside. Business first. Business always first.

"Yes?"

"The others you mentioned? Her son and daughter. Get their names, please."

"I already have them, Joe and April Worth."

Q closed his eyes, the name April tumbling through his mind. *April . . .*

For the first time in days, his smile was real. Now he remembered more than her green eyes, now he remembered *her.*

April girl. Her stubborn little face, how she'd screamed, bit his hand, kicked his ankle—before he'd tied her to a chair in Victor's den. She'd toppled the chair, he remembered, and when he'd set it to rights, she'd spit at him. All the time tears streaming down her grimy little face.

"You're certain these two people are following Worth to this place, this Tofino?" He'd quickly considered his options. Now that he knew precisely who to look for, he may not need Mercy and her sister. Perhaps he could do the job alone. Although it had been a long time—and if there were several people in the way . . .

"They seem to be working on the same information we have. So yes, I'd say it's a strong possibility that if they're not there already, they're on their way."

"Find out exactly where they are, and keep me apprised of their whereabouts. I'll see you in a few hours." He hung up the phone.

He picked up a Montblanc pen, tapped it on the desk, and mentally reviewed the latest data: The three of them, Worth, her son, and the April girl together. Yes, that would work. Work rather well. All of the targets gathered in one acceptably remote location—in another country. Tidy. And very doable with a limited chance of witnesses—except Mercy and her sister, of course. He'd have to take care of them in due time. But for now, things looked positive. The precision of it—the exactitude—very nearly warmed his heart.

What was that expression? As easy as shooting fish in a barrel. Quinlan Braid smiled again.

It was the second time today.

Chapter 20

Phylly, after a winding drive through mountains, much of it bordered by streams, rocky cliffs, and friggin' trees—glowering trees, tall enough to intimidate the nastiest choreographer she'd ever worked with—finally came to a crossroad. Simple enough—to the left, the last gas station attendant had told her, was a place with the unlikely name of Ucluelet and to the right was Tofino.

They'd also told her to turn right. She did.

More trees, endless trees. Only now, this close to the ocean, the winds off the Pacific mauled them, making them bend and thrash their branches around like boneless arms—as if they were pissed off at being disturbed. Even though the sun was still fairly high, the tall trees were a wall of dark on the western side, their shadows sprawling across the road ahead of her.

It creeped her out. God, when the sun really went to bed for the night, this place would be black as a coal mine. More and more she felt, not as though she'd driven a car to another part of North America, but that she'd boarded a spaceship to another planet. That was homesickness, no doubt about it, making her feel so weird and dislocated. And she missed Cornie something awful.

Shaking off her sad and useless thoughts, she sped up, knowing she had another half hour of driving at best.

Which meant she was almost at Noah's place, a realization that put her brain into meltdown and made her stomach a bag of thumbtacks—all of them electrified.

It was going to take every thimbleful of confidence she had to face Noah again, plus whatever acting talent she had—not much—to even look as though she were in her right mind. Taking a drink of water from the bottle in the cup holder, she reminded herself she had it all figured out. If Noah was married, she'd do the old-friend-passing-through routine. She looked out the window at the unfamiliar landscape, the darkening trees, heard the low howl of the wind. Jesus, she'd have to be Meryl Streep to carry that one off!

God, please don't be married, Noah. I just need a soft place to fall—just for a while. I'll figure out how to fix things, then it's back to Vegas where I belong. A Vegas without Rusty . . .

She took another drink of water, refused to cry. Rusty would hate the idea of her wasting that fresh makeup job she'd done in the restaurant ladies' room a while back—and she'd really hate the tears. *I don't know what I'm going to do without you, baby.*

She sniffled and forced herself back to thinking about Noah, what she'd do if he *wasn't* married which, while it might be the best-case scenario, also set her nerves on high-speed jangle. No matter how many lotions and potions she'd used against Mother Time—the bitch—it had been over fifteen years. She was definitely frayed around the jawline. Not that she'd come planning a seduction. No way. All she wanted from Noah was a safe hidey-hole until she could figure out what to do about Henry Castor. She and Noah had parted friends, and it was a friend she needed. And you didn't mess with friends. You were straight with them—as straight as you could be.

Twenty minutes later, she stopped in Tofino and peered out the car window. Christ, this wasn't a small town, it was a village. She spotted a gas station which she hoped would provide the quickest route to his address. If she could've done that Google thing Cornie was so good at before heading out on this insane safari, she'd already have it. But even if she could commune with a computer—which she couldn't—she hadn't laid eyes on one since scurrying out of her apartment like a rat given advance notice of pest control.

The lone gas attendant was reading some kind of fancy comic book. "Excuse me," she said.

He looked up—and up. His eyes widened, and if he had a tongue, he was having a hard time working it.

Maybe she was overdressed for this tree garden. But, damn it, she'd tried to dress down: Jeans with a single line of studs down the sides, gold mesh belt, a leather jacket with faux leopard skin lapels. But other than her diamond studs—which she *never* removed—she wore zero jewelry and a plain beige Tee. Pretty simple really. But her height and platinum hair she couldn't do anything about. Although maybe the hair—her trademark—would have to go. She didn't want to think about that.

She glanced at his name patch. "You do have a functioning voice box, don't you?" She said with a smile. Didn't want to insult the natives.

"Yeah . . . sure, uh, I'm Mike, what can I do for you?" He coughed, came around the counter, where his eyes immediately dropped to her feet and stayed there. Barely a three-inch gold heel, and he was acting as if he'd never seen feet before.

"I need some directions—but I'm not sure of the address."

He pulled his gaze from her feet and looked up at her. "Who are you looking for? This is a pretty small place, I might know them."

"Noah Bristol?"

"Oh, sure, I know Noah." He summoned up a shy kind of smile. "Nice guy. Writes books and stuff."

That was news to Phylly. She smiled back. "Really, and what's his wife doing these days. God . . . I've forgotten her name." She feigned a frown.

"I don't remember. She's been gone maybe five years now."

"Gone," she repeated. "Not as in dead, I hope." Her heart tripped. *Oh, Noah . . .*

"No, as in divorced. She didn't much like it here, I guess."

"I'm sorry to hear that." *Yes!* She set aside her shaft of guilt over her gleeful reaction, and asked, "But I'd appreciate that address—and maybe some directions?"

He went back behind the counter, reached under it, and pulled out a map. "Sure, but . . ." He still held the map.

"Uh-huh?"

"You've got to hear this all the time"—he turned a flamingo pink—"but you really are beautiful."

God, she pinked right along with him. She had her share of compliments in her time, but for some reason this one broadsided her. Hell, maybe when a woman was staring into the jaws of serious middle-age, she got a little desperate—had to be when a compliment from a twenty-something gas jockey in Road's End, Canada, made a woman feel like she was fresh from an Extreme Makeover. "Thanks," she finally mumbled, waiting for the directions he'd promised. But it seemed he'd used his current supply of words on the compliment. All he did was look at her. "Uh . . . Mike, that address and directions?"

"Oh . . . yeah." His blush did an encore as he flattened the map over the countertop. It was one of those with cartoons and ads they used as placemats in small-town diners.

Phyllis listened attentively—the last thing she wanted to do was get lost—and from what the boy was telling her, Noah was off the map.

* * *

A half hour and one wrong turn later, she found Noah's property. There was no gate, just a lamp sitting on top of a stone pillar, its neck curving to light one word: Bristol. Thirty acres, Mike had said, five of it facing the ocean. The road in, too long to be called a driveway, was gravel and ran parallel to the shoreline.

It was, of course, lined on both sides by trees. She took a deep breath, then another. Neither stopped her from shaking.

This was it!

Phylly drove the twisting length of the driveway, and concentrated on the uneven road. The shafts of brilliance from the sun on her left turned the road into a light show. Blinding when it pierced through open slots between the trees, black where a tough grove of them banded together to block its way.

The road started to climb. Not long after that, she saw it.

Noah's house perched like a glass nest on a cliff overlooking the ocean. You could see into it, and you could see through it. Its deck was massive, prow-shaped with a point that jutted from the land the house sat on and over the cliff's edge like a stubborn jaw. One side of the house, where the sun reflected itself on walls of glass, was drenched in gold; the other side, all beams and angles, rested in shadow. Behind the house was a wall of forest. If there were any lights on, she couldn't make them out. But then, any kind of man-made light would wash out under the glare coming from the full sun, descending now to meet a glowing, sunscorched ocean. A set of wide stairs led up to the house level.

When she was unable to get any closer by car, she parked beside a couple of cedar trees that looked older than sin and turned off the motor. The surging roar of the surf below replaced its mechanical growl.

She opened the car door and stood, feeling woozy and off

balance. When she got the beat of her heart under some kind of control, she took her first shaky steps toward the house.

Leaving the cover of the trees, the sun momentarily blinded her. She shielded her eyes and glanced up.

He was standing on the deck.

Phylly's stomach kicked, and her heart did a monkey-in-a-cage routine. From this distance and with the sun mostly behind him, he was in shadow. Phylly didn't know whether his back was to her or his eyes were on her. But she assumed the latter, put her shoulders back, and made for the stairs. Easier said than done on pebbly gravel over uneven ground— even in her mini stilettos—mini being anything under five inches. When she wasn't listing to one side or another, her heels kept sinking into the earth under the gravel. *God, she probably looked drunk.*

The shadow on the deck didn't move. She didn't know why, but she was sure his arms were crossed over his chest. A dog sat beside him, big and golden, and as still as he was, except for an occasional sweep of his tail.

With Noah watching, it made the short trek to his stairs a hundred times harder than any bare-ass, bare-breasted strut she'd ever done on a Vegas runway.

"You need new shoes, Phylly."

At the sound of his voice, the smile in it, she looked up from the bottom of the stairs. She still couldn't make out his face. "And you need some asphalt."

When she stepped onto the deck, the dog stood and wagged his tail. Phylly put her hand out, let him sniff her, before stroking his head. As a temporary diversion, he was a soft one.

"His name's Chance," Noah said.

"He's nice."

Phylly stopped petting the dog and faced Noah, and for a long moment neither of them spoke. Phylly didn't know what he was seeing, but what she saw made her breathless.

Noah looked as if the years had skipped over him. Oh,

his dark hair had some gray, and there were a few new lines forking out around his eyes, but he was as lean and . . . potent as she remembered. When she'd thought of Noah through the years, it was never his physical presence that came to mind—in that he was ordinary compared to most men she'd been with. No, it was always his personality. Strong, decisive, and focused, that was Noah then, and she had the sense it was Noah now.

He took her hand, stood staring at her. "You're more wonderful than I remember. The same fantastic dream. But this time come to life."

She bent to kiss him. "Don't you know you're supposed to say, you haven't aged a day?"

He smiled at her. "You're telling me 'wonderful' and 'fantastic' aren't enough? You want me to lie as well."

She laughed. "Bastard."

"Come here." He pulled her into his arms, held her. "I've been waiting to hold you since Mike called me. The kid could barely get the words out, but when he said the most spectacular woman he'd ever seen was coming to knock on my door, I knew exactly who he meant."

God, she was going to cry. His arms felt so good, so safe. "Oh, Noah, I've missed you so much." She let herself relax for the first time in days. "I never stopped thinking about you."

He stood back from her. "And I thought we never lied to each other." He said it without ill humor and stroked her cheek.

Phylly's thoughts flew to Cornie, the daughter he didn't know they had. As lies went, that one packed the wallop of an A-bomb. Instead of answering, she smiled, put her hand over his.

"I've been right here, Phylly. All these years," he went on, resting his warm hand on her neck. "I waited for you. For a long time. A very long time."

She didn't know what to say to that, so she said nothing.

"I married. A few years ago now," he said. "It didn't work out."

"I know."

He raised a questioning brow.

"Mike told me."

Shaking his head, he smiled, his expression wry. "Small towns. Gotta love them."

Phylly wasn't so sure about the small-town thing, especially the idea of everyone knowing your business. "I'm sorry—that it didn't work out. Knowing you, that would have been tough to take." She swallowed and added, "Any kids?"

"No, which, as things turned out between us, was probably for the best." He ruffled the dog's head. "There's just Chance and me."

She nodded, unable to read anything into his pat phrasing, while wondering why she'd asked the question in the first place.

His thumb moved over her throat. "But none of that matters now. You're here, and that's not 'tough to take' at all."

"No questions?"

"A million of them."

"Think you can hold off on them for a while?"

He studied her, with that calm expression she remembered so well. "Sure, I can do that," he said. "After all, we have all the time we need to get to them."

No, we don't, Noah. We don't have any time at all.

It was as if a dark fist clasped Phylly's heart and squeezed. She closed her eyes and again went into his arms, hugging him fiercely, not wanting him to see the fear in her eyes. Holding him, feeling the strength and goodness of him, she was suddenly paralyzed by the realization that she'd run to him blindly, without thought—that she'd put him in danger.

Noah hated lies, and she'd come to him with two: One

painfully tangled—Cornelia, and one life-threatening—Henry Castor.

The truth? Now?

Impossible. She wouldn't know where to begin.

Noah ran his hands down to her waist, set her back from him, his expression puzzled. "Are you okay, Phylly?"

"No," she said, dredging up some showgirl verve and a smile as real as silicone implants. "What I am is tired and hungry. So if you've got something trapped in a can somewhere, how about letting it out, and tossing it in a pot?"

He didn't answer right away, only stared at her for an uncomfortably long moment. "Food it is, then a night's sleep." He put his arm around her and started toward the glass doors leading into his house. Before sliding the door open, he added, "Like I said, the questions can wait. But you will answer them, Phylly. Something's wrong or you wouldn't be here." He paused. "We were more than lovers, you know. We were friends—even though you were, and obviously still are, the world's worst liar."

Chapter 21

Joe, April, and Cornie arrived in Seattle in the late afternoon, and the three of them were standing outside Julius Zern's mansion on the hill—at least that's what it looked like to April—within an hour of leaving Sea-Tac.

Kit answered the door. Doors, really. Massive doors. Made of oak planks. High and wide with burly black wrought-iron hardware, they looked as though they were built to withstand a battering ram.

"Everything a go?" Joe asked Kit, herding April and Cornie into the house ahead of him.

"First thing tomorrow morning," Kit said. "A hop to Vancouver, then another to Tofino. You should be there by noon. And I've arranged a car."

"Good."

April and Joe exchanged glances, grateful that Kit's answer was vague enough that Cornie wouldn't figure out the reservations were for two. Time enough for that incendiary information later.

Joe said, "Is Julius home?"

"On the back patio." Kit jerked his head toward a half-open door, but kept his eyes on Cornie. His eyes behind his glasses looked both curious and hesitant.

Joe made the necessary introductions, and while April listened, she couldn't stop her head from swiveling. The foyer was white, its floor black marble, and the art on the walls a clash of colors and style. All of it expensive. A round table sat in the center of the foyer, but where she would have expected an extravagant floral display, there was only a soft, worn leather briefcase. There was no other furniture. Julius Zern's house was seriously minimalist and stunning. April was impressed.

Cornie, after she stopped frowning at Kit—for God knew what reason—and scanned her surroundings, actually looked cowed. "One guy lives here?" she asked. "In all this?" She waved a hand to encompass the massive foyer.

"One guy, two dogs," Kit answered, before looking at Joe. "He's been waiting for you."

Joe, familiar with Julius's house, started toward the far end of the foyer. April, Cornie, and Kit followed in his wake. Midway to an entry that obviously led to the patio, he stopped, gestured to a door on his left and said to Kit, "Why don't you take Cornie to tech central, show her around."

Cornie's expression turned suspicious. "You trying to get rid of me?"

"Uh-huh." Joe's expression, until now preoccupied and intense, softened when he looked at the girl. "I've got some business to discuss with my partner, Cornie—and it's not all about Phyllis Worth. We'll only be a few minutes. Promise."

"I don't—"

Kit interrupted, "Trust me, they'll bore you stupid."

Cornie's mouth went in motion before her manners. "And you won't?"

He blushed a fiery red. "I might . . . but Julius's magic room won't."

"I didn't mean . . . I'm—Oh, hell," she said, gesturing with her head toward the door Joe had indicated. "Let's go." To cover a blush even pinker than Kit's, she shot Joe a firm look. "Fifteen minutes tops," she instructed then strode off.

Before Kit followed Cornie, he gave Joe and April an unreadable look, then stated firmly: "Fifteen minutes or I go on triple-time."

Joe strode the last few steps to the door at the end of the hall, opened it, and let April pass him into an expansive living room. The room, its drapes closed and with no other light, was cavernous and shadowed.

One step inside the room, and Joe had the door closed and April pinned against it. He took her face in his big hands and devoured her with a kiss so hot, so hungry, and so potent, she didn't even try to breathe when he finally set her free.

"I've been waiting to do that all day." He rested his forehead against hers. "And because I set a timeline for my bossy adolescent sister"—he smiled and brushed another kiss across her lips—"I'm going to stop now, because if I don't, there won't be any stopping until"—another brush of his mouth against hers, then a long harsh exhalation—"forever."

"Joe, I—"

He kissed her again, addled her brain enough that whatever she was going to say floated away like petals in the wind.

"Tonight," he murmured in her ear before taking her hand and leading her across the stadium-sized room to a set of French doors.

They stepped out into the brilliance of a late afternoon sun. Its searing intensity bore down hard on the west-facing patio; the luminosity obliterating the darker shades and casting the area in simmering hues of ashen pastels.

April momentarily closed her eyes against the light and used the time to steady her breathing. Joe's kiss—fast, hard, and promising—hadn't only taken her breath away, it also took away her ability to think straight. One touch of his mouth, his lips against hers, and her brain had gone from cool and logical to crazed and frenzied.

In the best possible way... She looked down as if to shield her eyes from the sun's glare, touched her mouth, and smiled.

"You okay?" Joe said, his tone thick with innocence.

"You," she said, "are a very bad boy. And I owe you one."

"I sure as hell hope so." His grin was easy and seductive—and quick.

Beside the pristine pool, a man rose from a chair and made his way toward them. April had both her smile and hormones under control by the time he reached them. The man nodded at Joe, then looked at her. "You're April," he stated and offered his hand.

She took his hand, noting his grip was strong, his hand cool. "And you're Julius, Guardian B... or A depending on who's in the office," she said, remembering the odd signage in their office.

"That's me."

With his back to the sun, his features were a blur of shadows. Her first sense was how tall he was, even taller than Joe. Standing between them made her feel like a shrub between two oak trees. When Julius released her hand, she lifted it again to shield her eyes, to see him more clearly.

Lean, darkly tanned, a hard face, maybe thirty-five. His smile was swift—*little used*, she thought—and showed even white teeth. Not handsome, not like Joe, but compelling in a dark, shadowy way. She could barely make out the color of his eyes, but put them somewhere between gray and green, with straight slashes of eyebrows above them. "Come out of the sun," he said. He indicated the table and chairs he'd just left. Sitting beside the pool, they were shaded by a tan umbrella. The table held some books and papers.

Heading for the shade, Joe asked, "Where are the dogs?"

"Kenneled. I leave tomorrow. The client moved up their departure date."

Joe grimaced, rubbed his forehead. "Shit! I'll be at least a couple of days."

"No sweat. I can handle it until you're done."

April looked at Joe. His mouth moved, as though in concern, then tightened in acceptance. "I owe you," he said to Julius, echoing her words of a few minutes before. It seemed the ripple effect of Phylly's mad dash to nowhere had no end, even interfering with Joe's work.

"Yeah." His partner's answer was noncommittal.

They were barely seated at the table before Joe asked, "Did you get it?"

Julius nodded. "Address and phone number. Tofino's a small place, some fifteen hundred people—a lot more during tourist season. Whale-watching, surfing, ocean kayaking, that kind of thing. Noah Bristol lives outside the town a few miles. He's something of a naturalist. Writes books on wilderness gardening." He shoved two books across the table toward Joe and April.

One of the books had Bristol's picture on the back, a good-looking man, medium height, with a warm smile. Maybe midforties, with quiet, thoughtful eyes. April glanced at the book titles: *Wild Interior Gardens* and *Wilderness Landscapes.*

This whole thing, Noah, Phylly, just did not *compute,* she thought. How had Phylly, all flash and brass, ever got involved with such a man? And why had she never once mentioned him?

Phylly was never tight-lipped when it came to man-talk, nor was she above the occasional boast. But this man she'd kept to herself, which made him the exception. And if Tommy's hunch was right, he was also Cornie's father. Not wanting even to think about that complication, April put one book neatly on top of the other and pulled her hands down to her lap, interlocking her fingers to stop their shaking. The chance that Noah Bristol was Cornie's father both scared and excited her. She knew Cornie would welcome the truth, that she'd face it head-on. But considering Phylly had known all along where her father was and had told Cornie he'd "just run off," she'd have a few million words for her mother, and none of them would be pretty.

All of which you'll deserve, Phylly. And I'll probably add a few myself. Even so, it was Phylly's job to tell Cornie about Noah, not April's, so until everything was sorted out, she wasn't about to put her oar in that pool of unknown water—or take Cornie to Tofino.

Julius went on, "Bristol is something of an expert in his field and an avid environmentalist. Travels a lot. Does speaking tours, university lectures, that sort of thing." He passed a single sheet of paper to Joe. "Here's my notes, everything's there. Everything but a concrete link between him and your mother."

"Phyllis Worth," Joe corrected without looking up from the paper.

Her stomach did that odd little pitch and roll it had taken to doing whenever Joe denied his mother. "I'd like the telephone number please." April nodded at the paper in Joe's hand.

"And your plan is?"

"To call Noah Bristol and ask if she's there. And if she is, to speak to her."

Joe cocked an eyebrow. "She's liable to take off again."

April shook her head. "If she is at Noah Bristol's place— which appears to be in the back-of-beyond somewhere, she's already taken a room at her last resort. She has nowhere to go."

He handed her the paper. "What do you plan to say?"

"That I'll be there tomorrow, and if she takes off, there'll be more than one person on her tail trying to kill her."

"Funny," Joe said, but he didn't look amused.

"Sounds to me like Phyllis Worth has met her match."

Julius slid an amused glance Joe's way, "You, too." Then he stood. "If you'll excuse me, I've got some work to do. But when you're done here, Joe, we should talk about that Miami connection."

"You've got more?"

"Some. Still inconclusive, but you'll be interested."

The two men exchanged secret-service glances. Julius arched a brow. Any other day, April might have been curious—one of her major faults—but all she could think about right now was talking to Phylly.

"Give me ten," Joe said to Julius.

Julius nodded, added. "Take whatever rooms you want," he said. "There're plenty of them." With that he headed for the house.

April watched him go, her attention caught by the tall man walking away from them. "I don't get it."

"What?"

"Him"—she waved a hand to encompass the glistening pool, grounds, and grand house—"this. It's hard to understand the Guardian B thing."

"Family money. Buckets of it. More since Julius took over managing it. I didn't find out about it until we'd turned in our boots. Started the business." He shrugged. "The Guardian thing? All Julius ever said was he wanted to do something worthwhile. We both did. So we do." He stood, looked down at her. His jaw worked, but no words came out.

"What?" she finally asked.

He rubbed his chin. "Has it occurred to you that we might not be the only ones to have found Worth's little hidey-hole?"

"Yes, but it doesn't change anything—other than we need to get there before they do."

"You know what I think." It wasn't a question.

"Yes. That I'm the real target, because I'm the only one who can identify the man who bought me and—"

"Worth can't." His gaze, which was fixed on her, intensified. "So consider yourself in lockdown, because you're not leaving my sight from the moment we leave this house. We clear on that?"

"Joe, you don't—"

"Are we clear?" he repeated, his voice dangerously low.

"We don't have time to argue, but—"

"Right, we don't."

"Is that how you run your business, ordering your clients around?"

"You're not a client." It looked as though he was going to say more, until he sealed his lips into a tight line, a slash of masculine determination.

"Then what am—" she stopped.

She'd had the insane urge to ask: *If I'm not a client, Joe Worth, what am I?* But it wasn't the time, and her own feelings were too hot and fuzzy. If this thing with Joe had emotional signposts signaling the next stage, where you took the leap from great sex to something unexpected and unknowable, she hadn't found them. What she'd found was confusion in having such terrifyingly strong feelings for a man determined to loathe his mother—and hers. So, she stood, shaded her eyes against the sun and said, "I can take care of myself," she said. "And I'm not about to do anything stupid. I understand we're in this together, and I'm good with that." *Grateful . . . as long as you don't get hurt.* "But I *am* going to call Phylly."

He nodded, one quick dip of his chin. "When you call Phyllis, what are you going to say?"

"Exactly what I said I'd say, that we're on our way, and if she moves one inch, she's roadkill."

He put an arm around her shoulder and started toward the house. His expression was oddly flat. "You plan to tell her about me?"

She stopped, thought about it for a minute, and decided. "No. While my threats might hold her in place, her knowing you're in the picture might—"

"Make her take off regardless?" His tone was dry.

April hesitated, not wanting to cause more hurt where there was enough already, but she couldn't lie. "Yes, something like that."

"Smart," he said.

"Smart but"—she touched his arm—"are you okay with it?" It had to be emotionally painful, believing your mother will run in the opposite direction if she knows you're coming. In Joe's case it must be like scratching a wound that had never quite healed.

Before he could answer, Cornie and Kit showed up. "Ready or not, your fifteen minutes are up," Cornie said. She walked up to Joe and tilted her head. "I saw Mister Magnificent going up the stairs. That mean you're done with your business?"

"Will be after I check out one more thing with"—he grinned as though at a private joke—"Mister Magnificent."

"Good." Cornie's head swiveled to take in the patio area. "Wow, this place is amazing."

"Do you want to have a swim?" Kit asked.

"I don't know . . ."

"Go for it," April said, glancing at Joe. "I've got a couple of phone calls to make." She hoped he'd get the hint to keep Cornie busy for the next while.

Cornie's expression turned instantly curious. "Like who?"

Deciding a half truth was a thousand times better than telling her she was going to call their mother, she said, "Like Tommy for one. I promised him I'd call." And that was true. Plus she really did want to know if he'd dug up anything on Henry Castor. "Have a swim, Cornie, I'll only be a few minutes."

"I don't have a suit," Cornie said, looking at the crystal water in the pool, this time longingly. "I wasn't, like, planning a vacation or anything."

"Julius has plenty of suits," Joe said, then added for April, "and use the study—just off where we came in—for your calls. Kit can show Cornie where the suits are while I talk to Julius." He turned to Kit. "Grab me one, too. I won't be long."

April gave him a silent thank you and headed to the house. She would call Tommy first, then get her thoughts in order before calling Noah Bristol.

The page with his telephone number on it firmly in hand, she went into the house.

Chapter 22

Noah handed Phylly a glass of red wine. The only light, a half-dozen candles in the table's center, lit the wine briefly as the glass changed hands, catching the deep ruby color in a soft, quick glow.

"Can I get you anything else?" Noah asked.

"No, thanks, I'm fine."

"That you are." Noah settled back in his chair, raised his glass toward her and drank, not taking his eyes off her.

Phylly didn't drink. She cupped the base of the long-stemmed glass and held on, afraid that if she lifted it to her mouth her hand would quake. "Dinner was great. Thanks for that, too. I don't remember you being such a good cook."

"As I remember food was low on our agenda back then."

Oh, no, I'm not going there. She smiled at him, said nothing, and—coward that she was—looked away from him to the view outside.

Noah had told her how abruptly the weather could change here, going from serene to wild, clear to misted, on the whim of the air and currents coming in off the northern Pacific. He was right.

Where last night had been late August warm and still, tonight was windy, the air thick with rain. Noah had set the table just inside the window. The only thing between them and the roiling ocean was clear glass. *Noah's house was a crystal box,* she thought, *set into nature like a diamond set in a gold band.* At first Phylly hadn't been sure she liked it, had felt more exposed than she ever had strutting topless across a Vegas stage. But this morning, waking up to a pair of eagles sitting on top of a tree off the guest room deck— peering in at her like a couple of stage-door Johnnys—she'd felt safer than she had in days.

Outside it was gray, the clouds tumultuous, and below, the ocean tore at the shore, roaring and crashing like a mad thing. *It was crazy,* she thought, *for it continually to beat its watery fist against stone.*

Phylly shifted in her chair as ridiculously nervous as she'd been last night when Noah had shown her to the guest room. As she had been today when he'd taken her for a walk in the woods—wearing a pair of his sneakers!—with him and Chance. As she'd been every single time they'd come within sensing distance of each other. Dear God, the scent of him, all forest, moss, and musk, made her crazy. And it made her mad, at him for being the same irresistible man he was fifteen years ago, and at herself, for being as attracted to him now as she was then. God, she was a nitwit when it came to men, despite the last few years and her feeble attempt at getting her act together.

She sipped her wine to hide her nerves. She hadn't come here to think about Noah that way, and she sure hadn't come here to screw up his life. Ugly, bald fact that it was, she'd come here to save her own skin.

Between her scattered thoughts and the awkward silences straining the air between her and Noah, she was strung taut. Too taut. But she'd asked him not to ask questions, and he hadn't. That meant silences. The trouble was she was full of answers, damn it. They were bunched up inside her like a bad lunch, and they were dying to get out.

You can't do that to Noah, you selfish bitch. He's got a

good life going here. Don't mess it up because you can't keep your big trap shut. Messing up his life won't make yours better. Won't make Castor and whoever else might be after that journal go away. So shut the fuck up! Hear?

The first splash of rain hit the glass and some horns blew a crescendo on the CD—some classical thing—that Noah had put on for dinner music. Then, other than the sound of rain on the windows, the house fell to silence.

"You're going to have to talk about it sooner or later, you know," Noah said. Although he'd sat back in his chair, it was as if he'd moved forward, entered her space.

The candles sputtered in a sudden draft, and a whiff of their light vanilla scent wafted to her nose. She was glad of it. Glad that for a brief moment her senses were caught by something other than the man across the table from her. She tried to lighten the mood in the room, so rife with her tension and Noah's curiosity. "And give up my woman-of-mystery gig, not a chance."

"Phylly. Please. Tell me what's going on?"

She lifted her glass, shook her head, and tried to smile. If the feeling that it was paste on her lips was any indication, she failed miserably. "You promised, Noah. No questions."

"So I did. But I was coerced."

She tilted her head in question.

"A beautiful woman arrives on my doorstep—out of nowhere—and doesn't want to talk. What man in his right mind is going to argue with her?" He paused. "She could have aced the deal, if she'd come to his bed last night."

"You didn't ask."

His expression turned serious. "Would you have come if I had?"

"No." *Oh, but I'd have wanted to . . .*

He smiled—a bit of a grim smile. "I didn't think so."

"It's not about you, Noah. It's about me, and that—us sleeping together—it would only complicate things."

"As complications go, I'll take it."

She tried to smile back, but didn't pull it off.

"Phylly, for God's sake, you're in trouble. You have to be or you wouldn't be here. I want to help, but I can't if you won't tell me what the hell's going on."

Words filled her mouth, a stew of words with no starting point anywhere, and all of them ringed by fear. "Noah, there's so much I—"

The phone rang. *Thank the goddess of mouthy broads everywhere. It had to be a sign,* she thought, *telling her to keep her mouth closed.*

When it looked as though he was going to ignore it, she said, "Go. Please go."

Reluctantly, he pushed away from the table.

Two minutes later, he was back, holding the phone out to her. "For you. She says her name is April. She says she knows you're here, and that if you don't take her call she'll—" He arched a brow. "Let's just say she was colorful."

Phylly closed her eyes. "Damn, damn, damn." She'd planned to call April, but in her own time. This wasn't it.

Noah continued holding the phone out to her. "Whoever she is she sounds concerned. Either you take the phone, or I'll do the talking—and listening—for you. You want that?"

She took the phone.

For ten minutes she listened while Noah watched, his face deepening with concern. April was mad, bossy, worried, mad again, and . . . she'd be here tomorrow. But not Cornie—thank God, not Cornie.

When she clicked off, Phylly, knowing she couldn't trust her legs, did not rise from her chair. She knew, from looking at Noah, her face must have paled to an ashen white even her makeup couldn't hide. Could April be right? Was it her Castor had come after?

"Phylly, what's wrong?"

Looking away, still gripping the phone, she started, "It's not about me, it's—" she stopped, knowing that what she had to tell him would show her for what she was: A fool, a thief, and a blackmailer. But knowing, too, that either she told him or April would. Still, it was as if her mouth was fused shut.

Noah, who'd been standing over her, took her hands and urged her up from the chair. He led her to the gray leather sofa facing the dark fireplace. Chance, who'd been playing dead-dog in front of the fireplace since they'd started dinner, lifted his head at their arrival, but when no attention came his way, he went back to dog sprawl.

When Phylly was settled on one end of the sofa, Noah took the other, and said one word: "Go."

Where to start . . . "I came here because there was a . . . man after me. I thought—"

He waited.

She took a breath. "I took something—a long time ago. A journal. I thought that's what he was after, because I didn't think . . . I didn't think the other thing mattered. Not anymore. Not after all this time."

"What other thing?"

"The girl I took—and kept."

"You kidnapped a child." Surprisingly, his voice was calm.

She swallowed. "Not exactly. It was more of a . . . rescue thing, a kidnapping from the kidnappers." She was botching it, like she knew she would. "That was her on the phone."

His eyes widened briefly.

"Jesus, it was over twenty years ago." She massaged her tense neck.

"Before me."

"Before you." She rubbed her hand on the arm of the sofa. "I, uh, usually kept her separate. You know . . ." While her words trailed off, he drew in a deep breath.

"From whatever man you were seeing."

She nodded. "She was just a kid. I thought it was best."

"Depending on how many men there were, I'd say that was a wise idea." He turned his head away for a moment and rubbed his chin. When he turned back he gave no hint of what he was feeling. What he was thinking. "But that's not the whole story, is it?" he asked.

"No."

"Then start at the beginning and don't stop until you get to the end."

She got to her feet, walked to the window, and looked out on what looked to be a angry wind. It was dark now and the rain was hitting Noah's glass house in intermittent shots as if a lover were throwing pebbles.

Putting her hands flat to the glass, she rested her forehead against its hard, cool surface.

Yes, Phylly, start talking and keep talking—until he hates you. Until he sees you for what you are: A selfish, vain woman who's lived most of her life as if it were a party and she was the A-list guest; a woman who's known too many men, and was too dumb to say yes to the one man she'd ever come close to loving. A woman who'd kept his smart, beautiful daughter a secret from him for fifteen years. That she'd save for later—or not at all.

She took her hands, chilled now, from the window and faced him, rubbing her upper arms. "When I was in my early twenties I was a lap dancer at a club in Seattle. I met a man named Victor Allan." She took a breath. "He was rich. I was young, vain, and unbelievably stupid. . . ."

For an hour Noah listened, his face impassive. Whatever effect her miserable story had on him, she had no idea. Occasionally he asked a question, with a who, what, or when lead-in, but he never commented beyond that. By the time she'd finished dredging up Victor Allan, the ugliness called Henry Castor, and her friend Rusty's death, she was spent, a rag doll—minus the stuffing. Nothing she said made her look good—or feel better. She sat down, taking the seat she'd left when she started her sorry-assed saga. Noah got up, went to get them both a glass of wine, and joined her on the sofa.

"That was tough," he said.

Gratefully, she sipped the wine. "Yes, it was—and if you want me to go, I'll get my things."

He looked genuinely perplexed. "Why would I want you to go?"

She shook her head, weary now. "Oh, I don't know, Noah. Maybe because I'm a fucked-up woman who stole a kid, property that wasn't mine—"

"The blackmailer's journal."

She nodded, added, "And to cap it off, I did a little blackmailing myself. Could I have been more stupid?"

"On that issue, probably not. Big mistake." He sat with his arm along the back of the sofa, his other hand balancing the wineglass on his thigh.

"I was broke—scratch that! I really didn't have an excuse."

"No, you didn't. Like you said. Stupid."

"Rub it in, the salt on the wound thing feels terrific."

"What's in the journal?"

Oh, God—she closed her eyes—the question she was dreading, coming straight from the man who she'd hoped would be the last person in the world to ask it. To top it off, she was blushing, her face as hot as the noon desert.

He tilted his head, frowned. "Phylly?"

"I don't know what's in the damn journal."

Now he looked confused. "I don't get it."

"For one thing, I didn't have to know what was in it. It was open on Victor's desk the night I took April, so I grabbed it. Added insurance, I figured." She hesitated. "To, uh, get money out of Victor. Him just knowing I had the damn thing was enough. All I did was threaten him, tell him if he didn't pay"—she looked away briefly, ashamed—"I'd slip the journal to the cops. And I only did it twice, maybe three times max—way back—when things were tough for April and me."

"You must have been curious?"

She shrugged, heat shooting up her neck like it was fired from a blowtorch. "Not so much."

Noah eyed her skeptically and waited.

Shit! She took a breath and looked him straight in the eye, tried to get past all the letters he had behind his name, past all the books he'd written, the speeches he'd given, and said, "I can't read. All right?"

"Jesus."

"Not that good man's fault. My parents took me out of school in second grade."

Noah grimaced but said nothing.

"Seemed like a good idea at the time, I guess. They passed me around to aunts, uncles, and miscellaneous cousins for odd jobs—that they collected for. If there was such a thing as a truant officer in Bayton, Tennessee, he never came a-calling. And if he did, chances were I was slopping hogs at Aunt Lou's or beating rugs at cousin Ollie's."

"You're kidding." He was shocked and let it show.

She forced a grin. "I never did beat any rugs. I'm not sure any of my relatives even had them. It's one of those metaphor things. I did the hogs, though. I kind of liked them. Maybe because they had better table manners than most other members of my family."

He ignored her lame attempt at humor, his own expression dark, angry. "You're telling me your parents put you out for hire—when you were eight."

"I was tall for my age. No surprise there. One of those big strapping gals." She got up, walked to the fireplace, gazed into its unlit black hole. "And you know, at the time

I didn't mind so much. The bit of school I had was a disaster anyway. Like I said, I liked the pigs, and I got more creds bringing home enough to buy whiskey, chips and dip, than, as Mama said, reading some silly book."

She looked at Noah, but had to turn away. The man looked positively traumatized.

She went on, determined to get it over with. "I split for Knoxville when I was fourteen, took off for the west coast not long after that. Never did go back." She decided to skip the sagging middle of her story. He didn't need to hear the section of her bio covering her street time, the clubs, the men. . . . Her stomach tightened painfully. And he didn't need to hear about her giving up the son she'd had when she was in her teens because she'd married goddamn Ivan the Terrible whose idea of Saturday night fun was giving her twin black eyes before tossing her on the floor and pulling her pants off. Something she'd put up with for four years—maybe even thought she deserved. But when he'd turned on Joey, their three-year-old son, she was out of there. Her breath snagged. *And Joey was out of my life. Forever.*

Noah rose from the sofa and walked to where he could stand in front of her near the mantel. He turned her face to meet his, looked into her eyes, and used his thumbs to stroke her cheeks, just under her eyes, where despite her best efforts, a few tears had spilled. "I'm not going to ask you about the years after Knoxville. We'll get to that later."

Later? There was going to be a later? Phylly wasn't so sure about that. She took a deep breath. "There's one other thing you should know." Her words made her think about Cornie, and her stomach started to ache as if it were punched. Well, maybe two things, she added to herself. But for now she could find the words for only one: "April's coming, and she's bringing someone with her. Someone she says can help. They'll be here tomorrow morning. She says she has a lot to tell me, but over the phone wasn't the place to do it."

"Considering the situation, she's probably right." He led her back to the sofa, and they sat together. He held her cold hands in his warm ones, massaged her knuckles. "I'm glad she's coming. And I'm glad she's bringing someone who can help. That makes four of us. All that brainpower, we'll figure something out."

Phylly didn't feel the same. Because if April found her—thanks to Noah's brilliant daughter rooting around in Phylly's things—chances were, so had Castor. The name hit her chest like an ice floe. Jesus, the man had already killed Rusty; she couldn't bear the thought of him hurting Noah. Or April if she was here. Her heart raced. She held Noah's hands in hers and squeezed them hard.

She had to leave.

Tonight—right after she made love to Noah.

Chapter 23

Quinlan arrived at the Las Vegas Executive Airport at 8:17 P.M. Ten minutes later he was striding to where he'd told Mercy to meet him outside the terminal. He'd instructed his pilot to expect him and a guest for an early flight to Vancouver in the morning, and to arrange a charter for them from there to Tofino. Even if it were possible for his Lear to land at the miniscule airport, it would attract too much attention. Now the only item on his agenda was finalizing his disposal plans for April Worth. Mercy would assist in that—if she impressed him in person as much as she had in their arm's-length dealings.

Q spotted the black Mercedes and walked toward it, shifting the one soft leather bag he'd brought with him from one hand to the other.

Mercy was on the driver's side, leaning against the automobile, with her back to the terminal exit. If she were impatiently awaiting his arrival, she didn't let on. She was on her cell phone and didn't notice him until he'd almost reached the car.

"Mister Braid," she said, clicking off her cell without saying goodbye, her tone cool, her words unhurried. The gaze she settled on him was oddly assessing, as though she were measuring him against preconceived judgments. Her eyes were a strange shade of blue, close to turquoise. Colored contacts, he was sure. Perhaps a crude effort at disguise. What she hadn't tried to disguise was her near perfect body. She wore shape-hugging denim—a fabric he loathed. But at least it was high quality denim, well cut, and effective in accenting her physical potential.

He didn't offer his hand nor did she. "Interesting to put a face to the voice I've heard so often on the telephone," he said, anxious to get time-wasting pleasantries over with.

"Yes." She barely smiled, before walking to the back of the large sedan and opening the trunk. She didn't offer to take his bag, merely stood there waiting for him to come around and stow it. Odd that the deference so obvious on the telephone was so noticeably missing in person.

Yes, I'll have her. Later. After everything's in place. It will ease my tension.

While placing his bag in the trunk, he asked, "I assume you've made hotel reservations?"

She closed the trunk. "Yes. At Wynn. As you instructed, a midrange suite, not to attract attention."

"Good."

"And for only one night. I take it we'll be leaving in the morning?"

"As early as possible." Q walked to the car's passenger door and got in.

When they were underway, he asked, "Have you located Joe and April Worth?"

Making a turn, she said, "They left Las Vegas today." Having completed her turn, she cast him a quick glance. "For Seattle."

"Seattle." He repeated the city's name, his blood slowing in his veins. The city he grew up in. Victor Allan's city. The city where Q made his fortune on the weak backs of the stupid, the greedy, and the addicted—where he'd killed those who others paid to have dead. And the city he'd left as far back in his past as space and time would allow. "Why Seattle?" he asked not letting his reaction to that city's name show.

She shook her head. "I don't know. But it's irrelevant. Because what I do know is that they're headed for Tofino. Black was clear on that—and at the time he relayed that information, he was in no position to lie about it." She lifted one shoulder, dropped it. "By the way, you'll be interested to know there are two daughters. April, the oldest, is maybe thirty. The other is fifteen or sixteen. She left Las Vegas with them."

This news somewhat disturbed Q. He did not like the idea of more collateral damage—too dangerous. The son was enough. But, of course, he'd do what he had to do. "And the son? What have you found out about him?"

"Nothing. No one in Las Vegas knows anything about him."

Q frowned. He'd like to have been better briefed on this late-entry adversary. Still, when he considered the woman beside him, the hard line of her jaw, her keen intelligence and muscular physicality—her and her sister's sterling although violent reputations, he remained unworried.

"Charity will be joining us as planned?" he said, requiring this final confirmation.

"Yes, she's gone ahead to Tofino to reconnoiter and set things up."

"Including the necessary weapons?"

"Yes. Charity will have everything we need when we arrive."

"Good." Naturally, he'd brought his own weapon, but hearing about Mercy's added arrangements was welcome news. "Have you discovered anything more about Phyllis Worth's connection to this particular town?"

"No." She flipped down the car's sun visor. "But it's a small place. Charity will have located her before our arrival. All we have to do is show up, Mister Braid." A ghost of a smile played over her mouth. "But tonight we rest—if that's your pleasure."

He cast her a sideways glance. "My pleasures are simple, Mercy. And should they include you, I'll let you know."

She met his eyes briefly, her expression hard to define. When she again turned her attention to the road, Q turned to silence.

In minutes, the brilliant bronze façade of the Wynn Hotel Casino came up on his right. Minutes after that, barely looking at the Wynn's extravagant tree-lined entry, Q was heading to the elevators, Mercy a step behind him. The room was under her name, or whatever one she'd chosen, so there was no need to check in.

The suite was lavish with a view of The Strip that, if you cared about such things, you'd find stunning.

Q didn't care.

Nor, apparently, did Mercy. Walking across the suite's black marble floor, she kicked off her shoes, shrugged out of her jacket, and began unbuttoning her white shirt. The rounds of her breasts and a fine strip of blue lace quickly came into view. "Shall we shower first," she said. "Or do you want me to get you off and shower later?" She pulled a pin from her hair, and rich brown curls tumbled to her shoulders. Long and lustrous, her hair, unlike her eyes, appeared natural.

Ever since Q had confirmed she looked as good as she sounded, he'd planned to have her, but in his own time. In his own way. He certainly hadn't expected her to make the first move—and such a sudden and aggressive one at that. No one approached Quinlan Braid with such force, such . . . brass.

Although he did like her approach. It was efficient. And certainly the more businesslike the arrangement, the less it interfered with his sexual attachment to Giselle. At the thought of Giselle, anger bit into his usual steely poise.

She'd gone. He hadn't wanted her to go, but she'd left anyway. He still didn't know how he felt about that, why he couldn't let it go. He didn't know why Giselle was such a presence in this room when a new and promising female was on the banquet table. The idea that he cared for the woman on some unknowable level was ridiculous—upsetting. Perhaps even threatening.

Q slipped out of his light Hugo Boss jacket, folded it, and placed it on the arm of the pure white sofa. "You take a rather overt approach," he said, purposefully noncommittal.

"I see no reason not to. We can wait, if you prefer, but when I saw you I decided I didn't want to." She shrugged. "And we could waste time on the will-she-won't-she game, but there's no real point to that. Because the answer is I will—and so will you. What you've got there"—she looked boldly at his crotch—"will be in me sooner or later. I prefer sooner. And I never play games."

"Obviously, you don't *fore*play either."

She unclasped her belt, slipped it through its loops, and tossed it on top of his jacket. "No. You touch me in the right place a couple of times, chances are I'll come. And if you don't, I'll take care of it myself." She pulled down the zipper on her jeans, exposed a Vee of blue silk, low on her taut belly. It matched the blue satin covering her breasts. Exposed to him frontally, from her undone shirt to her undone zipper, she put her hands on hips. "You can watch, or you can participate," she said.

He didn't move and wasn't sure he wanted to, feeling, as he was, some new, unexpected responses to such an earthy and direct sexual come-on. His tendency was to analyze them, put them in proper perspective. When it came to sex, Q always took the lead, assumed control. He should hate this, should tell her how underwhelmed he was by her crassness. Yet, unbelievably, he was getting hard.

"Take off your clothes," she instructed, her eyes again

on his zipper area, some of the cool now replaced by heat. "Or I'll do it for you."

Carefully, slowly, he breathed deep. "Let me guess, behind your rib cage, beats the heart of a dominatrix."

"And let me guess, behind your expensive zipper, beats the cock of man who wants exactly what I want." She peeled her blouse off, dropped it on the floor, closed the few steps between them, and turned her back. "Unclasp me."

He obliged. Her shoulders were straight, her upper arms threaded with firm, clearly defined muscles. Weight-lifter muscles. A strong woman. A powerful woman. He itched to reach his hands around her, cup her breasts, test the weight and firmness of them, but he resisted. Folding the lacy bra, he tucked one cup inside the other and when she turned to face him, offered it to her.

She didn't take it. "I'd heard you were a control freak," she said, "but that"—she nodded at the folded bra—"takes some kind of prize."

"May I ask how you heard I was a 'control freak,' as you put it?" He placed the bra on the coffee table. The curl of excitement low in his belly, knotting into suspicion.

"Our mutual friend Victor. He said he'd never seen you sweat. Not about a job, business, or a woman." She tilted her head. "Especially a woman. He said the two of you shared pussy on more than one occasion, and that you never so much as grunted."

He relaxed. Trust Victor to spread old gossip. "You don't like foreplay; I don't like noise." Except from Giselle. God, he loved it when she screamed.

Naked to the waist, Mercy put her hands on her hips, her odd-colored eyes fixed on him intensely, her gaze speculative. "So . . . do you want to fuck, Mister Braid, or do you plan on being faithful to the girl back home?"

Q met her gaze. "What do you know about 'the girl back home'—or even if there is one?"

"A man like you? Unless there's a boy, there's a girl." Her gaze increased in intensity. "And I doubt it's a boy."

"You'd be right. But neither is there anyone else of note—which doesn't mean I'm yours for the asking." Briefly, his lie bothered him.

Mercy took two quick steps, her expression now bordering on savage. "You don't get it, do you? I'm not asking." In one fluid moment, she tore off his five-hundred dollar shirt. Buttons hit the marble floor with sharp little clacks. Then she worked his belt. Slipping the fine leather through the loops of his slacks, she tossed it over her shoulder as if it were a bone from a Viking table. He glanced at his torn shirt, discovered he didn't care.

He let her proceed unhindered—or his erection did; it was thick with need, greedy for what was to come. Either way, she was right; what she was offering, he wanted. So, he'd have it. Still he didn't move, content to let her take charge, relaxed under the deft movements of her hands.

He looked down at her agile fingers as they unbuttoned his slacks, and breathed contentedly, savoring the heat and power infusing his penis—those little thrusts and surges so insistent in their demands.

The ambient light in the suite played shadow tricks on Mercy's strong, corded arms, and accented her physical strength, a feminine power Q had never encountered before. She was new. This experience was new. He wanted her to have him. What was the harm. When this was over, she'd be dead, along with everyone else connected with the forthcoming kills—and his past. He'd go back to his Giselle and life as it should be.

He'd consider this a goodbye party—he just wouldn't tell Mercy.

She undid his zipper, slid her hand into his pants, and grasped his fully engorged organ. "So," she said, squeezing him firmly and meeting his eyes, "do we fuck or fold laundry?"

"We fuck," he answered, the word strange on his tongue, but instantly understood by the erection encircled in Mercy's strong hand. It jerked, pulsed to even greater girth. Perhaps there was something to this gutter talk during sex after all.

Leering at him, she released him. "My way?" she asked, cocking her head.

Q worked to ignore his hard, throbbing penis, jutting from his slacks; abandoned by her hand, the cool air of the air-conditioned hotel suite now heralded its imminent collapse. "Your way." His voice was uncharacteristically hoarse, his excitement level dangerously high, his body drum-tight with anticipation. He needed this raw sex—the coming kills. This was why he'd come here—to feel old feelings, to gasp and grasp—to feel potent again.

Her smile, arrogant and self-satisfied, held the warmth of a specter. "You're a man, after all, aren't you, Braid? Just like I told Charity." He didn't miss that she'd dropped the mister, but couldn't bring himself to care when she went back to stroking his penis as if it were a prized pet, her sole possession. "The woman actually thought you wouldn't like my style."

"What do you mean—"

She seized his upper arms and forced him down on the sofa.

"Make yourself comfortable," she ordered. "Because if I do this right—and I usually do—it'll take some time." She fell on him and worked her way down, lapping his chest, licking his nipples, his stomach, lower—

Dear God, what was she doing? . . .

Pulling, tugging, sucking . . .

If he'd had a question about her remark about Charity, it was lost in her sexual attack—and his inability to think clearly in the midst of it.

He bucked, reared like a rutting stag, gave himself to her talented, voracious mouth—oral sex the likes of which he'd never experienced before. She pulled him deep, deeper . . .

Panting, thrusting, he threw his head back, the cords in his neck popping like cables snapped from under the water. His hands, tangled in her thick tumble of hair, fisted involuntarily. His mouth slackened, but still he held back the roar poised on his tongue. Every sense he had lay strangled in the depths of her relentless mouth.

Her teeth grazed him, threatened the soft tissues they scraped, only to heighten his pleasure. A harsh hissing sound slid over his lips.

Sliding her hands under his buttocks, Mercy lifted his hips, brought him closer to her insatiable mouth—and Quinlan allowed her to take him, all of him, in a way he'd never been taken before.

Chapter 24

Joe, tense as hell, couldn't sleep. For Cornie's sake, April had taken the room across the hall from him, saying something about how she didn't need Cornie knowing more of their business than she had to.

If Joe was tense, April made him look Zen by comparison.

She'd been quiet all through dinner, her smiles forced, her words equally so. He knew she was distressed by not being able to raise Tommy Black, either at the Sandstone or on his cell. She'd even tried the hospital, but he hadn't shown up there either.

She left messages wherever she could, but at the point they'd all headed up for bed, Black still hadn't called. Joe hated that he couldn't do anything about her stress, do *any- thing* to make her feel better. He'd even toyed with the idea of telling her about the possible line on her brother, think- ing it might cheer her up—but as Julius had confirmed dur- ing their earlier meeting, the information on Gus Hanlon was still unconfirmed. So that idea wouldn't fly.

Knowing it was a guy thing to figure hot sex would be the perfect cure-all, he was left with accepting—*manfully*, he thought, *considering he wanted her with an ache border- ing on terminal*—her decision to head for her own room. Damn it, she'd looked exhausted, more tired and fretful than he'd seen her since this . . . quest, for want of a better word, had began.

His mother was putting her through hell. It was April's call to her that started her downhill mood in the first place. Whatever they'd talked about, she hadn't shared it with him. Expected him to ask, maybe. He didn't. He didn't want to talk about Phyllis. Nor did he want to tell April that the closer he got to meeting her, the more antagonistic he became; or that his gut got so tight it felt as if it were wrapped in barbed wire. For a man who'd written off his mother years ago, having her emerge as a priority was like being tossed into a sealed room with an open crate of snakes.

Ensnarled . . .

Remembering Riggs and his horoscope, he damn near smiled. If Donny Riggs got wind of Joe's serpentine thoughts, he'd never let him live it down, be yelling fortunes at him all the way down the block.

But neither April nor Cornie would like the snake analogy. He didn't much like it himself, but it was what it was. They were crazy about their mother; Joe was . . . not.

So he and April had ended up walking to her door like a pair of teenagers on a first stilted date, holding hands, him full of wishful lusting, her mind God knew where. Hell, even their kiss was adolescent, all need and confusion, as if a parent lurked beyond the door. When it ended, she'd put her hand on the doorknob, looked up at him, and said, "Later, okay?" Then blew him a kiss and went to her own room.

He was counting on that "later" of hers. He'd been counting on it for two endless hours! Mister Joe Cool hadn't sweated over a woman like this for as long as he could remember.

Hell . . . never!

Tipping back the last of his beer, he ambled out to the balcony overlooking the pool and looked down from his second-floor vantage point.

Ringed in low-voltage garden lights and softly lit from

below, the water in the pool shimmered in the small waves made by its lone swimmer.

April.

Joe's stomach took a hit and he went totally still.

She was swimming easily, lazily, from one end of the pool to the other. It wasn't exercise, it was mindless communion with the water. He watched her do a final lap, pull herself out of the water, and sit on the tiled edge of the pool. *Easy flexible strength*, he thought, *all her movements fluid, graceful, and unhurried.* Pulling her long hair to one side, she wrung it like a towel and flipped it back, letting its thick wet coils settle against her back. The lights from the pool danced over her pale skin, shifting and shining, making her features wavy and indistinct. The swimsuit she'd selected, from Julius's storehouse of them, was a black two-piece—and the body wearing it as damn near perfect as a body could be: Endless legs, toes she laughingly said were too long, feet she said were too big, the silver-dollar-sized birthmark on the inside of her left thigh that she described as her personal map of Ireland.

April lived in her skin with a grace that beguiled him, always holding her shoulders straight and using her tall, strong body with unapologetic confidence. It was a body he knew and wanted to know again—and again. Like he wanted to hear her laugh, give him a hard time, and look at him with that take-no-prisoners look she was so damn good at. April was all woman. All his woman . . .

She took his breath away. He shook his head. *Sap!* Had to be if he was thinking words like goddamn *beguiled.*

Sap or no, he didn't take his eyes off her. His heart pounded, his muscles, nerves, and skin vibrated from wanting her. *This is nuts!* He rested both hands on the railing, breathed deep, held fast, and rolled his head. He was full of her and empty of her—and it made him animal-crazy.

In that instant, seeing her lit by wavy pool lights and midnight shade, he was absolutely certain of one thing: He wanted her now—and he'd want her on every tomorrow to come.

Was it love? Shit, he had no idea. He didn't know love, didn't know what to expect from it. All he knew was that there was an elephant on his chest, and it didn't seem to be leaving anytime soon.

He was still looking down, sorting through whatever it was he was feeling, when she looked up and saw him.

She smiled immediately—did that gimme thing with her hand like she did when she wanted his credit card—and cocked her head. As invitations went, it would do.

When he got there, she was sitting in the same place at the edge of the pool, but she'd put a towel under her butt and left enough of it beside her for him to sit on.

Joe, wearing a sleeveless Tee and shorts, took his place beside her and put his feet in the cool water. Cool as it was, he knew Julius had turned on the heat for his guests, because while he swam in it winter to summer, he never heated it.

Leaning back on her hands, April smiled at him. "I was coming to you," she said. "I just wanted to ease up first."

"And I was waiting for you."

Looking pleased at that, she nodded and looked away. Despite her swim, he saw her tension still lingered.

"It's going to be all right, you know," he said. "Everything's going to be all right."

She turned to look at him again. "I know," she said, sounding more certain than she looked. "And it was good to hear Phylly's voice tonight, confirm that she was okay. Now if I can just get Tomm—"

He pushed her into the pool and followed—in time to be there when she came up sputtering. "What was that?" he asked, feigning innocence and holding her by the waist. "I didn't quite get it."

She sputtered some more, then grinned at him. "That was mean."

"That was a distraction. If I can't get you into my bed, dunking you in the pool was my next best shot."

She put her hands on his shoulders while they both treaded water. "I worry too much, don't I?"

About his wild and selfish mother? Absolutely. But he wasn't going to say that. "Yeah," he said, his hands squeezing her waist. "So how about another distraction. Three laps, length of the pool, and the winner gets to be on top?"

"On top of what?" she asked, not even trying to look innocent.

"Whatever—and whoever—strikes their fancy."

"I think that's a win-win scenario."

"That's the idea."

She tightened her grip on his shoulders, looked perplexed. "You really hate to talk about things, don't you?"

"I hate to worry about things that I can't do anything about—until they're in my face."

"Like tomorrow."

He nodded.

She paused before answering then, as though making up her mind, she said, "You're right. About that and the distraction." Her beautiful face turned impish. "Make it two laps, and you've got yourself a deal."

"Fair enough."

"And one other thing."

"I'm listening."

"I'd very much like to win." She gave him a shot of pure sex from her green eyes. "I could use a good ride."

Already semi, Joe steeled up, and grinned. "You want a head start, say twenty minutes."

She laughed and backstroked away from him. "Nope, just stay on my ass, big boy. And I'll make it worth your while."

He was happy to oblige.

* * *

It didn't take twenty minutes before they were in Joe's room, dripping water all over Julius's expensive carpets, and heading for the shower.

Joe pulled his wet Tee over his head, and stepped out of his shorts. He tossed both items in the bathtub and turned on the shower, so they could rinse off the chlorine.

April wasn't in such a hurry. She stood and watched him from the doorway, her skin glistening, still wearing a wet swimsuit that looked glued to her body. She looked like some kind of misplaced sea goddess. And she was studying him.

Slowly, and with keen interest, she scanned every inch of him—every fuckin' inch. Or inches wanting to fuck, if you cared to get your English right. He was vaguely embarrassed. Damned if guys weren't at a real disadvantage when it came to the sex game. What they wanted always made a damn show of itself, right out there for the woman to see; nothing mysterious about it. For a second, he wondered if there'd been an available fig leaf would he have strapped it on—until he saw she was enjoying herself.

"I could spend a lot of time looking at you, Joe Worth," she said, running her tongue over her lower lip. "I keep thinking, if I were to design a costume for you, what would it be?" She tilted her head, again looked him up and down. "Maybe a highlander outfit. A kilt would be good . . . And there's always that no underwear thing." She took a step toward him. "Or maybe a Roman senator. A soft white robe—again no underwear. Or a biker—yes, one of those dangerous-looking types who wear tight jeans and—"

"No underwear." The bathroom was steaming up from the running shower. Joe was steaming up period. But the lady wanted to play, so he'd play. For a couple of nanoseconds.

She laughed softly. "I think we're on the same page."

"Not quite." He closed the short distance between them. "I like looking, too." He gestured with his chin at her two piece swimsuit. "And I've already designed a costume for you."

"Let me guess . . ." Her suit had a front close, and she unhooked it, baring her damp breasts, before dropping the bra top to the floor. "Would that costume be flesh-colored?"

"Definitely."

"And would it be trimmed with"—she peeled off the bottom of the suit, left her dark blond curls to wetly glisten in the bathroom light—"anything?" She stroked the curls at the top of her thighs.

Joe could barely breathe, and even if he could, he wouldn't hear it over the thumping going on in his chest. "You're killing me, you know that?"

She took the final few steps between them and touched his mouth with her index finger. "Killing you is the last thing on my mind." Her eyes softened, and she was so close he saw her pupils dilate. "Make love to me, Joe"—she backed him into the double shower—"right now. Right here." She lifted her face to the warm water coursing over them both, shoved her hair back, and looped her arms around his neck.

He slid his hands over her hips and cupped her bottom. Spreading his legs for balance, he lifted her and braced her back against the shower wall. "I've been waiting to make love to you since . . . Hell, I think I've been waiting forever."

Wrapping her long legs around him, she nestled her head beneath his ear and kissed his neck. "Then take me fast and hard." She bit him—not gently. "We'll do the slow stuff later," she whispered, licking then kissing the bite she'd given him, before moving her mouth to the rose in his tattoo.

"You ready for that?" They might be drenched in shower water, but that wasn't the moisture she needed.

"Oh, yeah," she murmured, the words vibrating against his skin. "I'm more than ready, I'm waiting."

Joe's brain fogged, his muscles hardened, and he slipped into pure testosterone fueled sex drive. He went in the way she'd asked him to: Fast and hard. She took him deep, her breasts against his chest so tight they were a blur of softness, her arms and legs gripped him like a vise. The rounds of her rear firmly in his hands. Throwing his head back, he plunged mindlessly, water splashing and splattering the glass shower stall with every thrust and jolt. His eyes closed, his mind shorted out, and he raised his face to the shower, and . . . mated. Free, primal, and possessive. He thrust, pulled back, thrust again, and again; each deep hard stroke numbing him, crazing him.

Brain chaos.

April under his hands, her skin water-slicked and hot. Her inner walls stroking him, taking and taking . . .

He couldn't hold on, didn't want to hold on.

A hoarse rumble starting low in his throat, the final surge building, overtaking him. Muscles straining, taut to max. Breath tangled in his lungs. Mind a blizzard.

He crushed her to him and plunged home, to her center . . . groaned . . . held her to him. His blood still popping in his veins, sweat rushing off his back under the shower's cascading water, he grasped for air. His muscles slackened. His legs quivered.

It was over. Finished. *Just beginning.* Joe's overheated brain couldn't figure out which.

His breath still a four-fisted brute pounding against his rib cage, he cursed softly, kissed the hot wet skin of April's shoulder, and waited for the cool-down to begin—and hoped like hell it never would.

It had been a wild, hard possession that was over in a time that had to be his personal best—or worst, depending on your point of view.

April, clinging to him like a rain-soaked vine, hugged him tighter. "Nice," she whispered in his ear.

"For me, yeah. For you, not so sure." His voice was low and uneven. He cleared his throat.

April loosened her grip on him enough to pull back and meet his eyes. "I asked for it, didn't I?"

He was still holding her, still in her, and distracted by the sensation of going soft inside her, he was seriously considering giving up his real life and staying there forever—or at least until he was hard again. The thought did nothing for his voice box, but it did bring a flicker to his depleted sex. Something suspiciously like a grunt came out of him. *Give it up for the Neanderthal,* he thought grimly. Joe liked slow, liked smooth, liked taking his time with a woman . . . but shit it was good to just get off once in a while with a woman on-board with it.

"Joe?" She was still waiting for an answer.

What was the question again? Oh, yeah, about her asking for it. "Just afraid it might have been one of those be-careful-what-you-wish-for-because-you-might-get-it kind of things." He reached behind her to turn off the water.

"It wasn't. Because I had an ulterior motive. " She smiled, wiggled her brows. "Now you owe me."

Lifting her and taking a steadying breath, Joe withdrew himself from her heat. When he had her feet on the floor, he dug up a smile of his own, cupped her breasts and thumbed the hard tips of her nipples. "A debt I'll be happy to pay." *Over and over again.*

Under the play of his fingers, her nipples peaked. He leaned down to take one in his mouth, let his tongue take over from his fingers.

April gasped when he sucked on her, sank her hands into his hair, and arched to give him full access.

He switched to her other nipple, lapped at it then took it between his thumb and index finger. Lifting his head, he looked at her closed eyes, the softness of her skin, made rosy by the warm shower, the flexing of her lips reacting to his touch, slack one second, tight the next. He heard a purr, and she shifted against his lower body, showing her need openly. No barriers, no shyness. God, he loved that.

It was a deep part her, he thought, *the openness—to sex, to caring, to loving.* He didn't stop toying with her nipples, but he eased up and gentled his touch. "That was a gift, wasn't it?" he said. "That fast-and-hard thing we just did."

She opened her eyes, and he could see the heat in them, see how he'd left her wanting. Aching. She put her hands over his, crushed his big paws to her breasts, and for a second looked away from him. When she looked back, her gaze was less cloudy with sex, more filled with purpose. Still she hesitated before shaking her head and saying, "Kind of a test really."

He cocked his head.

"Not of you. Of me. What's going on between us . . . it's too hot, too fast, and too bizarre for me to wrap my head around. And the sex . . . well, the sex was so good between us in Vegas and you were such an expert lover. I was afraid it might be just some slick—"

"Technique?"

"I thought if I got you to just—"

"Go at you like a wild bull. I'd demo that I'm the usual jackass male." *Which I did.*

She frowned. "Quit finishing my sentences." She took a breath. "But, yes, that's exactly what I meant. I thought if you did—what you just did—I'd get real. See you as just a guy. Maybe not like you as much as I'm starting to."

"Did it work?" he asked, not sure he wanted the answer.

She tightened her lips briefly, but apparently couldn't stop them from turning up into a quick smile. "No."

"Then you like me as much after I nearly embedded you into Julius's shower tiles as you did before?" Something way back in his sex-addled brain told him he should be asking about why she didn't want to like him. But he figured that would be too much information. Plus being naked with an equally naked woman in a cooling shower stall had a direct bearing on his priorities. It didn't include sticking an oar in murky waters. That was best left to a time when eye contact was the only option.

"I guess so." She looked up at him, rubbed her arms as if for heat, then crossed them under her breasts.

"Come here," he said. He pulled her out of the shower and wrapped her in a bath sheet. He massaged her back, her shoulders, her arms. When he had her warmed up, he turned her to face him, and lifted her chin. "I don't know why your liking me bothers you—"

"It's a—"

He touched her mouth. "And I don't want to. Not tonight anyway." He lowered his head, caught her eyes. "You good with that?"

"We should—" she started then stopped herself. "I'm good with that. We'll leave it until after."

He knew she meant after finding Phyllis Worth, but the last name he wanted mentioned in context with what was going on with him and April was that one, so he let her statement hang. "Can I take you in there now"—he gestured toward the open bathroom door showcasing his king-size bed—"and start paying off what I owe you?" It was the best he could come up with to give her a choice. "With interest," he added.

"That's the thing." Her brow furrowed as though in confusion. "I shouldn't, but that's *exactly* where I want to be—in that bed. You all over me and me all over you."

"All those shoulds and shouldn'ts must be tiring." He ran a finger down her cheek, and sensing a win, didn't hide his grin. "But it's your call."

She pulled the towel tight around her, eyed him, then as if she couldn't help herself, she grinned back. "How much interest?"

"As much as you can take."

She dropped the towel.

Chapter 25

April woke up in Joe's arms, her head and one hand on his broad chest, her hair snagged under his arm. She didn't move, didn't want to move. This was the finest cocoon she'd ever spun for herself, and she was in no hurry to leave.

God knows it wouldn't last. She had the nagging sense that she and Joe were heading for a crash and burn. And Phylly would be at the root of it. At the thought of Phylly, her mood darkened, but she didn't let the worry take hold. She was okay, safe for now, and would be until she and Joe got to her. And like Joe said, worrying, when you couldn't affect things, was a waste of time. She did wonder though, what Phylly would think of her stolen daughter sleeping with her abandoned son—or that daughter teetering on the brink of falling for him.

She peeked over Joe's shoulder to the bedside clock—almost six. She should probably get up, repack, and start some coffee. The trouble was she wasn't in the mood for *shoulds*; she was in the mood for Joe Worth and had been—not from their first meeting when he'd been what Cornie accurately called a jerk—but from the moment he strode into that cheap motel room, trying to pretend he didn't give a damn about family, even while his stubborn gaze filled up with equal measures of panic and awe on sight of his true sister. He'd acted like a father handed a five-pound new-born, enthralled and terrified at the same time.

Yes, that's when he had her . . .

And he'd been having her ever since. She had the dull ache between her legs to prove it.

God, what a night . . .

He stirred under her hand and the heart under her ear beat easily. Too easily, considering her heart was ticking like a broken clock. Smiling, she ran her free hand down and over his hard, rippled abs, lower, lower still.

"You know what they say about not going into the kitchen if you can't take the heat," he said, his voice morning husky.

"I like heat." She looked up at him. His beard was rough and dark, and his eyes, peering at her from under narrowed lids, were nickel bright. "Anyway, I was just going to pull up the covers," she lied, keeping her hand where it was and making circles with it.

"And I believe you, even when those busy fingers of yours are now well below the cover zone."

"Hmmm. Guess they slipped." Still smiling, she slid her hand to its final destination, encircled him, and watched his eyes. They closed.

"Jesus, what a way to start a morning." He lifted himself to her caress.

"We've got a few minutes before we have to start getting ready," she said. "Any ideas what to do with it?" She pumped him gently, loving the way he grew into her hand, his lazy thrusts when he got her rhythm.

"Ideas are a dime a dozen, baby"—he quickly took control, flipped her onto her back—"what you've got here is a man of action."

"April? Are you in there? April, come on. We've got to go."

Cornie.

"April, I know you're in there. I know Joe's in there. So get over it. Kit's made coffee for you guys."

Joe and April looked at each other, both shock-eyed, both still as rocks. Joe blinked first then sucked in some air. Very noisily. "She hates me, you know that. Why else would she have my sex life wired into her GPS system?"

April tossed the covers back and sat on the edge of the bed. Even though she was as disappointed as he was, and felt as if someone had thrown a bucket of ice water on the bed they were in, she had to smile at his irritation. Hell hath no fury like a man denied morning sex—twice. "She hasn't got anybody wired. She's just anxious about her mom, and she's right, we should get going."

April put her hand to her mouth. "Oh God, she still thinks she's coming. She's going to be so disappointed." Which meant seriously ticked off as only Cornie could be—a condition that brought sass, sulks, and stubbornness to new and glorious heights.

Joe pulled himself up, didn't bother covering what she'd had her hand around mere moments before. Her breathing hitched. "Disappointed?" he shook his head, ran his eyes over her. "That kid doesn't know what disappointment is." He paused. "But I'll take care of it, don't worry. It'll be my chance to get even. I'm pretty sure Julius has a dungeon equipped with various weights of chains."

She gave him a long look. "Know what?"

"What?"

"You sound just like a brother."

He looked disgruntled. "Maybe because—like it or not—I am one."

"You like it well enough." April thought of Gus. They'd had their fights, she and Gus, mostly because she'd get, as he called it, all pissy and grabby. But he'd always looked out for her, and while he might call her names, God help anyone else who did. If he'd been there the night the black-eyed man came, things might have different. She'd screamed for him—oh how she'd screamed—but he hadn't come. And for a long time she'd blamed him for that—until she'd grown up, got some perspective, and realized there was nothing a twelve-year-old boy could have done, no matter how he might have tried.

Joe slid back down the bed, snapped his fingers in front of her. "Deprived male here. Hello."

She smiled at him, brought her attention back to Julius's beautiful room, the bed with the deprived male in it. "I was thinking how lucky Cornie was to have found you."

"Hmmm." He rolled out of the bed, magnificently naked, his hair rumpled, his unshaven jaw a dark sexy shadow, and looked at her with his mother's silver blue eyes. "She won't feel so lucky a half hour from now, when I tell her she's staying here."

"No, she won't"—she went to him and wrapped her arms around his narrow waist—"but I'm sure you'll handle her with your usual diplomacy and tact."

He enclosed her in a powerful embrace, kissed her forehead. "Uh-huh, right after I have her in those chains."

Everybody was in the kitchen when she and Joe got there. Kit and Cornie were sitting at the far end of a long table eating cereal. April's stomach dropped when she saw the bag packed and sitting at Cornie's side. Her disappointment would be spectacular.

When Cornie's eyes met April's, the girl raised her eyebrows and glanced at Joe. Her gaze shone with the light of teenage triumph, making April the tiniest bit squeamish. When it came to men, April had always been discreet, particularly around Cornie, and considering her relationships were few and far apart, it had been easy enough—until Joe. With Joe nothing was easy, nothing was the same as before, and Cornie, like it or not, was right in the middle of it.

She'd have to talk to her—but not now, not today. Not only did she not know what to say, she didn't have the emotional reserves even to begin to think logically about what was going on between her and Joe.

She'd tried to do that last night, going to her room alone, taking some time to herself, a solo swim. Then she'd sensed him on his balcony, felt his eyes on her—and she'd wanted him so badly she'd shaken with it. All her thinking had only made things worse—or better if she considered what she and Joe had done after the swim. Her body warmed at the memory. She glanced at Joe—talking to Kit now—his clean-shaven jaw, his firm mouth, serious this morning and set with purpose. The kitchen light turned streaks of his shower-damp chestnut hair to dark gold, and when he caught her gaze, his eyes glittered with intimacy.

Her knees weakened simply looking at him. She shifted her gaze, told herself her ill-timed attraction to him didn't matter right now. Priority one was finding Phylly, making sure she stayed safe.

It wasn't like April to procrastinate, to delay or dither over decisions, but she'd never fallen in lo—serious like with her mother's son before.

God, all of it together made her head pound.

And coffee. I crave coffee.

As if on cue, Julius handed her a cup, black and steaming, exactly how she liked it. He did the same for Joe.

"I've called a limo. It'll be here in ten minutes," he said.

"Perfect," Joe said, taking a solid swig of coffee. "And that other thing?"

April gave Joe a questioning look; he ignored her.

"Done," Julius said. "There'll be a parcel for you to pick up, along with your rental car, when you arrive in Tofino."

Joe just nodded.

Kit glanced nervously at Cornie, then said to Joe, "Your Sea-Tac flights are booked, too. The info's by the phone."

He jerked his head toward a phone on a desk area at the end of the granite counter.

The kitchen was as massive as the rest of the house—and a chef's dream: Hanging pots, bronzed-steel appliances, triple ovens, and enough gas elements to cook for a regiment. April had never dreamed this big, this grand, for the home she hoped to have one day, but she could still appreciate it.

Joe looked at Cornie. "Will you get that, Cornie?"

Cornie took a last spoonful of cereal and went to the desk. She picked up the paper with the flight information, and automatically scanned it—her eyes shot to April, then Joe. "This is for two," she accused.

April braced herself for the explosion.

Joe set his coffee down, walked over to her, and gripped her arm. "Let's take a walk."

"I don't want to take a walk." She shook the papers and pulled out of Joe's grasp. "I want to know about these."

"And I want to tell you. Outside," Joe said.

Their gazes locked, new brother-to-be and stubborn-scared teenager. "Talk all you want. It won't do any good," Cornie said. "Because I'm coming. She's my mother. Not yours."

"You're right about that last part. Which is why I think you deserve an explanation." He nodded to the door. "Which is what I'll give you. Outside."

Cornie looked at April, her expression angry and confused.

"Go with him, Cornie," April said. "And remember, everything we're doing, we're doing for Phylly."

She stood there indecisively, then turned her back on them and went out the door. Joe followed.

A half hour later, a limo pulled up outside Julius Zern's entrance. Ten minutes after that she and Joe were in it. It was a woman driver, and she smiled at them as Joe closed the privacy panel between the front and back seats.

As the limo pulled away, Joe gave a cursory wave. April swiveled to look at the group on the doorstep: Julius, Kit, and Cornie, standing soldier-straight, her arms crossed over her chest. When April waved, she waved back, and nodded her head.

April turned to Joe. "What on earth did you say? She's positively . . . docile."

Joe cocked a brow. "I wouldn't go that far."

"No, really. Tell me."

"I told her the truth."

"Your version of which is?" she prodded.

"That we didn't know what to expect when we got there, and that I was going to have my hands full protecting her mother—and you. I told her having to look out for her increased the risks for everyone—that it might even endanger her mother."

"And she bought that?"

"Got it in one."

April's cell phone rang, and she looked at the call display, barely hiding a sigh of relief. "It's Rusty's number at Hot and High," she said to Joe before hitting the talk button. "It must be Tommy." It was Leanne. God, the poor woman must be a wreck, losing her cousin, police all over the place, and trying to keep the business running. It was a wonder she could think straight. Something that April also lost the ability to do after the first sentence out of Leanne's mouth.

It was as if someone suctioned out every energy unit in April's body. Slumping into her seat, she put her hand on her forehead, let her head fall back. "No! When?" She straightened up, listened so hard her ears hurt, unable to do anything other than mumble the occasional incoherent reply to indicate she was there. Finally she hung up.

Her eyes felt sharp and dry when she looked at Joe, and she couldn't make herself speak. She was numb. Totally numb.

Joe's eyes, full of questions, were glued to her.

"Tommy's dead. They found his body in the desert a few miles out of town."

His face went cold, not shocked, just flat and still, like a computer taking in information before processing.

"Castor's dead, too," April added, splaying her hand over a heart that wouldn't settle.

"Castor?"

"Some kids were dirt biking—late yesterday afternoon—they found the bodies. The police left Leanne maybe an hour ago. They didn't tell her much, so she called in a favor—a friend in the LVPD. From what she said, it looked like Castor shot Tommy—he was still carrying the gun—then some 'unknown person or persons' killed Castor and shot Tommy again. They said the guns were different calibers."

"Just what we need—more players in the game."

"They said Tommy was"—she swallowed, but her mouth was so dry the effort was worthless—"shot several times, knee, shoulder . . . stomach and head. Like he was tortured. My God, who would do such a thing? Rusty, Tommy . . . I can't believe it. And I don't want to think about what this will do to Phylly." She tried not to, but she started to cry. Joe put his hand on her shoulder, squeezed.

"Don't," he said softly. "Please." Then he pulled her to his chest, kissed her hair then stroked it. The limo had tissue in a receptacle behind the driver's seat; he pulled a couple out and handed them to her.

April rested a moment, daubed at her eyes, and took a deep breath. Tears and fear made a chilling combination and a paralyzing one. They did nothing to help the situation, and she knew she couldn't afford the indulgence. She blotted some more, lifted her head from Joe's shoulder, and said, "Sorry."

"Crying for a friend is nothing to apologize for." He again stroked her hair, adding quietly, "I think we should call the men in blue, tell them—"

"No!" She shook her head. "No police. I promised Phylly." Phylly had made her swear, said there were things about that night April didn't know, things Phylly had done that would get her in a lot of trouble.

"I think this has gone beyond any promises you made to Phyllis Worth."

She wanted to say how tired she was of hearing him always use her full name, objectifying her, but knew she'd be wasting her breath. That it would only take them down Joe's own bitter road, a road pitted with resentment and misunderstandings. A road she hoped would . . . straighten out once he and his mother met, had a chance to talk things through. So she just nodded again, and said, "We'll be with her in less than three hours. We'll call the police—after we talk to her, tell her about Tommy."

The look he gave her was heavy with disagreement. "Your call," he said. "For now."

"Thank you." To change the subject, she added, "The thing I can't figure out is who would kill Castor—and why?"

"Money would be my bet. Big money. Maybe someone wanted to take over his show—eliminate the middleman."

"Maybe we don't need to know who," she said. "Maybe it's all over. If Castor was the one looking for Phylly and someone killed him"—she lifted a limp hand, couldn't believe she was talking about a murdered man as if he were a character in a play—"maybe that's the end of it." Her rationale held more wish than logic and she knew it.

"You don't believe that, and neither do I." He glanced out the window at a sign telling them they were nearing the airport. "Castor was a thug and a loser, good at carrying out orders, but useless on his own. His record proves that. He had to be working for someone else. And that someone else decided he was expendable. Someone with balls, motive—and a lot at risk."

"You think it was the man who kidnapped me?"

The driver of the limo switched lanes to make the turn into Sea-Tac. "I'm saying it's a possibility, because if Castor found Phyllis—then you, he'd be a threat. So, yeah, I think our John-Doe kidnapper is the man behind all of this. And I think he'll do anything to protect his sorry ass."

The black-eyed man . . .

After all these years, he'd come for her again—had killed, and would kill again to find her. Because she knew his face. Would never forget his face.

Anger churned and thickened in her belly. She looked out the window but couldn't see through the darkness clouding her vision. *No! I won't let it happen. I won't let him hurt Phylly or me—ever again!*

He'd terrorized her young life, taken her from her brother—the only person who'd ever cared about her. With a cold frightening clarity she hated him. She closed her mind against the hate, the ugliness of it, forced herself to set it aside. She would hold it in reserve—like a shield. But right now, there was nothing to do but get to Phylly, make sure she was safe, and put the pieces of the puzzle together. For that they needed Phylly.

Thank God, they knew where she was.

Phylly came awake just after five. Outside was black as hell. Noah's house might be made of glass, but with its back to an eastern forest and its decks facing full west, the morning sun arrived late, and the evening sun stayed until the last drop of shine was wrung from it.

The totality of the darkness outside the window made Phylly squeamish. She didn't want to go out in it, didn't want to leave the warmth of Noah's bed—leave behind, for always, the heat of what they'd shared last night.

She didn't want to leave Noah . . . ever.

Closing her eyes, she took a deep breath and dug around in her sparse supply of character traits for what she needed: Courage.

That she shouldn't have come here was obvious. All she'd done was bring lies and danger into Noah's beautiful life.

It wasn't fair. She wasn't fair.

For a moment she listened to his breathing, quivered when its warmth wafted over her bare shoulder, then she lifted his arm—the one draped over her waist—and slipped from underneath it to the edge of the bed. She looked back at him, at the face she'd never been able to forget—and the face she'd never see again.

His eyelids fluttered. "Where you going?" he mumbled.

"Bathroom."

He nodded in his sleep. "Hurry back."

Phylly padded toward the chair where she'd left her clothes last night. Gathering them up, she disappeared into the bathroom and got dressed without turning on the light.

She'd packed her bag before going to Noah's room last night. It sat waiting for her inside the door of the guest room she'd slept in the night before.

She picked it up and moved silently and steadily to the front door. Feeling like a second-rate sneak thief, she slipped outside. Black, cold, and misty, the night reminded her again of how far from Vegas she was.

She was immediately chilled to her desert bones.

The car was where she'd left it two days before, and she quickly opened the driver's side door, tossed her bag onto the passenger seat, and got in, closing the door as quietly as she could.

Taking one last look at Noah's crystal box, she turned the key and started out of the driveway. There was no way of being a silent runner on the gravel road, so she sped up, anxious to make the first turn, put the house out of sight. She was almost there—

She slammed on the brakes.

Her breath jumped in her throat, her left hand flew to her chest to stop her thumping heart from leaping out.

There, in her headlights, stood a bear the size of a not-so-small elephant. After Phylly got over her initial shock, she realized she wasn't in any danger—as long as she stayed in the car—but there was also no way around him! She nudged the car forward, hoping he'd take off; instead he increased his bright-eyed scrutiny of her and didn't budge an inch. And while they locked eyeballs and played chicken, someone rapped on the passenger-side window with enough noise and force to crack it.

It was Noah. *Damn, damn, damn!*

When the bear turned its attention to him, Phylly quickly hit the unlock button.

"What the hell are you doing?" he asked, tossing her bag into the backseat and sliding in beside her, wearing nothing but a pair of boxer shorts.

"I thought I'd drive into town, pick us up some bagels and Starbucks." She said it lamely, as half lie, half joke, because she had to say something and the truth, as usual, was complicated.

"Even if there were a Starbucks within a hundred miles of here, it wouldn't be open and you damn well know it." He looked out the window at the stupid bear and rubbed his arms. "Jesus, it's freezing out here. Put this thing in reverse. You can tell me the rest of your lies over breakfast." He leveled his gaze on her. "But get something straight. I'm not letting you go until you've told me the truth, the whole truth . . . so help you God. Do we understand one another?"

He stared at her; she stared back. Phylly cursed, rude and crude, but all she got in response was an arched brow. "Reverse," he said again.

She touched the steering wheel with her forehead, then lifting her head, seeing the unmovable bear, she slammed at the horn. In the quiet of the dark forest its sudden, get-the-hell-out-of-here honking hit the air with the earsplitting blast of a missile warning. Phylly didn't know a bear could move that fast. *Bastard!*

Jolting the car into reverse, she was back where she'd started from in seconds. She turned on Noah. "I do not *have to* tell you the truth about anything. So you can stop ordering me around."

Without a word, he took the keys from the ignition, reached for her, and pulled her into his arms for a rough, demanding kiss. When he was done, he held her face in his hands, and said, "I can't lose you again, Phylly. No, make that *I won't* lose you again. Whatever the hell made you run from my bed, we'll handle it. Together." He let her go. "I love you, Phyllis. Have since the day I set eyes on you with fifteen pounds of feather and glitz on your head. You were the most beautiful woman I'd ever seen—still are. Maybe the time wasn't right for us back then, maybe you needed to do"—he lifted a shoulder—"whatever you felt you had to. But that was then. This is now. It might be cliché to talk about second chances, but damn it, Phylly, that's what we have. A second chance. I don't know about you, but I don't intend to waste it."

"Oh, God . . . Noah." She closed her eyes against the intensity in his. Her heart faltered, her brain faltered, and her will had a serious breach. "I can't . . . You don't know—"

He touched her mouth, shook his head. "Don't say anything. Because until we clear the air between us, it won't mean a damn thing." He touched her cheek briefly. "Now, unless you're intent on me freezing my balls off out here, can we go into the house?" His expression firmed. "And dig out that damn journal you've been packing around. It's past time you knew what was in it."

Chapter 26

When Quinlan woke, it was to the muffled sound of Mercy talking on her cell phone. She was sitting on the edge of the bed naked, her straight, well-muscled shoulders lit by a slash of light coming in the hotel room window. It was barely 6 A.M.

She looked over her shoulder at him. "Hold, will you?" She lowered the phone from her mouth. "It's Charity. She's located the Worth woman. No sign of the son or daughter though."

"Has she arranged accommodations for us?"

"Yes, a place called Crystal Cove Beach Resort."

"How far from our target?"

"Maybe fifteen miles. Worth is with some man who has an oceanfront house out of town. Very secluded, she says. Nothing around for miles. She says she could take her out herself, save you the trip." She watched him closely.

"No. Absolutely not." His voice was sharper than he intended. "She's to keep her distance."

"Can you tell me why? Charity's suggestion certainly makes things simpler."

"Why is no concern of yours." He got out of bed and stood over her. "It's enough for you to know I want the woman alive." *Until the assembly is complete. Until everyone associated with April girl and his past was dead.* Including Mercy and her sister. They would all die by his hand—and it would be done to perfection. He would leave nothing to chance. "Make sure your sister understands that. She *must* wait for our arrival."

"I expected that's what you'd say." Mercy went back to the phone, looking smug.

Q frowned. *Odd woman.* And much less sexually appetizing than he had felt last night. While he might attribute his feelings to sexual satiation, it was more likely she was simply like every other woman he'd had before Giselle: Disposable.

"He says to leave the woman alone," she said to her sister. "Look, but don't touch. We'll be there this afternoon. A charter." She faced him, the phone tight to her ear, her calm gaze fixed on him, her expression pleased. "Yes, we did," she said into the phone. "Does that surprise you? . . . He was very good. Like a fine dessert after a bad meal." She turned away, half-smiling at whatever Charity had said. "Aren't they just?"

She shifted from amused to businesslike. "I'll call from the plane, but we don't want to be met. Just leave a car and keys at the airport. You can tell me what to look for when I call. The less we're seen together the better." She hung up.

When she stood, Quinlan grabbed her wrist. Naked, they stood toe-to-toe. "What were you talking about?"

"I was organizing our arrival."

"Before that." Last night, her direct approach, her unfettered female aggression had aroused him, this morning, her set jaw and hard-eyed gall angered him—as did her arrogance. Surely the woman wasn't foolish enough to believe that what had transpired between them last night had in any way altered their relationship.

"You," she said. "We were talking about you."

"Go on."

She lifted her chin, her odd turquoise eyes meeting his

squarely. They seemed sharper in the morning light, her face tougher. "She wanted to know if we fucked."

"And you informed her we had."

"Why not?" She arched a brow, not in the least cowed by his cold glare, which by the freezing in his veins and distaste roiling in his stomach, he knew to be frigid and intimidating. Q might have had intercourse with this woman, but he didn't like her. Her high-handed attitude was too big a price to pay for a bout or two of oral sex—no matter how temporarily satisfying. *Stupid woman!* Quinlan had learned long ago that the fleeting pleasures of the flesh paled against the steady and reliable rewards of power and control.

He tightened his grip on her arm. "I don't share details of my sexual activities outside the bedroom."

"Neither do I." Using a sudden twist and jerk move, surely that of a trained professional, she easily freed her arm from his grip. "Other than with my sister. We share everything." She eyed him, looking highly amused. "Particularly men—if they're worth it." She grabbed his testicles, squeezed to a point that an ounce of added pressure would bring pain. "And I think you're worth it." She eased the pressure on his testes and began to stroke.

When his body betrayed him with the stirrings of an erection, he grasped her hand, interlaced his fingers with hers and bent her wrist back—a hold not so easy to break. He, too, stopped flexing at the point of pain, but hovered there. "I believe last night has led to a misunderstanding between us—as to whom exactly is in charge." She stood very still, her face showing neither pain nor fear. "Have no doubt, Mercy. I am." He bent her wrist near to breaking, an action that brought a faint whitening to her lips. "If you want to continue assisting me in the Worth affair, you'd best remember that." He gave her wrist a final bend, saw her grimace of pain, and released her. "Do we understand one another?"

She rubbed her wrist, and he watched while she composed herself by taking a series of deep breaths. She reminded him of a threatened animal, a dangerous animal. The look she gave him was pure loathing. "I understand that men in general are assholes—and you're the leader of the pack."

"Then perhaps you no longer wish to work with such a despicable example of his sex? If so, I'll happily release you from further obligation." *And your ability to breathe.*

She stopped rubbing her wrist, turned her back on him, and walked toward the bathroom. Once there, she faced him. "We're in this together, Braid, so don't get any fancy ideas about going ahead on your own." She smiled, her lips warping under the effort. "You arrive on that plane without me—and Phyllis Worth is a dead woman."

Cold snaked over Q's neck and shoulders. "What are you talking about?"

She ignored him, dipped into the bathroom briefly, and came out tying a robe around her slim waist.

"It means Charity and I have a retirement plan, and it means the four million you promised that idiot Castor has just been doubled—or Charity kills Phyllis Worth."

Q stared at her, every survival instinct he possessed quivering to alert. Now that he had April's name, it didn't matter if the Worth woman was killed, but Q wanted things done his way, with exactitude. He did not want April finding Worth dead and going on the run. He wanted them in one place—and all of them dead within the next twenty-four hours. He processed possibilities, quickly decided that if the insane woman in front of him thought Phyllis Worth was her leverage—and that would keep her alive until the others arrived—he'd leave her to think just that.

He molded his face to impassive, walked past her, and retrieved a robe. "Do I even want to know how you came into possession of that four million dollar figure?"

"You're not the only man with an itch." She met his eyes, smirked. "I told you in my report that Castor hired a hooker—I just neglected to mention it was me." Her expression turned to disgust. "The hardest five hundred bucks I ever earned. That man gave new meaning to the word pig." She walked to the granite bar. A sink was inset there, and she ran herself a glass of water and took a long drink. Folding her arms across her chest, she leaned against the counter. "You really should be more discerning in your choice of colleagues, Q. The man was damn near salivating over the 'four mil' he was about to get from, as he said, a guy so rich—and with so much to lose—he was the ripest pick he'd had in years. Of course, Charity and I already knew that much."

Q lifted a brow. "Aren't you clever."

"Yes, we are. We've had you pegged as our sugar daddy ever since Victor gave us to you for that job last year. We had to work on Victor to get the details—but the old fool did love two in a bed. You must remember that?" She took another sip of water. "He put your net worth at a billion plus. He was always exact about numbers, as you know, so I assume he was correct?"

Quinlan said nothing. He had no intention of validating her data, either sexual or financial.

"Sad about Victor, really," Mercy went on. "We had some good things going. A couple of well-paying married senators, some local politicians. Charity and I set them up, Victor did the rest."

"Where was Castor while this was going on?"

"Sidelined. We never met the jerk. Victor was phasing him out, taking the business in a new direction, developing a more sophisticated clientele. A 'cleaner business,' he said. The kind of business where Castor's kneecapping and bone-breaking skills were no longer required. Victor liked the industrial espionage thing—like what Charity and I did for you to get that SEC data you were so hot after a year or so ago."

"Victor recommended you highly," Q said, his tone deliberately flat, his words unhurried.

"I'll bet." She shook her head. "Not much to it though. Give a high profile married CEO some head, snap a few pictures—suggest a little chat with the wife and kids . . . You know how it goes." She shrugged. "Not exactly brain surgery."

"And not enough financial return for your efforts, I assume." Victor wasn't known to be generous. "So you decided to do some freelancing."

"Very good, Braid. And very right. Charity and I had been planning on doing our own thing for a while, even before Castor did his number on Victor. Because if there was one thing Victor had, it was connections." She eyed him. "It was those connections that had us, uh, offering our services to Victor in the first place. You in particular." She smiled. It was ugly.

Q let her go on.

"Those journals of his? Hell, if you knew how to work them, they were a freakin' gold mine. We wanted them."

"And Castor got them all."

"Yes. For a few days there, we figured we were shut out," she said. "Then we heard he was heading for you— the biggest whale in Victor's ocean."

"You learned that how?"

"Charity. Damn that girl is good! She picked up Castor in a bar." She lifted a careless shoulder. "Wannabe players like Henry are the easiest of all, small pricks and big egos with mouths to match. Hell, even then he was going on about *his* Q."

"Hence your little sales call on me."

"A calculated risk that you'd need discreet assistance when Castor showed his ugly mug." She looked at her nails, the gesture irritatingly casual. "Charity and I? We plan ahead."

"And had it failed? Had I not called on you?"

She smiled. "Rather a moot point, Q—because you did call us, didn't you?"

Q was tired of circling her cache of knowledge, and enraged by her supercilious attitude, but he needed to evaluate his risk, and to do that he needed to know everything she knew. "What did Henry Castor tell you about Phyllis Worth?" Waiting for her answer, he tensed.

"Enough for us to know, she isn't your main target—which by the way, you confirmed by not authorizing an easy kill." She paused. "She's a lead. A very important lead. And you want her alive."

Q's stomach tightened, but he didn't respond; he waited.

Mercy pushed away from the granite counter, came to stand in his face. "Castor said all he had to do for his four mil was find one 'growed up' little girl. It doesn't take more than putting two and two together to know Phyllis Worth knows where that 'girl' is. What we don't know is why she's so important."

He stilled the choler and oily panic roiling in his stomach, even though it oozed like a running sore, and maintained his silence.

When he didn't answer, she laughed. "Not that it matters, because I'm sure Phyllis Worth, with the appropriate coercion, will give us the information we need. And if there's one thing we learned from Victor it was the power of information."

"Which means your plan is to attach yourself to me—until you have what you need." *Then suck at my financial resources for as long as it suits you.* It was exactly what Q had expected.

"Got it in one, babe." She looked at the silver watch on her wrist. "We should get going." Again her lips formed a maddening smirk. "Our private plane awaits." She ran her finger down his bare chest exposed between the gaping lapels of the robe. "You live well, Q. Charity and I are very much looking forward to doing the same. And from what I hear that mansion of yours has plenty of room." She eyed him head to toe. "And the sex wouldn't be bad either."

Dear God, was she serious? The woman sickened him. "I could kill you here, now. Save myself a lot of trouble—and money."

"You do that, and my sister wreaks her own brand of havoc on Phyllis Worth—and after she's done with her, Mister Quinlan Braid, she'll do you." She snickered. "It's a sister thing, you know."

He watched her disappear into the bathroom and forced his mind to cool, to level out. He stood still, breathing slowly, deeply, but his lungs seemed encased in iron bands. His mind was slow to accept a loss of power, temporarily unable to identify solutions. He continued to breathe.

He heard the sound of the shower—the sound of singing!

Rage surged, billowing through his chest like thick scudding clouds and causing his body to quiver and chill. The all-powerful Quinlan Braid clenched his fists at his sides, worked to tamp his wrath into a dark hard place.

Morning light cut sharply through the open drapes, and the room grew brighter. Q turned his face to the sun's unstoppable power, took another, deeper breath, and let it go.

I have grown soft. Grown old. Grown sloppy. All truths that burned him as a torch would burn.

In his prime he would never have found himself in a situation he didn't control. He'd been careless and what had it brought him? *Parasites:* Mercy and her sister. But no matter. He was here to challenge himself, to feel, to recapture the essence of what he once was. A killer. A taker of lives.

They thought him trapped, impotent, a hostage to his own criminal past. They were wrong. He'd kill them all: The

Worth women, the son, the sisters, and everyone else who threatened him. And he'd kill them perfectly. And enjoy every second of the bloodletting.

But to ensure that outcome, he'd need some assistance. He picked up the phone.

There were only four people on the Cessna unloading at Tofino's airport. Joe and April were two of them.

April came down the plane's metal steps carrying a blue carpetbag with everything she needed for what she assumed—and prayed—would be a short stay. Joe slung a soft brown leather duffel over his shoulder and followed her down. On the tarmac, he reached for her bag. "Here. Let me take that."

"No, it's fine. I never pack more than I can carry." In a like move to his, she hoisted her bag to her shoulder and headed toward a graveled area behind a barbed-wire fence. She guessed the fence was either the airport's stab at security or its way of keeping the wildlife off the runways. If there was any kind of terminal, she didn't see it, only a couple of smallish trailer-type buildings representing local airlines.

They'd had delays in both Seattle and Vancouver, so they'd arrived later than planned. The afternoon was heavily overcast, and leaves, early casualties of the coming fall, lay scattered across the gravel parking lot. The air held the clean salty scent of the ocean, but it was damp and still, and mist had gathered like a crowd of ghosts at the far end of the runway. "Aren't the dog days of August supposed to be hot and humid?" April looked at the gloomy sky, shivered in her light jacket.

"Not here, obviously," Joe said, also looking up. "I'll get the car." A Budget Rent-a-Car office, consisting of a blue and white portable building, maybe twelve feet long, was settled on the gravel receiving area on their right. There were cars parked beside it. "Wait here."

"It doesn't look as if there's anywhere I could go, without being lost for months." The airport was ringed by trees with mountains forming a distant backdrop. From the ground the trees looked like a tidy green fence, but April knew from looking out the window during their descent, the trees—and the ocean beyond them—went on forever. Ten feet into that dense forest, she'd be search-and-rescue fodder. What in God's name Phylly was doing here was more of a mystery than ever. Feeling displaced, as if she'd touched down on another planet, it occurred to April, an avowed city girl, that other than a foray or two into the desert surrounding Las Vegas, this was as close to nature in the raw as she'd ever been. She wasn't sure how she felt about it.

"You going to be okay?" Joe asked.

"All I need is Toto. I feel like Dorothy. You know . . . 'not in Kansas anymore.' The sooner these sneaker-clad feet see high heels and pavement again, the happier I'll be." The other couple from the plane, apparently met by friends, were already loaded into a giant Escalade and on their way.

While Joe was getting the car, April—feeling tense and oddly nervous—scanned the weedy, leaf-strewn parking area. Her attention was caught by two vehicles coming into the lot from the pitted road leading to the airport: One an older pickup, the other a dark blue Ford Explorer. A woman got out of the Explorer, reached in again to retrieve her bag, then fiddled with the visor. It looked as though she was trying to lodge something behind it. When she was done, she moved back from the car, and looked around the empty parking area. When her gaze connected with April's, it lingered a moment before skipping away.

The woman was stunning, dark-haired, with pale, clear skin and a movie-star face. The kind of face so exceptional it brought second looks from men and women. Not too shabbily dressed, either. Although leathers weren't April's thing, the ones worn by this woman caught her eye. Maybe because they were of a cut, style, and quality more likely to be seen on Rodeo Drive or The Strip than in this remote northern rain forest.

"Set to go," Joe came up beside her, waved a set of keys. He followed her gaze, and asked, "What's so interesting?"

"Her," April said, making the slightest possible gesture with her chin. "She's beautiful, but . . . kind of out of place, don't you think?"

Joe glanced in the direction she'd indicated. They both watched the woman get into the pickup truck. It had a sign on its side: Dario's Motel and Resort.

"Probably a tourist," Joe said. "The resorts around here bulge with them at this time of year. Plus there's some pretty exclusive private getaways on the oceanfront." He looked away. "Ready?"

She nodded, settled her bag more comfortably on her shoulder, and followed Joe to a gray Taurus sedan. They tossed their bags in the backseat.

Over the top of the car, before they got in, Joe said, "The guy at Budget was closing up, by the way, said there are no more scheduled flights until tomorrow. Some mechanical problems. Good for us, maybe not so good for whoever's on our tail."

"Unless they don't use a scheduled flight." She looked up, swore she heard a plane in the distance somewhere.

"Yeah, there's always that." Joe followed her gaze, looked to the sky then back to her. "Let's go."

Chapter 27

Joe drove, while April studied the map and pointed him in the right direction. Within forty minutes they were staring at a painted sign that said: Bristol. A narrow road lay in front of them, rimmed on both sides with giant cedar and hemlock, a low lying mist snaking around their bases. Through the trees on their left patches of roiling ocean were visible.

Before Joe could make the turn into the driveway, his cell phone rang. It was Julius. He pulled off to the side of the road and listened. "Good," he finally said, adding, "How's Cornie doing?" He nodded. "Also good. Thanks." He clicked off.

April was waiting, her eyes questioning.

"Julius said there are a couple of charters due into the Tofino airport today. He doesn't have exact times, but said they'll probably be early because there's fog rolling in."

"Fog, this time of year?" It was August for pity's sake. Late August, but still . . .

"It happens. This close to the northern Pacific the weather doesn't always play nice."

"About the planes. How does Julius know—"

"Don't ask. Just believe. Julius knows everything and everyone." He loosened his grip on the steering wheel. "He says they were chartered under the names Holbert and Belltaro. Either of them mean anything to you?"

She shook her head. "Nope."

"I didn't think they would. It's unlikely whoever's after you would use their own name." He put the car in drive, but kept his foot on the brake, looking at her to add, "He also said Cornie's fine. Says she wants you to call her, but other than that all's quiet on the teen front. Kit's taking her to the Space Needle and the music museum. Keeping her busy."

April let out a sigh. "Bless him."

"This is it," he said to April, turning onto the narrow road. "You ready?"

"If you call almost jumping out of my skin ready, I'm as ready as I'm going to be." She shot him a quick, tight smile.

Joe was in the same boat, although not about to admit it. He was trained to be alert, prepared—hell, he made his living protecting people, being ready for anything, but this business with Phyllis Worth, and having April at risk, added a dimension that set his teeth on edge. This operation was like going blind into one of those video bat caves Cornie liked so much. And the package Julius had ready for pickup at the rent-a-car office—a shiny new revolver, courtesy of Smith & Wesson—while appreciated, didn't make him feel a whole lot better. The idea of bullets and April being within whispering distance of each other made his gut ache.

Meeting his birth mother wasn't high on his want-to-do list either—and here he was maybe fifteen minutes away from a woman he'd freeze-dried into his past and left there. And now some freak from her dubious past wanted her dead. Life is all about smart choices/dumb choices; that's what his adoptive mother, Fiorella Stanzi, had drummed into him. She might as well have opened his brain and branded it there she said it so often. And she'd been right—not kind, not loving—just right, and reasonably decent to him until the day she died, a year after her husband. She was in her fifties somewhere; he was eleven. Dumped back into the system at that age, it was foster hopscotch until he was seventeen and joined the army. But he owed Fiorella for that snatch of wisdom about making choices, because it made sense. Too bad his birth mother hadn't had the same lesson.

He knew April harbored the hope that his meeting Phyllis Worth would change things, that there'd be a joyous reunion of some kind, an instant mother-son bonding. Tears and the whole bit. But there wouldn't be. Not going to happen.

That ice cream sandwich melting in his hands was the only memory he had of the woman who brought him into this world. It was enough.

He hit a pothole, and the Taurus bucked and shuddered. April put a hand on the dash as if to steady the car. He slowed down, muttered, "Sorry."

He rounded a turn and there it was. Joe let out a noisy breath. "Jesus!"

April looked at Noah's glass house, silvered in the cold gray light. "It's beautiful," she said.

"It's that all right. It's also a perfect shooting gallery." If Joe had been asked to design a more exposed or defenseless structure, he couldn't do it. Visualizing Phyllis and April behind that glass with darkness outside it, was like seeing them set up in a department store window. "And this is where your mother came to be safe."

"It does look kind of open."

"A very bare-assed and vulnerable open." One thing was certain, they couldn't stay here. He hadn't seen a gate at the head of the driveway—and it didn't look as though there were any neighbors around for miles. Whoever this Bristol guy was, he must be some kind of hermit. "I don't like it."

"I think it's fabulous. Like a beautiful stage set."

Before he could respond, tell her he was talking about the situation not the house, a man and a very tall woman stepped onto the wraparound deck. A big dog, the color of hay, and of no discernible breeding, stood beside the man. The woman waved.

"That's Phylly," April said.

He shot her a glance. "I kind of guessed that."

"Yes . . . of course you would." She looked faintly embarrassed. "I'm just—nervous. For Phylly and for you."

"Afraid I'll throw another tantrum like I did in that ER she left me in? Word is it went into the record books."

"No. I know you won't do that. It's just that by bringing you here, I've broken her trust. She's under a lot of stress, and you being here . . . now. On top of everything else. It's not going to be easy. And even though you're acting the part of the big strong man who doesn't give a damn, you do, which means it won't be any easier for you." She shot him a direct look.

Acting the big strong man . . . psycho-babble. He'd let it lie. He wasn't about to let his feelings, or lack of same, for Phyllis mess up what was going on between him and April. So he'd keep his mouth shut. That he knew how to do. "Maybe it'd be a good idea to remember we're not here *looking* for my long-lost mother. We're here to *look out* for her. Make sure she—and you—stay safe." He leaned over, gave her a quick kiss—wished it were more, like he always did when he was within a hundred yards of her—and opened his door. Before getting out the driver's side door, he added, "You good with that?"

She didn't move. "Like it or not, you are going to meet her, Joe, and it's going to be . . . *emotional*. For everyone." She met his eyes, put her hand on the car's door handle. "So the question should be, are *you* good with that?" She got out of the car.

He sat a second and shook his head. In the last-words competition, she was the clear winner. He followed her out of the car, opened the back door, and retrieved both their bags.

Phyllis stayed on the deck, the man came down the stairs to meet them. "Noah Bristol," he said, taking a good hard look at both of them, before offering April his hand. "Glad you're here April. Phylly's been anxious."

She nodded. "Thanks for having us."

He offered his hand to Joe. "And you are?"

"Joe," he said, glancing at the woman on the deck. *Fuck it!* It was now or later. "Joe Worth." He dropped Noah's hand and gestured with his chin to Phyllis Worth. "And to say I'm not expected wins this year's prize for understatement."

"Joe is Phylly's son," April said, filling in the blanks.

Silence. Then Bristol said, "She didn't tell me she had a son." He didn't look pleased, he looked pissed. *Join the club.*

"Probably slipped her mind." Joe knew Phyllis couldn't hear him, but he sensed her eyes fixed on him like a pair of lasers. He shook Noah's hand, because he was still holding it, and let it go.

Bristol didn't waste time getting into things. "Phylly's told me most of what's going on about this Victor/Castor business, April. Is there a chance you've been followed?"

"Yes. A good chance. I'm sorry we arrive with so much baggage—of the trouble kind."

"You're in Phylly's orbit, you've got trouble. In Vegas they'd call that a sure thing." He smiled slightly, but he still looked pissed, and for some reason Joe felt as though he were the cause of it. "Come in. I hope you're hungry, because we've made lunch."

They followed him toward the house, as if they were normal guests in a normal situation. April walked ahead with Bristol, and Joe followed them, but he took his time, studying every detail of Bristol's steel and glass home. The house, sitting in a clearing, was flanked on three sides by dense forest and underbrush, allowing maybe ten-million possibilities for cover for anyone wanting to blow out a few windows—and the people inside. Stopping at the bottom of the stairs, he shoved his hands in his pockets and shook his head, convinced the only safe place to be was as far down the road as they could get. The house was a damn snow globe.

And April was putting herself inside it—along with his mother. The thought tightened the knot in his gut. A knot that had started turning in on itself the closer he got to Bristol's place.

April didn't know it but, when it came to Phyllis Worth, that "big strong man" thing wasn't working well.

He looked at the first step leading to the deck where she was waiting—a step he had serious trouble taking.

So far thinking about logistics had kept his mind off the tall woman at the top of the stairs, but with a suddenness that staggered him she took over his brain—and all he wanted to do was run away. Like a boy who'd broken a window, a boy who'd torn his best pants, like a . . . goddamn boy!

When he made it to the deck, it was on legs and feet as weighted as sandbags. Once there, three people stared at him as if he were an alien who'd just oozed out of the trees at the back of the house. So many glances were exchanged, between the three of them, so quickly, they were indecipherable. It was like a tennis match with a dozen balls in play.

April looked as if she were going to bite her lower lip off.

Bristol looked as if he wanted to bite someone's head off.

And Phyllis Worth just looked, and looked, and . . .

Then she fainted.

Quinlan and Mercy checked into the Crystal Cove Beach Resort within a half hour of their arrival in Tofino. Q's cursory look around the accommodations Charity had arranged left him satisfied. It was a freestanding log cabin, tastefully appointed and the last in a row of them, given privacy by a natural fence of low shrubbery and trees. Perfect.

He glanced at Mercy, who had tossed her bag on the sofa then sat beside it, immediately taking out her cell phone and calling her sister who, Q was advised, was at a motel closer to town and their ultimate quarry. He left Mercy to her call. He saw no need of further conversation with ı woman who from his view was nothing more than a walking corpse. And he certainly had no interest in Charity, who, when this was over, would also be counted among the dead.

That the death toll was rising he accepted, had already calculated the added risk that came with each one. Risks he'd already set about mitigating.

Mercy looked up at him, but didn't remove the phone from her ear. "I'm going to see Charity, get the Worth woman's exact location."

He noticed she'd neither sought his advice nor his permission, but he let it pass. For the moment he needed her, or to be more precise, he needed the location of the two women and the future site of his killing field. He thought of the godlike work ahead, his power over the blood and finality of death. It had been too long since he'd felt such power, such passion. Except with Giselle . . . Faintly troubled by how often she invaded his thoughts, he frowned.

"What are you going to do?" she asked.

He settled his eyes on her. "Wait for you to return, of course." Turning his back on her, he chose the largest of the two bedrooms and went in, closing the door behind him. He carried three items: A structured canvas duffel, an aluminum case, and his rifle in a leather sleeve.

Placing the duffel on the bed, he unzipped it and surveyed its perfectly arranged contents, exactly what he'd instructed Jerald to pack. Jerald always did as he was asked—to the letter. It was reassuring having such competence and loyalty in one's employ.

While unpacking his clothes, Q considered the steps to be taken before the killings could commence, finding the site, a reconnoiter—

The outer door closed; Mercy leaving to visit her sister, to confirm the details. Good.

He wanted no surprises. He hoped the site wouldn't be

some bunker-style dwelling made of logs as was common in such heavily wooded areas.

He hung two crease-free shirts in the closet along with a pair of dark brown cotton twill pants. A light vest with both inside and outside pockets followed. Setting his hand-sewn Arrow hunting moccasins immediately below the vest, he aligned them in the closet's center. He'd always preferred the softer, quieter shoe over the noisy crunch of a hard, in-flexible boot. Doing such trivial tasks calmed him.

It also made him think of Giselle, the disturbing fact that he missed her. Missed her even more since having his sexual tryst with the unsavory Mercy.

After surveying the closet and ensuring the items were uniformly spaced, he turned back to the aluminum case on the bed. He removed three boxes of ammunition, and clicked it closed. The hunting rifle, in a fine leather case worn from years of use, was a .338 Winchester Magnum, a hunting rifle legally cleared through Canadian Customs. He loaded the gun and propped it against the wall beside the bed. Q hadn't hunted in quite some time, but he'd kept up his skills at the shooting range, and he was certain his choice of gun, able to drop a bull elk from 400 yards, would be up to the job. Not that he'd rely on it exclusively—backup was always wise.

Having completed his tasks, he put his cell phone on the side table, and glanced at his watch. Stretching out on the bed, he closed his eyes and waited for his call.

He didn't wait long. When the phone rang he picked up immediately. "Jerald?"

"Yes, sir. I'm in place."

"You understand your role?"

"Yes."

Q clicked off, smiled, and closed his eyes.

Chapter 28

"That went well," April said, standing with her arms crossed, watching Joe stride off along the road they'd driven in on.

Noah glanced at the opaque glass door leading to his bedroom, a room constructed of glass bricks—where Phylly now hid like a frightened cat. "How long do you think she'll stay in there?"

April followed Noah's gaze. "Hard to say. The last time she melted down like that, it was three days at least." April looked from the door to Noah. The man looked shell-shocked, so she added, "But this time, I don't plan on giving her that luxury." She rubbed at the lines forming in her brow, which did nothing to ease the frustration rippling through her stomach. What she wanted to do, more than anything, was shake Joe and Phylly until their brains dropped into place. Until they healed. But with a deranged killer on their heels, it was hardly the time.

"And him?" Noah waved a hand in the general direction of Joe, who at that moment rounded a sharp bend in the road and disappeared from sight.

"Even harder to say. I don't know him all that well." *Except in bed*. Which of course made her a complete idiot. She should have seen this coming, should have been ready—or at least got some kind of promise from Joe about how he'd act when he met Phylly. Not that he'd done or said anything terrible, but God, did he have to look like Dr. Death when he came up those stairs? He'd been as rigid and straight as the steel girders supporting Noah's wild see-through house. Phylly had taken one good look at him and collapsed *a là* the most delicate of Victorian maidens. Then, after Joe had helped Noah and her get Phylly onto Noah's bed, he'd taken off without another word.

April should have known Phylly would recognize him instantly from his striking silver eyes—so like her own. The family resemblance was uncanny—as it was between Cornie and Noah Bristol, which made April doubly grateful Cornie hadn't come along to complicate things even further.

Standing here, cold and edgy, looking through a glass wall, with the father Cornie didn't know she had, her mother in meltdown, and the man she'd come to care about more than was wise traipsing around in the woods somewhere, April was coming to believe their unknown stalker was the least of her concerns.

She didn't know the precise moment her coping skills had evaporated, but they were long gone, leaving in their place only impotence and the sense she was tapped out. Dry. "Could I have a glass of water, please?" Better water than more of Noah's questions.

"I'll get it."

He was back within seconds. Handing her the water, he said, "And you, April? Will you be all right?"

No. And I won't be until Phylly and Joe are. Which might well be never. That thought entered stage-left and she hated it, for Phylly's sake, for Joe's—and for her own. She sipped some water. "Yes, I'm okay. Thanks," she finally said. And she was okay—for now. If Phylly and Joe didn't come to some . . . understanding, she'd deal with it. She wouldn't want to, but she would.

"You knew about this? About Joe and Phylly." He jerked

his head toward the road Joe had walked away on. The day, what was left of it, was sinking deep into shadow, the cloud cover making it unusually dark and ominous looking. The curling mist between the trees, while still low, had coalesced into heavy gray billows of fog. Even the shine of Noah's bright pine floors was graying down in the pallid light.

"Some of it. Most of it, Phylly kept to herself."

"Why doesn't that surprise me?" Momentarily, he looked irritated.

"Phylly's idea of dealing with unpleasant or difficult things is to pretend they never happened. Her premise being that if you don't talk about it, it ceases to exist."

"I'm learning that—or at least I'm trying to."

"Her way works as well as any other, I suppose." April said, compelled to defend Phylly. And herself. She hadn't been above playing Phylly's denial game herself—until the name Victor Allan reemerged, like some rabid disease out of a long remission.

"Depends on what your definition of 'works' is, I guess. But all that keeping secrets has a price. Sometimes too high a price. I don't want that for her."

April saw the concern in his face. "You and Phylly," she started, choosing her words, knowing it really was none of her business, "what was between you was . . . special?"

"*Is* special," he corrected. He met her eyes, his own expression determined. "Very special. She just doesn't know it."

She raised a brow, wondered if Phyllis had told him about Cornie, but sensed she hadn't. She also sensed Noah Bristol was a decent man, a stable, settled-down kind of man, who'd probably scared the sap out of the young, free-living, marriage-phobic Phylly. *You passed on a good one, Phylly.*

He went on, "But none of that matters right now. What matters is getting those secrets of hers out in the open,

whether she likes it or not." He glanced at the closed bedroom door where Phylly lay playing out her drama and
firmed his lips as though he'd made a decision. "Come with
me," he said.

Curious, April followed him upstairs and into his office,
really more of a glass box that sat atop the larger glass box
below it. The room faced a rolling Pacific Ocean. Stepping
into the room, April said, "This is beautiful, but why so
much—" she stopped, not her business really. But the idea
of living this transparent a life surrounded by water and
wilderness made her curious.

"Glass?" He finished for her while opening a bottom
drawer in his desk, a desk that sat center stage in the room.
Low shelves crammed with books formed a base on three
sides of the office.

"Yes. It's unusual." She took a couple of steps, turned
back to him. "You built it yourself?"

"I designed it and had it built." He put a burgundy-colored
journal with a cream spine on his desk, and began to leaf
through it, adding without inflection. "As a child I spent a
good portion of my time locked in a closet. This"—he waved
a hand around the airy room—"as a shrink would no doubt
confirm, is the result of that experience."

"A closet. Really?" April was aghast.

"Really." He opened the journal. "We all have things
that shape us—that closet was one of mine." He flipped a
few more pages, swiveled the book, and shoved it toward
her. "Chances are what you're about to read in this journal
will shape yours."

An hour later, April, with hands so shaky they barely
kept the thick journal she held from crashing to the pine
floors, took a breath, and opened Noah's bedroom door.
Although the room was dim in the darkening twilight,
Phylly hadn't turned on the bedside lamp.

She sat in shadow on Noah's bed, propped up by pillows, a box of tissue beside her and a wad of them in her fidgety hands. She'd obviously splashed her face with water, because her usually meticulously made-up face looked pale and tragic.

Clutching the journal to her chest, April walked to the bed and sat down on its edge. "You look like you were run over by a truck," she said to Phylly. "In forward and reverse."

"Thanks for that." Phylly's eyes found the journal. "Oh, God." She pulled herself higher against the headboard. "Noah's told you."

"Yes."

Her expression stark, Phylly said, "I didn't know, April. If I had—"

"You'd have told me. I know that. I'm not here to blame you for anything. This"—she patted the journal she still held to her breasts—"doesn't take away from what you did for me. You saved my life. I won't ever forget that. Ever."

Phylly's eyes went soft with tears. "In some ways, baby, I think you saved mine. Back then I was such a screwup, if I hadn't had you to look out for—make me act at least a little bit better than I might have without you—I don't know what I'd have done. What I would have become." She touched April's face. "I love you, kiddo, and I swear if I'd have known . . ."

"Will you stop beating yourself up. You didn't know, and it was a long time ago. Another time. Another place. So let's not go there." She rubbed the journal idly, her heart feeling thick and full—and scared. "Victor had someone go back for Gus, did Noah read you that part? But he was gone." April didn't know where he had gone, but at least it wasn't to the hell Victor planned for her. She hoped he'd found a safe place, a good heart—as she had with Phylly. Her heart ached with the desire to see him again, had ever since Seattle. She'd felt so close to him there.

"Good for him." Phylly dabbed at her eyes. "You always told me your brother was a smart one."

"He was. Very smart. And handsome—at least to my nine-year-old eyes. He was my best friend." *Only friend.* "He gave me a skipping rope . . ." Thinking—and hurting—at the memory of losing Gus those long years ago, she faltered. Everything was confusing and the pain of it heightened, mixed up as it was with new family, yet to be met. But later when everyone was safe . . .

Phylly's eyes were cast down, as though ashamed. She was twiddling with her tissue.

Resting the journal on her lap, April looked at the only mother she'd ever known. Her crazy, kind, wild, loyal, and loving mother-like-no-other—and her dearest and most cherished friend. "I can't believe I never caught on to you not being able to read." She paused. "Rusty knew, didn't she?"

"Yeah, Rusty knew." Nodding, she closed her eyes against the grief that came with the name, then coughed as if to shake it off. "Plus we illiterates are pretty damn smart," she said, shooting her a quick glance. "Not to mention sneaky. I got by with signs, a few simple words that I memorized, stuff like that, and staying close to home and friends helped. You helped, too." She smiled a bit. "Not that you knew it—you just thought when I asked you to read things to me out loud, it was reading practice."

"Definitely sneaky." She smiled in return, remembering how adamant Phylly was about her going to school. Getting her smarts, she'd called it. She had to be near death and running a thermometer-breaking fever before Phylly would let her miss a day. She'd go on and on about her report card, do a dance when she brought home A's and nag her with ferocity if a grade slipped. "But you cared—you always cared. And you let me know it."

The smile dropped from Phylly's face, and she grasped April's hand, held it tight. "Cared? Yes, but I wasn't smart.

Too busy covering up, playing the dumb blond party girl to go to school, do something about my own ignorance. If I'd done that, I'd have read Victor's journal, and I'd have told you about Gus . . . called your grandfather. You'd have had a real home instead of living with an airhead showgirl and having to earn your college tuition by doing the bare-assed Vegas thing. I mean that was okay for me—I didn't mind it. But you . . . I know how hard it was."

"It paid the bills, Phylly. And I loved that 'airhead showgirl.' She taught me"—she smiled a bit—"how to strut my stuff, not to be shy, or afraid."

"Now that, I'll take some credit for."

They smiled at each other and Phylly sniffled.

April tapped the journal. "And now, thanks to your thieving ways, I know I have a grandfather."

"He's probably ten feet under by now, April. That journal is over twenty years old."

She shook her head. "He's alive. Noah checked. And when this other ugly business is over, I'll go see him." She again rested the book on her lap, took a breath. "Funny, I remember my grandmother. She always smelled like flowers, and I remember her hugs and how she'd kiss my hair, but I have no memory of a grandfather."

"Your mother's dad, from what Noah read me," Phylly said, looking brighter now. "I guess the only reason that entry was in the book was because Victor found out he had money. That had him dithering about where he'd make the most profit, carrying out his original shipping plan or going for some kind of reward for getting you back to your grandfather. What's his name again?"

"Peter Malloy."

"Right." Her lips sealed tight. "I guess the Asian deal won out because the customer had already made a down payment on you, and Victor was afraid of getting his skinny throat cut if he didn't produce you on schedule." Her expression shifted to triumphant. "He had to give back the money, you know—after I took you. He was so pissed!"

"I'm curious, Phylly. If he knew where you were—after taking me—why didn't he come after us? Try to get me back."

Lifting a shoulder, she said, "Too late. It was a year before I, uh, talked to him again. And it wasn't as if I gave him our address, you know. And I went to him to get the money." She rolled her eyes. "God I must have been crazier than I was broke. Anyway, he did find out where I lived eventually, but me having that journal held him off. Funny, huh? Me not even able to read it." She shook her head. "Hell, he even asked me to come back to him. The sick bastard. As if! I made a lot of mistakes in my time, but taking up with Victor Allan was top tier."

"I won't argue with that." April hesitated to broach the subject of Joe, but someone had to. "Something else we need to talk about is Joe. Noah asked about him, and I told him everything I knew—which isn't much, as you know. But it's *you* who has to talk to Joe, Phylly. Only you. You owe him and you know it."

"Oh, shit . . ."

"And when you're done telling him—I want you to tell me. Everything." *Because I need to understand the man who I'm falling in love with*. When that wily, inescapable truth infiltrated her normal good sense, April's mouth went dry. If there was ever an inconvenient time to get dumb-brained over a man, this had to be it. Crazy people after Phyllis—maybe herself, the black-eyed man, a chance to find a grandfather she didn't know she had, it was too much. *I'm crazy. I don't have room for love* . . . but damned if love cared about her emotional space.

When Phylly started to turn away, April tugged on her shoulder, persisted. "After your face-to-face with him on the deck and that movie-star swoon of yours, Joe took off.

He's been gone for a couple of hours, but I just heard the dog bark, which means he's probably back. So get your beautiful self together and go in there."

"I can't."

"You can, and you will."

"He thinks I'm the bitch from hell, and he's right. I'm the mother who left him. He hates me, April. I can see it in his eyes." The tears started again.

"Eyes exactly like yours." April paused. "He has your eyes because he's your son. Your blood, Phylly. You owe him an explanation. Either he accepts it or he doesn't—that'll be his choice—but it's past time he got the chance to make it, knowing all the facts."

"God, I've fucked up so many lives, April"—Phylly squeezed her eyelids shut then opened them, her gaze blank, stark—"and I know I've got stuff to face. To own up to. But of all the things I've done—or not done—leaving Joey like that . . ." She lowered her head, looked away. "I just don't know where to start."

April squeezed her hand. "At the beginning, Phylly. It's the only place *to* start." April rose from the bed and looked down at Phylly. "And after you've talked to Joe, you have to talk to Noah. He's a good man—and he deserves to know that he has a fabulous daughter."

Walking out of the bedroom, she heard Phylly groan.

Noah opened the door for Joe and stepped aside for him to enter. Chance was at his side. The big mutt, obviously well trained, stopped barking immediately on Bristol's command. Now, his tail was sweeping the air in a friendly greeting. Joe ruffled the dog's head. "Where's April?" he asked.

"With Phylly. Talking."

"I'll bet." *Better her than me.* He'd spent the last couple of hours pushing Phyllis Worth and that stricken look she'd laid on him as far out of his mind as he could, concentrating his efforts on his job, which meant deciding either to wait here in some kind of last stand—or get the hell out of here. No contest.

"You want a drink?" Noah asked.

"Sure. A beer if you've got one." Joe's casual tone hid his concern, as he intended it would. The one thing he'd learned in his years of protecting people was that it never paid to panic them. You did that, they stopped listening, started getting stupid—and started getting dead.

Joe followed the older man into the kitchen, his nerves hosting a high-wire act. He didn't need a beer, he needed to get everyone out of here. Now. Before it got even darker. Joe's walk had covered the close perimeters of the property. It was too large to get beyond that in the time he had, but he'd seen enough to confirm the location was vulnerable. Their only choice was to get out of Dodge—as quickly as possible. Before that fog growing out there made things even worse.

He considered going in that bedroom and dragging the two women out, but he'd rather face a fuckin' firing squad. He'd do it when he had to, but not a minute before. And get Bristol on board before he made a move.

Seconds after Noah produced a couple of chilled Coronas, the two men were sitting on a long sofa.

"That must have been tough." Noah took a swig of beer. "Meeting your mother after all this time."

"Went pretty much the way I expected it to," Joe said, seeing no reason not to be upfront about it. Whatever residue of strangeness he'd had upon meeting Phyllis Worth, hours of walking in the woods had erased. Nothing had changed. She was still a stranger to him. There'd been no surprises, no tugs at long-buried heartstrings, no instant mother/son bonding. Nothing. He'd felt nothing. Exactly what he'd felt when he'd accepted she'd dumped him for good. They'd met. It was done.

Somewhere along the way, when the time was right, he'd have his say, get a few questions answered, and that would be it. Case closed.

"Do you know why she left you like she did?" Noah said.

Joe swigged his beer. Time for a change of subject. "No, and right now it's the least of my concerns." He waved his beer to encompass the airy glass room. "No offense, Bristol, but this is the perfect place to do a little human target practice. It'll be like shooting fish in an aquarium." He set his unfinished beer on the table. "So I'd appreciate it if you'd go in there"—he jerked his head toward the bedroom— "and get them out. We should leave before the fog cuts us off."

Noah looked at him, his expression skeptical, the look of a quiet man leading a quiet life, who can't grasp an evil that would interfere with it. "You're sure that's necessary?"

"I'm sure."

Noah studied his face a second or two longer, slowly nodded his head. "Then I'd better—" He broke off, glanced at his dog.

Chance, who, when the two men sat down with their beers, had curled up in front of the dark fireplace and settled into a luxurious sleep suddenly got up and padded toward the southern wall, his gait unhurried, but his head high. Alert.

Joe tried to follow the dog's line of vision to outside the glass, but with the lamp on inside, it was impossible.

Chance growled low in his throat.

"Douse the lamp," he said to Noah. "And hit the floor." Joe slid from the couch to the carpet and Noah did the same, snapping the light off as he went down. There was still enough daylight that the room wasn't totally dark, but grayness had enveloped the house like a shroud, making it impossible to see anything beyond the deck.

Chance, still at the window, went crazy—barking, growling, hurling himself at the glass.

April opened the bedroom door, the light behind her. "What's happ—"

Joe, staying low, propelled himself across the room and took her to the floor, covering her with his body. He saw his mother through the open doorway, starting to get off the bed. "Get down," he shouted at her. "And stay down." She obeyed instantly. *Thank God!*

Outside, a shot was fired. Chance freaked, running back and forth along the glass, teeth bared, mouth gaping and frothing.

"Chance," Noah yelled. "No! Come. Chance. Come!"

The dog stopped barking and moved toward Noah, but he whined like a mad thing, and Noah had a bitch of a time settling him down. While calming the dog, Noah pulled himself along the floor to where Phylly lay curled in a ball beside the bed. He turned off the single bedside light, plunging the house into deep shadow.

Beneath Joe, April squirmed and shoved at his chest. He gave her some wiggle room by shifting his weight to her side, then he edged them both toward the base of the sofa. Propped against it, he pulled out his gun and released the safety.

"What's happening?" April said, her voice raspy as though she were struggling to get her breath. Shit, he'd probably damn near smothered her.

A second shot answered her question. Glass shattered somewhere above them.

Chance, who Joe could see through the bedroom door lying beside Noah and Phyllis, whined and fell quiet, waiting.

April pressed herself to his side, shuddered.

They all waited. Listened.

A long silence grew in the glass house, an eye of utter calm.

"Bristol," Joe said. "Is there a phone in there?"

"Yes."

"Get to it. Call nine-one-one. You on that grid this far out?"

"Yes, but it's quicker to call the locals."

"Do it." Joe's eyes adjusted to the bad light. He watched Bristol pull himself around the bed, saw his hand reach up to the night table, grope for the phone. Tightening his grip on April, he waited.

"The phone's dead," Noah called from the bedroom. "No dial tone."

"Shit." Joe rifled in his pocket and got his cell. He cursed again.

"What?" April asked, lifting her head, which he immediately pushed down.

"No service. Chances are we've been jammed." Whoever was out there had come prepared.

"Which means?" April whispered from beside him.

We're fucked! "Which means we get creative."

Or we die . . .

Chapter 29

Quinlan reentered the living room from his bedroom, just as Mercy's cell phone rang. He'd heard her come back, but hadn't stirred himself, having no desire to spend any more time with her than was necessary. He carried his rifle, still in its sleeve.

Mercy listened for a time, then smiled. "Cool. Good job, Char. We'll see you ASAP." She clicked off, stuffed the phone in one of the pockets in her hunting vest, one much like his own.

When she looked at Q, the smile left her face. "We're good to go. They're all there, and Charity has them pinned down." She pulled an automatic handgun from inside her jacket, another from the back of her waist. Both were Glocks and both were equipped with silencers. She handed him one. "She says the situation couldn't be better. We should be in and out in fifteen minutes."

Q slipped the revolver into an inside pocket. A fine weapon the Glock—especially equipped with a silencer. He said nothing, and he asked no questions, because he had none. He knew exactly how things would play out. "Fine."

Glancing at the rifle in his hand, she gave him an odd, somewhat wary glance, before going to the window. Lifting the blind, she peered outside, where darkness and fog had fallen like a curtain.

A perfect night for murder.

Mercy dropped the blind. "As we expected, there are four people in the house, two women, two men. Charity has jammed their cells, cut the telephone landline, and immobilized their cars. She also fired a couple of shots to make sure they stay put. She says they've doused the lights and are now sitting there in the dark—probably shitting their pants—all ready for us." Again her ugly smile, her eyes bright with anticipated violence. "She'll keep them there until our arrival. There's one problem. She waited to call us until she was certain they'd tried their cells and because the jammer's battery is weak—so if they keep trying their phones, they might get lucky."

"Then we should go. Now."

She grabbed the car keys and Q followed her out of the cabin.

Five minutes later they were through what passed for a town, and fifteen minutes after that, they were maybe three-quarters of the way up Bristol's narrow pockmarked road. When they came to a wider section, Mercy turned the car until it faced the direction they came in on and turned it off. "We'll walk in from here," she said. "Charity's up ahead, on the west side of the road, not far from the house. She says we won't see her, but she'll see us. She didn't want to say more because she didn't want to risk leaving the jammer off to continue her call."

They stepped out of the car into the cold moisture-laden air coming off the Pacific. The day's final weakening light fought the massive shadows of the trees, the clouded sky, and lost. Their world was nothing but shifting shadows. Quinlan had never known such darkness, but he liked it, he decided. Liked the possibilities of it, the sins it would hide.

Mercy pulled her jacket's hood over her head. "Jesus, doesn't this stupid place know what the fuck time of year it is?"

Q winced at her foul language. "It's the northern Pacific—not Malibu. It doesn't come with summer guarantees. You have flashlights, I presume?" Quinlan asked, slipping his rifle from its case.

She reached back into the front seat of the Explorer. "Here." She handed him one, kept one for herself.

Q shoved the flashlight in a chest pocket of his vest. He'd use it only if he had to, preferring to let his eyes adjust to the dark. He patted his right pocket, confirmed the hard weight of the Glock resting there.

"Go ahead," he said, making a play of putting his rifle case in the car. "I'm right behind you."

She didn't move. "I'll bet you are," she said. He couldn't see her face clearly, but he knew it was set to hard. She went on, "And if you're thinking I'm disposable about now—think again. Charity expects to see my face. If she doesn't you're a dead man. You got that?"

"Understood. And rest assured I have no death wish. Now shall we go? There is the problem with the jammer, remember?"

Mercy stuffed her gun in her jacket, shot a beam of light on the rutted path—the rising fog making the light virtually useless—and went ahead of him up the road. No doubt confident her threat had sufficiently terrified him into obliging docility. It was amazing how wrong a person could be.

Q withdrew the Glock from his pocket and shot her in the back.

His reward was the sound of her body thudding face forward onto the gravel road. He put his moccasin-clad foot on her head, and ground her face into the sharp stones. He wouldn't give her the grace of being a beautiful corpse. "No one threatens Quinlan Braid," he murmured, savoring the hard powerful beat of his heart, the ease of his one-handed kill. "No one."

Shoving the Glock back in his pocket, he shifted the

Winchester to a more balanced position in his left hand—he didn't like carry-straps—and strode up the road.

Unlike Mercy his back was well protected.

April, Phylly, and Noah were propped up like dolls around the base of the bed in Noah's bedroom. Joe, demanding they stay silent, stayed near the bedroom door, and listened intently for any sound behind it. As did April, but all she heard was nature's mood music: The ocean's endless communion with the shore, soft but relentless, dulled by the night's mist and fog.

Noah had secured the patio sliders and pulled the blackout drapes on the outside wall of the bedroom that backed onto the dense forest. The bedroom's inner walls, thick glass brick, provided them all the protection they'd get. Not a hell of a lot. And whoever—whatever—was out there was keeping a close watch, firing another shot into Noah's second floor office just minutes ago.

April, sitting on the floor, her back against the bed, fought the invading, slithering darkness. They huddled in a brackish world, shadows to each other—a world growing blacker by the minute.

Basement black. Cellar black.

April had forgotten . . .

Forgotten how the dark pervaded, made her heart pound with a fearful expectancy. It was unknowable, the dark. It clawed at you, caged you as easily as iron bars.

As easily as a locked cellar door.

Joe, staying low, left the door and came toward them, gun in hand. When he was close enough, he put his strong hand on April's knee and squeezed it. "You doing okay?"

His gesture was reassuring, briefly making her forget the dark—the danger outside. She put her hand over his and squeezed back. "I am now."

"Hang in there," he whispered. "We'll get out of this."

"I know." *If Joe was right, and she prayed he was,* April thought, *she'd come full circle, first Phylly taking her from the dark, now her son.*

Joe's tone turned brusque when he said, "Jesus, Bristol, you must have a weapon of some kind. A rifle maybe?"

"No. I told you. Nothing," Noah answered.

He cursed softly. Other than getting them all into the bedroom, telling them to be quiet and keep low, Joe had barely said a word since the first shot was fired—except for the first time he'd asked Noah this same question. Now April sensed impatience, knew his mind was testing ideas, turning over plans, looking for a way out. His silence was deep, but deadly. This was a whole new Joe, no wisecracks, no easy smiles—just focused determination. When she touched his shoulder, his muscles were drum-tight.

"I have a gun," Phylly said. "A Kahr 9 millimeter. It's in my bag."

"Phylly!" Noah let out a long breath.

"Why the hell didn't you say so?" Joe said.

"I didn't hear you asking before." She matched his brusque tone, but still sounded defensive. "Things were a little chaotic after all."

While Joe let out a frustrated breath, April wondered how many years in prison Phylly had risked by carrying a handgun across the border. *Dear God!*

"Can you shoot it?" Joe asked.

"Damn straight," she said. "I took lessons. Stupid to have a weapon and not know how to use it."

"Then get it. But stay low."

April heard Phyllis dragging herself over the carpet, then rifle in either her bag or suitcase. "Got it."

When Phylly came back to the base of the bed, her shoulder again touched April's. "How you doing, April?" she asked, sounding remarkably calm. Maybe having your own gun did that. April only felt useless.

"I've been better." She didn't want to say sitting in the dark terrified her more than the insane, violent creature stalking them from outside Noah's transparent walls.

"Listen up, everybody," Joe said. "Whoever's out there is either waiting for backup or for us to make a run for it, so they can pick us off. Either way waiting around to find out nets us zero. I'm going out there—"

"No! Joe, you can't." April grabbed his arm, a shaft of fear tearing at her chest.

He touched her hand, his voice less clipped, more soothing. "This sitting-duck routine doesn't work, April. And if whoever's out there *is* waiting for backup, it's plain stupid to sit here until it comes."

"What if there's more than one?"

"I'll handle it."

"I'll go with you," she said. She'd borrow Phylly's gun; she could do this. She would do this.

"No." His reply was unequivocal. "I can look after myself, but I can't look after you—not out there." He gestured toward the window.

"Then I'll go." It was Phylly.

Joe's head shook again. "No. You stay here. Anybody gets by me, you use that six inches of steel you've got in your hand. And don't miss. Okay?"

"Okay, but . . . be careful."

"Yeah."

He moved away from April, and she chilled instantly. "Before I go," he said, "we're going to build a barricade. Move everything we can from this room and out there"— he pointed to the living room—"against these glass brick walls. It's not much, but it is better than nothing." His big shape moved toward the end of the bed. "Bristol, give me a hand with this mattress and . . ."

It didn't take long before three of the walls were stacked with furniture, sofas, chairs, table, lamps—everything they could find. All of the moves done with shoves and pulls from the floor.

The bed's mattress was now propped against the outside wall. Knowing they were less exposed did feel safer, and just doing something—anything—made them feel more in control.

When they were settled in the barricaded bedroom, Joe said, "Stay in here. And . . . Phyllis, keep that gun of yours pointed toward the door. If it's me coming in, I'll whistle. Once. Sharp. Like this." He whistled an example. "You don't hear that, you don't let anyone through that door. Anyone. You got that?"

She hesitated, then said, "I got it."

"Good."

"I want—"Phylly started. But whatever she was going to say, she thought better of it. "Shit. Just come back. Okay?"

After a beat of silence, he answered, "Yeah."

Noah said, "Remember to stay to the east. The bush is denser there. More cover. West is the ocean—you'll hear it—and the cliffs. It's misleading out there, even though both sides of the road in are heavily treed and the brush is dense, there's really only a narrow strip of forest on the west side. Not much of a barrier between the road and the cliffs, and it's about a fifty-foot drop, solid rock all the way."

"Thanks." That said, Joe was gone. The fog hushed the sound of his leaving. It did nothing to mute the pounding hearts of the two women he'd left behind.

Quinlan stayed on the tree and shrub-flanked road, walking the middle of it. His eyes scanned ahead, straining to see through the murk. The fog, pushed and prodded by drafts from the cold Pacific, was lighter in places, heavier in others. There were times he easily saw a few feet in front of him; in others, the dark mist closed over his path as solid as pewter.

Still he stayed with the dark rather than turn on his flashlight.

"Over here." A figure, ghostlike in the gloom, stepped briskly onto the road. "Can you see me?"

"Yes."

The figure immediately faded back into the trees on the west side of the road. Charity was exactly where her dead sister said she'd be. Good.

Q stopped, turned his ear to the road behind him, and listened. At first all he heard was the ocean's surges against the hard land holding it back; he waited until he heard a trilling whistle. Satisfied, he again moved forward, following the woman into the dense brush.

"Where's Mercy?" The voice came from somewhere in the trees.

"Coming up behind me." Unable to see his target, take his shot, he played along, even glanced over his shoulder. "She should be right along." He took another step.

"Stay where you are. Do not move. We'll wait for Mercy."

Her voice was sharp but familiar. *No . . . impossible. Unthinkable!*

"Of course," he said. Q stood in a compact clearing not more than five feet in circumference, and no doubt directly in her line of fire. Assuming a relaxed posture, he scanned the gray wooded area for form and movement. The fog was settled low here, massed in the underbrush except where it wound upward in spots to snake around the trees.

To locate the woman, he needed to hear her voice again. "How far are we from the house?" He asked the question genially, as if they were still a team.

"Sixty, maybe eighty feet," she answered.

His heart started to race. He worked to calm it. *That voice. It couldn't be.* "And it's secure? You're sure of that?" He turned his head, cocked his ear, and strained for her reply, even as his mind rejected the possibility.

She didn't respond. He waited, saying again, "I asked if the house was secure."

More time passed, then a figure stepped out from behind the tree, shapeless and hooded, a shadow within a hundred shadows. Surreal except for what was in her hand. The gun was very real indeed, and it was pointed directly at him. "She's not coming, is she?" The voice wasn't as steady as the gun. "You bastard. You sick greedy bastard! What have you done?"

Dear God! "Giselle?" The name shot out, a hoarse yelp born from a sudden, intense jolt of pain. Q's body jerked as his brain dulled to a mass of disjointed forms, in gray and sepia. "Is that you?" In his numbed state, he needed confirmation.

Giselle moved closer and shoved back her hood with her free hand. "Yes, Q, it's me," she said, her voice coolly amused. "Now, where's Mercy, you son of a bitch? What did you do to her?"

"Me, I—" He was mumbling, couldn't think. He took a breath. "She's behind me. As I told you." Even as he spoke a network of nerves misfired along his spine. Shock at seeing his lover clad in black and pointing a gun at him gripped him like a studded glove. He steadied himself until he was sure his discomfiture wouldn't manifest. "The better question is what are you doing here? With that." He pointed his chin at her hand, the gun.

"I'd think that was obvious."

You've betrayed me. At that realization, he felt a spill of acid into his stomach, an unimaginable pain cramp his abdomen. He swallowed deeply and set the pain aside. Let cool rage replace it. She had betrayed him. Nothing else was relevant. No one betrayed Quinlan Braid. "Not to me," he said in a soft voice.

She ignored him. Shifting her head, she looked behind him.

He smelled her hope—he had to think, to plan—use her hope to save himself. He reminded himself that Giselle was rash, easily manipulated. *His Giselle. She'd deceived him, used him. And she would die for it.* Bile rose in his throat, yet his tone was soft, unthreatening, when he assured her, "I told you, she's coming. But before she gets here, I'd like an answer to my question. Why, Giselle? Why are you doing this?" He hated that his question pleaded, hated the insipid need underlying it.

"Jesus! Money. Why the fuck else?"

"I gave you everything you wanted. More."

"You're an old man with money, Q—what the hell else are you going to do to get a woman in your bed?"

Her words were broken glass, cutting and razor-sharp. They entered him like fine shrapnel, first bringing pain— then rage.

"You were in it from the beginning," he said, refusing to acknowledge the tumult within.

"Mercy covered Castor. I covered you. When big money's at stake, you cover your bases. That's how Mercy and I do things."

"Is she really your sister?"

"Yeah. *Really.* And, damn it, I told her not to trust you—to be careful." Again she leaned to look behind him.

He couldn't see her face clearly, but by her rigid posture, he knew she was both afraid for Mercy and losing patience. His time was running out—as was hers.

Giselle glared at him. "If she doesn't show up, if you've . . . hurt her. I'll kill you—and fuck the money. I'm gone."

"You don't have to do this. You could put that gun away. I'll finish what needs to be done here and we can go home. I'll forgive you. We can go on as before."

"I don't want your damn forgiveness—I want Mercy. Here. Now." She steadied the gun. "Get back, Q."

He looked at the gun in her hand. "You could do that? You could kill me after all I've done for you?"

"Done for me—" She made a snorting sound. "A few orgasms and spa trips? A goddamn Brazilian wax! You're good with your tongue, Q, I'll give you that, but underneath the money and crap, you're a freak—in bed and out."

Something red and hot moved behind his eyes, stoked a latent viciousness in his gut. None of it showed. But he was through with conversation. "Have you ever killed anyone, Giselle? Or will I be your first?"

From behind her came a trilling whistle. If it registered with the stupid woman in front of him, she didn't show it.

"Third," she said, cocking her head. "But the one I'll enjoy the most."

"I see."

"You see shit. But don't worry, your rotten life is safe enough—if Mercy shows up."

"Too bad. Because yours isn't safe at all." He dipped his chin. "Giselle, my darling, you don't think you're the only one who covers their bases, do you?"

Like her sister, she went down hard, falling into a patch of rotting stump and salal at the edge of the clearing. Jerald had obviously seen fit to remove his silencer. Not a problem, of course, because there wasn't a soul within miles—who wouldn't be dead within the hour.

Jerald stepped into the clearing. He quickly checked Giselle's throat for a pulse, then picked up her gun and stuffed it in his belt. He stood. "Sir," he said. "Do you have further instructions?"

Q tore his gaze from Giselle's lifeless body and stared vacantly at his trusted accomplice. Yes, he had instructions; he always had instructions. Quinlan Braid always had a plan, always anticipated the next step. Quinlan Braid knew what to do about everything—except the tears sliding silently down his face.

Joe stopped cold, the sharp blast of the gun came from his right, ocean-side, fifty, maybe sixty feet away. And it signaled that whoever was after April and Phyllis was close to the cliffs. An advantage if he could figure out how to use it.

Moving closer to the road's edge, he listened in the direction of the shot, shutting out the sound of dripping trees, the swoosh of ocean against the shore.

Low voices. Male. Maybe two of them. No discernible words. Then the utter silence of the northern rain forest blanketed in ocean mist and fog.

He had his location fix.

Crouching low, he continued on his path, staying among the trees as close to the road as possible. Sooner or later he'd have to expose himself and cross that damn strip of gravel, but he figured getting behind the two men was his best shot at crossing unseen.

Two minutes later, he was on the ocean side of the road. Sixty seconds after that, he was on their asses. Two shapes, moving as he had, low and silently, inched their way forward.

Thanks to his earlier recon of Bristol's property, Joe already knew where their route would take them—to about thirty feet from the house. At that point the trees and underbrush gave way to moss-covered rock and the clearing that held the house. From there a slow rise led to Bristol's glass box.

The gravel road ended at the clearing, and except for the darkness, so did the cover. Joe guessed they'd stop behind the final row of trees; they did.

Whatever plans they made were whispered, inaudible. Again they did what he expected they'd do—what he wanted them to do—they separated. One man heading east—angling toward the back of the house—the other staying put, looking relaxed as he leaned against the last tall tree before the clearing. Had it not been oil-slick black out here, the asshole would have been easily seen from the house. As it was, the only thing visible was their plan; covering the house front and back they didn't intend for anyone to come out alive. His gut balled. Jesus, he hoped to hell everyone in there stayed put.

The shape leaning against the tree stayed stone still—just waiting for Joe's forearm to cut off his breathing . . .

Every muscle in Joe's body tensed, readied. He had just a few feet to close and—

"No! Don't move." The words were low, guttural and urgent—and poured into his ear at the same time a gun barrel was shoved into his kidney.

Chapter 30

"Phylly! I said you're not going out there." April, her own nerves strung to snapping, barked out the words. All she wished right now was that Phylly would calm down, give her time to think.

"You think I can sit here while Joey is—"

"Yes. That's exactly what you're going to do. Because there's nothing you can do out there to help him. Nothing." April ground the words out for what seemed the hundredth time since they'd heard the gunshot. Just minutes ago, although it seemed like hours. "He knows what he's doing," she added, bringing her voice down. "All you'll do is mess things up." Even as she said the words, she prayed she was right. Prayed even harder that Noah was right when he said the shot was farther from the house than the one fired into his office. Whoever fired the shot couldn't have picked up on Joe that fast. Joe would be farther to the east not the west where the shot had come from. But nothing either he or April said would calm Phylly.

"I can help out there. I'm good with this." She lifted the gun, waved it. "Damn good!"

Her movement was one April sensed rather than saw, because even with her eyes fully adjusted to the darkness, everything in the barricaded room was shape and blur. When Phylly made to get up from the floor, April grabbed for her and held her down.

Noah said, "You're not going anywhere, Phylly. You'll stay here like your son asked you to, and you'll use that gun of yours to protect yourself and April—if it comes to that." He got to his feet; Chance stood immediately as he did. "I'll go. Check things out."

"Noah, no!" Phylly said. "I'm the one with the gun, remember."

"And I'm the one who knows this property, every damned inch of it. It's rough, unpredictable terrain—especially at night." He let out a breath. "Jesus, you're probably still in those damn heels."

"I'll change my shoes."

"Jesus," Noah said again.

Chance whined and Noah shushed him.

April, if the situation weren't so dire, would have laughed. Laughed until it hurt. Until she could feel something other than fear running along her bones. She knew exactly how Phylly felt—powerless—because she felt the same way. And she was desperate to know if Joe was all right. Her stomach had formed a hard ragged knot at the sound of that last gunshot, and every second he was gone it tightened. "I think we should stay here. Give Joe some time to—"

Chance yelped once, whined again. Growling low in his throat, he headed for the closed bedroom door—nothing but an opaque membrane separating them from the hall and living room beyond. In front of it, they'd piled the last of what they could move, a chair, some luggage, and the table from beside the bed. It wouldn't hold back a marauding teenager let alone an armed killer.

Seeing in the dark wasn't necessary to know that the three of them had their eyes trained on the presence and sounds of the agitated dog.

In the living room something crashed to the floor. The sound hit the charged atmosphere in the bedroom like an electrical storm surge. Everyone froze—except Chance. The dog went crazy. Alternating between barking and growling furiously, he lunged for the door, desperate to find footing in the accumulated debris at its base.

Someone was in the house.

Dear God, let it be Joe, April thought. Her hand flattening against her painfully clenched stomach, she waited for his whistle.

"Who the fuck are you?" Joe muttered the words into the air in front of him. He might have a gun in his back, but he wasn't taking his eyes off the guy leaning against the tree.

"Your new . . . best friend," a female voice whispered close to his ear. He smelled her heaving breath, hot and sick. He smelled blood. She was having trouble getting her words out.

"Yeah? And that gun in my back. What's that? Your calling card?"

She panted before answering, "You have to . . . wait . . . for the whistle." She stopped, took some breaths. "If Braid signals, and bastard number two here doesn't reply, he'll know something's wrong. That . . . someone's out here. We'll lose . . . our edge."

The pressure eased on Joe's back. She'd lowered the gun, so he risked a semi-turn. The woman's face was inches from his own, but her features were masked by the dark. "I repeat: Who the fuck are you? And who the hell is Braid?"

"Q." She huffed out some breath. "Quinlan Braid. The guy who"—the gun moved away from his back—"killed . . . my sister. And who's going to kill . . . everyone in that house. If we don't . . . stop him." Her breathing sounded like it was coming through a leaky bellows.

The name Braid meant nothing to him—but the bastard had to be April's kidnapper. Any other questions had to wait, because there wasn't time to make sense of any of it. The guy by the tree straightened, as though he were alert for something.

"So . . . what's it going to be?" she added, wheezing. "You going to look a gift horse in the mouth or—"

A trilling whistle came from the house. Joe's head snapped around. From the goddamn deck! Had to be. Which meant someone was either in the house or damn near.

"That's it . . . that's the signal." She coughed.

The shadow under the tree whistled in reply.

"I can . . . do that asshole. You go after Braid." She staggered to her feet, shoved the gun in her jacket and pulled out a knife. "Just make damn sure you kill . . . that . . . scum." He heard the rasp of her labored breathing just before she headed toward the man by the tree—like a goddamn lightning strike.

Already moving toward the clearing, Joe heard a thick groan, followed by a gasping watery gurgle.

He knew the sound, had heard it before.

Whoever his *new best friend* was, she'd done her job. From here on in, the odds were even.

In seconds he was at the edge of the clearing, circling toward the wooded area at the back of the house.

The whistle brought Phylly to her feet. "It's Joe, he's back. He's okay."

April wanted that to be true, but there was something about the whistle—it didn't sound right. "No," she said, shaking her head, convinced Phylly was deep into wishful thinking territory. For one thing, whoever had entered the house, had—so far—not come near the bedroom, where Joe knew they were waiting. No, whoever was out there had taken his own sweet time, walking around the house as though he were checking things out.

The dark-eyed man?

April's stomach took a sinking blow. She got to her feet beside Phylly. Noah did the same.

A light came on from the other side of the wall, and the glass bricks, visible between and above the collected dam of debris they'd created, suddenly glowed like backlit jewels, filtering a dim gold light into the bedroom.

The light was welcome, strangely reassuring; the voice following it was not.

"I know you're in there, and considering your protection is meager at best, you could save us all time—and me bullets—by joining me in the living room."

Noah spoke first. "Who the hell are you and what are you doing in my house?"

"You may call me Q. That will do for now," he said. "And my purpose here is to correct a mistake. I regret the damage to your house, Mister Bristol—it's a masterwork—but unfortunately it was unavoidable. But you can expect more of the same, if you don't do as I say. While I don't relish playing—who is it? Rambo?—I'll do so if necessary."

"It's me you want, and I'm coming," Phylly said. She was standing close to April, gun in one hand, April's hand in the other.

"For God's sake, Phylly." Noah gripped her shoulders from behind. "Don't be a fool."

Phylly turned on him. "This is all because of me. All of it. Rusty. Tommy." She shook her head, tears not fear in her vivid blue eyes. "I won't let anyone else die." Her voice was high but steady. "I won't."

"Forget it, Phylly, you're not going out there. So just be quiet, let me think," April said, then whispered as an aside, "Do you remember anyone who called themselves Q?"

Phylly shook her head.

Then it had to be him. The man who'd taken her from her mother. The man who sold her to Victor Allan. Her breath snagged deep in her throat. *It was the dark-eyed man—had to be.* And it wasn't Phylly he wanted, it was her.

"Very noble of you, Mrs. Worth," Braid said. "But I wouldn't want you laboring under the delusion your sacrifice will be rewarded. You must all die. As to your friends' deaths, those were Henry Castor's doing. Not mine. My interest is centered on April Worth. Such a beautiful child. I'll be interested to see how you've matured, April." He paused. "And you, Bristol, are simply in the wrong place at the right time—as is your son, Phyllis. You won't mind my calling you Phyllis, will you?" He paused, as though he were waiting for an answer, then went on. "At this point, the only choice any of you have is whether the route to your final resting place will be short or long."

He doesn't know about Joe—doesn't know Joe is out there. Which meant Joe was safe. April looked at Phylly and together they took a deep breath, sharing a sense of relief.

"We need to buy some time, Noah—or get the hell out of here," April's voice was barely a whisper. "We have to hold him off until Joe gets here."

"It won't be as easy getting at us as he thinks," Noah said, his voice equally low. "These walls are mortared glass bricks, and the entry door is safety glass reinforced with wire mesh." He glanced between April and Phylly, then at the patio doors, where the bed's mattress was propped upright. April got his plan instantly. *A way out. Yes.*

"It's a twenty-five foot drop," he warned, hesitating. "You'll have to shimmy down the uprights."

"Shimmy, I can do," Phylly said.

"Not a problem," April said. "Let's do it."

She and Noah went for the mattress, began pulling it to the side.

From the other side of the wall, April heard a brief chuckle. "I should add that if you're thinking of using the patio as a way out, you will probably be dead sooner rather than later. I do have a man outside."

Shit! April thought.

"Shit!" Phylly said.

"I think I've waited long enough," the man called Q said, adding, "My apologies, Bristol." He fired three shots in rapid succession into the glass door. The blasts were deafening, but Noah was right; the door held. Its opaque glass turned to a million shards within the mesh, but only a few pieces fell to the floor.

Phyllis cried out and fell to her knees, clutching her arm.

April followed her to the floor. "Phylly. Oh, my God. Are you all right?"

Noah went to his knees beside Phylly. "We've got to get her out of here. Jesus Christ!"

Phylly patted him with her good hand. "It's my arm," she gasped. "But it's okay. I'm okay." Her gun had fallen to the floor from a now useless hand. There was no way to make out the extent of her injury, but if blood flow was any indication—

Q fired again. This time into the glass brick wall just beside the door. The booming shots took out maybe a half-dozen bricks. Glass bulleted through the room. Shards caught Noah on the forehead, April along her jaw. She looked at Noah, the blood trickling down his face, then at Phylly, her shirt already blood-drenched. She touched her own cheek and looked at the ooze in her hand. Numb. The silence after the thunder of the rifle was absolute. Unreal. April panted to bring in air, rubbed at her bleeding face.

Phylly moaned. "That son of a bitch!"

Through the hole in the wall April saw Q, sitting about twenty feet away, a rifle propped against his chair. As she watched, he pulled a handgun from a pocket in his hunter-style jacket and rested it on his knee. He looked as calm as a man waiting for a bus. But this man was waiting to kill—with no more concern than he'd had years ago, when he'd given her mother money and carried her, nine years old and terrified, kicking and screaming into the Seattle night.

She would not scream again. Never again.

Enough . . .

April picked up Phylly's gun, stood, and walked to the

door, fear falling from her shoulders like a tattered, too thin cloak. "This is April Worth, Q whoever-you-are. I'm coming out." Phylly clawed at her leg. Noah shook his head violently. He'd taken off his shirt and was pressing it to Phylly's arm, ignoring the bleeding cuts on his own face.

"Just like that, April girl?" The voice was soft, low, simulating kindness. And like a scent it triggered memories. Poisonous, ugly memories. Memories she'd never have had except for this man named Q.

She loathed the sound of her name on his lips.

"Just like that," she said, her voice flat. "I come out—and you promise to let everyone else go." She had no doubt he'd make the promise and no doubt he'd break it. It didn't matter. What mattered was he was evil—and she had a gun in her hand.

"Why would I do that?"

"To save you those bullets you mentioned? And because no one other than myself knows your face, *Mister Q*. Which means they can't hurt you—but I can." She stood to the side of the damaged door, again looking through the broken wall. Now certain of his position, she tightened her grip on the gun.

"Very well," he said, standing, but not moving away from the chair. "As I said, it will be interesting to see how you look as a woman—those amazing green eyes. I've never quite forgotten them. You were a beautiful child."

"A child you kidnapped."

"A child I bought and paid for. A distinction worth noting, I believe. Although you were somewhat of a bargain. Your mother had other priorities, as I recall. Like putting a needle in her arm."

The amoral bastard! She wanted to be sick all over him. "Should I apologize for not recognizing the fine line between kidnapper and white slaver?"

"Not at all. Your bitterness—and perhaps latent taste for revenge—is to be expected. It's why I'm here. When Henry

Castor advised me of your continued existence, I really had no choice but to do what was necessary to protect myself." He paused, but—thank God—stayed where he was. "But enough talk. Let's have a look at you."

"Yes, enough talk." April, ignoring Noah's protests and Phylly's soft crying, threw aside the chair and luggage against the door, and stood in front of its cracked façade. She inhaled to steady herself. She knew where Q stood, and that gave her one chance to get him before he got her.

Another inhalation.

One chance . . .

Holding the gun waist-high, she opened the door and fired. At an empty space.

"Ah," he said from beside her. "You brought a surprise." His hand closed over her wrist. "An unpleasant one at that."

He wrenched the gun from her hand.

What happened next was a blur . . . Phylly threw herself on Q's back. Noah went for his feet. Chance followed his master's lead.

Q went down under a tangle of bodies, but their advantage ended when he made one snakelike turn and pressed a gun into Phylly's temple. "Get off. Get off now."

They fell back, and Q got to his feet, pulling Phylly up with him, the gun fixed on her temple as if cemented there. "And get that animal under control, Bristol, or I'll do it for you."

Noah jumped to his feet, locked his fingers around Chance's collar and held the dog, his mouth foaming and snarling, by his knee. "You son of a bitch. You hurt that woman and—"

Q fired a shot into Noah's thigh. Noah fell back against the wall, slid down. Chance lunged, but amazingly, Noah held on. "No, Chance . . . No! Stay."

"Noah," Phylly screamed. Q tightened his arm across her throat, cutting off her words.

"Just do . . . as he says, Phylly." Noah's face was tense

with pain, and his words came out haltingly. He pressed one hand against his bleeding thigh, and used the other to hold fast to the alternately whimpering and growling dog. "Chance, easy. Easy boy. Sit."

"Well done, Bristol." Staring down at him, Q added, dispassionately. "And from what I'm told bleeding out isn't such a bad way to go."

"It's me you want, let them go." April took a step.

Q drilled the gun barrel into Phylly's head. "That might have been possible before your little stunt." His voice hardened. "Now the only choice you have is who goes first, you or this stupid woman"—he jerked his arm across Phylly's throat—"who caused all this inconvenience in the first place." He frowned then, and his cold dark gaze flitted over them, around the room. "Although we do seem to be missing a player."

Chance, still sitting obediently beside Noah, barked once. Q registered it with a flicker of his lids.

"That would be me. Toss the gun, Braid. And let the woman go. *Now.*"

Oh, God . . . Joe.

April's bones weakened with relief. Joe stood near the sofa, a few feet away. How he'd entered and crossed the room without being seen or heard, she had no idea. But it didn't matter. What mattered was—he was safe. He was here, and he had a gun pointed at Q's back.

Q appeared unfazed. *God, the man was ice.* He didn't turn, and he didn't take the gun from Phylly's head. "The son, I presume."

"You presume right. Now let her go. And put the gun down."

"I don't think"—with a half turn and a step back, Q faced them all—"that would be wise on my part." He straightened the gun, moved Phylly in front of him, and pressed the gun even harder against her temple. His black gaze settled on Joe. "I suggest you're the one who should put his gun down. Joseph, isn't it? Unless you want to see your mother's brains leave a stain on this fine wood floor."

"What I want is you dead, Braid. Just like your friend out there." He gave a quick jerk of his head toward the dark world beyond the glass.

Q frowned at that, looked annoyed, then tightened his grip on Phylly.

Joe walked around to the front of the sofa. His voice was feral when he said, "Take your hands off her."

"Back off." Q's mouth flattened and his eyes turned coal hard. "Back off or your mother's a dead woman. Do you understand me or should I illustrate by putting a bullet in her?" Q ground the gun into Phylly's bleeding upper arm. She groaned and closed her eyes, looked as though she'd faint from the pain. Noah, sitting in a pool of his own blood, cursed and tried to get up. He couldn't.

The light in the room, provided by the single lamp Q had turned on when he came into the house, was dim. But it was enough for April to see Joe's eyes flick to Phylly's strained face, his jaw flex and harden.

"Don't listen to him, Joey." Phylly gasped when Q again tightened his stranglehold on her neck.

"I hope you recognize bad motherly advice when you hear it . . . *Joey*." Q's eyes blazed. "Now put down the gun or I kill your mother. Right here. Right now."

Joe, not taking his eyes off Q, slowly lowered his gun.

April saw the change in Q's eyes, the slight adjustment he made in his posture—the barrel of his gun shift toward Joe.

Oh, God . . . Q was going to kill him. April flew at him.

Q fired. The bullet seared along April's arm. Glass shattered.

"No!" Phylly screamed. She lifted her foot and brought her stiletto down on Q's arch, at the same time dropping her head and slamming the elbow of her good arm into his chest. April grabbed for the gun, but got a fistful of his vest instead. She pulled hard. Phylly brought her foot down again, so hard she broke her heel—still he held on, but the distraction gave Joe a chance and he took it. He lunged, tackled Q from the side. April heard Q's breath leave his lungs on a sharp gush.

A gun clattered to the pine floor and skidded across it.

Joe's? Q's?

April scrambled after it on her hands and knees. Phylly, released from Q's grip, reeled and fell backward, her shoulder hitting the wall with a loud thump. She groaned, clasped her bleeding arm, and sank to the floor.

Q was no match for Joe's superior speed and strength and both men toppled backward over the coffee table. It broke under their weight, and they rolled away from it toward the dark fire pit.

The gun. I have to get the gun!

Frantic, April ran her hand under the chair. Nothing. It had slid out of reach.

The two men, locked together, rolled back over the smashed table, their rotation so fast and jerky it was a blur. They tumbled hard against the table beside the sofa, knocking it over. The lamp, the only light in the room, fell with it, crashing to the floor and flickering uncertainly.

April, her hand still desperately groping for the gun, looked over and saw the cruel, determined face of the black-eyed man—under Joe!—with a gun pressed to Joe's throat.

"No!" She scrambled across the floor toward them over the splintered table. Only inches away. Seconds.

The lamp flared then died.

A bullet cracked the blackness, tearing into flesh and tissue—even in the darkness finding its mark, and leaving only grim silence in its wake.

Phylly screamed into the utter blackness of the room.

"Joe!" April's mind blank with terror, she reached through the darkness, her hands feeling blindly for what her eyes could not see. *Yes!* Her fingers touched warmth, muscle—a strong arm—quickly traveled upward to the curvature of a shoulder. She clapsed it tightly, squeezed. *Dear God, it had to be Joe. Had to be.*

The life and shape beneath her hands slackened, collapsed and fell away, hitting the floor with a dull thud.

April pressed her hands to her face, unable to breathe. Frozen in her fear and the impenetrable darkness.

"It's okay, April. I'm okay." Joe's hand, big and warm, clasped her knee. "But I'm guessing we can't say the same for the other guy."

"Oh, God . . . Joe, I thought—" When she covered his hand with hers, he took a deep breath, then got to his feet, pulling her up with him. Her heart was so full, her chest so tight with left-over panic, she couldn't finish her thought, didn't even remember it. All that mattered was that Joe was alive. Joe was here.

A light came on in the kitchen, and April looked over to see Phylly teetering back into the living room wearing her one good stiletto and holding a towel to her arm. She came over to Joe and April, looked them both over, and said to Joe, "You sure you're all right?"

He nodded, then went to his knees besides Q's body. He checked for a pulse. "He's dead." Looking up at her, he added, "We could use a blanket."

"I'll get it." April was back in seconds with a dark blue blanket; Joe quickly covered the body.

Phylly glanced down at Q's dead shape and shook her head. "Bastard." With that she went back to Noah, where he lay against the bedroom wall clutching his leg. Putting her good arm across his chest, she started crying. As he stroked her hair, soothed her, their blood mingled on the floor beneath them. The man was the color of bleached linen.

Joe shoved his gun into his jacket pocket, and went to kneel beside Noah and Phylly. He quickly checked both of them out, looked up at April. "Get me a sheet, some towels."

She was back in seconds, and while she secured the towel as best she could around Phylly's wound—which, thank God, seemed to have eased off bleeding—Joe tore the sheet apart and made a rough tourniquet for Noah. He tightened it and said, "Can you hold it there?"

Noah nodded.

Again Joe looked at April. "We need a doctor and we need one fast."

Phylly raised her good hand and pointed to Q. "And someone to take out the garbage."

Joe nodded, his expression unreadable. "That, too."

"Royal Canadian Mounted Police in Tofino . . . fastest way," Noah murmured.

April, her chest thick with panic, looked at Phylly and Noah, both pale and bleeding. From what she could see of Phylly's wound, she'd be able to hang on, but if it was Noah's femoral artery, every second counted. She gave Phylly a reassuring hug and got to her feet. "I'll go."

"Wait," Joe said. Taking his cell phone from his pocket, he hit 911. He put the phone to his ear. "Worth a try." He looked at Noah. "Will they patch it through to local?"

Noah nodded.

They waited. Lives hinging on the sputtering of sabotaged technology. April sent a silent prayer . . . *just one little break, God, that's all I ask. Just one—*

Joe let out a noisy breath, briefly closed his eyes, then spoke into the phone. "We need a doctor and the police. Stat. Gunshots. We have at least three people dead and two injured. One of them is my mother. . . . Noah Bristol's place. Tofino. The locals know it. . . . Good." He looked at April, touched her hair, and bent to kiss her forehead. Not taking his eyes from her, he again spoke into the phone: "Joe Worth. Home address, Seattle. Yes. We'll wait."

He clicked off the phone and pulled her into his arms.

Chapter 31

Joe draped his arm loosely over April's shoulder, careful to avoid the burn left by Braid's bullet, and watched the cop car lead the ambulance down Bristol's narrow road for the second time tonight, this time carrying Braid and his accomplice. It'd been a damn long night—and it wasn't over yet.

The preliminary examinations by the local doctor, who'd come along in the first ambulance, were tentative. Phylly was going to be okay, the wound was clean, mostly tissue damage that would take time to heal and leave a hell of a scar, but Noah wasn't so lucky. Braid's shot missed the femoral artery, but even so, the bullet had done a real number on his leg. The plan was to 'copter him to a hospital trauma center across the island as soon as the fog lifted.

Noah was set for surgery and major rehab, but all he seemed to care about was Phylly. And for the first time since this insane *quest* began, Joe was getting the message: Some good people cared a hell of a lot for the woman. Yeah, he was getting it. He just wasn't sure what to do about it. When she'd slammed that heel of hers into Braid's foot— when she'd set herself up to take the bullet meant for him, he'd damn near . . . hell, it was like his heart was set to leap from his chest. He'd felt crazy. Confused. Panicked.

He didn't like thinking about the thoughts and feelings

that had ripped through him, too many, too fast—like lightning on the brain. Not only could he not put things together, he didn't know how. Moving from the mother who'd walked out on him to the one who'd saved his ass, was like trying to run from zero to sixty wearing a full kit and army boots.

Then there was April, the woman standing beside him—the woman he wanted in exactly that place for as long as he could keep her. Because of her—and his mother's dumb shoes—he was still breathing.

"How's the arm?" he said to her.

"Fine. Whatever the good doctor put on it, it took away the sting." She gingerly touched the small bandage that the doctor had applied, along with his instruction that she drop by his office first thing in the morning.

When the taillights of the ambulance were lost in the fog, and the sound of both cars vanished into its smothering darkness, April looked up at him. "I should have gone with Phylly." She worked her lower lip. "She might need me."

"She'll be okay. Besides Noah asked us to secure this place as best we could—and drop off our friend here." Chance lay at their feet, his attention still fixed on the road that had taken his master.

"I know but—"

He touched her mouth. "She'll call as soon as she knows where they're taking Bristol. We'll head out at first light, right after we drop off our buddy at Noah's friend's place, check with the RCMP and you see the doc. Fair enough?"

Silence, then, "Fair enough." More silence. "Looks like it's her and Noah for now, anyway." She smiled a bit at that, then looked into the fog which had absorbed all traces of the landscape. Rubbing her upper arms, she winced when she hit the bandage. "When will the police officer be back, do you think, for the, uh, woman?"

"An hour, if he can get some help, later if not. The one

left behind is doing what he can to secure the scene. Keep an eye out for—" he stopped, deciding April didn't need the graphic.

"Animals, I know."

"Yeah."

"I wouldn't want his job—in this." She lifted her chin at the grayness that enfolded the property, deeper where it shrouded the forest beyond the deck.

Joe's gaze followed April's, while his mind conjured the death behind the mist, and the woman who'd lived long enough to give him the edge he'd needed.

How the hell she'd found the strength to take out Braid's accomplice—he'd never know. Judging from the hole in her back, she must have been running on an ounce of blood. And she'd used the last of it—and a whole lot of mean— when she'd cut out that guy's Adam's apple. She'd hung on long enough to tell the cop Braid's plans for the people in Noah's house, how he'd killed her sister, cried about how she was too late to save her. The doctor had done what he could, but she'd died before the tears for her sister had dried on her cheeks.

"It's hard to think about," April said, her voice low, halting. "Knowing there's dead bodies out there in the fog—because of me."

"Hey." He turned her toward him. "Put that thought away and put it away now. Because what happened to them had nothing to do with you. It had to do with Braid taking a little girl from her mother. It had to do with a son of a bitch who wanted to steal your life, April—then get away with it by taking even more."

"I know." She took a deep breath. "But there's a part of me that's having trouble buying it."

"Buy it—and swallow it whole, because it's the truth— and because feeling rotten about something you had no control over is a waste of time. Zero net."

"Why does that sound like the voice of been-there-done-that talking?" She paused. "Phylly? Right?"

He opened his mouth then closed it, recognizing uncharted verbal territory when it hit him between the eyes. "You're shivering. Let's go inside."

She didn't move. "When you and Phylly met—before all this awfulness started—she fainted. Right into Noah's arms. And you, you walked away, Joe. Just walked away. How could you do that?"

His throat felt as if there were a wire around it. "I . . . couldn't do anything else."

She frowned up at him, her lips twisting as though she were trying to understand.

"I was frozen." This wasn't coming out right.

April kept her curious gaze on him, said nothing.

He gripped the railing. "She fucking terrified me. Okay?"

"Why? She's your mother."

Turning to her, his chest hard, he said, "Yeah, but I didn't know that until I saw her. Until then she was a ghost, a stranger I'd . . . waited for, then taught myself to forget, because it was better to let go than feel I'd been dropped off because I wasn't worth keeping."

"Joe, that's not—"

"Look, I was probably still mewling and wetting my damn pants when she dumped me. I grew up. I got that kids are a load of trouble, some of them more than others. I just figured I was one of them. Carried that load of crap around for quite a while, but then—like I said, guilt has zero net, so I traded it in for not giving a damn. Telling myself it was no big deal not to have family, that maybe it was even kind of cool. I think I was about thirteen when I latched onto that idea—from there I moved on to her getting rid of me as being her damn loss. I was going to be an okay guy in spite of her—and she could go to hell." He took a deep breath. Anyone who said this talking crap was easy once you got the hang of it was out of their damn mind. His mouth was dry, his brain sizzling, and his chest an empty sack. "I kind of stuck on that last one."

"And now? After tonight?"

"You won't let go, will you?"

She shook her head. "I've got a stake in you, Joe. And I've got a stake in Phylly. So, no, I won't let go—unless I have to."

His brain spun around her words: *I've got a stake in you.* But it took him a nanosecond to respond. "Care to define 'stake'?"

"It's probably too damned early to say it, but hell, I'll say it anyway. I'm falling in love with you, Joe Worth—"

He reached for her, wanting to drag her against him, to hold her, feel her—use her to stop his heart from jumping clean out of his chest—but she pushed him away. He wanted to tell her he was long past the falling; he was done. He was taken. He'd hit the love ground hard. But before he could speak, she raised her hand.

"The operative word in that statement is *falling*, Joe." She gave him a fierce look. "But I'll grab the skinniest tree branch I can latch onto to stop that fall if you can't—" Again she wrapped her arms around herself.

Against the chill? Against him? They faced each other, her chin lifted, him frowning, half in frustration because he couldn't hold her and half in confusion over her stubbornness. He leaned back against the railing. "If I can't what, April?"

She squared her shoulders and finished: "If you can't resolve your feelings about Phylly." She met his gaze. "You know how I feel about her, what she did for me. I want her to be part of my life forever. She's my mother in every sense of the word. I can't let myself . . . love someone who can't—or won't—feel the same. I can't see a future with the two people I care about the most not caring about each other. I wouldn't know how to make that work."

He looked at her a long time, tried to read between the lines, see behind her eyes. Past her invincible loyalty to his mother. He wanted to say the right words, the words she wanted to hear, but he couldn't find them. And he wasn't about to offer glib promises—before he'd sorted some things out, talked to his mother.

April closed her eyes against his silence, drew in a breath.

"That's not all of it, is it?" he asked. "It's not just about Phylly and me." He ran his knuckles along the smooth skin on her jaw.

"Maybe not. And maybe I can't say exactly what I feel. I only know it makes me sad—and afraid."

"Afraid?"

"To think you're . . . an unforgiving man."

April heard Joe on the phone when she passed his door on her way to the kitchen. She was busy making coffee when he joined her a few minutes later.

What light there was—the fog had thinned but loitered—was a cool pearl gray, but growing warmer as daylight broke behind the lingering mist.

He came up behind her and put his arms around her. Carrying the moisture and scent of his shower, he smelled as fresh as the cedars on the other side of the glass. "Good morning," he said, nuzzling her neck.

She turned in his arms and kissed him, rubbed the pad of her thumb over his mouth. His eyes were dark, urgent—as she suspected her own were.

They hadn't slept together. And wouldn't until what was between them was fixed. That was Joe's idea; she hadn't felt quite so noble last night, especially when he'd walked into the shot-up bedroom, and she'd gone into the undamaged one where she'd tossed about in a sleepless night. Alone. What she'd wanted was to lose herself in Joe's arms, push away the fog outside as well as the fog within. What she'd said surely hurt him, confused him as much as it confused her. But it hadn't occurred to her to not say what had to be said.

"I'm ready to go. You?" he asked.

She gestured at her bag sitting by the table, then left his arms. "I found a Thermos. We'll take the coffee with us. I put Chance in the car, and I called the doctor. They took Phylly and Noah out half an hour ago."

"Good. I've arranged for the plane, so we're right behind them." With that, he grabbed her bag and his and went outside. It was a while before he came back. "Somebody messed with the wires on the car, but I got it going, so—" His cell rang, and he pulled it from his pocket. When he heard who it was, an eyebrow shot up, and he looked at April. From that point on he listened, acknowledging what was said with the occasional uh-huh or murmur, finally saying, "It's all good, so suck it up. And stop worrying." He clicked off, smiling. "Want to take a guess who that was?"

She shook her head.

"The wise and terrible Cornie. She's on her way to the hospital."

"Oh, God." And that was all there was to be said, because from here on in, it was up to the heavens to call the shots. It was Cornie, after all. "How did she—"

"Phylly called her last night, right after they got Noah settled. Must have been quite a call, because she knows everything. She says Noah's her father. That true?"

"Yes, but damn it! I'm going to kill Phylly. That's not something you tell a girl over the phone. Cornie must be half out of her mind." April took a few steps, hoping to calm down. It didn't work. "Sometimes that woman is so incredibly thoughtless, she makes me crazy."

Joe raised a brow. "Be careful. That's my mother you're talking about."

She looked at him, felt her eyes widen, a quick soft flutter near her heart. It was the first time Joe had openly acknowledged her as his mother.

"And as for Cornie," he went on. "She's as pissed off as you are. Seems Phylly's good at bringing out the inner beast in people she cares about."

"And who care about her." She stared at him, hoping he wouldn't look away. Maybe she was pushing it, maybe it was too soon to hope.

Silence filled the glass house, even as some early rays of sun bounced off its reflective surface. "Cornie's not the only one who's talked to her mother." He looked at her, his expression grimly humorous. "She does good phone."

"Yes, she does." She held her breath.

"We're going to—and here's that word you love so much—*talk* when we get to the hospital. We're going to goddamn Starbucks."

"Phylly loves Starbucks."

He came to her and took her face in his hands. "I wasn't so good with the words last night. I'm sorry for that. But there's one thing I want you to know. I might not get all soft and gooey about finding my mother—I'll work on that— but that forgiveness thing you're fretting about? I don't think you should worry about that anymore." He stroked her cheeks with his thumbs, bent his head to brush his lips lightly across her own. "How could I not forgive a mother who not only saved my life but gifted me with a teenage sister who holds the record for the biggest mouth in America— and who"—he kissed her again—"rescued and kept safe for me the woman I love—and the woman I want to spend all my tomorrows with?"

Breathless now, April murmured, "That would be hard."

"It would be impossible."

Chapter 32

"How are you fixed for boiled oil-slick this morning, Riggs?"

Donny Riggs looked up from his morning newspaper. "Hey, Joe. Back from away are ya?" He swiveled his chair enough to deal with his coffeemaker. A big, new shiny one he'd ordered from Italy. *Grazie, Italia.* Riggs had finally figured out it was a felony to serve bad coffee in Seattle—which didn't mean Joe had quit giving him a hard time.

"Where ya been, anyway?" Riggs asked.

"In the last couple of months—pretty much everywhere. Until a few days ago Mexico City."

And when he wasn't traveling for business, Joe was carving a mile-deep rut in the I-5 between Seattle and Portland, spending every possible moment with April. But in a couple of months, she'd be finished with her costume design internship then—hallelujah—they'd start planning a real life. Together.

"What about that pretty woman you got? She gonna like that—all that traveling you do?" He put the steaming coffee in front of Joe and watched him cap it.

"It's what I do. And she's good with it." He shoved a fiver across the counter. Like I'm good with her getting that job offer from Hollywood. Hell, if that's what she wanted—where she wanted to be—that's where they'd go. He could work from anywhere.

"So if you've been home for the last week, how come I haven't seen ya?"

"Now you want to see my punch card?" No way was he going to explain to Riggs that he'd been spending his time checking out a special gift for April, making sure everything was exactly right.

He glanced at his watch. April said she'd be at his office by eleven, which meant he had twenty minutes, so he'd better move his ass. He headed down the street.

"Joe?"

Joe stopped, waited for the inevitable. "Yeah?"

Donny poked an index finger at the morning paper. "Says here you gotta be ready for the unexpected today. Says things aren't going to go as planned and that there's only one right answer to a woman's question." He squinted at the paper. "And it says—and I'm not kidding—there's going to be a new man in your life." Grinning, he looked up. "You got something you're not telling me?"

"No snakes this time?"

"No snakes."

Joe lifted his coffee cup in salute and turned the corner. Again he looked at his watch. Then he flipped open his phone. "Julius?"

"I figured it would be you."

"Are they there?"

"They're here."

"Good. If the I-5 doesn't do a number on April's ETA, we should be right on time."

He clicked off, shoved the cell into his inside pocket, and tried to ignore what else was in there. If he thought about *that*, he'd get the shakes. And today wasn't about that. Today was about April. A minute later he was in the stairwell and starting up the first set of stairs leading to his office.

"Hey, big boy, wanna have a good time?"

The low, sultry voice came from behind him. Turning, he cocked his head. "Depends on whether the price is right."

"The price is whatever you're willing to pay."

"And I can have it here? Now?"

"You can have it any way—and any time—you want it."

"Now that's a deal any man in his right mind wouldn't refuse." Joe pulled April into his arms and kissed her until neither of them could breathe. When his lungs got their groove back, he said, "You're early."

"I was worried about the traffic so I got an earlier start." She wrapped her arms around him and rested her head against his shoulder. "You okay with that?"

His answer was to pull back so he could lift her face and kiss her senseless again.

"Hey, Joe. I guess saying have a good day would be overkill, huh?"

A man's amused voice penetrated Joe's brain fog, but he didn't take his eyes from April, the laughter in her eyes. "My day couldn't be better." And it could only go up from here.

April stepped back and smoothed her hair behind her ear, still smiling. "A neighbor."

"Office down the hall." He copied her action and smoothed her hair. "You ready?"

"Where are we going exactly?" She tilted her head. "And why all the mystery?"

"Answer to first question—Julius's for lunch. The second? You'll see when we get there." He kissed her nose. "No more questions. You've used up your quota." He turned her toward the exit door. "Now move that miraculous butt of yours."

"I love a man who takes charge—especially when they compliment my butt when they do it." She moved.

They were on the street almost to his car when his phone rang. When he reached in to take it from his pocket, his hand brushed the other small package—sitting in his inside pocket like a hard, glowing coal. He clicked on, arched a brow in April's direction, and said, "Yes, Mother Dearest, it's definitely coming down. Forty-five minutes tops . . . and, yes, I'll call. . . . How's Vegas—or more important—how's Noah's tolerance level? Is he missing his trees yet? . . . Uh-huh." He glanced down at April, ran a finger along her jaw. "She's right here. I'll ask her." He dropped the hand holding the phone. "She wants to know if we'll do a glass box weekend with them when you're finished interning?"

"Absolutely."

"You're on," he said into the phone. "Yes. I said I'd call and I will. . . . Now get back to taking care of that man of yours—while I take care of your daughter." He clicked off. The phone rang again immediately. Joe looked at the call display. "Cornie," he said, and clicked on. At this rate they'd never get to Jules. "Yes, *I'll call*. I promise. . . . You think that's a good idea? The guy's leg isn't a hundred percent, you know. You should take it easy on him. . . . Real easy." He looked up at the sky, wondered how he'd got from minus zero in the family/female department to thrice blessed—and dazed and confused—in under three months. And he wouldn't trade a second of it. "Bye, Cornball, see you soon."

"What's going on?"

"Noah's going riding with her this afternoon." He held up a hand to stave off the protests he knew were coming. "Noah knows his limits, April. It'll be fine." He hoped. Because if Cornie asked Noah to ride a hungry croc, the man would do it. Noah didn't just dote on his newfound daughter, he was certifiably gaga. He'd told Joe that finding Phylly and Cornie made his life complete. It was as if a circle had closed around everyone he'd ever loved, he'd said, adding, "I'd die for them, Joe—and I've never felt anything like that in my whole life." Joe knew the feeling.

They walked a few steps before April said, "You know that old saw, about there being 'fortune in mis*fortune*'?"

"Uh-huh."

"After all that horrible mess with Quinlan Braid. . . . Have you ever seen a situation where that saying fits more? There's been so many good things. Not just you and me— but you and your mother, Noah and Cornie . . . Phylly and Noah." She shook her head. "I mean, really, if those two came from different planets, they couldn't be more different. Noah with his attachment to the wilderness and Phylly with her love of . . . just the opposite." She chewed her lip briefly. "Do you think it will work out for them? Over the long-term, I mean."

They were at his car, so he took the time spent opening the door for her and walking around to the driver's side before he answered. "I think it will work—because they both want it to work, and they'll do what it takes to make it happen."

"You mean that living-in-two-places thing they've got planned."

"Yes."

"I guess." She didn't sound convinced. "But it's hard to visualize Phylly in hiking boots for six months of the year."

"Or Noah in a town that never turns the lights off?"

She nodded, smiled at him. "But it's going to be damned entertaining to watch."

"That it will be." *Like it will be entertaining watching you in the next hour—and for the rest of my life.*

It wasn't until they took the last step leading to Jules's massive front doors that April noticed how uptight Joe was. The closer they'd come to Julius Zern's place, the quieter he became. Now his lips were one straight line, and he looked as if he were heading for surgery rather than lunch at his best friend's home.

Not that April didn't have a worry or two of her own. She had a few things to say to Joe Worth before she headed back to Portland. But it would have to wait until they were alone. For what she needed to say—they needed privacy.

The door opened, but it wasn't Jules who answered it; it was a redheaded woman wearing jeans and a white shirt. Her too-curly red hair tied back with a—yes, atrocious— yellow scarf.

"Hi, I'm Keeley Farrell," she said to April. "Julius asked me to welcome you." Her blue eyes, oddly dark for a fair-skinned redhead, skipped from Joe to April—and filled up with questions. "And you're April." She shook her head. "I still can't believe it." Her eyes misted.

April glanced at Joe—who appeared to have donned an unreadable mask—but all he did was shrug. She looked back to Keeley Farrell, not sure what to say.

"Come in, come in." Keeley brushed at the moisture under her eyes and moved aside to let them in. "And don't mind me. It's just that I know he's been waiting so long."

April stepped into Julius's grand front hall. "You'll have to excuse me, but I have no idea what you're talking about." Again she looked at Joe, and this time he smiled.

"Not exactly how I had it planned, Keeley," he said to the woman. "But let's do it."

When he took April's elbow, she dug her heels in. "Do what? What's going on here?"

"There's someone here for you, April. Someone waiting for you."

"I don't understand. Who? Who's waiting for me?" Her heart did a sudden unexpected lurch.

A voice came from the study doorway. "That'd be me, April. And I've been waiting one hell of a long time."

She spun around to see a tall dark man standing in the doorway. His face was scarred on one side, and he was taller and leaner than she'd imagined him, but she knew him instantly. "Oh, God . . . It's you. Gus. It's really you." Her heart pounded crazily, like a hundred dogs throwing themselves against a cage. *Gus. My brother* . . . Her eyes saw him, her heart recognized him, but her feet refused to move. They were as heavy and solid as the marble she stood on. "Gus," she said again. "I can't—" The tears came in a rush, spilling from her eyes, blinding her. She thought of Phylly fainting on first sight of Joe. No, she wouldn't. . . .

Gus closed the distance between them. Clasping her shoulders, he lowered his head and looked into her eyes. He looked as though he might say something, instead he pulled her roughly to his chest. "Christ, April, I was beginning to believe this would never happen—that I'd never find you."

She hugged him fiercely, never wanting to let go. Over Gus's shoulder she saw Julius Zern, his face closed and stoic. Inexplicably sad. When their eyes met he smiled fleetingly, nodded, and went back into the kitchen.

Joe, grinning as if he'd bought California for a dollar, stood beside Keeley who wept openly. Pulling a pack of tissue from her pocket, she handed Joe one. He took it, but looked at it as if it needed instructions.

Keeley touched his arm. "Let's go into the kitchen, keep your partner company. I think those two"—she gestured with her chin toward April and Gus—"have a lot of catching up to do."

"Just a minute," April said, pulling away from Gus long enough to wrap her arms around Joe's waist and say, "You did this, Joe. I know you did. And I'll never forget that. I'll love you forever for it." The hug she gave him was even fiercer than the one she'd just given her brother. If she'd been holding back even the smallest piece of her heart from Joe Worth, in this moment, it was lost forever. "Thank you. Thank you."

"And Julius. I couldn't have done it without him," Joe said and grinned. "But I'd appreciate it if you'd make that love part exclusive." He kissed her forehead, held her away from him. "Now go. Keeley here—who by the way is soon to become your sister-in-law—is right. You and Gus have a lot of ground to cover."

With that Joe and Keeley went into the kitchen. April took Gus's arm, looked into his chocolate-colored eyes and said, "It was you, wasn't it, who came to my apartment looking for me? You talked to my landlady?"

"She said you'd skipped." His mouth tightened. "To think I was so close."

April swallowed, then breathing deeply, happily, she said, "That doesn't matter. Nothing matters except that we're together. I want to hear everything, Gus. Everything. . . .

Morning came, bringing crisp autumn air, sunshine, and the salt scent of the ocean coming off Puget Sound. Waking, the only problem Joe had was not having April in his arms. But he did have her in his line of vision. She was standing on his deck, leaning on the rail, and looking at the water— wearing one of his big ugly sweat sets that was miles too big for her slender frame. With the sun making her hair gold and her skin all pale and soft looking, she made his heart stop.

He pulled on some jeans, didn't bother with a shirt and went to join her. Coming up behind her, he wrapped her in his arms. "It's cold out here," he whispered in her ear.

She melted back into him. "Not anymore."

For a time they stood there, caught in the morning quiet, content with each other's silence, content in each other's arms.

Finally, she turned to look at him. "I've been thinking how in the past few months just about everything in my life has gone right, Phylly being so happy, meeting my grandfather—"

"Who you didn't like a whole lot."

Her brows knit briefly. "Yeah, well, I'm working on that." She paused. "Finding Gus again—"

"Priceless." He quoted the MasterCard commercial and she smiled.

"Definitely. And that brings me to you. To us." She put both her hands on his chest, rubbed idly.

"What about us?" he asked, stilling her hands so he could keep his mind on the subject—instead of what her hands were doing to his heart rate.

"I love you, Joe. Seriously and crazily love you."

"That's a two-way street, April. You must know that— God knows I've told you often enough."

She nodded again, slowly, thoughtfully, before saying, "If there's one thing Phylly taught me, it was to go for what you wanted in life. Up 'til now that's been simple, college, my design work—the internship . . ."

"And now?"

"It's not so simple. Because I want you, Joe. I want you to marry me. I want it to be you and me against the world, loving and legal—forever and always."

Joe closed his eyes. "You can *not* do this to me."

"I can't ask you to marry me? There's a law?" She smiled. The woman was damn sure of herself. And he was glad of it.

"I thought you didn't want to talk about 'serious stuff' until you were done in Portland." Her words exactly, which he'd set about choosing to ignore.

"I changed my mind. Last night when you closed the door behind us and had your way with me against the wall."

"The wall? That's when you decided you and I should get married." Okay, so his male brain wasn't getting this. The smart money was on keeping his mouth shut and his ears open.

"Uh-huh." She pulled down the gaping neck on the sweat top she was wearing. "And I've got the bruise to prove it. See."

He leaned in, looked hard. She was bruised all right, a tiny little square bruise the color of lilacs. Right at the top of her breast. She touched his chest, left side. "It was right about there, I think." She extended her right hand, did her gimme thing and raised a brow, her green eyes glowing with one-upmanship

She had him. But then she had since the day she'd walked into his life. "I guess branding you with the ring box was a bad idea, huh?"

"I love you, Joe. You branded me when you tossed me out of your office."

His breathing snagged low in his chest. "And I love you, April. Just not enough to hand over a ring . . ."

She tilted her head, waited.

"Without the accompanying champagne and violins."

"You're making me wait?"

"I plan on making us both a memory."

"Plans don't always work out," she said, inching closer and putting her hands on his bare chest, kissing where she'd touched.

"So I'm told." He thought of Riggs's horoscope, or tried to while April locked her arms around his neck and kissed his throat, under his chin . . .

"I have ways of getting what I want," she whispered into his ear, her breath warm against his jaw.

"Yeah, you sure do." He exhaled. "And I'm more than willing for you to try all of them."

She chuckled. "I'll bet . . . And by the way, you haven't answered my question. Will you marry me, Joe Worth?"

He smiled. According to Riggs, there was only one answer to that question. "Yes."

Don't miss Shelly Laurenston's
THE MANE EVENT,
available this month from Brava . . .

Dez closed her eyes as his hands slid down her body, across her breasts, lingering for a moment at her nipples, which caused her entire body to convulse. *Damn sensitive nipples.* Every time her ex had touched them, she practically ripped his throat out. That wasn't the response she had with Mace, though. She wanted him more than she ever had before. And she'd wanted him a lot before. Yet knowing he was only partially human had changed everything for her. She dealt with humans every day. Every day she found herself disgusted and appalled by their bullshit. Trusting human-Mace seemed like a stupid idea to her. She didn't trust, understand, or really even like humans. She knew what they could do. The damage they could cause.

Animals, though, were all about survival. Mating, hunting, feeding—simply keeping their species alive. They didn't hurt each other out of spite. They didn't humiliate others to make themselves feel better. When they hunt and kill it is only for food, and they never do anything morally reprehensible to the corpse afterward. Dez understood animals. She always had. Now she understood Mace, and that made all the difference in the world for her. He was the first man she could ever truly trust.

Although that particular thought made her want to pass out.

"You stopped breathing again, Dez." She let out the breath she had been holding. "Good, baby. Keep doing that and you'll be fine."

His hands slid around her waist and he crouched low, bringing them down the outside of her legs. He found her secondary weapon in an ankle holster and a small blade strapped to the other ankle. He took those and tossed them on the dresser.

He returned to his crouch behind her. "Spread your legs," he ordered. She caught that moan before it could pour out of her mouth along with the potential begging that might follow. Silently, she complied.

Mace slowly dragged his hands up between her legs, his right hand sliding between her thighs and pushing against her crotch. Her whole body jerked like someone attached a live wire to her. She knew she was wet. Now he knew it, too, if that very primal grunt of satisfaction rumbling up from his chest proved anything.

He rubbed his hand against her crotch, and Dez dug her short nails into the closet door. "Anything else I need to be on the lookout for, Dez?"

She didn't answer him. Instead, she shook her head.

"What's the matter?" And she could hear the smile in his voice. "Cat got your crotch?"

By far, one of the stupidest things anyone had ever said to her, and in response, she burst out laughing.

He turned her to face him, and she looked down into that gorgeous face.

"It's going to be okay, ya know. I promise."

His body, still crouched in front of her, seemed more naked than most. Not that she'd never seen a naked man before. Hell, she arrested a lot of naked males over the years. But none of them, even the best-built Marines, had ever been like this. Something so raw and male exuded from Mace, the thought of *not* fucking him was becoming an impossibility.

"Now, if you're not going to tell me if there are other weapons, I guess we'll have to get the rest of these clothes off you." He grinned. A wicked, evil grin that almost dropped her to the floor. "Just so we can get a closer inspection, of course."

He unzipped her jeans, pulling them down her hips and legs until they puddled onto the floor. He tossed the jeans aside while he pulled his body out of its crouch and kneeled in front of her. He slid his hands back up her legs as he kissed the exposed flesh above her red lace panties. His hands slid under the lace to grip her ass, his tongue swirling right under her belly button.

Dez bit her lip. "At this point, Mace, I'm not exactly sure what you're searching for."

Gold eyes, so dark with lust they seemed black, focused on her face. "Do you really care?"

She blinked. "Care about what?"

"You're not paying attention, Desiree." He nipped the sensitive flesh of her lower abdomen. "I guess I'll have to work a little harder to make sure you don't lose interest."

Mace slid her panties off, and Dez wondered what the hell was going on. What the hell was she doing? And what exactly was Mace doing with his finger?

"Mace!"

He stopped, clearly annoyed. Although his forefinger seemed damn happy to have slid past her clit and buried itself deep inside her pussy. "What now?"

"Maybe we should—" before the word *wait* could come out, Mace started slowly finger-fucking her. Dez's back arched off the closet door. *Tricky fuckin' cat!*

Dez dug deep lines in the wood of her poor door. It had been so long since she'd been with anyone. So long since she had a man touch her in any way but friendship or while trying to outrun her after doing something illegal. She didn't want to blow this, but to be honest she had no freakin' idea what the hell she'd gotten herself into. Add in the fact

Mace's cock was freakin' huge and you have a recipe for a Dez disaster.

Mace's free hand slid around her waist, pulling her close to him. He kissed and nipped her stomach and hips. "Touch me, Dez. I need to feel your hands on me."

Why did that surprise her? Maybe because Mace never seemed like he ever needed anything or anyone. "I thought cats didn't like to be touched, Llewellyn."

He licked her belly button. "Damn dog people. That's propaganda." He rubbed his face across her belly and thighs, his unshaven cheeks and jaw feeling rough against her skin. "We need affection, Dez. We just don't beg for it."

Dez grinned as she slid her hands into his hair. She now understood why Mace's hair was always out of control in high school. Because it had been growing into a mane. A real, honest-to-God lion's mane.

She closed her eyes and plunged forward. "I need you to kiss me, Mace."

Mace stopped moving. Even his fingers paused in their slow, steady movements.

"I loved the way you kissed me today." She looked down at him, brushing his hair out of his eyes. He watched her silently, and Dez realized how much she wanted all this. How much she wanted him. "Do you know I would have given anything for you to kiss me like that in high school? I would have given anything for you to even try."

Mace's gold eyes locked with hers. He slid his finger out of her and, as he slowly stood, he slipped it in his mouth, sucking it clean. Dez groaned as his exquisite body towered over her. He took her hands, their fingers interlacing. Palms against palms. Then he slammed them against the door, his body once again pinning her to the hard wood.

"I wish I'd known you'd felt that way, Dez." His mouth barely touched hers, and Dez briefly wondered if her lungs stopped working. "Because I've felt like that since the second I saw you. And I've never stopped." Then his mouth was on hers, and this time she couldn't stop the moan or the shudder that went through her entire body. Nothing had ever felt so good. Or tasted so good. Damn, but the man tasted so goddamn good.

Christmas just got a whole lot hotter in
I'M YOUR SANTA.
Here's a peek at Lori Foster's
"The Christmas Present,"
the first novella in this sexy anthology,
available now from Brava . . .

With each step he took, Levi pondered what to say to Beth. She needed to understand that she'd disappointed him.

Infuriated him.

Befuddled him and inflamed him.

In order to get a handle on things, he had to get a handle on her. He had to convince Beth to admit to her feelings.

He needed time and space to accomplish that.

Thanks to Ben's directions, Levi carried her through the kitchen toward the back storage unit, where interruptions were less likely to occur.

The moment he reached the dark, private area, Levi paused. Time to give Beth a piece of his mind. Time to be firm, to insist that she stop denying the truth.

Time to set her straight.

But then he looked at her—and he forgot about his important intentions. He forgot everything in his need for this one particular woman.

God, she took him apart without even trying.

Among the shelves of pots and pans, canned goods and bags of foodstuff, Levi slowly lowered Beth to her feet.

He couldn't seem to do more than stare at her.

Worse, she stared back, all big dark eyes, damp lips, and barely blanketed desire. Denial might come from her mouth, but the truth was there in her expression.

When she let out a shuddering little breath, Levi lost the battle, the war . . . he lost his heart all over again.

Crushing her close, he freed all the restraints he'd imposed while she was his best friend's fiancée. He gave free rein to his need to consume her. Physically. Emotionally. Forever and always.

Moving his hands over her, absorbing the feel of her, he tucked her closer still and took her mouth. How could he have forgotten how perfectly she tasted? How delicious she smelled and how indescribable it felt to hold her?

Even after their long weekend together, he hadn't been sated. He'd never be sated.

Levi knew if he lived to be a hundred and ten, he'd still be madly in love with Beth Monroe.

The fates had done him in the moment he'd first met her. She smiled and his world lit up. She laughed and he felt like Zeus, mythical and powerful. She talked about marrying Brandon, and the pain was more than anything he'd ever experienced in his twenty-nine years.

Helpless, that's what he'd been.

So helpless that it ate at him day and night.

Then, by being unfaithful, Brandon had proved that he didn't really love Beth after all—and all bets were off.

When Beth came to him that night, hurt and angry, and looking to him for help, Levi threw caution to the wind and gave her all she requested, and all she didn't know to ask for.

He gave her everything he could, and prayed she'd recognize it for the deep unshakable love he offered, not just a sexual fling meant for retaliation.

But . . . she hadn't.

She'd been too shaken by her own free response, a response she gave every time he touched her.

A response she gave right now.

They thumped into the wall, and Levi recovered from his tortured memories, brought back to the here and now.

He had Beth.

She wanted him.

Until she grasped the enormity of their connection, he'd continue pursuing her.

Lured by the sensuality of the moment, Levi levered himself against her, and loved it. As busy as his hands might be, Beth's were more so. Small, cool palms coasted over his nape, into his hair, then down to his shoulders. Burning him through the layers of his flannel shirt and Tee, her touch taunted him and spurred his lust.

Wanting her, right here and right now, Levi pressed his erection against her belly and then cradled her body as she shuddered in reaction, doing her best to crawl into him.

His mouth against hers, he whispered, "I need you, Beth."

Keep an eye out for Jennifer Apodaca's
EXTREMELY HOT
available next month from Brava . . .

"**A**re you trying to save me?"

She jerked back as if he'd slapped her. "I'm only interested in saving my mother."

His lips quirked in a half grin. "Liar. I'm your biggest weakness, sweet cakes. A dangerous, broken man that you can't control. Damaged goods." He took another step. "I'm *that man,* the one you warn all your listeners about in your safe little booth while hiding behind your microphone. I scare you."

Color crawled into her cheeks and she straightened her spine. But she didn't look away from him. "You're a bastard." She lifted her chin. "And for your information, I'm in control of myself."

She believed that. Interesting. He was close enough now to smell the fresh berry scent that clung to her, probably from her shampoo. It was enough to send his thoughts into hot and heavy naked territory. "That so?"

"Yes." She nodded vigorously.

"So if I pull you into my arms—"

She froze then stepped back. "Don't you dare!"

Her horrified reaction made him feel unworthy. Not good enough. Unwanted. He stepped closer to crowd her. "Don't what? Tempt you? Seduce you? Make you feel raw and aching lust? Make you burn for what only I can give you?"

She swallowed hard and squared her shoulders. "Trying to scare me off, Sterling?" Keep me from poking at your wounds? Don't bother, you're not worth the effort." She turned and walked to the door, then she looked back. "We have a deal. You help me find the murderer and I'll help you find the statues. I'll start doing financial searches on Trip and see if I can—"

The sight of her walking away from him spurred him into motion. He reached her before she finished talking. Curling his hand around her shoulder, he bent down to her ear. "Damned right we have a deal."

She turned to stare at the door. "I'm going home now to start searching. That's my part of the deal."

He felt the tremor in the muscles of her shoulder. He didn't think it was fear. Stepping closer, he pressed his body into hers, felt her warm softness mold to his harder angles. Hot lust raced through him, his dick rose and reached for her. The sense that they fit together, the hot flash of need, made him want to force an admission from her. "The truth, Ivy. Can you admit it? That you're attracted to me, that you want to have sex with me." He figured she'd run. Put some space between them.

Instead, she turned around and said, "Do you know what the biggest sex organ on a woman is? Don't answer, because you'll be wrong. It's her brain. And my brain says no." She lifted her chin, her blue eyes shinning with triumph.

He placed his hand on the doorjamb over her head and leaned in toward her. "That's a nice line of bullshit, sweet cakes. Your listeners eat it up. All the sex hex mumbo jumbo, your tidy little lectures about being in control of your hormones and finances sound so smart, so evolved. But you forgot one thing."

"Maybe when you're done flexing and trying to crowd me with your big manly muscles, you'll enlighten me as to what I've forgotten?"

He had to admit he loved sparring with her. He was doing exactly what she accused him of—crowding her, reminding her he was bigger and stronger. He hadn't missed the way she looked at him, she liked his body and his muscles. "If you'll stop lusting after my manly muscles, I will tell you."

"You wish."

He smiled. "The thing you forgot? Sex is a primitive, elemental drive in all of us. You can try to dress it up anyway you want, but in the end—it's a magnetic pull that all of us have. Even you." He dropped his gaze slowly, taking in her full mouth, and slid his stare down to the base of her throat where her pulse jumped. He lifted his free hand, draped his finger over her shoulder and stroked the beating pulse with the pad of his thumb. "Your body is reacting *primitively* right now." She swallowed hard, then said a little breathlessly, "But I'm still thinking. I'm still in control."

Her skin was warm beneath his hand, and the erratic dance of her pulse beneath his thumb matched the beat of his own heart. He knew that if he made love to her, he'd feel the same beat—a wet, hot pulsing—surrounding his cock. Lust squeezed his balls. He hadn't wanted a woman the way he wanted Ivy in a helluva long time. He admitted it, this was fun. He kept thumbing her pulse and lowered his face until he could feel her breath fan over him. "Then think about this. It's just sex. You're in control of your emotions, right? If that big brain of yours is in control, why not take what you want? It's not like you're going to fall for me. You know better."

She stared at him.

He left the thrum of her pulse to run his hand up her neck and cupped her warm skin beneath her ponytail. "Afraid? Worried you aren't in control? Or is it that you want me too much? The need to fix the broken man inside of me is just too much temptation?"

"No. You're just not my type."

He laughed. "I am exactly your type and that's what has you fighting so hard." The silky length of her hair spilled over the back of his hand. He pulled his other hand from the wall to press it on the small of her back and draw her closer into his body.

Where he needed her.